MW01631703

COILS OF THE SERPENT

COILS
OF THE
SERPENT

A Novel

Raymond Clark Lutz

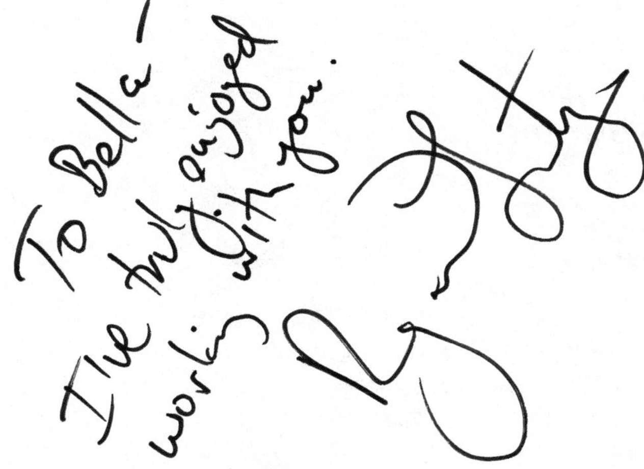

ISBN 0-7414-4228-0

Cover Art: Creative Graphics by Raymond Lutz

Stained Glass Depicting Adam and Eve,
Philippe Colombi - Getty Images

Enter the "Secrets of the Cover" contest!
Visit www.CoilsOfTheSerpent.com for contest rules.

Correspondence to the author should be addressed to:
RayLutz@CoilsOfTheSerpent.com

Published by:

1094 New DeHaven Street, Suite 100
West Conshohocken, PA 19428-2713
Info@buybooksontheweb.com
www.buybooksontheweb.com
Toll-free (877) BUY BOOK
Local Phone (610) 941-9999
Fax (610) 941-9959

Printed in the United States of America
Printed on Recycled Paper
November 2007

DEDICATION

To my loving wife Jill and sons Austin and Garrett.

EPIGRAPH

Jesus said, "Those who seek should not stop seeking until they find. When they find, they will be disturbed. When they are disturbed, they will marvel, and will reign over all."

— *Gospel of Thomas*

PREFACE

Coils of the Serpent promises to aid in your spiritual quest and challenge your understanding of life and the universe. It addresses the most significant of all mysteries: our very existence—life on earth. Although the mystery itself is factual, contemporary places, characters, and their situations are developed by the author. Any similarity of these characters to real persons, dead or alive, is strictly coincidental.

Information regarding the structure of life, DNA, and other cellular mechanisms is factual. Passages from the Bible, *Al Qur'an*, *I Ching*, *The Gospel of Thomas*, *The Book of Mormon*, and other scriptural documents are as written. The theory of evolution as debated by the characters is, to the author's best effort, presented fairly and objectively. Astounding connections between the biblical book of Genesis and the structure of DNA, its function, and the pattern of life are authentic.

PROLOGUE

On top of a small hill, a flashlight sliced an unsteady cone of visibility from the night. Two camouflaged men hovered over a youthful male body tied to a thick wooden beam with ropes. One man rhythmically pressed the boy's naked chest with his hands.

The other man beamed the flashlight on the boy's face. "You're wasting your goddamn time. He's history."

Tony pressed again. "I'm not ready... to give up."

"He got what he deserved. He's dead because he's a failure."

Tony continued pressing the teenager's chest with one hand clasped over the back of the other, counting the interval between each compression to simulate and encourage a heartbeat.

"For Christ's sake, you're wasting your time. We're doing God's work here, Tony. If one sinner dies along the way, that's what you call 'divine punishment.' He was tested by God, and he failed. He doesn't deserve to live."

Tony stopped giving chest compression and felt for a pulse on the boy's neck, the head lifelessly twisted to one side, exposing an unusual scar on his cheek. After a moment, Tony straightened up, finally resigned to the fact of death. "These boys come here for help, not to stare death in the face." He sighed and shook his head. "It's too much... too much."

"After the way you teased him the other day? Don't act like some sort of angel. If you want to blame anyone, look in the mirr—"

"Shut up, Carl. Just shut up!"

"Sure, I'll be quiet. But that doesn't change the facts."

"Facts? This dead body is the fact I'm worried about." Tony snapped his fingers, then held his hand open. "Where's that knife of yours?"

Carl pulled his knife from a black leather sheath on his utility belt and started to hand it to Tony but then pulled it back. "Hey man, I just cleaned it. What are you going to do? Don't get no blood on it."

Tony grabbed the knife with a jerk, turned, and then sawed his way through the blood encrusted ropes restraining the body to the rustic wooden structure as Carl looked on.

"Here's your precious knife. Don't waste time polishing it; I need your help."

Carl grimaced, took the knife, cleaned it with a swipe, put it back in his sheath.

Tony positioned himself over the boy's head, grasped under his arms, and began to lift him up. He pointed with a motion of his head. "Quick! We've got to get him out of here. Grab his legs."

The two men carried the limp, drooping body down the small hill, around the end of a compound of buildings and past head-high brush. They stopped at the brink of a steep bank littered with trash and garbage, culminating in a large pile of debris at the bottom. For a moment, they set the body down while they caught their breath.

Tony turned his head from the odor of the pit and waved a cloud of flies away. "Carl, on the count of three..."

They lifted the body and proceeded to swing it back and forth as Tony counted: "One... two... three..." Both men grunted as they released the boy into the air. The body twisted and turned like a rag doll, finally coming to rest amid the garbage pile face up but with the legs twisted around to the back. The boy's lifeless eyes popped open and seemed to stare accusingly back at the guards.

CHAPTER 1

What's that? Dan spun around and looked behind him, letting the door of the coffee house swing closed. He held his breath while his eyes darted over the familiar coastal village, looking for someone or something out of place. The tension and touch of fear was the same one he would get as a child, running in the dark from the garage to the house, the one he would get in the middle of the night, wondering about moving shadows or sounds, especially after his father's untimely death when he was only ten.

Leaves blew across the damp sidewalk around parked cars and into the two-lane street; some lodged in the gutter or cracks in the street; others blew up on the aging brick buildings. Massive, gnarled roots of two nearby eucalyptus trees cracked the brick-edged sidewalk with their zest for life. Above, limbs arched over the street and sidled up to the buildings. Dan looked down the street, past the antique store, the women's boutique, and out to the Pacific Ocean, flat and calm under solid gray overcast skies. A flock of seagulls swooped overhead, squawking and chattering as a group. The shops were still closed, not unusual for an early Wednesday morning, but something felt strange. *Why do I feel like someone is watching me?* Dan closed his jacket to block the light ocean breeze and turned back to the door.

He pulled open the rustic wooden door and looked over his shoulder. Half a block back, a bearded man holding a bag of cans and bottles stumbled from between two buildings and staggered off in the opposite direction without making eye contact. *Hmmm. Just a bum,* Dan thought. *That explains it.*

Dan entered the familiar, warm interior of the shop and pulled the door closed. He took one last look through the unusual round porthole window in the door—a door salvaged, perhaps, from the captain's quarters of an ancient sailing ship. The marine theme continued through the coffee house, with antiques, brass hardware, and artwork. Dan could still feel adrenaline in his blood; it would take a few more minutes to relax, even with the comfortable smell of roasted coffee beans and warm scones drifting in the air.

Lately, Dan had been reserving time in the morning for conversation with friends. This was a relatively new practice. For years, he had worked long hours every day at his Internet service company, a company recently sold for a comfortable profit. Finally, he was setting aside some time for leisure, friendship, and perhaps even love. Now, that would be a change.

Only a few customers sat here and there. After buying his coffee, Dan glanced at his two friends sitting as usual at the table where they all had met at the book club gathering several months earlier. Dan's friend John frowned and shook his head, and Dan smiled to himself—*Ah, the old argument again!* Dan approached the table, leaned down, and surprised Shannon with a hug from the back, reaching across her slender waist and dodging her healthy brown hair. She turned and laughed; her gold necklace glinted through the top of her blouse.

John's frown disappeared into a deeper crinkle of his permanent laugh lines. His vice-grip handshake prompted a short squeezing contest. Dan occasionally wondered if that customary death grip was a help or hindrance to John's insurance and financial planning practice.

Dan removed his jacket, placed it over the back of his chair, and made room at the table for his napkin and mug by pushing aside John's black leather Bible and Shannon's hardcover microbiology textbook.

"Scientists have been experimenting with genetic engineering and DNA technology since the '60s," Shannon said.

John picked up his gold pen and twisted it closed. "Huh? I don't remember that."

"People don't keep up with technology. Public awareness...it didn't shift for another twenty years."

"Shift? What shift?" John asked.

Shannon pondered John's question for a moment and sipped her coffee.

Dan's friends were so engrossed in their conversation, they didn't seem to notice his difficulty in getting settled. It seemed that again, John was the reluctant student, resisting all scientific advances and denigrating Shannon's technical biotechnology education. Dan looked out the window, through the trees, and out to the ocean. Birds flew under the clouds to join dark flocks floating on the surface of the sea, only appearing as tiny black dots in the distance.

An answer came to Shannon, and she blurted out, "The shift—I think 'Oh-Jay' did it."

"Oh what? Orange juice?"

"No, no, no. O.J. Simpson. You know, his trial."

Dan picked up and cradled his mug to warm his hands, sitting so he could keep an eye on the door and still be in the conversation—a conversation that could start to get interesting.

John twisted his pen open, wrote "OJ" on his napkin, and then circled the initials. "Right. O.J. Simpson. Sure, everybody remembers that. Don't they? I figured it was just another celebrity in a spat with his wife. Instead it was a huge production. Remember the thirty-five-mile-per-hour freeway chase and the thousands of idiot fans waving 'GO OJ' signs from the overpasses?"

Dan briefly recalled the so-called "trial of the century" that seemed to consume everyone in America and most of the world, one of the first big trials to be fully televised. The reality soap-opera—including everything from a football star, to the celebrity lifestyle, strange roomers, parties, and drugs—ran daily for months; seventy million viewers watched the anticlimactic verdict.

Shannon stirred her coffee with a red plastic stirring stick. "Prosecutors relied heavily on DNA evidence. You can't really argue with matching DNA samples, at least not with the overwhelming statistics."

"O.J. and his 'dream team' tried to blame poor Mark Fuhrman for everything," John said. "They were desperate."

"I wouldn't be so sure. DNA is easy to plant if you want to." Shannon held the straw-like red stirring stick like a laboratory pipette, her thumb over the end as if she were in one of her graduate biotech labs, to keep a few drops of coffee inside. "One drop..." she released a drop onto John's napkin, "...of blood..." she dropped another on Dan's napkin, "...and you've got someone framed. Blood samples from O.J.'s house even contained a blood preservative normally used by forensic labs, and they said they didn't add it. It seems possible that rogue cops planted the glove and the blood. It wouldn't be too hard. Remember? They said, 'We found this glove at the crime scene and a matching glove at O.J.'s house.' Yeah, right. If they planted the glove, how can you trust the blood?" Shannon licked her stirring stick and popped it back in her cup.

Dan set his mug on his "blood"-stained napkin. "Without the DNA evidence, what would they have? Not much, I would say. I'll bet they would've dropped the case," Dan said.

"Except for the bloody glove, you're right. They didn't have much," she said. "My point is that the O.J. trial exposed the general, nonscientific public to biotechnology. DNA, chromosomes, and genetic fingerprints became common during prime time for months. But it really wasn't new at all. DNA evidence was already standard practice in the courtroom, deciding life or death for years. The Simpson case merely brought it to the kitchen table."

"John, why do you have such a hard time accepting the reality of DNA?" Dan asked.

"What proof is there? We can't see it, right?"

"Even under a microscope, it's too thin to see in any detail, that's true. But you can see the chromosomes and there's a lot of supporting evidence. I'm really surprised you'd have any doubt of the existence of DNA at this point."

"I'm afraid our friend here is still hanging on to the Dark Ages."

Shannon patted John on the arm.

"John, you've got to wake up to modern times. It's a hard, cold fact, proven over and over," Dan said. "Is there really any doubt? Geez, in 2003, the Human Genome Project finished unraveling the complete sequence of human DNA. Anyone can view the entire genetic sequence on the Internet, all three billion bases."

Shannon added, "Yeah. Just click on genome.ucsc.org. It's overwhelming: a massive pile of genetic data, like a huge pile of unassembled jigsaw puzzle pieces. It'll be a long time—I'd say at least decades—before scientists decode the meaning of it all."

"Look, I'm no scientist. I'm willing to go along to get along. DNA probably exists. But so what?"

"DNA is not just a simple fact of life." Shannon leaned forward and tapped on the table. "It's the most significant discovery of all time, as far as life is concerned. DNA is at the core of absolutely every form of life, in all animals, all plants, all bacteria, and even viruses. No life form exists that uses anything else."

Dan added, "DNA essentially means life. Remember comparisons of animal skeletons in high school science class? A rat skeleton looks very much like that of a cat, a bird, a whale, and even man, with five digits in their paws, wings, flippers, or hands. All about the same, just proportioned a bit differently. The pattern of life is not just uniform at that level. Organisms are very similar no matter how closely you look. At the genetic level, all life uses basically the same DNA structure, DNA code, cell machinery, and procedures. To the big picture, there simply is no exception!"

The door to the coffee shop creaked open, and Dan glanced up.

CHAPTER 2

Knock, knock, knock.

Agent Russell Hall turned away from the door and looked out to the street. Noisy children rode their tricycles down the heavily cracked sidewalk just beyond a twisted and rusty chain-link fence. He glanced at his government-issued Ford sedan parked behind a faded-blue Camaro with four flat tires. *That car probably hasn't moved for months*, Hall thought.

Hall had seen a lot in his twenty-seven-year FBI career and this light investigative work was not too exciting, but it wasn't all that dangerous either. This easy, safe work was just what the doctor ordered, he reasoned, for a few more years until he retired anyway. Why not leave the danger of the more significant busts to the younger agents? But deep down, he still enjoyed the intensity and excitement of those busts.

Following his usual practice, he unsnapped his concealed holster and felt the hammer of his handgun, cocked and ready to fire. He really didn't expect any trouble, but he never let his guard down completely. His business suit may blend with the attire used in the financial district downtown, but in this rundown residential neighborhood, he might as well have worn a jacket with "FBI" clearly emblazoned on its back in eight-inch high yellow letters, perfect for urban target practice.

A crescendo of sound alerted Hall. Someone inside approached the door, and he turned to face it. The door opened only a crack, restrained by a security chain.

"Yessir, who's there?" the woman asked in a thick, uneducated, southern accent.

"Good morning, ma'am. Agent Hall, FBI." Hall pulled out his leather badge holder, opened it, and showed his identification card and shiny badge in one well-practiced move. "Is this the Freeman residence?"

The woman closed the door to remove the security chain, then opened it wide. "Oh, yes. Come on in. I'm Mrs. Freeman, Delia Freeman. I was told someone'd visit."

"Thank you; happy to meet you, Mrs. Freeman." Hall shook her hand and walked into the room as she held the door.

After he entered, she closed the door and engaged the safety chain, then darted ahead of him, clearing children's toys from the floor and moving a stack of newspapers and magazines from the couch. "Wontcha sit down, Mr. Hall? I won't be but a minute." She turned to three children peering through an open door. "Younguns, you get in that room, go on, get!" She hustled them in as if they were sheep, deposited the toys and newspapers after them, and then closed the door. Her hair was tightly braided and she touched it with her hand as she walked back. "Wouldja like somethin' to drink, Mr. Hall?"

"Oh, no. But thank you for offering." Hall waited for her to take a seat. He pulled out a small notebook and pen from his jacket pocket to take notes. "I'm new on this case Mrs. Freeman, so if you don't mind, please start from the beginning. My case file didn't tell me much." Hall always started an interview this way, even if he had been working on the case for years.

"It's just terrible. I got no trace of my son William at all. He's just up and gone." Mrs. Freeman's dark brown eyes glistened with worry.

"Your son William, how old is he?"

"Well, he's seventeen. He'll be eighteen in four more months, but it seems like only yesterday he was just a baby."

"Does he live here?"

"Well, no, not now. Ya see, William would get in and out of trouble and was falling into them gangs that hangs around here. Ya see, our family is God-fearing. There ain't no way we'd let William go on down that path of the devil."

Hall looked behind Mrs. Freeman to the large crucifix adorned with blood-red paint hanging on the wall.

"So, we enrolls him in that program, the one at that Pacific Institute of Theology for Youth—PITY, ya know. They call it PITY 'cause they takes pity on our kids and straightens 'em up. Ya know, it's one of them 'youth rescue' programs."

"Oh, yes. I've heard of that type of a program. Is that a school?"

"Oh, my yes, it's a boarding school, ya know. He was doing real nice, making good changes and all that. We were all happy as the dickens. He wrote me letters every single week for 'bout three months." She looked at Hall and shook her head, tears welled up, her voice rose in pitch. "Ya know, William's really not that bad inside. He wrote his Momma like I told him he had to. He said everything was just fine, he liked the place and all. But a few weeks back, he stopped writin'." She paused and looked at Hall. "They say he just left—if you can believe that. I know my William would write his Momma. I'm just sick!" Mrs. Freeman sniffed and cried, fanning herself with a magazine as if she were in a heat-soaked church in Alabama.

Hall didn't say anything immediately. He let Mrs. Freeman wipe the tears from the corners of her eyes and relax her voice.

"They said he just left?"

"That's the thing. You see, you don't just leave that kind of place.

They keep track 'round the clock. You do exactly what they say or you're in a heap of trouble. And most kids, they don't fight for long. William fought for a while. He just wanted to leave, but they said no. The next week, he was a bit strange. Just perfect, ya know, a perfect angel. We were surprised they got him going right straight so fast. We thought they'd give up on him. Nah, they broke 'im, and fast."

"I see. Do you have any of those letters he sent?"

"Oh my, yes, I saved 'em all." The tears started to flow again. "William's my first baby, ya know. I missed him even if he was a royal pain in the bee-hind." She got up and went to the other room, disciplining the kids on the way. She returned, holding a stack of letters.

"Thank you," he said. "If you don't mind, I'd like to keep these for the case file."

"I don't know, Mr. Hall. Those'd be the last letters I've got from my first boy. I don't want to lose 'em."

"Okay. I'll tell you what. I'll make photocopies, and I'll send them back tomorrow, okay?"

"Well, I guess that'll be okay, Mr. Hall. As long as I get 'em back. I been reading 'em every day."

Hall paused, then said, "What else happened?"

"Nothin', really. I don't know nothing more than that, I guess."

"How did you find out he was missing? Did the school contact you?"

"After I didn't receive no letters from him, I called that school. They said he was just missing, that he ran away, or something. I just can't believe it. I can't believe they would just lose track like that and say nothing, nothing at all!"

Hall noticed a picture on the bookcase behind Mrs. Freeman. "Is that a picture of William?"

"He's only fifteen in that one, but he's still about the same, only a bit taller."

"Is that a scar on his face?"

"From a real bad burn. He was nothin' but a baby."

"I see." Hall didn't push the questioning any further.

"Do ya think you'll find what happened to my William?"

"That's our job, ma'am. We'll do everything we can to find him." He reached into his pocket. "Here's my card. Please call me right away if you hear from William or from anyone from PITY. I'll be your primary law enforcement contact from here on out. Okay?"

"Oh, thank you, Mr. Hall. I most definitely will call if I hear anything, anything at all. Please, please find my William—and God bless!"

CHAPTER 3

Dan watched the door of the coffee house. A bearded, unkempt man in a dark-brown hooded sweat suit entered and stood silently for a moment. As Dan stared at the newcomer, Shannon's voice outlining the history of DNA starting in the mid 1800s merged with Dan's thoughts and the image of the stranger. The surroundings of the coffee house seemed to fade and change. Slowly, the brown sweat suit morphed into the tunic of the Augustinian Monk, Gregor Mendel. The walls of the coffee house became the aging walls of the Altbrünn monastery seventy miles north of Vienna in 1859.

"Brother Gregor, why do you no longer take any interest in your gardening? You've enjoyed tending and breeding your peas for thirty years. Now you completely avoid the garden. What happened to your love of nature?" The Abbot Cyrillus Napp patted Mendel on the back.

Mendel nodded and stared blankly out the window. "You said the Natural Science Society would be interested in the laws of heredity... True, they listened to my talk and clapped courteously. But no questions! No comments at all!" He turned to face the Abbot and waved his hands with emotion. "They still think everything is completely random. My research proves that heredity follows strict mathematical laws." He put his hands down. "They ignored it. They don't even understand dominant and recessive traits. It's the discovery of the century, but they just scoffed." He looked back out the window and stood silently, then continued. "I've discovered God's laws of heredity but no one cares. Tending the garden only reminds me of the humiliation." He paused and stabilized his voice, then turned back to the Abbot. "The Abbey needs my attention now." He put his hand on the Abbot's shoulder. "I know you're getting on in years, and...well, I realize you expect me to take over... when the time comes."

Dan jerked and shook his head to snap out of this strange hypnotic trace. Even as the modern coffee house reappeared, his thoughts lingered over his unusual daydream. Indeed, Gregor Mendel was far ahead of his time. Ridiculed and ignored, scientists would scoff at his breakthrough for another four decades, until it was rediscovered and proved again in 1900. Then, the march of science continued, marked by the discovery of the structure of DNA in 1953 by Watson and Crick, all the way to the Human Genome Project, which sequenced the DNA of a human, completed in 2003. The whole course of discovery didn't start until the microscope was sufficiently developed in about 1830, and the rest completed in less than 200 years, a historical blink of an eye.

By the time Dan returned fully to his senses, the bedraggled stranger had moved to the counter and ordered a coffee. When his drink came, the man walked directly toward their table. His worn baseball cap protruded from under his brown hood. Dan expected that the man might ask for spare change, a cigarette, or a bottle of whiskey, but he simply sat quietly at the table right next to theirs.

The three friends dipped their heads in a silent, uncomfortable greeting. Although Dan didn't want to, he readjusted his chair to give the newcomer a bit more room. Sitting just beyond the limit of Dan's peripheral vision, the stranger stayed quiet but could obviously overhear their conversation.

Was this guy following me? He's getting awfully close. What happened to his bag of bottles and cans?

"I've seen pictures of DNA, that's true. It's that thing that looks like a twisted staircase, right?" John sketched it on his napkin, right next to the drip of coffee and the word "OJ."

"Good job, John." Shannon clapped softly. "You say you hardly believe it exists at all. I'm surprised you have any idea what it looks like."

"Well, everybody's seen pictures of it, that doesn't prove anything."

Dan looked again at Shannon, admired her as a person, and was suddenly struck by the fact that he was deeply attracted to her. During his entrepreneurial years, Dan had been too busy for any relationship. Now, he was ready for something to happen. *I might have a chance with Shannon,* he thought.

The two men listened as Shannon elaborated on the wonders of DNA. With each sentence, it seemed Dan was drawn closer to her while John drifted away. "You've got about seventy trillion cells in your body, each an incredibly complex molecular machine," she said. "Each one of those cells has an identical copy of your genetic code, described by DNA molecules wound into forty-six chromosomes."

John leaned back in his chair and folded his arms.

"It's amazing how much DNA there is in each cell," Dan said. "Assume you could take all the DNA out of just one of those cells and lay it out straight, end-to-end, so it would look like that spiral staircase you just drew." He pointed at the diagram on John's napkin. "How long do you think it would it be?"

John raised his eyebrows; he certainly didn't know. Shannon almost said something, but Dan continued, not really wanting an answer. "I'll tell you... It wouldn't be one millimeter long; it wouldn't be one centimeter long; get this: it would be about six feet long. Two meters of DNA from one tiny cell!"

"Wow. That's longer than I thought it would be." John stretched his arms out to measure off six feet in the air, about as far as he could reach. He looked like a seated Vitruvian Man. "Are you sure that'll fit into one cell?"

"Even though it's as long as some people are tall, it's far from being visible. Remember, it's so thin that it can coil up into a very small cell, a cell so tiny that you can't even see it. I did the calculations the other day to bring this to something I could intuitively grasp."

"You're kidding," John said, letting his arms hang down in disbelief.

Dan had to be careful. Math and technology were fun and games for him, and he was used to being around other technically savvy colleagues. Lately, with his new nontechnical friends, he would catch himself going overboard, losing everyone around and lecturing to himself like a delusional genius madman.

"If you take that super-thin six-foot strand of DNA, the DNA from just one cell, and magnified it so you could just barely see it—say the width of a common human hair—guess how long it would be?"

"Right, right, as if I know," John said. "Okay, bright-eyes, how long?"

"Imagine a strand of DNA 'hair' that's five hundred miles long. That's from just one cell!"

"I knew it was long, but that *is* a lot of hair to keep straight!" Shannon said as she pulled back her dark brown hair into a ponytail, then let it fall naturally. She kept her hair about shoulder length and generally avoided cosmetics. As a gifted microbiology student, she had more important things to do. Dan didn't mind, that's for sure.

"No wonder it remains tightly coiled in our chromosomes. Can you imagine the job of untangling five hundred miles of hair? Talk about a bad hair day!" she said, chuckling.

John turned to face Dan. "I can't believe that you 'just happened' to do that calculation, Dan. You're such a nerd! I'm happy that I don't waste my time making math calculations 'just for fun.'"

"Yeah, we know. You just read the Bible, over and over!" Shannon said, patting John on the arm.

"Hey, if I'm a science nerd, then God is too," Dan retorted, cocking his head. "The scientific complexities of the world require the high intelligence of a nerd like me to understand them." Dan adjusted his collar. “I consider it a compliment, John. Thank you.”

John didn’t have a comeback.

Dan held his hands about shoulder-width apart. “Look at the bigger picture, I’d say it’s really the biggest picture. The sequence of bases in our DNA defines our looks, our height, our intelligence, and even our personality. I’ve read studies of identical twins separated at birth. In spite of different environments and life experiences, they led very, very similar lives.”

John continued to doodle on his napkin, writing “DNA” as Dan talked.

“I’ll never forget the story of identical twins separated at birth and raised in Ohio, eighty miles apart. Both bit their nails, chain-smoked Salem cigarettes, and drank Miller Lite. Both loved stock car racing and hated baseball. In school, they both were poor students and eventually worked as sheriff’s deputies. If that’s not enough, both married women named Linda, got divorced, and then married women named Betty. One selected *James Alan* for his son—with just *one l,* while the other picked *James Allan*—with two *l*’s. And, their dogs? Both were named Toy. Their hobby was woodworking in nearly identical basement workshops. Although no one else in their neighborhoods had them, each built a circular white bench in their front yards. All this, and they had never met. It’s a bit scary, if you ask me.”

Shannon grimaced. “Creepy, that’s what I would say. Creepy.”

“Stop right there,” John said. “Are you saying that absolutely everything about a person is genetically controlled?”

“Almost, but there are exceptions,” Shannon said. “For example, even identical twins have unique fingerprints. DNA doesn’t define those fractal-like swirls and patterns of the ridges on your fingers. Many personality traits are probably unique as well. If you experience a lousy family life, maybe you never learn to be a good parent. Then your kids also have lousy family lives. Does this mean it’s genetically controlled, or is it just learned? It’s difficult to know exactly where to draw that line between genetic control and environmental effect or even pure human choice.”

“I see.”

“But many genetically controlled diseases are clear-cut,” she said. “Some forms of diabetes are caused by a defect in the proteins involved in metabolism; sickle-cell anemia is controlled by a single defect in the hemoglobin protein. The completion of the Human Genome Project means that we might overcome these defects and have healthier lives. Science and medicine are poised at the edge of a very bright future. To me, it’s quite exciting!”

Ugh, kuk, kuk, ugh.

The stranger at the next table cleared his throat loudly enough to disrupt the whole coffee shop, and several other patrons looked over.

"Hah! You're missing the point!" he said loudly, with a voice of an older man, a bit broken and with extra white noise.

The three thinkers turned around, looked at him, looked back at each other, and then motioned for him to continue.

"You're...you're completely missing it!" He cackled, snorting through his nose.

There was silence. From the darkness under the bill of his worn-out baseball cap, he glared.

CHAPTER 4

Rebecca opened one of the large, white doors and stepped into Bishop Richard Ward's ostentatious office. Marble floors reflected light from the towering windows behind his huge desk, leaving his face in a shady darkness. She walked over to the side of the desk, about twenty steps from the door. Her black patent leather shoes clicked with each step; the sound echoed against the ornately carved vaulted ceiling and walls, all stark white.

Rebecca needed her job as the Bishop's assistant. But deep down, she really hated his disgusting quirks. For one, he required her to bow her head in apparent pious humility as she talked to him and then genuflect as she left his side. Even though she knew he deserved not one ounce of respect, it was a practice easily mastered; she could fool him every time. She would accept her place in the world, at least for now.

Most other executives used an intercom for their assistant to connect calls. Not so for the Bishop. He required that Rebecca walk in for each call and display the excessive reverence that he enjoyed so much.

"Sir, the 'General' is on line one." Her voice echoed off the floors, walls, and large glass semicircular bow windows that surrounded his desk, lost in the volume of the room. A call from the General was always important. Rebecca bowed her head and dropped her right knee to the floor for a moment, meeting the Bishops expectations.

The Bishop put out a hand to stop her from leaving. "One moment, Rebecca, I have something for you." He picked up the cordless phone with his manicured hand; his gold rings glistened.

Rebecca stood beside his desk and waited.

"Hello? Yes, General, how are you...? Just fine. Thank you for calling...Certainly, sir— ...We are— ...We are on schedule to deliver as discussed. No, I'm—" The Bishop fidgeted, unable to complete any sentence.

Rebecca could tell the Bishop felt pressure. Unusual. The Bishop usually had the upper hand, frequently bringing callers to their metaphorical knees.

"Sir, I can explain. Our training methods haven't changed and are still quite effective. Yes, one of our trainers was a bit overzeal— ...Sir, I understand that you're ups— ...There's no reason this should impact our arrangement. Trust me. This will never reach the light of day...Yes..."

His voice trailed off. He limply placed the handset back in the cradle and stared into space.

Rebecca enjoyed the novelty of seeing the Bishop reveal a weak side. Kissing up, begging, and then left listening to a dial tone—all certainly out of place with this power-hungry man. What was the Bishop upset about?

Something had gone wrong. Very wrong.

CHAPTER 5

"What's this 'point' you say we're missing?" Dan asked intently, surprised by the challenge of the bearded vagabond.

The man leaned toward the group and cleared his throat again. "Well, you say it's a fact that DNA and the details of life are the same for all life, right?"

"Absolutely." Shannon set her coffee down and picked up the stirring stick again; she waved it as she talked. "There's no debate about that. Scientists are amazed at the uniformity among—"

"Well then," the stranger interrupted, "is it also true that throughout history, life used exactly the same pattern? For example, were the humans of six thousand years ago also based on DNA and cells like we have today?"

"Without a doubt," Shannon answered. "Mummified remains from Egypt are at least that old. They've recently recovered DNA from Neanderthals, perhaps 30,000 years old. I understand that DNA may have been recovered from bones of a prehistoric animal—perhaps a dinosaur—from an 1,800-foot-deep coal mi—"

"Surface," he grunted. "You're just talking on the surface. You've got to dig in. Push your discussion deeper." He dug his hands into the air before him as if he were scooping out a hole.

The three friends scanned faces and waited for him to continue.

Wasn't our discussion already deep? What does this guy mean? Dan thought.

Shannon didn't say anything. She apparently thought 1,800 feet was already deep enough.

The stranger stroked his heavy beard. "Let me start with a simple question: Would God understand DNA? Would God understand this uniform underlying pattern of life?"

Oh great, a homeless beach preacher, just what we need, Dan thought.

"Okay, that's easy," John said, without delay. "Of course he would. God created the universe, earth, and all life. He would obviously know everything about DNA and how biology works. Indeed, since all life is built on this one pattern, I think it proves a single source of creation, the intelligent design of a single creator."

"Wait..." Shannon held up the red plastic stirring stick to make her point. "This single pattern—it's more likely the result of evolution from a single primordial life form. God could have used many patterns. Why use only one? Why would an unlimited God be limited to only one pattern? Evolutionary theory is much more strongly supported by this simple question."

"Shannon, we all know we'll never agree on this," John said in a condescending voice. "Let's try to answer this guy's question and not get sidetracked, okay? If you accept that God exists, he would obviously understand DNA, right?"

"Okay, John, fine." Shannon was abrupt. "Look, if you assume that God created life and knows all about it, then God would obviously know all about it. If he knows it, then he knows it. That's what logicians call a 'tautology'—a definition that simply proves itself. It's worthless!"

This introduction of religion into their otherwise peaceful conversation delineated a war zone between Shannon and John. Dan began to worry that this normally taboo topic would ruin the three-way friendship and bonding the group had developed since they first met at the book club meeting. Yet, it seemed he and Shannon were becoming closer in the process.

Dan wanted to find some middle ground. "Consider this: In spite of all our scientific understanding, the basic forces of nature are still quite mysterious; we have to agree on that. For example, magnetic fields can be defined and mathematically described to great detail—we have cell phones, radios, TVs—but scientists really don't know how such invisible fields can exist. They just do. Gravity is even more baffling. We are subject to its constant influence, but we don't know how it works. We can't manipulate the gravity field at all—at least, not yet. There are no anti-gravity cars or gravity lenses, or anything like that.

"Even though we don't really know how they can exist, these basic forces define how our world works. If evolution is factual, it also complies with these basic laws of nature, even if the ultimate source of those forces is unknown. Evolution doesn't explain why these underlying laws of nature exist, but it must still conform to those laws. I can understand how a reasonable person can rely on God as the creator of these invisible forces while still embracing the theory of evolution. It's not too hard."

"Since we have complete agreement on that question, let's move on." The stranger smirked, but beneath his cap his eyes twinkled. "You can believe what you want, but let's assume, for sake of discussion at least, that there is a god—a creator. God would obviously understand DNA and the secrets of biological mechanisms; that seems simple enough. But that's not really the question I was talking about." His eyes grew serious as he held their gaze.

"The question, my friends, is simply this: Are these biological facts ever described by sacred literature? For example, have you ever seen any mention of DNA and the basic pattern of life in the Bible?"

The room grew quiet. Ceiling fans turned slowly above their heads and the red second-hand of the clock on the far wall ticked off the seconds one by one.

Dan looked beneath the man's worn bill into clear, youthful eyes surrounded by wrinkles that hinted of a wealth of experience. His full, graying beard effectively concealed most of the rest of his face. *This can't be just a homeless vagrant. Maybe he's an ex-professor whose life was ruined by the bottle.*

"Well, you pose a very interesting question, my friend, but we don't even know your name. My name is Dan." He shook hands with the stranger.

"Hello, I'm Walker."

"Pleasure." Walker's somewhat soiled hand fit comfortably with Dan's, and he had an unusually disarming and solid handshake.

"This is Shannon and John." They shook hands in turn. "I don't think I've seen you here before. Are you new to the area?"

Walker rocked back in his seat. "Well, no, I'm not new in any respect." He cleared his throat. "Haven't been here recently, that's true enough." He didn't elaborate.

"This question about the Bible...I really think you're barking up the wrong tree." John shook his head and spoke a bit defensively. "You can't consider the Bible as some sort of science book. The Bible is about love, relationships, and the failings of mankind. It recounts the history of the Jewish culture and reveals the story of Christ.

"Plus, it sounds impossible to describe such modern-day technical information. You're not going to find technical jargon like what...? Oh yes: *DNA, chromosome, protein*, you know, words like that. Those words didn't exist six thousand years ago. I'm certain that the Bible doesn't describe that high-tech stuff. But just because you can't find scientific details in the Bible, it doesn't mean that it's any less true or inspired."

Dan shifted his chair a bit. "John, I agree with your point on terminology: We shouldn't expect modern scientific words in the Bible."

"You're absolutely right about that," Shannon added. "*DNA* stands for *deoxyribonucleic acid*, a term coined in the last century. That can't appear in any Bible, that's for sure."

"Yet, even though the words are new, the facts of life are the same now as they were then," Dan said. "DNA was the same then as now."

Walker raised his hand. "Consider this question: Could a story in the Bible explain the underlying principles of life without mentioning any advanced terms?"

Dan leaned back in his chair and looked beyond the group. "Now, *that* would be interesting." He talked slowly, pacing each word as he thought. "If the pattern of life could be found and clearly matched with modern-day understanding—wow." He sat back up and pointed into the air. "Any descriptions would have to be limited to general concepts only. Complex descriptions, covering minute details of biology, seem totally impossible, right? The details are much, much too complicated for these to be covered in ancient literature." Dan readjusted his position. "But, with all that said, I'm sorry to say that I'll have to disagree with your conclusion, John. It's possible."

"We should go one step further," Shannon said, almost interrupting. "The pattern of life is uniform, pervasive, and all-inclusive. It's the single pattern used for all life on earth. You can't get any more universal than that. If you talk about life, you *must* mention DNA. Any divinely inspired literature about life *must* describe that pattern for it to be regarded as legitimate. This information is so important, it's not optional. It must be included. I'll go along with you, John."

John raised his eyebrows and further opened his eyes.

She continued, "Look, I'm with you. I'm sure DNA won't be discussed in the Bible. It comes down to a simple fact, one that you'll probably never admit, John: The Bible is not divinely inspired. You won't admit it, but it's easy to prove. These universal secrets of life are omitted, like you said. They should be included, but they are simply missing. You've got to face it, John. Evolution is fact. Biblical creationism is a farce. The stories in the Bible are just that, stories to keep the masses in line and keep the high priests in power, nothing more."

John thought for a moment, his eyebrows lowered and brow furrowed. "Your point is a good one, Dan." He looked sharply at Shannon and then back at Dan, nodding his head. "I think I'm going to go along with it. There probably *is* a story somewhere in the Bible that could be interpreted as describing DNA and the fundamentals of life. I... I think that isn't too hard to imagine. No modern scientific terms, only common words, we agree on that.

"If you could find this passage and make a good case for how it describes the modern understanding of DNA, you would make history, there's no question about that. For one thing, that would authenticate the Bible like no other test."

He turned to Shannon. "Your absurd claim—that the Bible is all made up by humans to maintain control of the masses. Sorry, that's simply wrong. It's the *Word of God,* Shannon. Just read it. You'll know in your heart that it's true."

Shannon exhaled loudly and pressed her lips tightly together.

John paused and then went on, pointing into the air. "If we find descriptions of DNA, cells, and biological facts, it would put this issue to bed once and for all. You just said that DNA and these underlying patterns were discovered only in the last century or so. It certainly wasn't information available to Moses, Abraham, the Apostles, or anyone else who might have had a hand in writing the Bible."

"That's right," Dan said, dipping his head once.

Shannon threw her red stirring stick down onto the table. "You're both sounding ridiculous! Until you find the story and can clearly make the case for how it describes these life patterns, all this is just idle coffee-shop nonsense. If you can't find a good correlation to the underlying pattern of life, we should write the Bible off once and for all as religious tripe—superstitions—and that's it."

"Shannon, that isn't fair." John's voice started to get out of control. "You can't base your acceptance of the Bible only on whether you can find a description of DNA and biotechnology. The Bible has value as a guide to a good and moral life even if there is no support for this DNA crap. Countless believers find guidance through the Ten Commandments and the teachings of Jesus. That value is far greater than just a summary of some scientific theory." He swallowed some emotion. "I've known people whose lives were in the gutter, in a shallow pursuit of alcohol, drugs, and instant gratification. Christianity turned these people around to lead productive lives." His voice cracked only very slightly; he avoided their eyes and paused for a moment. "Do you want to debate the value of religion to people who have transformed their lives? And why would you want to do such a thing? If you show a tie-in between the Bible and DNA, it won't change the true value of religion as I see it."

Dan wanted to defuse the tension. He spoke dispassionately, "There's certainly merit in religious beliefs apart from any factual recounting of scientific details. We should agree up front that we don't want to challenge the value of personal transformation."

Tension in John's face relaxed; he took a deep breath.

Dan continued with a positive tone. "Still, I like Walker's question. Fifty years ago, no one could ask it. If the Bible describes DNA and other life mechanisms, then for the first time in history, that description could finally be located and understood."

Walker moved his chair closer to join the others. He kept his voice low and his head down. "Listen. You're obviously a very capable group with different points of view. That's good. You seem to be open to new ideas. That's also good. It's an openness you won't find in the ivory towers of the 'experts.' Take a look at this question. It's a mystery, the most important mystery you could ever solve."

Dan raised his eyebrows, cocked his head, and then nodded. "It's certainly an intriguing challenge. There's no crime in looking into this to see what develops. Maybe we should start with clearly accepted biological facts and then look for corresponding patterns in ancient biblical literature. Of course, we should avoid theories that are in question or primarily speculation."

Walker winked and leaned back. "That's the spirit!"

"This sounds like the age-old battle between scientists and Christians." John wrinkled his brow and waved his arms wildly. "Atheists want to rip apart the beliefs of Christians and replace them with a belief in naturalism or scientism. Scientists say the world formed an incredible five billion years ago, with the notion that life rose by chance from what? Random ooze? And then, also purely by chance, proceeded to plants, fish, amphibians, reptiles, mammals, and finally, man? It's insane."

Shannon folded her arms and frowned.

"Creationists feel that Genesis provides the obvious truth." John slapped his Bible. "The universe formed in the six days of the creation about six thousand years ago. I, for one, think that the 'by chance' concept is totally hopeless. The amazing complexity of the world implies an omnipotent creator. And, since no one was around to witness the creation, this mystery will never be solved."

"This simply isn't on the same level as the question of creation versus evolution," Dan said. "The practice of science as a culture has produced some astounding successes, unlocking the mysteries of nature like no other method. These are not just pie-in-the-sky theories without much merit, but facts of the natural world, the pattern of God's creation, if you will. DNA is not just a questionable theory. Walker's question is simple. If we look at the scripture with a new eye, will we see a 'pattern match' with biological facts? Those facts of life could be described even if the creation story is true. You have to admit, it is very enticing!"

"We're jumping the gun to think that the Bible actually describes such high-tech information," John said. "It's a very large book. This could be one of those never-ending projects. Just because you can't find those patterns doesn't mean they're not in there—somewhere. Theologians have been hard at work interpreting the meaning of the Bible for centuries." John looked at his watch and drank the last few drops of coffee. "I've got to go. I'm still interested, but I think this is going nowhere."

"Wait." Walker looked around to make sure no one could overhear, then moved slightly closer to the group.

CHAPTER 6

Agent Hall left the Freeman house, walked by the Camaro, and then got into his car, reviewing his interview with Mrs. Freemen. William is missing. There's no question about that, at least from the perspective of his mother. And just prior to his disappearance, he was enrolled in this school, the PITY. One possibility is that he could have just left PITY on his own. He could be happily walking the streets, unaware that he is missed at all. For that matter, why is this considered material for the FBI? Missing-persons cases are usually handled by local law enforcement. It doesn't become a matter for the FBI until it becomes an interstate issue or a chain of similar events.

Why should I worry about that? Hall asked himself, realizing that all too often, he was just a cog in the bureaucratic wheel. His assignments were out of his hands, an unfortunate fact of life in a hierarchical organization like the FBI. Higher-ups frequently misunderstood the situation, making poor decisions just because they're unaware of details lost because of rapid assignment changes.

He scanned the letters from William to his mother. The first few letters were defiant, full of objections to being placed in the institution, promising that he would leave and soon. As the weeks passed, William's tone changed remarkably from defiant to pious. The last letters were filled with blessings, "Praise-the-Lords," and comments about Christ's sacrifice. The regularity of the letters was amazing. Who would expect a defiant seventeen-year-old to conscientiously write his mother every single week?

Hall put the stack of letters in the pocket of his briefcase. So far, this case seemed very simple. Cut and dry. He pulled out the case information sheet and looked it over again. Indeed, this was not the only missing person or unusual accident related to the case. The case file listed a string of cases, all related to the PITY school or its parent, the PIT. Then, just like the time he first studied the case file, Hall saw something that made his gut react. On the list was a name of another missing person, *George Stanfield*, in a case from twenty-five years ago. But that isn't what got to Hall. The name of the investigator next to that case is what grabbed him.

Agent Russell Hall.

He looked out the window. Kids rode their tricycles back down the sidewalk and a heavy gust of wind swayed the trees next to the buildings. That was a long time ago. It was one of his first cases, and he still remembered how the Bureau dropped it—dropped it and covered it up with a bogus story.

I need to revisit the PIT.

CHAPTER 7

The vagabond continued with a lower volume, just over a whisper. He looked through his thick, bushy gray eyebrows, his beard moved with his words. "I must warn you. Be careful where you talk about this project. It could be dangerous. I'm serious."

Those words made the hair stand up on the back of Dan's neck. Not the words themselves, but how Walker said them. "Uh, really? Well, okay." Dan wrinkled his forehead. The others accepted the warning without comment but with similar quizzical expressions.

"John," Dan said as his friend put on his jacket, "with your commanding knowledge of biblical matters, perhaps you could whittle-down the likely books or chapters where we might want to look first."

"Yeah, thanks, Dan. Thanks a lot. It's like saying there's a pin in the haystack, and I need to find it. Well, I'll admit that I do like this sort of study, so I won't hold it against you. I'll try to come up with some suggestions at least." John grabbed his Bible.

"Great!" Dan said.

Shannon shook her head and stood up from her seat, holding her biotechnology textbook. "I'll do my part even though I'm certain this is a waste of time. I can put together some basic patterns of life, patterns we can look for. I should have something that will help us from my university classes—a high-level primer of the 'central dogma' of life from a biological perspective, you might say. It'll help me review, even if we never do anything with it."

"Ah yes, just what I was thinking, Shannon," Dan said.

"It's been, well..., interesting...meeting you, Walker," Shannon said with several pauses as she shook his hand.

"I agree, Walker. That question—I'll make a point to look into it," John said.

"See you tomorrow, okay?" they said to Dan.

John and Shannon both walked out of the coffee house and into the wind of the damp street.

* * *

Dan sat alone with Walker, contemplating the stranger with a challenging question and unusual way about him. Dan recalled his earlier sensation of having been watched. Maybe this guy was the source of that feeling. He wasn't sure.

"It's a mystery all right, one that may produce historical results, if you work it out. But, I can't stress this enough: Be cautious when and where you work on it."

"Right, you said to be careful. That's really just a bit ridiculous, isn't it?"

Walker looked around again to make sure no one could overhear and moved slightly closer to Dan. "Let's just say that I have a strong sense you'll find far more than you expect. What if you actually find a scriptural passage that clearly describes and explains DNA and the uniform pattern of life?"

"Sure, that's a remote possibility." Dan didn't feel like he needed to whisper. "But we haven't found such a passage yet. It may take forever to find it."

"Yeah, but that's not the problem you need to imagine. Consider this: What would the implications be? Now, that is the question, my friend. You see, *any* alternative interpretation of important passages in religious literature will challenge the conventional wisdom of the church. It's only human nature to resist changing long-held beliefs about anything, particularly the story of our origins and our relationship to God." Walker played with his coffee cup. "You strike me as a man with a scientific background, willing to let the cards fall where they may, without pushing your result one way or the other to support previous beliefs. Am I right?"

Dan leaned back in his chair and accepted the compliment. "Well, I like to think that's true, but I realize I'm subject to my own biased world view, just like anyone else."

"For you to be successful, you and your friends must not be part of the so-called 'establishment.' People who have climbed those ivory towers feel intense pressure to maintain the status quo—they'll never entertain new ideas. In ages past, if you questioned religious doctrine, you'd face execution. Even today, not everyone has an open mind. Those intolerant few will do whatever they can to discredit any results you might find."

"Yeah, that's probably true."

Walker continued. "Although we like to think we're in a world where almost anything can be published, the large publishing houses are controlled by those clinging to conventional wisdom. New ideas are ignored. Anyone lucky enough to get by those gatekeepers still have an uphill battle. They'll be confronted with an all-out effort to formally refute and discredit their ideas in the form of books, articles, and sermons. Their adversaries hope that any new viewpoint, no matter how true, will be conveniently forgotten, and people will return to the established world-view, no matter how false."

Walker paused and swallowed, then continued at a still lower volume. "If your viewpoint challenges the views of fanatics in the establishment, you could get on their hit list. Your only recourse is to abandon your identity and start a new life, avoiding the spotlight at all costs. That is, if you want to stay alive."

Dan looked at the repaired brim of Walker's cap, hand sewn with a contrasting thread, and then at the sweat stains in the crease. The ceiling fans turned slowly overhead.

"Wait a minute," Dan objected. "This is the twenty-first century. Sure, the church persecuted Copernicus and Galileo for their views, but that was in the 1500s. Sure, Darwin experienced a great deal of animosity over the years, but in this day and age? I really don't think so."

"Well, I only wish you were right." Walker looked down, apparently to conceal his reaction. He said nothing for a moment.

Dan looked out at the calmness of the ocean and drank the last few drops of cold coffee. *This guy must have had some first-hand experience to be this paranoid.* He looked at Walker. A man with educated enunciation and the ability to think and be productive. *Why does he go around looking like he just slept in a dumpster?* Dan's face flushed. He started to realize the full extent of the possibilities—that Walker himself might be running from those fanatics, and might have abandoned his identity, just as he described.

Indeed, even within relatively open-minded scientific circles, it can be difficult to get work published if it doesn't comply with the current thoughts of the high priests of science. And if the ideas challenge the beliefs of religious extremists, the risks could be much higher. Was Walker running from extremist forces? The idea seemed to make some sense.

Walker cleared his throat. "Although Darwin and others proposed contrarian views, they kept their work strictly in the scientific domain. They avoided measuring their work against any particular scripture or biblical passage. If you do that, you're making a direct challenge to religious doctrine. That's where this question differs from the approach of the scientists you mention. You're working directly with 'sacred' documents. That can be dangerous.

"Listen." He looked directly into Dan's eyes, then continued softly with tightened lips. "Work on your project only in private. Be ready to take evasive action if the worst-case scenario should start to develop. Don't involve the church officials any more than necessary. Don't give them a chance to get to you before your work is finished."

Dan looked at him and nodded his head in agreement and only mumbled, "Okay." There was a pause.

Walker straightened up in his chair. "Dan, what is your religious background, anyway?"

"Well, till I was ten years old, I was raised as a Christian. My father was a researcher at the Pacific Institute of Theology. He called it 'The PIT'." Dan snickered. "After he was killed in a car accident, we pretty much avoided religion."

"Your father worked at the PIT?"

"Till he died, like I said, when I was ten. That was about twenty-five years ago."

"Stanfield...You're Dan Stanfield, am I right?"

Dan blinked and then sat motionless. "Yes...how do you know my last name?"

Walker mumbled for a moment and finally composed a sentence Dan could understand. "Well, I knew a *George Stanfield* years ago. He also worked at the PIT."

"That was my father's name." Dan sat perfectly still. His father's death was one of those areas of unfinished business in his life.

Walker stared into blank air, remembering. "He helped me get back on my feet once or twice. He was a good man, your father."

Dan had only sketchy memories of his father and really no information about what his father actually researched at the PIT. His mother followed a strictly secular way of life, with strong moral values and a strong work ethic. She never attended or joined any particular church. Strange, given that Dan's father was a scholar in theology. Her sudden death from pancreatic cancer when Dan was a sophomore in college left him with no immediate family.

"On this project...I might have some ideas I could contribute, but I won't be able to work with you on a regular basis. Be here at this coffee shop in two weeks at about this time. I'll contact you then if possible."

"Wednesday, in two weeks? Uh, sure...I can make that. Okay, I'll meet you then."

Walker rose from his chair, shook Dan's hand, and then leaned over the table. "Remember:" again he looked straight into Dan's eyes, "what you're doing is essential to establish the truth and avoid the persistence of conclusions reached in medieval times. Throw everything out. Start at the beginning, and don't give up. Look at all the implications." Walker started to amble toward the door.

Dan raised his voice slightly, "You say you think we should start at the beginning? Do you mean in Genesis?"

Walker turned back as he walked. "Take a look at the *J-Account*."

"Huh? What's that?"

"*Luke 8:11* also might help."

"Huh?"

Walker didn't answer. He walked directly out of the coffee house.

Dan looked across at the empty chair. *Was he following me? He knew my last name and my father's name. That's pretty strange, all right.*

Hmmm... Luke 8:11. I'll have to look that up.

CHAPTER 8

KNX Radio, Los Angeles. Bong...Bong...Bong...KNX Traffic...A Jackknifed big rig on the 10 has traffic backed up all the way to the 15...

The news radio station sliced cleanly through the silence of Hall's car, still parked behind the faded-blue Camaro. He studied the next item from the case file, a glossy, colorful foldout marketing brochure for the Pacific Institute of Theology for Youth. On the back was what he was looking for—PITY contact information. He turned down the radio and dialed the number on his cell phone.

A robotic attendant picked up the phone almost immediately and played a pleasant recorded message. "*Welcome to the Pacific Institute of Theology for Youth. If you know your party's extension, please enter it at this time. For Administration, please press three. For Enrollment, please press four.*"

Hall pressed the four button.

"PITY Enrollment Office. All of our staff is either busy or on other lines. If you would like to attend a free introductory enrollment seminar, we have these daily at nine A.M. No reservations are necessary. If you would like to leave a message for our staff, please record it after the tone."

Hall hung up without leaving a message. *An enrollment seminar, he thought. That's a great idea. It's a few hours up the coast, but I can still make it to tomorrow's seminar. It'll give me chance to see the school and ask some questions.*

CHAPTER 9

John held the steering wheel with a white-knuckle grip. His divorce was final, and there was no chance his ex-wife would return; he knew that was true. For that matter, he knew reuniting with his wife was only a recipe for disaster. Now, Shannon seemed a possibility, but the stark difference in their religious views seemed to strike that concept down cold.

He wasn't used to questioning his beliefs. Leave well-enough alone, he would say. *Should we question what the Holy Scripture says? Does God worry that we might know too much?* He had maintained his composure in the coffee shop, but now he began to worry.

As a Christian who believed in the sacred Holy Bible, he did his best to lead a life following the teachings of Christ. *This project might prove that the Lord God of Genesis inspired the Bible. God would certainly understand the patterns of life that scientists are just beginning to unravel.*

To John, there was no question. God, the Creator, would obviously know the principles used to build every organism on earth. On the one hand, finding advanced technical information in the Bible would be amazing; on the other, it didn't seem out of line at all.

John flicked on the radio. The station played a song John had learned as a boy.

Oh, I wish I was in the land of cotton,
Old time there are not forgotten,
Look away, look away, look away, Dixie Land...

John thought of his days in North Carolina...

"John, you're going to be late for school. What are you doing?" John's mother Anne leaned out of the screen door and looked out onto the porch.

John continued to pluck away at his guitar. "I'm not goin' to school here, Ma. They're a bunch of jerks, nothing like my friends back in California. This place sucks. I'm just playing my guitar today."

"Oh, no you're not, young man. Look, it's going to take some time to adjust, but you've got to go. Now get your sorry-ass butt in gear and get on down the road before you're late."

"Eden...this town is just too small, Ma. If we have to be in this stupid state, why can't we live down in Winston-Salem. That's a much better town. This place doesn't have nothing."

"My family... you know I've got family here. We've already been over this, John. I have no one else to turn to after the divorce. Now put your guitar away, take your backpack, and get going!"

John reluctantly got up, set his guitar inside the door, and then took his backpack from his mother as she shoved it into his chest. Then, he walked closer to her and yelled into his mother's face, "I hate this place!"

"You'll get over it, John. Now, get going!" She gave him a shove out the door.

John left the house and started to walk across the small town to the local high school.

I wish I was in Dixie, Hooray! Hooray!
In Dixie Land I'll take my stand...

John took his hand off the steering wheel and mindlessly reached in his top pocket for his cigarettes. Only his gold pen occupied that convenient location. He remembered that after moving to Eden, that pack of cigarettes became his tool to fit into a town of tobacco worship. Not just accepted, it was a statement of patriotism to the southern way of life and a means to a full and long life. Tobacco fields surrounded the small rural town, and the economy of the area relied upon the weed for a majority of its jobs and revenue.

When John finally left Eden, he brought his two-pack-a-day habit back to California. Later, he learned it was a habit that was very difficult to break, almost impossible. But that wasn't John's only bad habit.

John punched the button of his truck's radio, flipping to a classic rock station.

If you got bad news, you want to kick them blues, cocaine...

The song brought back some of John's most difficult memories, of that time after he left his mother and returned to the West Coast.

Dammit, John, get your butt out of the house! We need MONEY!" John's wife, Julie, kicked John in the side and yelled at the top of her lungs, trying to penetrate the earphones covering his ears.

He sat on a beanbag chair, his eyes closed, playing his guitar into his earphones, high again and again completely unproductive. But he had

had just about enough of Julie and her incessant nagging. It was easier to just sit here and ignore that bitch than to get into another huge argument. As soon as she left the room, he snorted another line of coke, his favorite drug. A little on the end of a cigarette didn't hurt either.

Don't forget this fact, you can't get it back, cocaine...

John watched as if he were a bystander, watched his life go up his nose. He lost job after job. Soon, the only work he could maintain was his business selling drugs. There was no interview necessary for that job.

Julie, also a user, made it even more difficult for John to break his habit. He wanted to stop this downward spiral, but he didn't know how. When he visited his friends, they would always have angel dust on the mirror available for free. Not just a little—a lot. It was hard to turn down.

Impossible.

Hard to turn down not just because it was worth a lot. Not because John really liked the high of cocaine, which was not that big a deal to him. No, it was simpler than that. John's mind was addicted to the presence of the drugs. Addicted.

This went well beyond the stupid "just say no to drugs" slogan. At this point, John couldn't say no. He wanted to. He tried. After twenty hours of partying and being high, he would lie on his bed, unable to sleep and feeling like a failure, his head buzzing and throbbing with unavoidable activity. *No more. I'm never doing it again*, he swore.

Despite John's intentions, he failed. He watched himself helplessly violate his own promise and proceed to snort the evil white powder that he didn't really want. Each night, he made a new promise, a promise broken early the next day. His life continued in a steep downward spiral, the ground quickly approaching, the final crash within sight. Now, the pleasure of his next buzz guided him toward death. His life never veered far from the mirror on the table; he snorted and smoked that damn powder every few minutes to stay high.

If you want to get down, down on the ground, cocaine...

Then, John got sick. His constant nosebleeds got worse. He coughed his brains out—something like walking pneumonia. Air-conditioned rooms were the ultimate prescription for coughing fits. He would hang his head over the side of the bed at night and let the thick mucus ooze from his nose and sinuses into a bowl so he could sleep. Even a few minutes of sleep without coughing would be bliss. This went on for months.

John could still clearly remember the scene that will forever haunt his mind. With eyes bright red from burst blood vessels, head hung over the kitchen sink, the snot, spit, tears, and blood ran out of his nose, sinuses, eyes, and lungs. Through his bloodshot eyes, his vision blurred. He watched his bodily fluids oozing over the dirty dishes in the sink.

My life is shit. All I live for is that god-dammed drug, and I can't stop. This is not the life I want. Something has to change. I want out. John cried desperately.

Looking back, John credits that sickness as a last attempt of his body to get him out of his death spiral. He finally decided that the only way he could stop using the drugs was to avoid them entirely and avoid other users, people who he called "friends," but were really interested only in their mutual addiction. He had to make a huge change. But he needed help.

As a child, John had learned to pray. But, he never did believe it did any good. That day, he was ready to try it again. John blew his bloody nose, spit again into the sink, and dropped to his knees.

John clicked the radio off.

As his mind snapped back to the present, tears distorted his vision. He blinked his eyes clear so he could safely drive on. In the seat next to him sat his well-worn Bible, his guide away from his old life. John believed that his prayer had been answered: Every person he met, every action he took, now conspired to rescue him from a life spiraling toward an early demise. He felt he was being led by the Spirit of God. His prayers were not always answered the way he expected. Life was not perfect. John was not at all confused about the change he had made in his life. It clearly saved his life. He reached over and stroked his Bible tenderly, as if it could feel his touch. He held his hand on it as he drove.

He felt like the pirate in *The Count of Monte Cristo* whose life was spared by Edmond Dantes. The pirate became Edmond's servant for life. Because John knew that his life would have been over were it not for divine intervention that he received, he felt he was the unquestioned servant of the Lord who had spared him.

In a way, this commitment to his faith allowed John to entertain the challenge of Walker's question. Whatever the result of this inquiry, it would not alter the fact that his life had materially changed. It could not touch his strong faith. John was certainly not afraid of the truth, whatever it might be.

He also knew that *faith* meant that he would not know all the answers and that he would always have some uncertainty. "If I was absolutely certain, why would I need faith? I would not; I would just *know*. When I don't know for sure, *that* is when faith is important," John said to himself in a whisper. "God expects me to be uncertain. That's why Jesus talked so much about *faith*. God expects me to be uncertain of the details. I can be faithful only *with uncertainty*."

CHAPTER 10

Dan threw on his jacket and waved goodbye to the shopkeeper. As he walked the half-mile back home, he mulled over the encounter with Walker. In a way, Walker was right. Religious fanatics and scientific celebrities could be a problem if this project challenged beliefs central to the power structures of conservative churches. Dan shivered when he thought of author Salman Rushdie, marked for death by the Muslim world for publishing *The Satanic Verses*.

Would we be marked for death? If not, being ostracized from the community could be like a slow agonizing form of torture.

As Dan walked along his route home, he looked at the small Catholic church—*St. Jude's*—a church he had passed many times before, but never really took much notice. Today, he paused in front of the church and thought of the long-standing traditions it represented and the extent of its imposing influence over the past two millennia. Its primary symbol—a large crucifix—dominated the front courtyard. Beyond, the door of the church was open, so Dan walked through the courtyard and stepped into the still, cool air of the sanctuary.

Several parishioners sat in the pews near the front of the church before a crucifix even larger than the one outside. They chanted prayers in unison, switching between "Our Father, who art in heaven" and "Hail Mary, full of grace." Like Shannon had argued earlier, Dan viewed organized religion as perhaps more dangerous than the worst power-hungry corporations, using the threat of eternal suffering to keep the masses in line.

Shannon is probably right; there won't be any link between the Bible and modern biological science. These religions are based on a world view from antiquity that is now long obsolete.

Dan reflected on the history of the Catholic Church, which had ultimate power in the western world for at least 1,500 years. The church and the Roman Empire grew together, with similar organizational structures and a symbiotic relationship that enforced the power of both. Yet with all that power, not all was well in the western world. Indeed, during the first millennium after Christ, knowledge of the sciences fell into stagnation, with few, if any, notable discoveries in the period from

AD 400 to 1100. Dan knew that historians blame the rise of Christianity for the virtual absence of scientific investigation during that period. It made sense. The thinkers of the early church were preoccupied with more important problems: the Trinity, human sin and free will, the authority of the church, and other doctrinal matters. Experimental science was of no use on these pesky questions. As a result, the church avoided research into mathematics, human physiology, and astronomy, especially when that research could be regarded as part of the tainted legacy of paganism. Why investigate causal relationships when everything was under the strict control of Almighty God?

Dan looked over the accouterments of the church, the impressive architecture, arched ceiling, statues of saints, stained glass rose window, candles lit for Mary, and the basin of holy water.

The influence of the church was not all bad, he thought. The mind-set of both the Christian and Islamic cultures included the concept of a logical and reasonable god—a concept that encouraged a quest for universal truths, order, and simplicity. Those cultures promoted the idea that the natural world follows consistent and reliable laws, laws that are comprehensible to the human mind. These underpinnings promoted the eventual rise of a scientific world-view that has been so successful in recent history.

Walker's warning was just a hoax. In this day and age, the religions of the world are much more open to new ideas, right? Dan looked again at the parishioners chanting their prayers and wondered. He paused for several more prayers and then walked back out to the street.

Taking half strides to avoid slipping on the wet, uneven concrete sidewalk, he continued his walk home. After the September 11, 2001, attacks, the public allowed an increased emphasis on religion in government and a concurrent suppression of science. This trend made Dan reconsider his conclusion about Walker's comments. *There is a chance that his warning had merit. Walker could be trustworthy. After all, he did know my father.*

Dan walked up the final entry sidewalk to his house and up the front stairs to the large porch. He had a nice view of the ocean from this vantage point with the village and coffee house along his line of sight.

After he removed his jacket, he grabbed a Bible from the bookcase, sat in an overstuffed chair, and opened it to Luke 8:11.

Now the parable is this: The seed is the word of God.

Dan leaned back in the chair and let his mind spin. Clearly, a real seed is an amazing object, potentially a blade of grass or a huge tree. Inside every seed is DNA, the key to life on earth. Was this a hint that DNA is the word of God?

* * *

Dan looked over the rest of Luke, chapter eight, and realized that it went on to explain the concept that the word of God would grow in a man's heart, unless it fell on stoney ground. The hint from Walker was perhaps a bit off the mark, but it was interesting nonetheless. It was definitely a hint that no typical homeless vagabond could ever give. Dan was starting to trust Walker.

He went over to his array of computer screens and pulled up an Internet browser to review some of the history of science and religion. *Let's start with the Dark Ages.* He clicked his mouse and stroked the keys, accessing the informational wealth of the Internet.

After the difficulties of the Dark Ages, Thomas Aquinas initiated a return to scientific inquiry in about AD 1250. A learned theologian, Aquinas wanted to demonstrate that the universe is an ordered system whose laws can be studied and at least partially understood. His theological works touched on topics that are today within the realm of science—motion, gravity, celestial bodies, magnetism, and tides. Aquinas taught that the scriptures and the natural laws must be harmonious and that it is possible to understand God's laws of the natural world using the rational capacity of the mind. First, he stated that that there is no God, and then he proposed five proofs that God does in fact exist, proofs that are still often quoted.

There was never really any conflict between the scientific study of God's creation and pious worship. If this is indeed a master creation of Almighty God, what harm is there in finding out how it ticks? The corners of Dan's mouth turned up slightly as he read about the work of Aquinas. Human curiosity seemed reinvigorated after the sleep of the backward nature of the Dark Ages.

But the smile on Dan's face faded. He continued to read of the desperate attempts of the church to thwart this new thinking. In AD 1277, soon after Aquinas's death, the Bishop of Paris condemned several hundred philosophical propositions, many drawn directly from Aquinas's work. *New ideas are rarely fully embraced, especially at first.*

Dan clicked his mouse a few more times.

Aquinas was really not much of a challenge to the church institution when compared with Copernicus. At about AD 1500, fully 1,800 years after its original conception by the Greek Aristarchus, the "Copernican Revolution" threatened the views of the church like nothing before or perhaps since. Replacing the earth-centered, finite universe with a sun-centered infinite universe represented the most profound single event in the whole history of scientific thought.

Copernicus, a churchman with a very traditional education in canon law, had spent his life in ecclesiastical administration. But he had a special private interest: astronomy. His crowning achievement explained the motions of the heavens in a simple, elegant way, far simpler than the popular Ptolemaic—earth-centered—model. Unfortunately, for fear of retaliation, he left his great theory unpublished for some thirty years. It's difficult indeed for such a churchman to promote theories that challenge the central nature of earth in the solar system, and by extension, also challenge the central position of humans, God's ultimate creation.

It's not obvious, Dan thought, that the surface of earth is spinning and moving about the sun. It certainly seems stationary, that's for sure. Amazingly enough, the surface of the earth is moving up to one thousand miles per hour as it spins, and it flies along at 67,000 miles per hour in its orbit around the sun. All five senses testify the opposite conclusion. Dan again looked around the room. He saw his chair, his books, and his files sitting, visibly stationary, yet really moving at an ungodly 67,000 miles per hour. How could it be? Unless you were an astronomer, you would never conceive this revolutionary, yet simple solution to how the solar system works.

Another click of his mouse moved Dan to a discussion of the famous astronomer Galileo, who reintroduced the experimental method and clearly articulated the Copernican model. The year was AD 1590, and conventional wisdom asserted that heavier objects would drop faster than lighter objects. For example, if you simultaneously drop a ten-pound cannon ball and a marble, weighing only a tenth of a pound, which one will hit the ground first? It's simply "obvious" that the object weighing a hundred times more than the other will fall faster and hit first. This conclusion just seems right, that's for sure. And besides, at the time of Galileo, who would dare challenge the laws of physics developed nineteen centuries earlier by a famous authority like Aristotle? Unfortunately, those original Greek philosophers felt that experimentation—that is, actually touching the world like servants—was beneath them. They relied only on the purity of philosophical thought to derive the laws of the universe. No one had even tried the simple experiment, and everyone went along with the conclusion for nearly two thousand years, trusting mistaken conventional wisdom and so-called common sense.

Dan could imagine the seventeen-year-old Galileo releasing a cannon ball and a marble from the top of the leaning Tower of Pisa and thereby firmly debunking conventional wisdom. Indeed, except for air friction, if you drop the two objects, they will fall at exactly the same rate of acceleration, hitting the stone platform below at exactly the same time, and at exactly the same velocity—a tie. Galileo's experiment proved without a doubt that, in this case, conventional wisdom was dead wrong.

The significance of this historic event was not the debunking of the nature of falling objects but rather the method of debunking it. Galileo composed a simple experiment to test this law of nature so it could be repeated by anyone, thus allowing the conventional wisdom to be disputed not by opinion, but by observing nature itself. You don't need to be a philosopher or priest to drop two objects of differing weights and watch them fall.

In spite of his simple demonstration, Aristotelian adherents resisted the truth for many years, holding to the inertia of long-standing false conventional wisdom with all their might. Perhaps they tried the experiment themselves but nevertheless continued to assert their mistaken opinion so that they would not be seem weak, wrong, or uninspired.

Dan realized that, unfortunately, simple scientific experiments are not always possible. If time scales are very long or if objects are too big to work with, it's impossible to study them using experiments. Scientists resort to observation, thought experiments, and theoretical models. It's simply not possible to go back in time to the beginning of the universe to know exactly what happened, or to know exactly what will happen in the future. There is never any final proof in these sciences. However, we can look at other galaxies and stars and model the universe using mathematics and known physical laws. When a preponderance of evidence supports a given model, the model stands until someone finds reliable evidence to the contrary. If such evidence is found, the model is enhanced to fit the new evidence.

The origin of life is also one of those questions that cannot be tested by experiment. *But*, Dan thought, *it would be interesting to find a correlation in biblical literature. That book clearly describes the origin of life.*

Scientists know that our solar system is sun-centered, that we do indeed whiz by at nearly seventy thousand miles per hour in earth's orbit and spin at a thousand miles per hour. But the acceptance of these facts was not instant or painless. Galileo courageously supported *heliocentrism,* the sun-centered Copernican model of the solar system versus the popular *geocentrism,* the earth-centered Ptolemaic system. The church provided the stronghold for those who most fiercely fought to maintain the Ptolemaic system as the accepted model. It was simply incomprehensible for the sun to have a more central role in the universe than the earth. It seemed God would never create a world with humans as his crowning achievement unless that world was also in the middle of that universe.

Galileo published an easy to read book in AD 1632 presenting the Copernican system very persuasively and making the earth-centered adherents look foolish. But the authorities in the church didn't appreciate appearing weak and uninspired. In his 1633 trial, Galileo was asked to renounce his views of the Copernican model. He refused, and the church excommunicated him. The Catholic Church held to the Ptolemaic view for centuries, finally relenting and welcoming Galileo back into the church in 1992.

It took about 360 years for the church to embrace the truth, Dan thought. *How many other truths are in the same category? And, if we challenge other false beliefs, will we become like Walker, ostracized by the world?*

CHAPTER 11

John parked his Ford F-150 pickup under a leafy carrotwood tree, his usual spot at the Christ Advent Church. Far from the main building, John could rely on "his" parking stall every time he pulled in. He grabbed his Bible and leather portfolio, locked his truck, and hustled along the sidewalk. Lawns and trees created a park-like setting, separating the numerous buildings of the church campus.

After his divorce, John had completed a course in financial planning, discovered that he was reasonably good with numbers, and eventually found himself helping the church with their finances. Today, he was headed to the church finance committee meeting. John felt fine, but his mind was troubled.

He loved his church home, but it seemed all the nice women were taken. He shunned activities outside of his church, fearing they might prompt a return to his old life. Increasingly, he pinned his hopes on Shannon, but the new line of conversation about DNA and science, something Shannon truly enjoyed, revealed a widening gulf—a gulf he could not ignore. He wondered if he even wanted to meet with Shannon and Dan again.

John's route to his meeting took him by the office of the Reverend Montgomery "Monty" Wright, the pastor of the church. *Monty might be able to help me know what to do. He always says to drop in if you want to talk.* He hesitated by the door, unable to decide if he should go in. Finally, he pushed the door open just enough to peek in; Monty stood behind his large wooden desk—alone—apparently gazing out the window. John entered more confidently.

At the sound of the door, Monty turned, and John froze: The pastor was on the phone. Their eyes met and Monty motioned John to come in anyway, and then he motioned with his hand for John to take a seat. They shook hands, and John sat and leaned back into the chair.

Monty spoke into the telephone, "I understand, sir." John studied him, noting his full head of hair was strikingly white, with even less color than when they had met three years ago. Yet, in spite of the lack of color in his hair, Monty was still trim and fit.

"I will look over all the paperwork." Monty turned to the side slightly. "Yes... Say, if you don't mind, I have a member in my office who would like to talk to me for a moment. I will call you back a bit later..." He moved closer to the phone on the table. "Thanks," he said, and hung up the phone.

"I'm very sorry to interrupt your call," John said.

"No problem, John. How are you today?" Monty sat down in his black leather executive office chair.

"Oh, I'm doing...uh, well..." John stopped, as if he didn't know how to continue.

Monty leaned forward. "You look like you want to get something off your chest. Tell me, John, what's bothering you?"

"It's...it's really no big deal. You remember that gal I told you about?"

"Oh sure. What was her name again?"

"Shannon."

"Oh yes, that's right. Any progress?"

"Well, we're only meeting for coffee...with Dan, too. Not much beyond that."

"Don't worry. You can't expect an instant romance. These things take time."

"That's not exactly the problem."

"Go on."

"We got to talking today about religion. It seems she's quite an evolutionist, and just goes on and on about DNA and all that stuff."

"What does that have to do with religion?"

"Exactly. It's science, I know. But all this science talk worries me that we'll wind up questioning church doctrine. And this doesn't seem to be improving our relationship. It's only making it clear that we may not be cut out for each other."

"I see." Monty leaned farther back in his chair. "Aligned religious views are important to any relationship, that's certainly true. I thought you said Shannon was a Christian."

"Sure. Catholic. But she doesn't attend church anymore, at least not that I know of."

"Well, that isn't necessarily a show-stopper, John. Once the message of Christ has touched a soul, the heart will be at least partially open to the message of the Lord. This may provide just the opportunity you're looking for—to witness to Shannon and bring her back into the fold."

"I hope so, Monty. But, you know, I'm still not sure about this DNA talk. Both Shannon and Dan know about all this science stuff, but I'm simply not into it. And now they have this crazy idea to review the Bible for DNA patterns. They've asked me to give them an overview of the Bible and where we might find evidence that the Holy Scriptures contain references to DNA."

"I hope you're joking, John. The Bible doesn't talk about DNA. It's not a science textbook."

"That's what I said."

"Hmmm..." Monty tapped his mouth with his index finger. "I would advise you to look at this as an opportunity. If you are going to be reading the Bible, the fact that it is the sacred work of God will become apparent to your friends, and you'll find that they'll soon be attending church to learn more.

"But proceed with caution. If you are drawn into a strictly secular interpretation of the holy scripture, then you're probably out of line. Generally, if it varies from what you've learned here—our established and traditional church doctrine—you might be getting into trouble. If that happens, definitely let me know."

"I like the idea that this will probably be good for my friends. If you really want me to, I can let you know if anything happens, sure." John rose from his seat. "Sorry I barged in, Monty. I'd better get to the finance committee meeting."

Monty stood and shook his hand again. "Thanks, John, for coming in."

"You're the guy that deserves the thanks, Monty."

As John reopened the door, he glanced back and noticed the Reverend dialing the phone, and then he continued down the hall toward his meeting, confident that this DNA project might actually resolve his differences with Shannon.

Monty watched John leave with the phone to his ear.

"Rebecca? Hello again. May I speak with the Bishop?" He waited, listening.

"Yes, I'm back. Sorry for the interruption..." He flipped his pen in his fingers. "Nothing important, only a member worried about a conversation with his friends, I don't know, something about looking for patterns of DNA in the Bible." He stopped flipping his pen for a moment. "Yes, that's right." His hand stayed motionless. "Are you sure it's worth worrying about...? Oh really...? I don't think there's much to be alarmed about, but sure, I can keep an eye on them."

CHAPTER 12

"Good morning. Please find a seat, and we'll get started."

Agent Hall moved with a group of about twenty concerned parents from the foyer into a meeting room with cushioned chairs arranged in rows like a small theater. Today, his gray suit fit the situation perfectly: He was just another parent who had reached a dead end. The group was serious and very quiet, shying from conversation. Coming here was a last resort. Any strategies they may have had as parents had failed, and they weren't in the mood for small talk.

Hall took a seat toward the rear of the room so he could see the presentation and also observe the parents' reactions. A painted slogan dominated the center of the room, "Christ Died to Save Your Soul," and on either side, school emblems blazoned, each about five feet tall. Hall thought the logo was a bit disgusting: a Christian cross, looking exactly like a dagger, stabbed through the head of a serpent, apparently to symbolize the power of Christ over Satan. The serpent objected to the penetration with its snarling, forked tongue extended. Hall tried to ignore the graphic images, but their prominent location made doing so quite difficult.

On his way in, Hall had surveyed the facility. This part of the school was a set of rectilinear concrete buildings of neo-brutalist design situated just below the more ominous buildings of the main theological institute. Those buildings on the top of the hill reminded Hall of the abbey of Mont Saint Michel he had visited during his recent vacation in France, although they were not quite as extensive as that famous landmark. All the buildings were well maintained with what looked like a fresh coat of paint in a two-tone color scheme, at least several grades above what Hall had seen in other schools. Apparently, there was no shortage of money here.

"Hello, my name is Vivian Balma, and I want to welcome you to the Pacific Institute of Theology for Youth or 'PITY' for short." Vivian spoke well, with a slight South Pacific accent. *She probably majored in communication arts or marketing,* Hall thought. "Our school is designed to bring challenged youth back to the straight and narrow. We stress spiritual growth through strong biblical training. Our students perform well, scoring at or near the top in academic performance. But we are most proud of our success in rescuing young adults from a life headed for destruction. We find that a large percentage of our graduates elect to pursue a career in the military or law enforcement, instead of a life of crime, gang violence, drugs, and decay."

The parents sat in rapt attention.

"We have a twenty-minute presentation to introduce the program, and then I'll take any questions you might have." She walked to the back of the room and flipped a switch; a motorized screen rolled down out of a small slot in the ceiling at the front of the room. When it reached the bottom, she turned down the lights and started a video presentation projected on the screen from the rear of the room.

"Welcome to the Pacific Institute of..." The presentation began with a professional narrator and an aerial shot of the campus, the camera circling the white buildings on the top of the hill. This was not a simple, low-budget, one-camera production of a nervous administrator monotonously reading information about the school. It was professionally designed and produced, with many shots of smiling students interacting, doing schoolwork, exercising, praying, and kneeling before a cross. The individual clips were short in duration, only a few seconds each, artistically combined into a high-paced, persuasive marketing presentation that Hall felt would compare with anything put out by a casino in Las Vegas.

Persuasive? You bet. Hall felt an almost involuntary need to enroll someone. The slick presentation, as persuasive as it was, still left the exact methods used by PITY unclear. Were they doing anything outlandish or unusual to rescue these youth who apparently had no rudder to guide them through life? *Sure, this school seems to achieve results, but how?*

After several questions from this group of prospective clients, Balma gestured to two tables at the side of the room where half-a-dozen well-dressed and smiling workers sat ready to enroll the parents. Hall noticed that only a couple of parents lingered as the rest lined up to do the paperwork, a testament to the effectiveness of the video presentation. Or perhaps to the simple lack of other viable options.

Hall left the presentation room quietly to take a look around the campus on his own while Vivian was preoccupied with the parents. *Nice presentation, but I can't help thinking that there's something unsettling about it.*

CHAPTER 13

As Dan entered the coffee shop, he noticed John seated at the table, thumbing through his Bible and making notes on a pad in his leather portfolio. Dan bought his coffee, and then made his way through the coffee shop, passing only a couple of other customers who were preoccupied with their own conversations.

"Good morning, my good friend," he said, and shook John's hand as usual. John was smiling, but there was something different today. He seemed more distant, more uncertain. The smile didn't seem genuine.

John tapped his pen nervously on his pad. "I'm not sure what exactly we're looking for...some sort of story about DNA...what's that supposed to be...? The Bible is a very large book. This could be a huge project, you know."

I don't care what Walker says, I think this is a safe enough place to talk. No harm in having a Bible study in public, right? Dan decided to warn his friend anyway. "Listen," Dan said quietly and then looked around, adopting some of Walker's paranoia. He continued leaning toward John and whispered, "Let's keep our discussion only on the Bible for now. No talk of science when we are reviewing the Bible, okay?"

"No problem. I don't talk about science much anyway!"

Dan hoped this was what Walker meant. *Could reading the Bible in public rub extremist atheists the wrong way? No, that's ridiculous...Who really cares?*

"Okay. I was reviewing the general structure of the Bible from *a purely theological standpoint.* I'm sure you know something about the Bible, but I'll start with some simple stuff, to make sure. You can tell me the direction you think we should go as we discuss it."

"Actually, I like starting at the beginning. That way we won't miss any part of the larger pattern." He looked up. "Ah, just in time," he said as Shannon approached the table, her mouth over the small straw of her coffee, apparently on a cloud of chocolate and cinnamon.

Shannon grimaced, looking like she had smelled something terrible when she noticed John with his Bible open with numerous notes on his pad. "What is this, some sort of a church service?" Shannon sat down with hesitation.

"You guessed it! Bible 101," Dan said. "Let's talk Bible today and leave the rest for later." Dan winked. "And, since we're talking about touchy topics like religion, let's agree that we won't let it ruin our friendship, fair enough?"

She smiled a little and sipped her coffee. "Sure, as long as this doesn't turn into 'convert your friends to my way of thinking' day." Shannon looked directly at John. "Fair enough, John?"

"Deal. But, it's probably going to feel a bit strange for you." He smiled tentatively and then went on, "I think it's something you've avoided for a very long time, isn't it?" She frowned at him, and he hurried on. "Before I plunge ahead, it's fair to say that the Bible is probably the most important document to all western thought—"

"Let's not have tunnel vision," Dan interrupted. "The Bible is but one of a number of ancient religious documents. I mean, there's the *Koran*, the *Book of Mormon*, t*he I Ching*, t*he Bhagavad-Gita*, and t*he Teachings of Buddha*."

"Oh, come on!" John protested. I'm not hunting DNA in every book from here to the moon! I don't know anything about that ka-ching thing."

"Not my usual bedtime reading either," Shannon added.

"Okay, okay...Fair enough," Dan said. "We can stick to the Bible for now and see what happens."

John drank some coffee and collected his thoughts. "God's Word, that's what we need to work with."

Dan tapped his fingers on his mug. "That Bible...it's an artifact of an entire ancient civilization. Our culture developed stories and explanations that go along with the actual scripture to explain and expand on what's written. These stories are historical as well, generated and established in careful consideration of the ancient scripture. In other words, the document exists as an artifact, but there are also stories that interpret the meaning of that document. It's part of the surrounding culture and can be treated as a 'virtual' artifact."

"It's hard to understand some parts without the help of those other stories, I'll grant you that." John said.

"No matter what document you analyze, getting the meaning out of it is a whole science." Dan said. "I've done a lot of semantic analysis in computer programs."

"Perhaps," John replied, "but I'm sure that it's completely different for 'sacred' documents. They call it *hermeneutics*."

"John, if you need other stories to explain the meaning, how can you be a hard-core literalist?" Shannon asked.

"Hard core? Well, let's face it, we humans may not fully understand what is said in the Holy Bible. Just because we don't understand it doesn't mean it isn't true."

"So you're saying that the Bible may be literally true, but our *interpretation* may still be faulty, right?"

"Faulty? Well, uh...You'll get the idea as we get further." John went back to his train of thought, seemingly eager to avoid Shannon's attempt to "stump the professor." He continued, "The first books of the Bible are among the world's earliest writings. The major monotheistic religions—Judaism, Christianity, and Islam—all use them. Mormons—the LDS Church—they use them as well. For this reason alone, respect for these books as ancient artifacts is definitely proper and appropriate by anyone, regardless of religious leanings. Here, I brought two Bibles for you guys." John handed out black-bound King James Bibles. Dan picked his up, but Shannon left her copy on the table.

Bible 101, Dan thought with a sigh, as John started with well-known definitions— "the word *Bible* is derived through Latin from the Greek word *biblia* meaning *books*," and "only the books that are officially recognized by the Christian church are called 'canonical.'" And finally, he explained the difference between the Jewish Torah, what Christians call the Old Testament, and the Bible, which adds the teachings of Jesus Christ and the establishment of the Christian tradition.

Even Shannon nodded politely as if it was new information. *I'll bet she went to Sunday school as a child,* Dan thought. *John's enjoying every minute of this!*

"I'll be quoting from the *King James Version*," John said. "It's an English translation that's not perfect but is deemed quite close to the original Hebrew. It's the most common English translation ever used and is still probably the most popular in churches today.

"Most of the Old Testament tells the story of how the Jews established themselves in the area of today's Israel. The Hebrew language was the original language of the Old Testament, and it's still in use today—a fact that should help maintain the original integrity of the text."

"That's right," Dan said. "It's the official language of modern Israel, although for centuries it was spoken only in prayer."

Shannon seemed to take more of an interest, stirring her cafe mocha. "Do you know exactly when it was written?" She smiled slightly.

John patted his Bible. "The Bible is composed of many separate books, written by different authors at different times. Paul wrote over half of the New Testament well after Jesus's death, for example.

He opened his Bible to the list of chapters. "In the Old Testament, the first five books are *Genesis*, *Exodus*, *Leviticus*, *Numbers*, and *Deuteronomy*, also called the Five Books of Moses or the *Pentateuch*. The first chapters of Genesis include the famous story of creation and the start of life on earth."

Dan recalled Walker's suggestion that they *start at the beginning* and said, "In the beginning was the Word, right? Let's start there. I would think that any secretly embedded information would be provided earlier rather than later. It is so fundamental to all life, it should be in the most ancient part. Why wait?"

"Okay, we can start there. The creation is described in Genesis, chapters one through three," John said.

"Who wrote that part?" Shannon asked.

"Does 'The Five Books of Moses' give you a clue?"

"So, Moses wrote it? Does it say that?"

"I'm not sure why you're so interested in that one fact, but I will admit that the Bible itself doesn't clearly say who wrote it or where the information came from. For example, there's no story in the Bible where a person was given the Genesis story in the form of a vision or inspiration that was subsequently reduced to written form."

Dan looked up. "In contrast, the *Book of Mormon* and the Islamic *Al Qur'an* both provide explanations: The content was provided by angels, either in silver plates or by dictation. It's too bad the Bible didn't tell us how it came about."

John wagged his gold pen in the air. "All is not lost. Biblical scholars and historians are constantly researching the various sections of the Bible to determine who the authors were, when the books were written, and how they were compiled and standardized. They study tone and style of the writing and certain inconsistencies that exist in the text."

"Inconsistencies? Hey, I thought this was supposed to be the 'Word of God'?" said Shannon a little sarcastically. "Why is God inconsistent?"

"Inconsistencies sound like a huge problem for any literalist," Dan said.

"Well, yeah... It'd be much easier to argue that the Bible is divinely inspired if there were absolutely no errors or inconsistencies of any kind. It's understood that over time, translation and interpretation errors do occur."

"So, do we have any clue who actually wrote the Bible?" Shannon asked.

"Scholars began the search for the authors of the Bible in the 1700s, and we've been refining the work for three centuries. I'd bet people speculated long before then as well.

"From what I've read, Moses is obviously credited with the first five books. However, his own death and its aftermath are described in Deuteronomy. Here is that passage, in 34:7.

> *And Moses [was] an hundred and twenty years old when he died: his eye was not dim, nor his natural force abated. And the children of Israel wept for Moses in the plains of Moab thirty days: so the days of weeping [and] mourning for Moses were ended.*

"Unless he was just guessing at his own death, it would have been impossible for Moses to have written that section himself," Dan said. "Moses would have needed god-like foresight to know when he would die and what would happen afterward."

"Right. These books were first told by someone else, or perhaps Moses started the story and someone else completed it after his death. We can be sure they were told as stories long before they were written down anyway. Oral tradition could have allowed the stories told by Moses to be combined with those from others who lived after that time."

"Admit it," Shannon said, leaning forward. "We don't really know *who* wrote it, do we?"

John shook his head reluctantly.

"Do we even know *when*?" she asked.

"Historians say that the Pentateuch was probably put into written form by Jewish scribes during the exile to Babylon in about 560 BC, perhaps by the 'Chronicler'—that is, the same person who wrote the Chronicles." John wrote "560 BC" on his note pad. "The story of creation was likely handed down from generation to gener—"

" —And probably ruined in the process, like that telephone game, where you whisper a secret from one person to the next around a circle and see how it turns out at the end," Shannon said. "It's always all messed up."

"You're not being fair, Shannon." John protested. "In those days, storytelling was the only way to preserve cultural history. Stories were memorized word for word, with almost no change from one generation to the next. When you hear the term *oral tradition,* you should think of a reasonably reliable method of propagating a story. A good recent example is the oral history recounted in Alex Haley's *Roots*. The generations of slaves in the United States were often illiterate, and even if they could write, their masters would never allow it. The family history retold by Haley's blockbuster is a good example of the preservative power of the oral tradition."

"It still seems errors would likely creep in," Shannon said. "Especially if you figure the original stories were told long before. When do you figure Moses first told his story?"

"That's not too hard to figure out," John said. "Old Testament genealogies place Moses at about 1260 BC."

Dan was always quick with a calculation. "You said Jewish scribes finally recorded them in about 560 BC... Let's see, those the stories were retold and memorized for about seven hundred years, or at least fifty generations."

"Whew! That's a long time." Shannon said. "John, don't you think that *some* details of the story would be changed during a fifty-generation-long telephone game?"

"Couldn't it be," John suggested, "that God carefully helped the storytellers maintain the integrity of the story, so the meaning remained unchanged? You can't prove it one way or the other. In the end, most scholars admit some uncertainty in the fidelity of these stories. I'll go along with that."

"I don't buy the divine intervention idea, but at least you're giving in to allow some change. I was starting to worry about your sanity!" Shannon said.

"Yet, this question of fidelity, it's interesting. Especially if you look closely at the details of style and tone. For instance, there are two different accounts of the creation, each with slightly different emphasis and details. The first is the day-by-day account of the six days of creation starting in Genesis 1:1, known as the *P-Account*. The second version starts in Genesis 2:4, the *J-Account*. Dual stories also exist for the story of Noah and the flood and many others."

Dan's eyebrows went up. He watched John write a *J* and *P* on his note pad. Dan flipped through the loaner Bible and looked at the chapters and verses John mentioned. "They're here...and here," he said, pointing them out to Shannon. She reluctantly looked at his copy, leaving her own Bible untouched.

"Experts guess that the 'J' and 'P' authors received their information from two oral sources, with each version referring to God in two distinctive, but internally consistent ways."

"And what do 'J' and 'P' stand for?" Dan asked.

"'P' stands for 'Priestly' account. It uses the Hebrew word pronounced *Elohim*, a plural word meaning *Gods*. This is written as *God,* singular, in the King James Version. The P-Account generally presents an all-powerful and stern God who focused on names, dates, genealogy, and detailed measurements." John wrote the word *Elohim* next to the 'P' on his note pad.

"The first creation account uses only that name, *Elohim*, but the second account, the J-Account, adds the Hebrew word pronounced Yahweh." John wrote four letters—*YHWH*—after the 'J', and then he proceeded to write it, painstakingly, in Hebrew: יהוה writing from right to left.

"They call this the tetragrammaton," he continued. "The King James Version translates *Yhwh* as *Lord*. Written Hebrew of that period did not include any vowels; they were assumed from context. Without vowels, it can be difficult to know the pronunciation of ancient words, especially that one. Saying the name of God was severely frowned upon."

"Yhwh—okay, but why do you call it the *J-Account*?" Shannon asked.

"That's from the German translation, of Yhwh: *Jehovah*."

"And the personality of this god?"

"Was that of a loving God unconcerned with minor details and exact times and dates," John answered.

"Let me see if I understand." Dan looked through his Bible as he talked. "In Genesis, there are two distinct versions of the creation story.

The first is the *P-Account* in Genesis 1:1 through 2:3, as indicated by the use of the word *God.* Then, starting with Genesis 2:4, the J-Account uses the words *Lord God* that you say corresponds to the name Yhwh. You say also that many parts of the story are repeated and some parts disagree on details."

"And researchers believe these two versions were carefully intermingled throughout the Pentateuch by a later editor," John stressed. "The interesting thing is this: If each account is read alone, it is consistent in tone, focus, and use of detail. When the two versions are compared, they don't always agree on details, and some parts of the story are included in one version but are missing in the other."

"What a mess!" Shannon shook her head. "You said I would automatically start thinking that this is a sacred, error-free document. So far you're proving the opposite, my friend."

"It's not that bad, Shannon. The fact that the two accounts are *not* harmonized is actually a good thing. It implies a higher level of fidelity, not lower."

"Huh?"

"You see, it means that the editor of this section combined the two ancient stories by interweaving them. He didn't attempt to settle inconsistencies himself. That's good news for us," John said enthusiastically. "It means that each version will retain more of its original material. The integrity of the earlier artifact was respected by the editor, the 'Chronicler,' when this text was finally inscribed."

"How could inconsistencies be a good thing?" Dan asked.

"If all of the inconsistencies were settled by a later editor, we'd have only one version of the story, the version that happened to make more 'sense' to that editor, and the other one lost forever to the waste bin. Some people just ignore the second J-Account of creation. They say it isn't as clear as the step-by-step, day-by-day, P-Account. The fact that the ancient editor opted to respect both original oral traditions instead of picking one or the other means that we're left with accounts that more accurately represent both of the stories that were current at the time."

"Hmmm. I'm really starting to respect the work of this Chronicler," Dan said.

"Apart from fidelity of the story, there is still the problem of terminology," Shannon said. "Advanced scientific concepts would be impossible for storytellers from the time of Moses to include in those ancient stories. They had no words to express these modern concepts."

"Impossible? I beg to differ," Dan said, leaning back. "You can convey fairly complex ideas by using simple, common words, like those available when biblical stories were composed, if you use enough of them."

"Even in ancient times?" Shannon asked.

"I looked into this question a bit more last night. Consider numbers.

The word 'thousand' is frequently used in the Bible to represent any very large number. I understand that at the time, *thousand* was the largest number that had a name. *Million* and *billion* didn't come along until much later. If you wanted to precisely express more than a thousand, you were out of luck—*thousand* would have to do. That said, they could multiply thousand by thousand, or ten thousand by ten thousand, to get larger counts." Dan flipped his Bible open to the last book. "Revelation is one of the most recent books. Look, here's the number of elders, beasts, and angels in verse 5:11:

> *And I beheld, and I heard the voice of many angels round about the throne and the beasts and the elders: and the number of them was ten thousand times ten thousand, and thousands of thousands;*

"When I read that passage, I see 10,000 x 10,000, or 100 million. They couldn't say 100 million, but they got the point across." He turned a page or two. "And here, the number of believers allowed into heaven was explicitly stated:

> *(Rev. 7:4) I heard the number of those who were sealed: 144 thousand from all the tribes of Israel.*

"By today's standards, that is quite a small number, far fewer than the number of believers even at that time," Dan said. "The lack of a named numerical value larger than *thousand* may be the reason."

"If the number actually is larger than 144,000," John said, "that's good news for believers who worry that they may not make it into heaven."

"That's a very small fraction of the 6.5 billion people on earth today," Shannon said. "That's about the same population as Dayton, Ohio, near where I grew up."

John looked back at Shannon. "I would rather believe that everyone who follows Christ will be received."

"Too bad, that's not what it says! It's only one out of about forty thousand people alive today," Dan said. "You can tell the other 39,999 people to go to hell, no matter what they might believe. It sounds like hell is going to be very crowded! No wonder it's supposed to be so hot down there!"

Shannon shook her head. "Yet another admission that for some reason, God is limited in power. And you say he's unable to make room for everybody in heaven? Apparently heaven is a very small and limited place after all!"

"By my calculations, you're about twice as likely to become a professional athlete as you are to make in into heaven, at that rate. And I've given up hope becoming a professional athlete long ago," Dan said.

John shook his head with exasperation and looked down at his pad.

Dan pointed at the clock. "Today we have clocks. They didn't. With no clocks, there were no words for hours and minutes, just the morning, evening, and seasons of the year. John, you mentioned that Genesis was likely first written in about 560 BC. In that period, the Jews used the Babylonian calendar that divided the year into twelve thirty-day months. That gives you only a 360 day year, five days short. Those extra days were a problem, and so they became *holy-days*. That's how we got our holy-day—our *holiday—season*."

"I guess that explains the '*reason for the season,'* not the birth of Christ, but to explain those pesky five and one-quarter extra days," Shannon said.

"Let's face it. The Jewish calendar was really pretty lousy," said Dan. "The Mayans of Central America, on the other hand, relied not only on the sun and moon but also the planet Venus, to establish 260-day and 365-day calendars—only six hours off the accepted solar year instead of over five days off."

"Aren't the Jews God's chosen people? Why did they wind up with such a crummy calendar?" Shannon asked.

"Shannon, please!" John took a deep breath. "Let's not be too hard on these ancient cultures, okay? My point is simply that the words in biblical scripture won't be modern words, especially since the King James translation was composed in AD 1611." He took another breath and slowed down a bit. "Another approach is to discuss the terms indirectly—to describe the effect or use of the concept."

Both Dan and Shannon nodded in agreement.

John said, "Of course, from another angle, there can be outright errors of translation when concepts easy to state in one language are difficult in another. Words may have several meanings. The meaning of a passage can change when the words are translated using the different meanings. If a word can be interpreted in two distinct ways, translators tend to choose the one that most closely complies with the story as held by biblical schools of thought at the time—and discard the other. Over enough translations, the story may *drift* toward one, and only one, accepted interpretation."

"I guess it's possible to avoid that error by turning to the original document," Dan said, "assuming such an original is available and that we know the possible meanings for the Hebrew words of that time. John, do you know if there is such an *original* for Genesis?"

"Sorry. Archeologists have never found any such *original* physical document. The Pentateuch was written on papyrus, parchment, and animal hides that decay relatively quickly. On the other hand, the Jewish scribes carefully copied the scripture from any deteriorating scrolls to new ones and ceremonially destroyed the old scrolls, so the content should be about right. Each Hebrew character has a numerical value, and with each new copy, the scribes would add up those values in the rows and columns and count all the characters on each scroll to make sure that they matched the previous document. Assuming the original copy was correct and that the painstaking copying process maintained the fidelity of the document, it's possible to review the 'original' Hebrew scripture word-for-word."

"We're not out of the woods, people," Shannon cautioned. "The definitions of words change all the time. Can you really know all the possible Hebrew words that were mistranslated?"

"Umm. True," Dan said. "Take the word *day*—we assume we know what that word means because we use it specifically to mean a single twenty-four-hour day. But, did the word *day* mean even something different in ancient times? It may be impossible for us to know."

Shannon grinned wickedly. "You say it will be impossible for us to know... Tell me, do you mean 'know' in the biblical sense?"

To Dan's surprise, John blushed a hot crimson and lost control of his Bible, dropping it to the floor.

CHAPTER 14

Agent Hall slipped quietly out of the orientation room and walked down a wide, shady arcade of the PITY school. His black leather oxford shoes tapped rhythmically on the patterned tile walkway. He passed several classrooms and casually looked in open doors and windows when he could. He figured his presence wandering the campus should not be particularly unusual; other parents would surely visit and tour the school from time to time.

Hall stopped outside one door wedged open to let in fresh air. He stood so that he could see the class, but their backs were to him, and the teacher was just out of sight. Given that these students were considered "at risk," he was a bit amazed at how well they had adapted: They looked well dressed, attentive, and healthy. Desks and chairs were aligned in exact rows, and the students sat bolt upright, with hands folded. Whenever the teacher would pose a question, the class responded in machine-like unison.

The repetition was hypnotic. *They're like Stepford Wives*, Hall thought, recalling the movie with always attentive robots that replaced the real women. *These kids are just too perfect!* He made a mental note of the machine-like regularity of the students, and continued down the arcade.

Hall turned into a main hallway running perpendicular to the others with doors on either side. On his left, he saw another open door, entered, and found a modest auditorium with high ceilings and a stage at one end, about four times longer than wide. Hall imagined that this room might have been the original sanctuary, which the school had apparently outgrown. Several students arranged lights and props for a play or other performance. They paid no notice to Hall, so he strolled over to the stage—close enough to see what they were doing.

One student had tattoos or brands on the backs of his hands. Hall found himself staring at them. *Those were probably gang-member markings made before he came to the school.* But he wasn't sure. They resembled in size and position the stigmata—the scars of Christ. It would be an unusual school indeed if it promoted such tattoos.

"Gonna be a good show?" he asked one boy jovially.

"I'm a sinner!" the boy yelled out, then started crying for no reason. The boy stopped crying suddenly and returned quietly to his work, almost as if nothing had happened. The other students had no reaction.

Hall was stunned. *Just a simple question, and the kid breaks down in tears... Something is strange here.* He backed out of the room and left the students to their work. Farther down the corridor, he came to the newer main sanctuary courtyard. He walked through whisper quiet glass doors that could have been found as the entryway to any retail store and into the sanctuary narthex. Remarkably, no one was around. There was plenty of equipment, open boxes, ladders, and lifts in the area. Absent were the wooden pews of older churches, replaced with modern cushioned, fold-up theater-style seats, arranged in an arc facing the altar.

Gone were the days of a simple wooden lectern in front of hard church pews with a gesticulating minister throwing his voice to an enraptured congregation. This place had an elaborate sound system and dozens of theatrical lights filling racks covering the ceiling. Hall imagined elaborate productions far exceeding the church experience of his youth. *Times have changed.*

Hall left the sanctuary, aiming for another classroom-lined hallway.

He got no closer. A balding man, barely five-feet tall, stepped from a doorway, almost colliding with Hall.

"Sir! May I ask what you are doing here? Are you lost?"

Although startled, Hall had rather expected that someone might object to his stroll through the campus. "Uh, can you tell me where the administration office is?"

"Don't you have a campus pass?"

"Uh, no."

"Sir, you shouldn't be on campus without a proper pass. Please follow me." He turned sharply, gesturing for Hall to follow. "Are you from the orientation meeting?" Without waiting for an answer, the man went on, "We run a very tight ship here. We can't have people randomly walking the halls."

"I understand completely."

"It's very disruptive...to the students. I'm sure you understand."

They turned the next corner, and the man pointed to a door marked 'Administration.' The man watched him open the door and enter before walking off in the other direction.

Typical of any school administration office, a high counter separated visitors from the efficient clerical workers behind it. A woman of middle age, dressed in a high-collar dress walked over to the counter. A pearl necklace fell in an arc over the front of her dress.

"May I help you?" she asked, looking over her black half-frame reading glasses, silver chains draped around the back of her neck.

"I'm Agent Hall with the FBI." Hall pulled out his identification folder.

She tilted her head up to look at his badge through her glasses. "Oh my! How can I help you?"

"Your name is?" asked Hall.

"Oh, yes, excuse me. I'm Nancy Bellwether, office administrator." She offered her hand to Hall. Her handshake was businesslike and firm. Hall noticed a brass nametag with her name engraved next to the stabbed-serpent school logo. "Is there a problem?" she pulled off her glasses and repeatedly opened and closed them.

"I have some questions about one of your students."

"I'd be happy to help you any way I can." Nancy continued to play with her glasses.

"Let's see..." Hall acted as if he were reading the name for the first time. "Did you have a student named...uh...William Freeman?"

"Just a moment, I'll look him up." She slipped on her glasses, sat back down and rolled her chair to the computer, typed on the keyboard, read some information, typed again, and finally looked up, her finger on the screen to keep her position among the many lines in the report. "Mr. Hall, yes, here he is. William Freeman is on my list." She clicked the mouse. "Okay... Hmmm... Oh my! He's no longer enrolled. Apparently, he... uh...withdrew from the school about two weeks ago."

"Withdrew? What does that mean?"

"Well, just what it says; he's no longer a student."

"Ms. Bellwether, is that a usual procedure? Does a student normally just withdraw from your school?"

She stood up, pulled her glasses off, and spoke defensively. "We have policies and procedures, and we follow them, Mr. Hall! It's rare, but not unheard of, for a student to withdraw. Is William having a problem?"

"Do you have any record of why William actually withdrew?"

She sat back down and looked at the screen again through her glasses. "We usually have a note saying why students leave..." She took her glasses off for a moment and rubbed her eyes and then put them back on and looked at the screen again, typing at the keys. "Gee, I don't see one. I'm sure it's just a simple oversight; it has to be!"

"Since that record doesn't say anything, did you hear anyone say anything about why he left?"

"Well, no. In fact, this is the first time I realized he wasn't in the school. Someone else must have handled his withdrawal."

"Who else might work with these records?"

"I'm the only one, except, of course, for the Bishop or his personal staff."

"You say 'Bishop?'"

"I mean Bishop Richard Ward. He is the Executive Director and Master of Theological Policy."

"Is he available? I have some additional questions, if you don't mind."

"I'm not sure if he's in. His office is up the hill... the PIT... sorry... the *Pacific Institute of Theology*. Let me call and see." She picked up the phone and hit a single button. "Hi, Rebecca? Is the Bishop in today?" She listened. "I have a Agent Hall from the FBI. He has some questions for the Bishop... Yes, I'll hold."

Nancy kept the phone to her ear but swiveled the mouthpiece down to talk to Hall. "His assistant, Rebecca, is checking to see if he's in."

He's screening his visitors. I'm sure Nancy will report back that the Bishop is unavailable. No one likes a surprise visit by the FBI. A few moments elapsed.

Nancy swiveled the phone back up. "Yes, certainly, that will be no problem... Thank you, Rebecca." She set the phone into the cradle and stood up. "I can take you to his office, up the hill. Please follow me."

A pleasant surprise. I thought this would be more difficult.

Nancy slipped through a waist-high two-way swinging door in the counter, then led Hall out of the Administration Office, locking the door behind them. Parked on a wider concrete path were several small electric vehicles much like golf-carts. Nancy stepped into one and invited Hall to sit in the seat next to her. She then drove up the hill, slowing for the speed bumps on the road.

Ahead, wrought-iron gates insulated the institution from contact with the outside world. Their design reminded Hall of a bygone age, of medieval churches and Europe during the Inquisition. Symmetrical, the height of the gate was lowest at the hinges, rising in a smooth arc to the central point where the two gates met. Christian crosses adorned the center of each gate, each a part of the same logo, each cross stabbed through the outline of a serpent's head. Nancy waved to the guard in the guardhouse, and the gates swung back electronically, an incongruous touch of modern technology.

White masonry buildings with red tile roofs covered the entire top of the hill. Walls of the outer buildings were anchored directly to the sheer rock face like an extension of the sides of the hill. As they got closer, Hall thought the whole place reminded him of Alcatraz or Hitler's eyrie at Berchtesgaden, with a sheer drop from any window.

Ms. Bellwether pulled the vehicle right into the central courtyard of the facility, parking in front of a very prestigious looking building at the north end of the square.

"The Bishop's office is in here." She got out of the vehicle and motioned to Hall to follow her. She walked up the granite steps to tall and venerable wooden doors. The doors had the same archway design used in the driveway gates. Nancy struggled to pull open one for Hall, and he sprang forward to help her. He held the massive door while she entered into the reception area. Rebecca was waiting.

"Rebecca, this is Agent Hall."

Rebecca nodded briefly to Hall, then turned to Nancy. "Thank you,

Nancy. I'll take it from here."

Nancy returned a quick nod and a nervous smile, and then turned back to Hall. She said, "Nice to meet you, Mr. Hall," and left the room through the same doors.

"Mr. Hall, please have a seat for a moment while I notify the Bishop." Rebecca motioned to an uncushioned, Elizabethan-style armchair. She turned and walked through doors at the far end of the hall.

Hall didn't really feel like sitting, but he wanted to be cooperative. The chair was as uncomfortable as it looked.

After a moment, Rebecca returned, walking silently all the way to where Hall was sitting.

"Would you please follow me?"

The elaborate entryway to the Bishop's office was adorned with religious paintings of the Renaissance period. Probably priceless, but they weren't the kind of artwork Hall would consider for himself. It was a sequence of paintings by the Cretan-born painter, El Greco, including *Christ Carrying the Cross*, *Christ on the Cross Adored by Donors, The Holy Trinity*, and *The opening of the Fifth Seal of the Apocalypse*—all depictions of Christ's suffering, crucifixion, resurrection, and visitation by apocalyptic horrors. If Hall felt torture and pain were inspirational, he supposed he might consider them attractive. Instead, they only made him even more uneasy about his visit to the PIT.

At the end of the gallery, Rebecca pulled the doors open and gestured for Hall to enter. She led Hall across the marble floor to the front of the Bishop's gigantic desk, held her head low and announced, "Your Honor, this is Agent Hall."

CHAPTER 15

Dan looked at the modern conveniences in the cheerful coffee house, the lights, fans, marine-theme artifacts, and recorded music in the background—all things alien to ancient times. *It's going to be hard to grasp the mindset of ancient writers. Their concept of the world was much different from ours.*

Shannon set her coffee mug down on the table. "John, you say the story of creation was preserved as an oral tradition until it was finally recorded in written form in about 560 BC during the Jewish exile in Babylon. If we're not sure who first told the story, where did it come from? Do you know?"

"Well, it's obviously not possible for anyone to witness the creation firsthand, that's for sure. One possible scenario is that Moses could have acquired the original story by way of a vision. You've heard of his encounter with the burning bush on Mt. Sinai?" John asked.

Dan snapped his fingers, then shook a pointing finger. "Exodus somewhere, right? The burning bush, yes... it could be simply a film or video projected into the dark shadows of a dense shrub—like the televised Yule log at Christmas-time. Moses would see the projection as a magical fire that did not consume the bush. I could easily make that today using inexpensive video equipment, and to a man of that era, anyone who could create something like this would be declared an angel."

"Sure, or a hologram would do it. I think you're going a bit far in casting yourself as an angel. Let's concentrate on mechanics," Shannon said with a grin.

Dan grinned back. "A movie might be the most convenient way to express complex information to anyone who could not understand terminology or concepts. Anyone can watch a video. Think of this: If indeed the first chapters of 'Earth Science 101' were presented to Moses in a video presentation, then each of the events outlined in the first chapter of Genesis might have been split into presentations that lasted one day. If it took six days to complete the video summary, then the term *day* would not refer to the time that God spent creating but instead to the days of the burning-bush presentation. No correlation with real time at all, only to the length of the presentation. It explains the encounter Moses had on Mount Sinai, resolves the burning bush magic, and it conveniently resolves the debate over the word *day*."

"Bravo, Dan." Shannon clapped. "Your theory takes care of the mystical fire and the source of the story of creation in one fell swoop; plus, it finally puts the question of angels to rest. Good job."

"I don't buy it... I don't like it. You're taking all the mystery out of the story!" John said.

"Why not? Once we understand the structure of the world, is there anything mystical about it?" Shannon asked. "Sure, we may not understand everything, but to stick to an old story just because you prefer a mystery is crazy!"

"No, I think it's crazy to postulate a time-traveling video player and a boxed set of National Geographic documentaries. But for the sake of argument, the burning bush could be a video, so long as we eliminate Dan as the angel. But, let's talk about another option." He paused, perhaps to get the image of Dan with wings out of his mind. "The source of the creation story could have been *divine intervention.* The author was inspired by God directly—and every word was written as God intended."

"That's a ridiculous idea, John," Shannon said. "If God inspired the writer directly, the text would be error-free. God wouldn't make mistakes, would he?"

"Well... uh... no."

"I have to agree that that's really an impossible theory, John," Dan said.

"Fine... I will admit that even theological scholars say it's implausible," John said and then paused for a moment. "Thomas Paine summarized all these issues in his work The *Age of Reason*, published just as the Declaration of Independence was being signed. But in the case of divine intervention, God would certainly not use words his listeners wouldn't understand."

Dan made a note in his small, black notebook. "I'll have to look up Paine's *Age of Reason* on the Internet when I get back to my office. It should make interesting reading."

"I'm sorry I mentioned it," John said. "Thomas Paine is a royal 'Paine' in the neck. He misses the point that the Bible must be taken as a whole and that the creation is later explained by the other books of the Bible, or by Christ himself in the New Testament."

"Right. The 'Whole Bible' theory. I've heard that before, but I don't buy it," Dan said. "Here's why: If the later writers didn't know about the hidden information, they would just support the customary view and that would persist until sufficient scientific understanding became available to allow a reader to interpret it correctly. Those later views are used by some to bolster the credibility of the traditional viewpoint, but without the advanced scientific understanding, they are both off track."

John scratched his head. "I'm not sure I'm following you on that. Still, it's common for scriptures to be applied in different ways by different readers... one of the amazing powers of the Holy Bible."

Dan stroked his chin with his finger. "Here's another way to think of this: Even if the later interpretation is wrong, it is still an essential part of the puzzle. It preserves the earlier story and points back to it as important. You can't look for hidden scientific meaning if the story is lost. Those later stories kept the earlier ones around for us to scrutinize."

Michael, the coffee shop owner, came by the table. "Look at all these Bibles! Planning to start your own church? Please no hymns in here! Anyone need a refill?" They accepted the offer, laughing with the barista.

Shannon pushed her cup over for a refill. "John, I have to admit I've probably forgotten just about everything about the stories in the Bible. I remember being bored stupid in Sunday School—the nuns just droned on and on, and once they got clothes on Adam and Eve, the people just got dull."

"Think of them as characters in a novel, if that's easier," John said.

"Oh, all right—go ahead, let's hear what you've got." She smiled at him.

John beamed as if he had struck oil, sitting up in his chair. "The first and obviously most important actor would be God during the creation of the universe, life, and man." He wrote *Creation* on his note pad.

"A very long time, indeed. Definitely the longest time period covered in the Bible, although it gets only a few paragraphs," Dan said, half smiling. "Since God is defined as eternal, he would have existed for an eternity into the past.

"A man once asked St. Augustine: 'What did God do with all that time—an eternity—before he created earth, life, Adam, and Eve?' St. Augustine said, 'God was busy, very busy.' But what was he doing?' asked the man. St. Augustine scratched his head, then said adamantly, 'He was making hell for people like you, who ask ridiculous questions like that!'" Everyone chuckled.

John wrote *Adam* on his pad. "Adam was the first human, created by God *in God's image* from clay. He lived in and cared for the Garden of Eden. Adam named all the animals but could find no suitable partner from those animals. At this point, God's creation was perfect, and there was no sin.

"The next human was Eve, created by God not from the dust, but from one of Adam's ribs, so she could be Adam's partner.

"Now, Satan was originally the angel Lucifer, who disagreed with God and revolted. God initially sentenced Satan to the pit of hell, but Satan wound up getting stronger and becoming free to reign over the earth.

"Early in the book of Genesis, a story is told about the relationship between God and man, perhaps one of the most influential stories in the Bible. God warned Adam and Eve not to eat the fruit of the Tree of Knowledge of Good and Evil or they would introduce sin and die. Eve was deceived by Satan to eat the fruit, and she then convinced Adam as well. They ate the fruit against God's warning. This is the original sin and the *Fall.* God kicked them out of the Garden for their transgression and sentenced them to a life of toil and misery. At birth, each person inherits this sin, making mankind inherently sinful and wicked. Newborn babies must be baptized to eliminate that sin."

"That is absolutely ridiculous," Shannon said. "How can a newborn baby be sinful? It's mind boggling."

"Could you wait until I get done before you rip this apart?"

She shrugged and subsided into silence, sipping her newly poured coffee.

"After Adam and Eve were ejected from the Garden of Eden, the world became increasingly evil. God decided to kill off all the evil by causing a worldwide flood. He told Noah to build the Ark for himself, his family, and a pair of each of the animals of earth. At the end of the 150-day flood, God used a rainbow to signify that he would never do this again. Based on this story, it would be the case that all humans would be related to Noah and his family, so they're certainly key characters as well.

"After Noah, Abraham and Moses are perhaps the most prominent characters of the Old Testament. Moses received the all-important Ten Commandments during the Exodus from Egypt. In those days, the blood sacrifice was essential for atonement.

"There were many other characters in the Old Testament—for example, Solomon, David, and Job. But these figures do not rise above the importance of Abraham and Moses in the grand scheme of things. However, King David is frequently mentioned in later scripture. He was perhaps the most successful Jewish king, ruling over Judah, an empire that took in the entire coast of the Mediterranean, from Egypt to the Euphrates. Later, the Jews always looked back to the time of David and of his son, Solomon, as a golden age. David's dynasty continued for four centuries. The Jews never stopped believing that some descendant of David would return to rule over them.

"I'm going to turn now to the New Testament. It's centered on Jesus Christ, a descendent of David and born to Mary, a virgin mother, fulfilling scriptural prophecy of such a Messiah. Jesus had many followers, a potential problem for the huge Roman Empire. At the time that empire extended from west of Italy to the region we call 'Israel' today, making it difficult to rule, especially during those days of primitive communications and transportation.

"Jesus was a pacifist. He stressed nonviolence to his followers. Eventually, he was crucified and more important, resurrected, as proof that he was the Son of God. The sacrifice of his life is offered to Christians to wipe clean the original sin of Adam. Jesus joined his father in heaven, and the Holy Spirit continues to be present on earth. The Father, Son, and Holy Spirit, compose the 'Trinity' of Christianity.

"Living a life with Jesus Christ will allow the Christian to live forever in heaven. Denying Christ his proper place in your life means you'll revert to your sinful nature, as established by the original sin of Adam, and will be sentenced to an eternity in hell. The second coming of Christ and the final judgment will determine whether a Christian will live out eternity in heaven or hell. As I mentioned, some churches believe that only 144,000 believers will be offered a life in heaven; other churches believe that the only prerequisite is a belief in Jesus, and that all believers can live eternally in heaven.

"That's pretty much the story, but we should mention Paul, the second-most important character in the New Testament. According to researchers today, he wrote more than half of that part of the Bible. His missionary travels helped establish the Christian church across the Roman Empire. Remember, Jesus was a Jew, and the Jewish religion required strict adherence to Jewish custom and the law of the Torah. It was very difficult to get converts to Judaism, as compliance with the law was a bit onerous. Particularly difficult was convincing men that they should be circumcised."

"A very difficult choice to make as an adult!" Dan laughed, crossing his legs, but his joke didn't seem to catch on with the group.

"Well, that's about it for a basic overview. I hope that helps, Shannon."

She nodded. "Yes, thanks for the overview. It's pretty much what I remember from Sunday school."

Dan spoke in a quiet tone of voice, just over a whisper. "That guy, Walker... have you ever seen him before?"

"Sorry, I don't frequent homeless shelters, Dan," Shannon said.

John shook his head.

"Well, he made some peculiar comments to me after you left. It's strange, but he seemed sure that we would find a connection between stories in the Bible and DNA and other advanced biological concepts. He warned that we should be extremely careful when and where we talk about it. He's concerned that the church and scientific establishment might overreact. With recent threats by religious fanatics, I would feel more comfortable if we took some precautions. That's why I insisted that we not talk both science and religion at the same time."

"I was wondering what you meant," Shannon said. "Walker might be dreaming. Come on, the coffee house? What is it, bugged or something?" She started singing the theme to the Twilight Zone very softly "da-da-da-da, da-da-da-da... Big brother is watching!"

"Very funny, Shannon. I'd be surprised if it is, but in this day and age, it's not impossible. Let's be more careful, okay?" They nodded. Dan raised his voice a bit to a normal level. "Shannon, did you have any time to find your summary of biological 'dogma?'"

"Not yet. I know I have a short summary somewhere that might be about right from one of my classes. There's been so much discovered in the last few years that I'll have to leave a lot out to get to the core information. I'll try to do as good a job as you did, John."

Dan said, "To be safe, we should meet in a new location. What do you think about meeting at the University Deli—the one next to the campus bookstore?"

"Sure, the East Deli... that'll be fine with me. I should have something by tomorrow," Shannon said. "That should prepare us with the facts of life, so we can prove that they are never mentioned by your sacred scripture!"

CHAPTER 16

Hall stood in front of the Bishop's desk, watching the seated man sign several documents in a deliberate, unhurried hand, making the point clear that he could easily ignore the agent.

Finally, he looked up and tapped the papers into loose order. "Yes?" he asked coldly.

Hall decided not to reflect the same measure of rudeness. "I'm Agent Hall, with the FBI." He flashed his identification and badge to the Bishop. "I'm very sorry to disturb you without an appointment, but it would help me if I could ask you a few questions."

"Certainly, sir. We're always happy to cooperate with law enforcement. We are in fact in similar businesses, my friend. The influence of the devil is obvious as we look around us. Without him, your services would never be needed, would they?" Bishop Ward held his finger points together, as if they were a church steeple.

Hall cleared his throat. "Bishop Ward, I wanted to compliment you on the wonderful school you're providing here for the youth—'PITY,' is it? I was able to take a peek earlier. It's truly amazing how well the students are enjoying the school."

"Thank you, but I'm sure you're not here to compliment me on the school. What do you want?" The Bishop moved a stack of documents off the table and into a drawer.

"I'm working to complete some paperwork on a student of yours, a..." Hall took out his note pad to look at the name, as if to refresh his memory, "...oh yes... a... William Freeman."

"Didn't our administration office have that information?"

"I did talk to Ms. Bellwether."

"She is usually very efficient."

"Well, she had the basics. I was hoping you might be able to shed more light on his disappearance."

The Bishop grimaced. "Disappearance? I do know many of the students by name. But I don't recall this William Freeman. Don't you think you're being a bit hasty to call this a disappearance? It sounds more like a runaway to me."

"Certainly, I understand. I wouldn't expect you to know all the students at the school by name. Perhaps you can tell me if it's a normal occurrence for a student to be released from the school prior to graduation and without the consent of the parents."

"We never do that. Our rules are strict and comprehensive. Students don't leave without a proper release. I'm sure everything was properly handled."

"Ms. Bellwether couldn't find any note of what happened in his record—no mention of when or why he left." Hall thought the Bishop's brow looked a little shinier than when he walked in.

"Runaways are extremely rare, but—" he shrugged—"they can happen. We'll look into the matter."

"Of course. Well, I guess that will about do it. Here's my card. Please call me if you come across any information that I might include in my report." Hall turned, walked to the door with Rebecca and then turned back to face the Bishop.

"You say it sounds like a runaway," he broadcast across the room. "I wonder how you got that idea?"

"I said, we'll look into it, Agent Hall. And if and when we find some additional information, we'll certainly share it with you. Good day!"

Hall was escorted by Rebecca out of the Bishop's office, down the artwork-lined corridor, and into the entry area.

"Please wait here. Ms. Bellwether will be up to get you in a minute."

"Thank you. By the way, Rebecca, if you remember anything about William Freeman, would you please call me?" He handed his card to Rebecca.

She took the card and nodded once, with some hesitation, looking directly at Hall, and then quickly turned away.

Hall waited for a few more minutes, looking over the unpleasant artwork. After the drive back down the hill with Ms. Bellwether, Hall handed her one of his cards as well, with the same suggestion.

He walked out of the facility with more questions than he had when he entered. The perspiring Bishop almost certainly knew more about William than he admitted, coming up with the idea of a runaway without even recalling who the student was.

You don't just release a minor without informing and coordinating with the parents, especially on such a tight ship, as they proudly call it, Hall ruminated. He caught sight of the complex in his rearview mirror and his stomach churned. His earlier experience with the PIT did not cheer him up.

As he drove out of the long driveway, he noticed a bearded man with baseball cap under his brown sweatshirt hood walking toward the facility. *He's a little old for this PITY—maybe he thinks they can help him. Or maybe I should warn him.* Hall drove on.

CHAPTER 17

The University East Deli could be reached only by serpentine concrete paths, winding among manicured lawns between towering hardwood trees. Dan and John met in front of the University Library at the foot of those paths.

"It reminds me of a county courthouse," John muttered, looking up the wide granite stairs at the library building.

Dan glanced up at the imposing white columns. "A little intimidating, eh?"

John nodded, and they walked off together toward the deli. Even on Friday, it was packed. Waves of people purchased snacks or lunches and walked off or sat to eat. Students, professors, teaching assistants, and visitors filled the tables, eating, talking, and studying.

"Do you see Shannon anywhere?" asked Dan.

"I'm looking. Tell you what. You look on that side and I'll take this side." John used his finger to keep track as he scanned the tables.

Dan spotted Shannon at a far table. "There she is!" They zigzagged through the tables to where she was sitting, dodging chairs and students, each taking a different route.

"This place is packed!" John said, looking around.

"It's grown quite a bit even since I've been here. Biotechnology—my major—is severely overcrowded. The industry is booming. Everyone is planning on hitting the jackpot. They're no longer in it just for the pleasure of science or for the good of humanity. High-paying careers and the promise of lucrative stock options can twist priorities severely."

Shannon cleared her throat. "Last night, I pieced together a summary of the biological mechanisms of life. Then I realized it would be even better to just take you guys to the *Museum of Life* here on campus."

"Oh really?" asked Dan. "That sounds like fun! Where is it?"

Shannon tossed her books and notebook into her backpack. "I'll lead you. Follow me."

The two men trailed her out the side exit onto a little-used side road where they could walk three abreast with no interference from cars and only a few bicycles.

"After all," Shannon said, "the big picture is all we'll need. Universal, core principles are what we're looking for. That's all we'd expect to find in any ancient document, right? Details included in most textbooks are certainly far too detailed. Biology is exploding with advances, and I'm pretty close to the action. The museum presents the information at a level perfect for us to get a handle on this stuff without getting lost in the detail."

"Great... great idea, Shannon," John said, a bit uneasily, his face showing some additional creases of reluctance.

Shannon had a spring in her step. There was no sign of the foot-dragging she exhibited during John's Bible study lesson. She seemed delighted, ready to delve into her area of expertise. "Remember, this is still a relatively new field, so some concepts are disputed and differing theories are competing for attention. I'll mention those when I think they're relevant. But by and large, this information is quite settled."

They approached a massive, century-old, weather-stained building constructed of brown and gray granite. The entrance looked like a castle with round towers on each side of wrought iron gates. Large windows filled the upper story, each having twenty individual panes. A pair of granite stairways rose to the entrance. The group walked up the stairs, around a number of students reading or talking on cell phones.

Outside, the building showed its age, but surprisingly the interior was fully remodeled. The light from the large windows kept it bright and enjoyable. Familiar classical music—Bach's *Violin Concerto No 1 in A Minor*—played lightly in the background. A sign above the first arched interior doorway read

MUSEUM OF LIFE

They walked under the sign and entered the first gallery, "The Material of Life."

The first display had two compartments, one displaying *organic* and the other *inorganic* material. An informational sign informed the three friends that ancient alchemists learned to separate material on earth into two general classes, based on how they behaved when first heated and then cooled. *Inorganic* materials—like salt, lead, and water—return to their former state after cooling. When hot, salt will glow red, lead melts, and water evaporates. When cooled, they appear unchanged.

In the second compartment, the display explained that *organic* material doesn't return to its original state after heating. For example, sugar will char, olive oil remains a vapor, and wood turns to charcoal. Heat-resistant inorganic materials come directly from the earth, air, or sea. Organic materials are derived only from living organisms.

John turned to his friends. “I thought ‘organic’ meant it was grown without using pesticides. This says that virtually everything that’s related to life is called organic, right?”

“The confusion isn’t helped with food products marked ‘*organic,*’” Dan said. “All food is organic!”

“Hmmm. Well, that’s an example of another word that has many meanings, and I’ll bet most people don’t know the scientific one,” John said. “Gee, I’m looking forward to having some *organic* potato chips and a greasy *organic* hamburger. I feel healthier already.”

The group chuckled.

The next exhibit described the steady march of science as chemists worked to break substances down and group them into similar properties. In the center of the exhibit, the periodic table was displayed prominently, lighted with halogen spotlights. The culmination of centuries of research by chemists and scientists, the famous table of elements was discovered in the 19th century.

Just past the periodic table, the molecular structure of matter was shown using little balls of different colors and sizes connected by sticks. Models of inorganic material, such as salt, water, and lead, were very small and simple. Salt, NaCl, had two balls—one atom of sodium and one of chlorine. Water, H_20, had two atoms of hydrogen and one ball-atom of oxygen. Lead, Pb, had one large ball.

The organic compounds, on the other hand, used many, many balls of only a few different colors in complex configurations. The display began with simple molecules, such as the simple sugars, fructose, glucose, sucrose, and lactose.

John turned the corner and stopped: “Wow, look at this one!” he exclaimed.

In front of them was a monster: hemoglobin, one of the most important proteins in life. The model was mostly composed of only four different colored balls—carbon, hydrogen, oxygen, and nitrogen—but it was huge, having 574 amino acids. Each amino acid was composed of about twenty atoms, totaling about 11,000 atoms in all. Each of the four chains looked like a single ribbon spiraled and twisted around to make a very complex three-dimensional structure.

Shannon read from the label: “‘A pocket in the middle of this giant molecule is the secret of its life-giving function. It carries oxygen from the lungs to the tissues and carbon dioxide from the tissues back to the lungs. Without this molecule, large oxygen-breathing organisms would be impossible.’”

John stood back and looked over the hemoglobin model. “Now that... that is a huge molecule. It winds all over the place, randomly turning this way and that. Now, I understand why organic molecules can’t recover after heating. It’d be impossible to get all those balls back in the right place.”

"That's true, but it isn't really random. Look at this display," Shannon said, pointing ahead, "*Amino Acids*."

In the mid-1800s, scientists discovered that proteins could be decomposed into only twenty amino acids, which fit together in long chains. All amino acid molecules start with identical "backbones," consisting of the same atoms every time—two carbon, two hydrogen, one oxygen, and one nitrogen. They are arranged in a standardized three-dimensional tetrahedron—a triangle-based pyramid—that allows one amino acid to connect with the next in long chains, chains called *proteins*.

Dan was working on his cell-phone calculator. "Let's see. Given the twenty different amino acids and the average protein length of five hundred amino acids, it would be possible to produce... uh... 10^{600} combinations. That's the number one followed by six hundred zeros. Googol to the sixth power. Indeed, life would have almost infinite possibilities."

John leaned over and looked at the result on Dan's phone.

"I'm sure that the set of useful sequences is far less than that," Shannon said. "It's like an alphabet of twenty characters in gene sequences of about five hundred characters or about a hundred typical English words. There are many paragraphs of a hundred words that make sense but far more that make no sense at all.

"Like a hundred chimps hunched over typewriters randomly hitting the keys, statisticians say that given enough time, those chimps will eventually compose all the works of Shakespeare. But even getting a hundred words 'just right' is something a writer may sweat blood over for weeks. The same is true for the sequence of amino acids in proteins. We're not talking about just getting something that will barely make sense, it must be functional in the organization of the cell and organism. It must be *just right*."

The three friends finished the displays in the first room and passed through a door to a round room outfitted with displays of complex protein structures supported artistically by clear plastic cylinders. The entire room was a model of a cell, including the major structures within it. Shannon walked through the room as if she were showing a house to a prospective buyer. "With this model, you can easily imagine the cell, composed of thousands of proteins, each about the same complexity as the hemoglobin protein we just saw. The organic molecules are the building blocks of the next level, the level of the cell. All organisms use cells like this. Some have one cell and others have trillions of them, from the simplest single-celled organisms to the largest beasts, including humans. There are about 260 different types of cells in humans, but all are fundamentally about the same, typically smaller than the eye can see or in some cases several feet long, such as in the spinal cord."

They walked over to a big green plastic blob in the middle of the room. "This must be the nucleus," Dan said. "That's where the DNA is stored."

Shannon looked into the blob and mainly talked to John. "See those X-shaped molecules? Those are the *chromosomes*, where the cell keeps your DNA. There are twenty-three pairs of chromosomes in humans, forty-six total. Each chromosome is a single DNA strand wound around a protein support structure. They vary in length but average about a hundred-million units. If you add it all up, there are about three-billion units that encode your genetic traits."

The group looked around the other models in the room, especially noting the ribosomes, where proteins are built, and the mitochondria, systems that help provide energy for the cell.

"This is really a remarkable display," John said.

"I feel like I'm a tiny microbial parasite swimming inside the cell. It's great!" Dan said.

"Being in this display gives you an idea of the scale of the cell and all the proteins that make it up. Follow me now into the 'DNA Room.'"

The DNA Room had a very high ceiling, and it blazed with light. Centered in the room, a giant model of a DNA segment dominated the scene, about three feet in diameter and twelve feet tall.

Shannon continued acting as the host. "DNA is a helical molecule with two backbones spiraled around each other. I love this model of it."

Dan and John walked around the display, inspecting it from all angles.

Shannon said, "The two backbones are connected together with pairs of *base molecules*. Those are the ones in the middle, see?" Shannon pointed to the central molecules. "Four bases are used—*Adenosine*, *Thymidine*, *Cytidine*, and *Guanosine*. Scientists usually use only the first letter to represent each one, that is A, T, C, and G."

"If you don't mind, I'll stick to the letters," John said. "I can't even pronounce those other words."

"The important thing is that A bonds only with T and C bonds only with G," she said. "See right there, that's an A and a T hooked together, and next to it is the C and G. It's the order of the pairs that determines the information in the strand."

"Okay... I get it. That's pretty simple," John said.

About halfway up the model, they show the two strands splitting apart, with each half having another strand being built on to it. DNA can be unwound and separated like a zipper into two halves, complementary opposites. Then, a second half is built on each of those halves, producing two strands that are exactly the same.

"That's called 'replication,' and it's a key aspect of life. But it's not as easy as it looks. DNA won't replicate on its own. It needs DNA *polymerase*, a special protein that works like a creative zipper head, moving down one side of the zipper-like strand and creating the second half. Once replication is complete, the cell can split in two, with each having the exact DNA sequence of the original cell. That is perhaps the most important feature of DNA. It can duplicate itself exactly."

The friends ambled over to a display labeled *Genetic Code.*

"Here is the DNA sequence of one half of the DNA molecule." Shannon pointed to a gray block of letters, all seeming to fade into each other:

```
TGAGCCTCCCACGCCTCAGTTTCCCCTGCAGAAAACACCCTGCATCCAANACGGGCCTTG
GTGTCCAGCCCTGGGGCGGAAACNCCGNACGCATGTCCACACACGTGTAGGCACGCGGGC
ACACACAGGCTCACATGCCTGNACNCATGCGCGCGCACGGACACACACACACACACAC
ACACACACACACACACACACACACACGGGTGTTACCAAAACGGCCCCGCCTGAATCGC
TGAGGCCTCGACCCAAGGCCGGAAAAGTCCATGACGCTGGAGCAGGGATGAGGTNCCATT
CCAGCAGGCTGGGGGAGGAGAACCTCTCTTTTAAAATATTAGGTCAAACCATGNAATTGC
TGATAATTAACCGTTTTGGTCCTACCAACAATACACACACACACACACACACACACAC
ACACACGTGCAGCAAGTTCAGATAATTCAACATTATATGCAGCCATAATATCAAATTCTG
AATCTTTAATGCTGGTCAGAGGATTTTGAGGAGCCCCGCCCCAATTTTGGAGAGGGAAGT
GTGTGTCGCTGCCACTGTGCCACCTTCCTCCCCCACAATTGCAGCAGCACGGAGTGGACA
GNACGGATGTGTGTCNAGGTGCTGNANGGATGTGTGTGACAGCTGATTATTTCAATGCTC
ACAAATATTTATCCAAAGGGTGCTTCTCTTGGGGGTTGCAAAACATCCCCACGAGTAGGA
CACTGGAGCCCTAGGGGTAACCTGTCCATAGGAGCCGTACTTCTTTCTCAGTCACTGAGG
TTGGAAGAGGGGAGAAGGGCCTGACCGATGTTCACAGACACACACACACACACACACACA
CACACACACACACACGAGAGGTTGGAATGCCACCTCTACAGCCATGGAGACGCTCCCATT
TCATTTCCAGGCCCGGCGGCACACTGCTTGCATCATGCAGTTATTCAATCATCCTTTCAA
TGGTTGCCATTAACAACCCGATTCTTTAAAAATAATACTAAAAAAGGCTCATACGCTTTC
TGAAAAGCTAGCTAAAACATCAACTCTCCCCTGTGTTTCCAGCCTGTGGGCCCATGATGA
AGATTCTGGACTTGCCAGTTTCCATAACCACGTGAGCCAATTCCTTAAAACTTCAGCAAC
CCCTATACACCACACACACACACACACACACACACACACACACACACACACACACATCCT
ATTGCTTCTGTTTCTGTACATAGTCCCTAAGGCTTATTGGGGTTTGAGCTAGCTGTGTGC
ACACAACATGANGGGGCACACATGCACATGCACACATGCCCACATGCATATGCACACACA
CACACACACACACACACACATTCATGCCCAAGCACGCCCACCCTCATGTCTCACCATGTG
CACATAACACACAGTCACATATACCCTGGCACACATGCCCACATGCAGACACGAAACACA
GGCCCACGNTTNCATGCACACAGGTATGGGCACACATACCATGCACACATAANGACAAAT
ACCAGGCCAGACATGATTTGCCCCTGCTGGTGTCACTGTTAAGTGTGACAGACAAGCAGA
GGACACACACCCACCTGGGACGCGGGGCTTCAGGAGAGAGGCAGACCTAATAGGGCCCGG
ATTCGGGGCTGGGGAGGCTATTCGGGGCTGGGGAGGCTA
```

Dan read the informational plaque out loud. "There are 1,600 characters printed above, representing 1,600 base pairs, enough for many proteins. If we printed three times this amount per page—that is, 4,800 characters—we would typically need about twenty thousand pages to represent a single chromosome and nearly a million pages to represent the entire human genetic code—about the same as five hundred Bibles."

Next to the display were stacks of Bibles, twenty-three stacks, with roughly twenty in each stack corresponding to one chromosome. Above each stack was a number and a picture of that chromosome. The pictures each looked like a stretched-out "X".

"I guess each stack of Bibles represents the amount of information in each chromosome?" John said as a question. "I know that the Bible is the most commonly printed book, but why use *that* sacred book in *this* secular display."

"What is your problem with it, John?" Dan asked. "You said God created everything. Wouldn't he be proud that we are understanding his creation?"

"I concede," Shannon said, "you don't usually see Bibles in a museum like this. Someone might accuse the curator of desecrating the Holy Scriptures. I think they might honestly be safer to use Darwin's *Origin of the Species* if the want to avoid a lawsuit by religious fanatics."

"What's this?" John pointed to a portion of DNA strand, printed row-by-row, winding down the wall, ignoring Dan's challenging question. The first row was about five feet long, reading from left to right. Then it made a hairpin turn, continuing right to left another five feet and so on, going back and forth sixteen times. The ATCG characters were small, about 10 characters per inch.

"That's a gene," Shannon said. "Printed with 10-point characters, it's about 83 feet long and has about 10,000 A-T-C-G base units. A *gene* is an active area of the DNA strand that encodes a protein or has some other active role."

"Wow! One gene is pretty long!" exclaimed John.

"But it's only about two pages in one of those five hundred Bibles, so there are a lot of them," Dan said. "And you'd need at least six pages to encode the hemoglobin protein we just looked at, about 250-feet long when printed like this. It says there are 10,000 to 20,000 genes in each of twenty-three chapters, for a total of about 40,000 to 80,000 gene 'recipes.'"

"Recipes? These are more than just recipes!" Shannon protested. "The physical sequence of the information allows the genes to mechanically construct the proteins, enzymes, and infrastructure that make up the organism itself. It's like a recipe that makes itself. We'll probably get into that in the next display."

"Wait, Shannon," Dan said. "This might be important: *Junk DNA*, base units with no apparent purpose interspersed between and within functional genes. The long strand we just saw on the wall? Here it is again with the green parts showing active DNA, called the *exon*, and the red part showing junk, called the *intron*. There is quite a lot of junk around and within the active genes, if you ask me."

"They say that junk DNA has no purpose, but this is an area that is still in flux," Shannon said. "Researchers may eventually find that junk DNA has some purpose. Some animals have almost none. It's a strange exception that we can probably ignore as we look for the larger patterns. But what I think is truly amazing is that in humans, *almost all* DNA is junk. Some say only five-percent of the strand is active, with only 1.5 percent actually used to make functional proteins."

"Shannon, are you sure about that?" Dan asked. "That would mean that ninety-five percent of the human genome appears to be included for no purpose." He turned to look at John. "John, this is going to be a huge problem for your *intelligent designer* theory. Why would God throw in so much junk in our DNA sequence just for fun? Another mistake by Almighty God?"

"Maybe it's not really junk. It might be of some use, right?" John answered.

"I agree; it doesn't sound like God is very intelligent if he accidentally left in so much inactive DNA." Shannon said. "But, I will admit that there's still a lot of discussion and research, as you can imagine. I'm not going to be able to settle that one. Put that in the 'to be determined' category. Let's move on. We need to understand how DNA can define how the cell and the larger organism are built. Come into this next room."

While looking around at the remaining displays, they followed Shannon into the next room, called *"Central Dogma."* Shannon stopped in front of a long display showing the mechanism of life—how DNA determines the structure of huge proteins.

"This is the most amazing part of the whole thing, the central dogma of our theory of life. It's found in all life forms and should be something we can look for in any sacred documents. Let's start with this first step here on the left."

Shannon walked up to the first display showing the DNA strand separated and an RNA strand built onto it, inside the confines of the nucleus. She described the model to her friends without reading the description.

"First, a portion of DNA that's to be used for making a protein is unwound, and a helper molecule, *messenger RNA—mRNA*, is built onto the exposed base molecules of one half of the DNA strand, including only the gene being activated. DNA is confined to the nucleus, which it never leaves, but mRNA can get out. It has the same sequence as the DNA strand, except that, during this step, junk DNA is remarkably omitted. The mRNA molecule then has only the sequence necessary for building the protein."

"That's interesting," Dan said. "Somehow the mechanism that makes mRNA knows how to omit all the junk. It's almost as if the junk is somehow required and understood."

"There may be something intelligent about the design of junk after all!" John said with a smile.

"What's next?" asked Dan, prompting the group to look at the next display.

"That's an mRNA molecule moving from the nucleus to the ribosomes, where proteins are built. Remember, I pointed out the ribosomes in the model of the cell. Messenger RNA uses roughly the same base sequence as DNA, but there is one key difference—RNA has only one strand. It doesn't have the two backbones of DNA, and it falls apart relatively easily. mRNA only has so long to do its work."

"And then it decomposes, right?" Dan asked.

"That's right. The mRNA is used and then quickly falls apart. It's not tightly held together like DNA."

They moved to the next panel, and Shannon continued. "This exhibit shows how proteins are built in the ribosomes from the twenty *amino acids*. Here, mRNA is used by the ribosomes like a punched paper tape used in computers in the 60s. Amino acids are joined together using the mRNA sequence as a guide."

"I get it; I get it!" John said. "That's how those incredibly huge molecules are made exactly right! The DNA sequence determines the mRNA sequence, and it in turn determines the amino acid sequence."

"Yea, John!" Dan and Shannon clapped in unison.

"You've got it now, John," Shannon said. "And that amino acid sequence is the protein. As we saw earlier, amino acids have identical backbone structures, so they link together into chains that bend into three-dimensional structures that give the protein its useful properties, building the structures and mechanisms of the cell. They're chains much like DNA, but instead of a boring linear helical structure of A-C-T-G bases, they're all twisted up like that hemoglobin protein."

Shannon continued with a professional air. "Three mRNA bases are grouped together to form a word, or *codon*. There are sixty-four possible triplets—far more than needed to specify just twenty amino acid ingredients. Some specify punctuation, to indicate where the proteins start and stop, and others redundantly specify the same amino acids again. These codons are the key to understanding how the DNA sequence describes which amino acids are combined into the proteins."

Dan interrupted, saying, "You said the other day that all life on earth uses almost exactly the same DNA molecular structure."

"It's much more than that, Dan. All forms of life uses the same DNA structure, the same mRNA transfer mechanism, and the same ribosome machines to build proteins from the same four bases, the same three-base encoding scheme, and the same twenty amino acids, which have the same mirror-image polarization, by the way. The mechanisms are virtually identical for all living cells and all life forms. Sure, there are some minor exceptions here and there, but they are only wrinkles in this uniform pattern."

"There is no exception?" asked Dan.

"Not of any consequence." She looked back toward the rooms they had explored together and gestured with an outstretched arm. "This is the underlying basis for life. Any scripture that is truly inspired by a creator, a designer, should—no—*must* describe this essential pattern of all life."

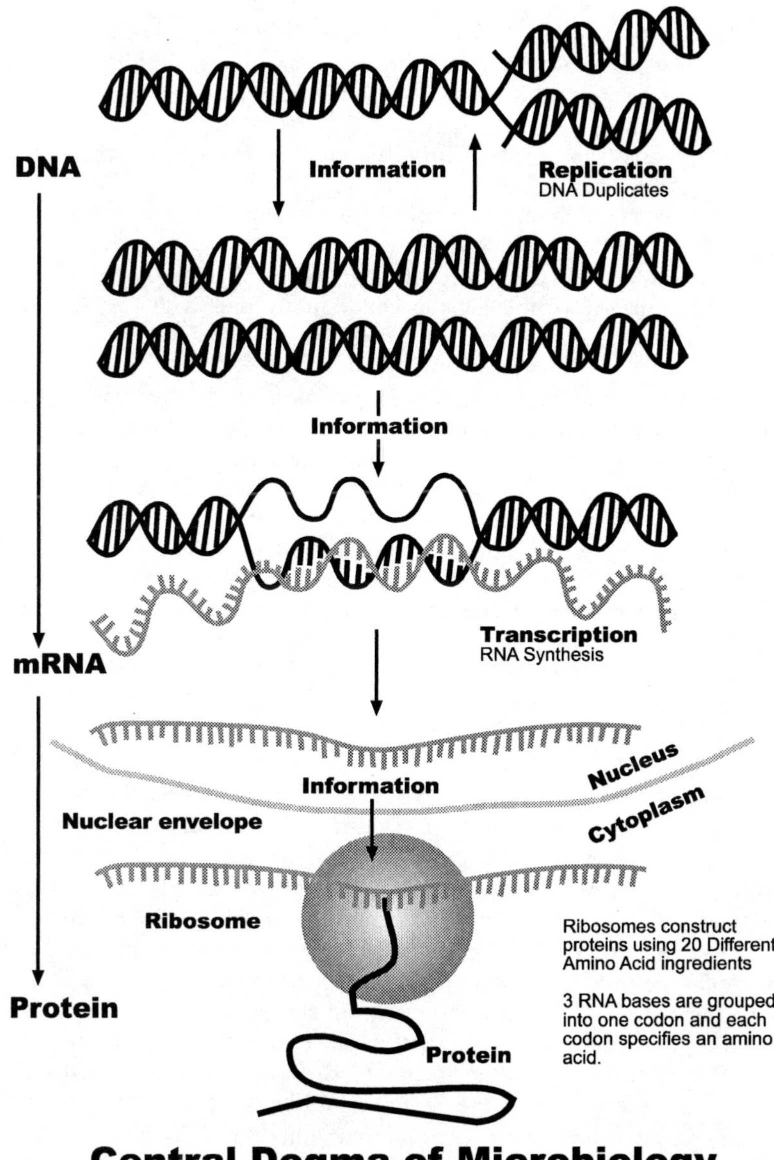

Central Dogma of Microbiology

The threesome stood in silence. Classical music continued to play in the background, mostly unnoticed in their conversations. A skylight overhead allowed natural sunlight to brightly illuminate the room.

Dan said, "It would seem that the three-base encoding would imply that all life is intimately related, right?"

"Research indicates that the correlation between a given three-base codon and its associated amino acid seems absolutely arbitrary. If it is arbitrary, why choose this particular encoding for all life forms, without exception? That's a great question. If it is arbitrary, then you are absolutely correct to say that all life on earth is intimately related—the same pattern, the same image."

"The image of God," John said. "Like I said, all life started from a single intelligent design, and this proves it."

"I knew you were going to say that, John," Shannon said. "But to me, the uniformity of the genetic code simply means that we are all evolved from the same ancient simple organism."

"Oh come on!" John exclaimed. "Give it up."

She said, "Whatever your bias on this question, the fact remains that if you boil any organism down to its simplest expression, you're left with its DNA sequence. Granted, other cellular mechanisms are required, such as the ribosomes, to be able to do anything with DNA. But those structures are coded and built from the information in DNA as well. Even with that coding, without the mechanisms of the egg from the mother, DNA is as worthless as dust. It can't produce anything without the pre-existence of the other mechanisms. You can't use DNA if you don't already have the ribosomes to construct any other proteins."

John said, "It sounds like the old 'chicken and egg' problem brought down to the lowest level. You've got huge problems without a creator to start the process!" John looked like he thought he had hit a home run.

Shannon didn't have a direct answer. "Here, take a look at this sequence of human life." Shannon pointed to the next display. "A human starts as a single fertilized egg—a huge cell, as cells go—about the size of the head of a pin. This stem cell is not the start of life but simply a continuation of life from the two parents, containing genetic information from each parent. Most of the egg is almost all an exact replication from the mother, even though half of the genetic information in the nucleus is from the father. It then divides many times, replicating the DNA into each cell, until trillions of cells result in the typical adult. As the cells are added to the organism, they begin to differentiate to form different tissues. Once they take on the particular attributes of that tissue, they're called *somatic cells* and can't change into other types of cells. Scientists still don't fully understand all the details about how cells decide what type of cell to become, or how that change is made.

"We know a lot, and those things we just saw are far from being in any dispute. All in all, we're far from knowing everything there is to know about life, that's for sure," Shannon said.

"It's pretty complex, that I'll hand you that," John said.

"And it presents a huge mystery to researchers. But the most profound mystery about life is not about life at all."

"What do you mean?" asked John.

Shannon looked straight at her friends. "The biggest mystery about life is very difficult indeed. I'm talking about death."

CHAPTER 18

The tidy and conscientious mind of Nancy Bellwether was troubled. Clearly, she was a worker who could not tolerate a pencil or paperclip out of place on her clean and immaculate desk. The incomplete record of William Freeman was troubling enough, but a visit from an FBI agent made the issue an obsession. She had never before talked to such an agent, or at least not that she could remember. Students, parents, teachers, even gardeners, yes, but FBI agents, no.

The information on William Freeman in the school computer was indeed a bit unusual, and she knew it was not her doing. But what had happened? How did the record get changed unless she was involved? Then, she felt a shiver of realization roll down her spine. *Oh my, I forgot to check his other records!* The brief record Nancy had checked when Hall visited was just the high-level database entry, not the full student file. Nancy sat back down at the computer, placed her glasses back on her nose, her forehead glistened from sudden perspiration. *Oh my, oh my—I didn't show him that boy's CSR file. Is it breaking the law to forget to show an officer some things?* Her fingers trembled.

Nancy clicked nervously through the folder hierarchy, searching the Complete Student Record files. *There it is, the folder "Freeman, William." These records should clearly give William's grades and teacher comments, awards for good behavior, or punishments. Oh my, how stupid of me! I should have checked this earlier.*

She scrolled rapidly down. *Things seem to be in order. Here's his admittance record—oh dear! Selected for PITY Ranch. I know they send some students to the Ranch, and usually they're released to join the military or private security firms from there.*

Nancy went over and over the files, looking for the usual progression—PITY, PITY Ranch, military service—but for Freeman, any details of his time at the Ranch were missing, and he was released much earlier than she usually recorded. *How strange! Oh my, I don't understand this at all.* Should *I contact Agent Hall?*

Nancy's fingers trembled on the keyboard, and her stomach churned with the realization that her records were incomplete. *Did I miss some entries, or... did someone else?* Her thoughts trailed off. *I'd better ask Rebecca about this.* She picked up the phone, and dialed Rebecca's extension.

"Bishop Ward's office, Rebecca speaking."

"Yes, Rebecca, uh, this is Nancy. I know it's late in the day, but... do you have a minute?"

"Yes. Of course, Nancy. What's the matter?"

"Oh, I was thinking about the questions Agent Hall was asking, and I looked into the files again. It seems the record is incompl—"

"Nancy. Nancy." Rebecca interrupted. *"Uh... Please hold..."* Nancy waited on the phone listening to the silence of the hold button. Was Rebecca talking it over with the Bishop? Or was she getting another call? She worried about the idea of that secondary facility—PITY Ranch—she had never visited. It was a secret facility, one that was never to be revealed to visitors. That was unusual, but it was no big deal, she thought. Their school did turn lives around. To serve those in need made her sure she had the right job. The line remained silent.

"Nancy?" Rebecca's voice interrupted the silence.

"Yes, I'm here."

"What did you find again?"

"I'm so sorry!" Nancy's voice rose in pitch. "I should have checked the Complete Student Record when the agent was here. My record shows William being assigned to the Ranch, but I don't see that he was released, and there is no discharge paperwork. It's very odd."

"Have you told anyone else about this?"

"No... No one."

"Okay, good. Let's keep that information strictly between us, for now, okay? I'll fill you in later."

"Sure, I can keep it quiet. But Rebecca, I'm worried. I don't know what happened. Maybe something terrible happened. Don't you think we should call that FBI man?"

"No, not yet. Nancy, I'm sure everything is just fine. God is looking out for us; he'll guide our future. Have faith."

"Thank you, Rebecca. I will pray about it." Nancy put the phone on the hook.

I told the agent I would call him if anything unusual turned up. But Rebecca works for the Bishop, so surely she knows if this is really "unusual" or not. I guess I should let Rebecca handle it. She clicked and closed the computer folder and tried to put it out of her mind. She continued to get ready to go home for the day. Before she closed and locked the door, she thought, *Oh my!*

CHAPTER 19

"What is death?" Shannon asked, looking over her friends for an answer. They stood in a hallway of the museum, just after the Central Dogma room.

Dan hesitated. "Uh... death... death *is* mysterious. It's something that will probably never be fully understood, that's for sure. I don't see too many dead people walking around to explain what it's like."

"Come this way," Shannon said, leading them into the next room of the museum. They walked through the door and under the sign:

THE CYCLE OF LIFE

The first exhibit dealt with death at the cellular level. Some cells die for one reason or another and need to be replaced. In some cases, the body triggers these cells to die as a reaction to disease or pathogens, thereby protecting the remaining cells of the body. The dead cells can be replaced by replication of nearby cells.

John said, "Sure, individual cells might die and be replaced, but that's not the whole person. If cells simply divide and replace any cells that die for one reason or another, it seems we would be able to live forever. From that explanation, I don't see why we have to die at all."

"This may answer your question," Dan said. "Listen to this information." He read from the sign over the display. "DNA may play a key role in death. Most cells will divide roughly fifty times before entering a resting state known as *senescence*. For more than a decade, researchers have suspected that *telomeres*—sections of DNA at the tips of chromosomes—control that process."

The display showed chromosomes mostly blue but with their tips red.

"On the end of each chromosome, there is a sequence called a *telomere*, between 100,000 and 300,000 bases in length—that's about... about the same as forty pages in those stacks of Bibles we just saw. In 1973, Olovnikov proposed that cells lose a small amount of DNA—maybe about a page—following each round of replication. DNA polymerase, the zipper-head protein that functions to make exact copies of the DNA strand, can't fully replicate chromosome ends, the telomeres. Each DNA copy is a bit shorter than the ones before. Eventually the telomeric ends of the chromosome are used up, and a critical deletion of genetic information on the DNA strand causes cell death. If this is indeed the case, there is a defined limit to the number of divisions, with aging and cell death following."

"That's an interesting story," John said, "a story clearly supported in the Bible. God planned a normal life span of seventy or eighty years as shown in Psalms 90:10:

> *The days of our years are threescore years and ten; and if by reason of strength they be fourscore years, yet is their strength labor and sorrow; for it is soon cut off, and we fly away."*

"Very impressive, John," Dan said. John smiled with pleasure.

"This telomeric deletion stuff is certainly interesting. Not all life forms use it," Shannon said. "Many simple one-celled organisms do not have a predetermined death. Given favorable conditions, such as enough food and space to grow, they can live and divide forever. Their DNA is maintained in loops with no ends. They can replicate without any limit in number, with no telomeric loss." She pointed at the display of the circular DNA found in simple organisms. "See, the DNA is not organized into X-shaped chromosomes residing in the nucleus but as circular loops attached to the cell wall, and no nucleus is exists in those cells.

"I've heard the idea of repairing the telomeric shortening in chromosomes, so that cells could reproduce indefinitely. I imagine that if scientists ever learn to repair the ends of the chromosomes, a form of eternal life or more correctly indefinite life may be possible. I say *indefinite* because even if you don't grow old, you may die for other reasons, such as murder, accident, or disease. The single-celled creatures that use looped DNA will typically continue to replicate, increasing in number until they encounter overpopulation, dying from lack of resources, or from an inability to dispose of waste. The same would happen to people if we tried that."

"I bet most people would want to try to live forever, if you told them they could," John said.

Shannon said, "The bottom line is it would be great if the cells could divide indefinitely, but they can't. For humans, death is unavoidable. If we're lucky, we get the seventy or eighty years you mentioned, John. Or, if we're really lucky, about 100 to 115 years at the very most. You just don't hear about people living to 150, 200, or 900 years."

"I'm really not sure I would want to live that long," John said. "I've had enough trouble with my life as it is."

"Of course, it isn't purely luck. Consider the body as a huge colony of seventy-trillion individual cells, balancing the needs of each cell with the needs of the whole body. Individual cells can die and be replaced but the larger organism will continue to appear roughly constant. The danger is that some cells will start to bias their actions based on their own success instead of the success of the overall colony."

Dan said, "Renegade cells do nothing for the body as a whole, although they are highly successful when viewed as individuals. But we don't want cells to seek individual success."

"What happens if they do?" John asked.

"Well, that's not a good thing at all," Shannon answered. "You see, that's the problem known as *cancer*."

The friends stopped talking, and an uneasy quietness enveloped the room of the museum. The classical music that had been playing was silent for just that moment, then restarted with another Baroque-era selection.

"I'm curious about this idea of unlimited life. What would happen?" John asked.

"If we offered unlimited lifespan to everybody, one thing is certain," Shannon said, "sexual reproduction would have to be banned and children avoided. If reproduction continued to occur, rampant overpopulation would be the sad outcome. Death due to inadequate resources—starvation—would be rampant, eliminating the idea of eternal life from a different direction.

"Just imagine a finite world such as ours, with people living indefinitely," she continued. "At first, people would continue to have kids, but no one would die. The population would rise geometrically. Resources would be rapidly depleted, and starvation would be widespread. We do a poor job of feeding the current population as it is. Thousands die of starvation every day. But if no one dies naturally, things would get bad, really bad. It would be a dog-eat-dog world—literally." Shannon looked in their eyes. "I don't think I want to live in that situation and certainly not indefinitely."

"It's probably more likely that a small, powerful group would gain this information, perhaps the scientists who first develop the technology. Then, they would keep the mechanism for unlimited life secret to maintain their power," Dan said.

"Purely hypothetical," Shannon said.

"If the mechanism were widely known," he continued, "sterilization, contraception, and abortion would be the law to avoid any new children. Fortunately, it's not an issue yet."

Dan led them to the next display, *Genetic Adaptation*. John lagged behind, apparently somewhere between uninterested and uncomfortable. Shannon, in contrast, beamed, at ease in the intellectual discourse.

Dan continued, "Really, in a way, you can live indefinitely through many generations: Just have kids. Your genetic traits are inherited from your parents and their parents—a mixture of traits from your mother and father—due to recombination. What we don't need is each individual to live—"

"Why even bother with recombination?" Shannon interrupted. "At that point, people could make identical copies of themselves."

John looked appalled. "You mean *cloning*?"

"Yep. Some people relish the idea they might make duplicates of themselves, a process foreign to our natural life cycle. But a form of cloning is used in nature all the time."

Dan pointed at the next display. "Yeah, look here. Simple single-cell organisms divide and produce identical clone offspring. If you've ever used a cutting to start a new plant, the new plant is an identical copy of the first, a clone, if you will. It's a method of propagation especially common for plants but not so common in animals, except for single-celled animals or fungi.

"Here's a good example of cloning in plants—the seedless navel orange." Dan pointed to the information on the display. "It's been said that all seedless navel orange plants are genetically identical with a single parent plant developed in Brazil around the year 1800. In 1873 farmers in Riverside, California, received three seedlings of the *Bahia* orange from Brazil. Offspring—identical twins—of these original seedlings spread all over the United States and other parts of the world with the name *Washington Navel*."

The next display showed a picture of Dolly the sheep, one of the first mammals to be cloned, and other examples of cloning, including cats and dogs.

"More recently, cloning of humans has been proposed, allowing identical offspring to be produced and perhaps giving people the misconception that eternal life could result. Identical twins are genetic clones, but they're clearly not the same person. If you were cloned, your clone would be a separate identical twin and would not be *you*. To get a new *you* would require a way to transfer your memories and thoughts to the young clone, something that's certainly far fetched, indeed."

"But you and your clone would be genetically identical, and as I mentioned, identical twins are very, very much alike," Dan commented.

"The reason for the fear of cloning," John said, looking at his friends, "is that cloning isn't natural. People don't trust scientists to get it right. They would rather trust the teachings of the Bible to guide them in this area. Cloning is not discussed in the Bible, so it's something we shouldn't do."

Shannon shrugged. "Neither is flying in an airplane. Should we give up on jets, cars, or telephones?"

Without waiting for an answer, she went on, "Apart from sex, many reproductive strategies are used in nature, including exact replication—

cloning. They're certainly not discussed in the Bible. Just because you can't find it in the Bible, that doesn't mean it doesn't exist or that it isn't natural. That's crazy! For example, some earthworms have a means to reproduce asexually. They are *hermaphroditic*—that is, they have both male female sex organs. Offspring can be produced even if the worm can't find a mate, and if it does find a mate, each can act as both the male and female. So even though they will mate with themselves in a pinch, when two worms eventually meet, they can always mate."

"I guess we shouldn't expect issues over gay rights in the earthworm arena," Dan joked. The others chuckled uneasily, apparently a little embarrassed that they thought it was funny.

"Worms are a simple form of life, yet they're quite advanced when it comes to reproductive strategies. What are the odds of finding mates as they crawl aimlessly through the mud? It must be quite exciting to meet another worm. I'm not sure how evolution originally solved that problem, but the result is certainly interesting: the gender of the other worm is always just right. They *both* get pregnant!" The three laughed.

"Sure, that's fine for worms. What about something a bit higher on the food chain?" asked John, quicker to stop laughing this time.

"Higher forms of life use strict sexual reproduction, of course. We're all familiar with that, aren't we?"

"Oh, please explain, Shannon," John said. "Or... should we just read the display?"

Dan lifted his eyebrows.

"Yeah, yeah, very funny." She pointed at the display as she talked, but she looked at their faces and seemed to be self conscious.

Dan felt that she was noticing for the first time a change in the chemistry among the three.

She continued, "Male and female organisms each contribute half of the genetic information when a new generation is formed. In this way, we don't see identical copies—clones—of the higher-order creature, but instead we see almost infinitely varied sets of traits. Single-celled organisms don't have a way to 'have sex' in the usual sense. They *can* contribute traits to one another though, by trading DNA information from one cell to the other when in proximity. Sexual reproduction formalizes this process." She coughed slightly.

The sign on the exhibit went on to explain the special cellular division process that occurs to support sexual reproduction. Shannon read it. "In *meiosis*, chromosomes from the mother and father *cross-over*—that is, combine, including bits and pieces from each one and allowing the offspring to somewhat randomly include genes from either the father or the mother. Without these recombinations, all children in the same family would be the exact combination of their parents with no variation whatsoever—all identical twins. Instead, children are an elegant combination of traits from the mother and father. This impressive and essential process provides the variation in offspring, possibly to allow for evolutionary change.

John said, "I could have told you that. My kids are each very different people."

"Sexual Reproduction" was the title of the next display, and the friends each read it silently. In humans and many other animals, the gender of an individual is determined by a single pair of chromosomes. In humans it's the 23rd chromosome pair. There are two kinds of 23rd chromosome, arbitrarily denoted as *X* and *Y*. Shannon pointed to the display where the larger X and tiny Y chromosome were displayed. She explained that the X-chromosome is roughly the same size as other chromosomes but its partner, the Y-chromosome, is one of the smallest.

Two eggs were displayed, one marked XX and one marked XY. In females, the 23rd chromosome pair includes two X-chromosomes. As the female develops, only one of these X-chromosomes is used in the definition of the woman, with the other X coiling up into a tight bundle known as a *Barr body*.

"I didn't know that," Dan said, a rare admission. "I guess that means that only one X-chromosome is really needed to define the female."

"Right," Shannon said, proud of one-upping Dan. "Males have the XY pair, with the Y-chromosome donated by the father and the X donated by the mother. Apparently, the super-small Y-chromosome does very little, only selecting portions of its partner to be used or not used, thereby changing the female into a male. Females are, in essence, the *default* result of the X-chromosome and males are a *perturbation* of that natural result, modified by the action of the tiny Y-chromosome."

"You're always fighting for women's rights, aren't you," Dan said, smiling and shaking his head. "Females may be the 'default,' as you put it, but you'll have to admit that females lack the Y-chromosome. They don't carry a complete genetic template. Men carry the information for both sexes and determine whether it will be a boy or a girl. Sorry, my dear!"

Shannon pretended to pout, eyes smiling at Dan.

As they moved to the next display, *Natural Selection,* Shannon giggled a bit and held John by the arm as if to hold him up. "You'll need to keep an open mind here, John. Don't faint! And, I don't even want to hear the comment that this isn't mentioned in the Bible."

John kept silent and remained serious.

Shannon explained that the heredity of traits is key to natural selection, an extremely powerful means to adapt to the environment, combat disease, and resist predators.

Dan looked at the displayed information and took over seamlessly from Shannon. "Charles Darwin performed the classic work in this area, based on his observations of nature during his voyages on *The Beagle* in the early 1800s. Combined with Gregor Mendel's work on heredity, the science of genetics supports the concept of within-species natural selection. Nature continually makes mistakes in the ongoing attempt to find a better fit to the environment—and the mistakes die off—leaving the fittest to create the next generation.

"We're familiar with man-made 'artificial' selection, used for centuries to selectively breed dogs, cats, and cattle as well as untold other animals. It's not a difficult stretch to see that such an effect can also occur under natural circumstances—that is, *natural selection.* Today it's acknowledged as fact."

"Fact? I think you're going overboard, there, aren't you Shannon? Evolution is nothing more than a theory," John said.

"John, natural selection is not the same as evolution. The concept that natural selection allows individual species to adapt to the environment has been easily shown experimentally. Dog breeders can select specific traits within just a few generations. There is no question that natural selection is fact. Extending this concept over long periods results in evolution, a concept most scientists accept as fact, but indeed, it can't be proven experimentally."

The three friends walked back out to the granite entryway of the building. They paused there, able to enjoy the fresh air and the view of the campus. The day was bright with numerous puffy clouds blowing across the sky. Shannon leaned against a waist-high rock wall framing the entryway.

"I learned a lot in that museum, I have to admit," John said. "Walking through the cell and seeing DNA up close... Those were great presentations."

Dan said, "With your brief summary of the Bible, John, I think we're ready to try to put the pieces together, to try to find patterns of life in the Bible. I've got an appointment I need to get to, and it's probably smart for us to sleep on all this information before we do any more."

"Shannon, before we leave," John said, "let's write down the important numbers, of life and of scripture."

"Okay... I can easily list some numbers about life," Shannon said. She took a notepad out of her notebook and wrote down a list:

- 3 bases per codon
- 4 different bases, 2 pairs
- 20 amino acids used in proteins
- 23 chromosome pairs in humans
- 46 total chromosomes
- 64 possible codon triplets

She gave the notepad to John and he wrote down his list.

- 3 elements of the Trinity; 3 synoptic gospels; 3 hierarchies of angels, 3 in each level
- 4 evangelists or the 4 gospels
- 5 — the Pentateuch
- 6 days of the Creation
- 7 is a sacred number
- 9 Angels in the three hierarchies of three each
- 12 tribes of Israel (12 sons of Jacob); 12 apostles; Jesus was 12 years old at the temple incident
- 14 stations of the cross
- 27 books in the New Testament
- 30: Age of Jesus when he started his ministry
- 39 books in the Old Testament
- 40 days of rain in the Flood; Jesus's 40 days in the wilderness
- 150 days of water covering the earth during the Flood

"I don't see any sort of amazing match with your numbers game, John," Dan remarked. "Except for that match of four bases and four gospels. Is that useful?" Dan wondered out loud. "I seriously doubt it!"

"There may be some connections," John suggested. "For example, you said that there are four bases that make up the DNA strand and that three of these are used at one time to designate a specific amino acid, right?"

"Right. Each codon is three base pairs. The numbers four and three are both essential to understanding life."

"Yes, and three plus four is seven. The sacred number seven is a way to express both the four bases and the fact that they must be used in groups of three. Maybe the *seven seals* in Revelation is actually about the information in DNA."

"What is this about the seven seals?" asked Dan.

"A black and white movie by Ingmar Bergman, wasn't it?" Shannon asked.

"That was *The Seventh Seal,* a story about a knight returning from the crusades who played a chess game with Death to delay his final demise," Dan answered. "I hope that's not what John is talking about. That was a pretty boring movie, even if the critics loved it."

"No, it's not the movie. I think they quoted it in that movie, but other than that, I didn't like the movie either. The seven seals are talked about in Revelation. It's key to understanding the prophecies of the apocalypse and Christ's second coming," John said. He pulled out a small Bible from his pocket. "Here let me read the verse:"

(Rev 5:1) *And I saw in the right hand of him that sat on the throne a*

> *book written within and on the back side, sealed with seven seals.* (2) *And I saw a strong angel proclaiming with a loud voice, Who is worthy to open the book, and to loose the seals thereof?* (3) *And no man in heaven, nor in earth, neither under the earth, was able to open the book, neither to look thereon.* (4) *And I wept much, because no man was found worthy to open and to read the book, neither to look thereon.* (5) *And one of the elders saith unto me, Weep not: behold, the Lion of the tribe of Judah, the Root of David, hath prevailed to open the book, and to loose the seven seals thereof.*

"This passage talks of a book *in the right hand of him that sat on the throne.* But, what is this book? Perhaps to read the 'book' means to decipher DNA, and you would need to understand the secret of the seven seals. You said that DNA uses four bases organized in groups of three, and four plus three is seven," John said. "Those are the seven seals. If you don't know the secret of the seven seals, you can't read the book—the book of life: DNA."

The others were silent in amazement. A gust of wind blew through the hardwood trees of the campus, rustling the leaves. Several students walked by on the sidewalk below.

"But that's not all." John's expression darkened.

"What do you mean?"

"Once the seventh seal is broken, the end of the earth starts—the apocalypse." John's eyes narrowed and his lips trembled slightly as he spoke. "Once the book is opened, seven angels sound seven trumpets, wreaking havoc on the earth. I'm talking hail and fire mingled with blood burning the trees; mountains exploding into the sea, the sea changing into blood; a star called Wormwood, probably a meteor falling from heaven, which made the water undrinkable; the sun, moon, and stars obscured by smoke; scorpion-like locusts coming out of a bottomless pit that torment all men who don't have the seal of God on their forehead; and finally, the end of the earth as we know it. The end of days. That's what worries me."

"I'm sure that's just a story, a fiction," Dan said, shaking his head.

"I wouldn't be so sure, Dan. If we do find a pattern that authenticates the Bible, isn't it possible that Revelation is inspired as well?"

"Please! Let's not jump the gun, guys," Shannon said.

"How about this connection," Dan said grinning with excitement, attempting to change the subject. "The Hebrew name for God, Yhwh, has four letters, but only three of them are different; or, perhaps we should consider the four evangelists, and the three whose names are composed of four letters: Mark, Luke, and John. Oh, boy, the numbers four and three again! And they add to seven! Not only that, but Matthew has seven letters!"

Dan suddenly shook his head. "Sorry, folks, this just isn't what we're looking for. I'm not much into trying to find just tricky number matches. I have a strong feeling there is something more to this."

"Almost all the information about life is available on the Internet," Shannon said, mostly to John. "In fact, you can even access whole biotechnology textbooks on-line. Search for the *Human Genome Project,* and you'll find a site on human DNA available to read at the click of a button. You can also compare it with the DNA of the mouse, the chimp, and other animals."

"Do I have to? I admit, I'm not a biotech expert."

"Well, I'm just the other way, John," Shannon said. "I'm going to have to brush up on biblical matters. I guess that's probably all on-line as well. Tell you what. I'll read over the first few chapters of *Genesis* again if you at least take a look at that web site."

"Fair enough. We may just have to get together to compare notes."

Shannon laughed uncomfortably and shot a glance to Dan.

"I've got to get going too," she said. "Bye guys."

As Dan walked off campus, he thought, *are we loosening the seven seals, the keys to opening the "book" of DNA? I wonder if we are worthy to open the book? And... are we ready for the apocalypse?*

CHAPTER 20

"Sir, the General is on the phone. I'm sorry it took so long to reach him, but he just wasn't available."

"Thank you, Rebecca."

The Bishop turned from Rebecca toward the telephone, picking it up and swiveling his chair to face the semicircular bow windows. He looked out over the rose garden and beyond the far wall to view the ocean.

"General, thank you for taking my call." He paused and his voice grew stern. "The FBI visited—to discuss the matter I mentioned before... it was an Agent Russell Hall... I want this stopped, and now." He waited without moving, listening for some time. Rebecca could almost hear the General's voice on the amplified earpiece. "Uh, no sir, I don't mean to be rude... it's just that I don't want this to spiral out of control, that's all... Good... Thank you, sir."

The Bishop hung up the phone, got up, and stood in front of the large window, thinking. Carlos, the head gardener, quietly groomed the rose bushes just outside the windows. Rebecca meekly backed out of the room without making a sound and returned to her desk.

Something has happened. I don't remember the student that Agent Hall asked about, but he could have been one of the many boys the Bishop sent to that Ranch place. I know things don't always turn out when that happens.

Rebecca knew that the Bishop used his powerful position and contacts with the government to do things others would not be able to do. She was content to look the other way when students were sent to the Ranch. She didn't even want to think about what was going on.

CHAPTER 21

Shannon climbed the steps to Dan's house. "So this is where you live!" She turned to look at the view. "Wow, you can see the whole village and all the way out to the ocean. I wish I had this!"

John was sitting in an Adirondack chair on the porch, just to the right of the door. He got up when Shannon arrived and gave her a hug. Dan lightly hugged Shannon as well, then took her hand, and pulled her into the house, and John followed.

"Welcome to my humble abode!" The front room of the house spanned the entire length of the building, with the view still visible out large windows extending to the open-beam ceiling. Hardwood floors could be seen here and there among stacks of papers and file folders, some piles reaching several feet in height. Nearly in the center of the room, a dining table stood with half of its surface clear and the other half filled with stacks of paper and files. Several piles on the floor nearby hinted that they were probably just cleared from the table. Across the entire wall at one end of the room, a large conglomeration of computers stood with numerous displays, wires, and flickering lights. It was a configuration expected for a software guru like Dan, but even so, it seemed excessively large and imposing. To one side of the computers, several bookshelves were packed with technical and historical books. Through the door in the back of the room, a hanging bicycle could be seen.

The three friends sat down, with Shannon sitting directly opposite Dan, and with John sitting at the end of the table. John put his Bible and portfolio notepad in front of him as Shannon set up her laptop. Dan already had a laptop set up in his spot.

Shannon studied her chair. "Dan, I love this table, but I notice you're still using these 'high-quality' green plastic lawn chairs. Haven't you noticed the rest of the world keeps these out on the patio?"

"I still have the designer chairs... they're right over there." Dan pointed to several chairs against the wall, their designer backs extending into the air, their seats filled with file folders and boxes. "I used them at first, but they just weren't for me. I was going to throw out these comfortable green chairs, but I rescued them just in time. Don't you think they're comfy?" He demonstrated how they flexed with his weight.

"You're too much! Oh yes, these are *very* comfortable," she said, smirking.

John tested his chair. "They do give with your weight a bit. The designer chairs look stylish, but those straight backs do look rigid and a bit too flat for me."

Light streamed through the front windows, hitting the floor and forming bright rectangles next to the table. Outside, a Bower vine billowed over part of the window, slightly reducing the field of view. Music played lightly from speakers somewhere near Dan's computer, probably from a digital play-list.

Dan looked at his friends. "Well, we have a lot to do and not much time, so we should get started. Our first step will be to decide where to begin. We have these two stories or patterns before us—the biblical story and the pattern of nature. Is there a link? Does it make sense to think that the single pattern of all life would be discussed in scriptural literature? Assuming that God exists, he would know about this pattern. If he also inspired the Bible, the pattern might be expressed somehow. We all buy into that concept, right?"

John kept his arms crossed and forehead wrinkled. "I'm curious what 'presuppositions' we will be working with. Are we starting with an atheistic assumption, from a position of scientism, where science is assumed true and when there is any conflict, the Bible false? Or, do we start with the traditional assumption that the Holy Bible is the sacred word of God, to be followed when there is any conflict?" It was clear by the tone in his voice that he preferred the latter.

Dan thought about John's question. "You pose that question with the assumption that only two possibilities exist. Perhaps we could view the starting assumptions as a continuum between two extremes." Dan gestured with his hands to make his point. "On one extreme is the assumption that the Bible is the Sacred Word of God, complete and sufficient for all information. The other extreme is pure naturalism—science—with no belief in the sacred nature of the scriptures. I think we're balanced somewhere in the middle rather than at either endpoint, if that makes sense."

"In the middle?" John asked.

"Look. It will be of little interest for us to work at the first extreme. For thousands of years theologians have analyzed biblical literature from that traditional point of view. I doubt that we'll be able much better. On the other extreme, scientists work with theories of evolution and the formation of life by chance and avoid any mention of the Bible at all. We're not planning to do that either.

"Instead, we find ourselves somewhere in the middle of the continuum, allowing both biblical and scientific views to be considered true and valid. I don't think we need to denigrate any belief in the Bible as a sacred document or assert that science provides the only reliable source of knowledge. But, we must respect the power of science when it generates knowledge that is clearly acknowledged as fact.

"In other words, I would hope that we can respect both paths to knowledge and examine how they support each other, rather than examine how each disagrees. From my experience with the laws of physics and nature, the reality we encounter is rational, consistent, and, amazingly enough, understandable. The truth in this case should be no different."

John uncrossed his arms. "I'm willing to see where all this leads."

Shannon nodded without looking up from her computer, apparently still booting up.

John opened his Bible to Genesis. "The creation in Genesis is our best starting place. It's the most famous description of creation, one of the few instances in religious literature where we have a full recounting of the formation of the universe, earth, and life."

"John, since we already know the basic story, can we skip to the good part?" Shannon asked.

"Sure. Take a look at the verses that talk about life, starting on the third day of creation:" John read aloud, mentioning the verse references as if they were part of the scripture.

> (Gen. 1:9) *And God said, Let the waters under the heaven be gathered together unto one place, and let the dry [land] appear: and it was so.*
>
> (10) *And God called the dry [land] Earth; and the gathering together of the waters called he Seas: and God saw that [it was] good.*
>
> (11) *And God said, Let the earth bring forth grass, the herb yielding seed, [and] the fruit tree yielding fruit after his kind, whose seed [is] in itself, upon the earth: and it was so.*
>
> (12) *And the earth brought forth grass, [and] herb yielding seed after his kind, and the tree yielding fruit, whose seed [was] in itself, after his kind: and God saw that [it was] good.*
>
> (13) *And the evening and the morning were the third day.*

"What do you think of that section?" John asked.

"Well, it has a very interesting way of discussing the creation of the plants," Dan said. "The text doesn't just describe the plants. It goes into a great deal of detail about the *seed after his kind*. In my reading last night, I was a bit intrigued about this, since it would have been simpler to just say that plants were created. Why is it necessary to talk about seeds and more particularly, *seeds after his kind*?

"The concept that the seed is the container for DNA is something that seems to be a clue. Walker mentioned it at the coffee house as well. So, I used my computer-based Bible to search for all uses of the term *seed*." Dan rose from his seat and walked over to his desk as he talked. "It's a good example of a word that's used symbolically—that is, to represent something other than the literal concept. A literal definition of *seed* would be a grain of wheat or a nut. But in the Bible, that's not usually how it's used at all. Here, let me show you what I found." Dan grabbed a computer print-out, returned to the table, and proudly displayed a chart of information about the word *seed*.

"First of all, the word *seed* is found in 245 verses in the King James Bible. But only one out of six times is the word clearly used to refer to a physical seed. About three-quarters of the time, it's used to represent genetic progeny, offspring, or bloodline. For example, Jesus is said to be of the *seed of David*, meaning that he was genetically related to King David—not David's nut!" They chuckled.

Shannon said, "Using the word *seed* to represent progeny or bloodline makes a lot of sense. Ancient farmers understood that plants would spring from planted seeds and they would be related to the parent plant. In the same way, related families were of the *same seed*."

"Right. There is indeed quite a bit of talk about the fact that the seed of Abraham was blessed," Dan said. "The practice of circumcision is said to reduce some diseases, such as AIDS, but it would also have the effect of further maintaining the purity of this bloodline. Any woman could easily notice if her partner had the desired background. Not circumcised? Sorry, big boy, not tonight!"

"Right!" Shannon said.

John asked, "Does the New Testament continue to use the term seed that way? It seems that at least Jesus was referred to as the *seed of David*."

"Yep. It does, but to a lesser extent. In the New Testament, seed is used about half the time in parables to represent the *Kingdom of God* that may germinate in the soul of man, should it not *fall on stoney ground*. The study of this one word illustrates a major shift in religious thought, from the emphasis on Jewish bloodline through Abraham, that is, the primary use of the word in the Old Testament, to the concept that the seed of the Kingdom of God can germinate within a man if he's receptive to it, regardless of the bloodline of that individual. That's the primary message in the New Testament."

"Bravo, Dan," John said, clapping lightly. "You've defined a crucial difference between the Christian and Jewish religions. The 'Old Covenant' was based on being blessed by bloodline and adherence to the laws of the Torah. The 'New Covenant,' expressed in the New

Testament, requires that the *seed* of the Kingdom of God germinate in the heart of the believer—that is, the believer must accept Christ as the Son of God."

"Listen to this example, Matthew 13:31." Dan read a portion of the verse out loud.

The kingdom of heaven is like to a grain of mustard seed

Dan continued with some delight. "A key point here is that the words used to express things in the Bible are frequently not used in their conventional literal sense. Progeny or bloodline is a much less concrete concept than a literal seed of a plant. But it's also a great example of the meaning of words evolving over time, so that in the New Testament, the word *seed* is primarily associated with the Word of God accepted by the receptive believer.

"It's mind-blowing to compare the parable of the sower, where *seed* implies the Kingdom of Heaven, with what is encapsulated by real seeds. Inside a seed is the genetic pattern for the plant and more generally, the fundamental building block of life—DNA. This could be our first possible dovetailing of the concept that DNA is the fundamental description of life and its container, the seed!

"My favorite verse is this one, which lays it on the line:

Now the parable is this: The seed is the word of God.

"It may be more than just a parable!"

CHAPTER 22

Dan jumped out of his seat. "We're probably interested in seeds of a literal sort, my friends—the crushed seed of the coffee plant! I'm sure the coffee is ready. Come on!" They followed him happily into the kitchen and filled their cups, doctoring them up before they returned, again sitting in the green plastic patio chairs, sipping their coffee in heavy, hand-made pottery mugs.

"Let's go back to the first reference to seeds in Genesis:" Dan tapped on John's Bible.

John turned back. "Okay." He read.

> (Gen. 1:11) *And God said, Let the earth bring forth tender grass, the herb yielding seed, the fruit tree yielding fruit after his kind, whose seed [is] in itself, upon the earth: and it was so.*

Dan put down his cup. "That verse may describe both a physical seed and progeny. A*s I mentioned, t*he word *seed* is actually used to mean *offspring*. These verses were not attempting to differentiate between seed-bearing plants and those that use spores. The verse doesn't mention seeds to imply that plants using spores, like ferns, fungi, and mushrooms, were not also created."

"I see what you're saying." John looked at the verses. "The word *seed* is used in a more general sense than to specify seed-bearing plants, even to the point that it might mean DNA-based life. The tie-in between the *seed*—implying *DNA*—and the *Word of God* is very cool. But, I hope we can find more of a connection than that. If that's the only connection, then I'm afraid our 'project' is an utter failure."

"I'm not ready to give up," Dan said. "We've read only a couple of verses. Take a look at the next day of creation."

"Right, we're looking for references to life, and life is certainly mentioned here." John said, and then read the verses in Genesis, chapter one.

> (Gen. 1:20) *And God said, Let the waters bring forth abundantly the moving creature that hath life, and fowl that may fly above the earth*

in the open firmament of heaven. (21) *And God created great whales, and every living creature that moveth, which the waters brought forth abundantly, after their kind, and every winged fowl after his kind: and God saw that it was good.* (22) *And God blessed them, saying, Be fruitful, and multiply, and fill the waters in the seas, and let fowl multiply in the earth.* (23) *And the evening and the morning were the fifth day.*

"This story starts with life in the waters, the oceans," Shannon said, "just like all scientific theories of evolution. But, that's where the correlation stops. The Bible says birds were next. Straight from the ocean to the birds, skipping the amphibians, dinosaurs, and reptiles. No scientific theory agrees with that!"

"According to evolutionary theory, animals developed gradually on earth, with many species appearing in some strata and not in others," Dan said. "From the evidence of fossils in the geologic strata, there is little debate about the actual order of appearance, which is far different from what is stated in the scripture. To be fair, we should probably chalk this up to inexact wording rather than a direct confrontation between the scripture and science."

"One thing you said is definitely true, John," Shannon said. "The Bible is not a science book. It gets this stuff dead wrong. But I'm willing to look the other way."

"Oh, thank you, Shannon," Dan said, with relief. "In this section, I note the words *after their kind* frequently repeated, supporting the concept that each species of animal is distinct, never changing to another type. Evolution from one species to the next is the linchpin of Darwin's *Origin of the Species*."

"You can't have it both ways," John said. "Either we were intelligently created according to these sacred scriptures, or you've got evolution strictly by chance. I have a hard time believing that I'm just an accident."

"Have you ever asked your parents about that?" asked Dan, smirking. "They might admit that you were just a mistake, a late-night slip-up!"

They chuckled.

"Well then, let's consider the final day of creation, which has the longest description." John read:

(Gen. 1:24) *And God said, Let the earth bring forth the living creature after his kind, cattle, and creeping thing, and beast of the earth after his kind: and it was so.*

(25) *And God made the beast of the earth after his kind, and cattle after their kind, and every thing that creepeth upon the earth after*

his kind: and God saw that it was good.

(26) *And God said, Let us make man in our image, after our likeness: and let them have dominion over the fish of the sea, and over the fowl of the air, and over the cattle, and over all the earth, and over every creeping thing that creepeth upon the earth.*

(27) *So God created man in his own image, in the image of God created he him; male and female created he them.*

(28) *And God blessed them, and God said unto them, Be fruitful, and multiply, and replenish the earth, and subdue it: and have dominion over the fish of the sea, and over the fowl of the air, and over every living thing that moveth upon the earth.*

(29) *And God said, Behold, I have given you every herb bearing seed, which is upon the face of all the earth, and every tree, in the which is the fruit of a tree yielding seed; to you it shall be for meat.*

(30) *And to every beast of the earth, and to every fowl of the air, and to every thing that creepeth upon the earth, wherein there is life, I have given every green herb for meat: and it was so.*

(31) *And God saw every thing that he had made, and, behold, it was very good. And the evening and the morning were the sixth day.*

Shannon pushed her laptop to one side. "The first two verses of this section continue the creation of the animals, progressing to land animals. Again, they were *after their kind*, further restricting the variation of animals within their own species, like you suggested."

"True enough," Dan said, "but there is again some disagreement with regard to the leading theories of evolution. What do you really think of this, Shannon?"

"Well, I have had a number of courses on this topic, and I've read Darwin's *Origins.* The basic theory of evolution, as postulated by Darwin, assumes minute random variations from one animal to the next. Then, natural selection selects the best of each generation—a process that results in gradual change, adapting the population to environmental and competitive pressures. The logical extension of this principle is full-blown Darwinian evolution, where, over millions of years, one species gradually changes into another."

"And, humans are the final step of that evolutionary tree, with the ability to change the world like no other animal in history. And, the final result of human innovation is... the cookie." Dan unwrapped a package of bite-sized cookies from a local health-food store and offered them to his friends. Each took a cookie.

"I guess I don't have to ask if these are organic," John said. "I eat only organic foods now, you know."

"I'm so proud of you, John. You didn't forget a thing from my museum tour!"

Dan finished a bite of his cookie. "Let's turn back to Genesis, my healthy friends. The rest of the sixth day is about the creation of mankind and his relationship to the other life forms. Don't you find these words interesting: *make man in our image, after our likeness?* God talks of himself using the plural our instead of my. The Elohim was not a single god, but a group or a population. And the concept of image may mean that this group was substantially similar to humans, albeit certainly more advanced from a cultural and knowledge standpoint. Could this mean that humans were originally designed using the same DNA patterns used by the multiple 'gods' that were our precursors?"

"Most Christians believe this mention of *image* simply implies that God and man are intimately related," John said while chewing.

"And apparently God is not a single entity but perhaps a whole race," Shannon said. "Why else would you say *our image*?"

"Well, it probably refers to the Holy Trinity," John said, always quick with an answer. The others took some time to enjoy their cookies.

Dan cleared his mouth. "Let's look at this again. At this point, there is a reference to the plants introduced on the third day. It's an important fact of life that animals can eat only plants or other animals. Animals can't eat rocks or dirt. Remember, those are inorganic. Of course, salt is an exception, but don't try to live on it! If we had the task of introducing life on a planet, we would first need to find a planet suitable for life. Then, plants could be introduced and established. Plants generally don't need animals to survive; they can generate their own oxygen through the use of photosynthesis. But the animal kingdom requires the plant kingdom for both food and oxygen. Plants must be firmly established before animals can be successfully introduced."

John took a couple of deep breaths. "Wait, I thought that plants breathe in carbon dioxide and exhale oxygen and animals do the reverse. Wouldn't plants need animals to provide their carbon dioxide?"

"Well, that's mostly true, but there is a bit more detail. Plants have two processes. The first is *photosynthesis*, arguably the most important chemical process on earth." Dan sounded like the resident professor. "Photosynthesis uses water, carbon dioxide, and light to produce energy and waste oxygen. *Respiration*, the second process in plants, is just simply breathing, requiring oxygen and producing carbon dioxide, just like the animals. Plants breathe like we do! The photosynthesis process in plants fortunately produces a bit more oxygen than they need for respiration. Some is left over for the animals. The fact that plants generate more oxygen than necessary is vital to the prospect of the animal kingdom. I imagine it might be possible to design plants so their photosynthetic processes generated just enough oxygen for their own use, instead of enough for plants *and* animals. In such a world, animals, as we know them, would simply be impossible."

"Thank God for the plants!" John said, looking up to heaven.

"If you were faced with this task of establishing life on a lifeless planet, it would be necessary for plants that generate an excess of oxygen to become established first so that they could provide oxygen for themselves and also eventually for the animals. In addition, plants are an important food supply for the animals, stated as *the fruit of the tree* and *meat* in these verses. Since photosynthesis extracts energy from the sun, it is without a doubt the most significant chemical reaction on the planet. Life depends on it."

"God created light as one of his very first acts," John said. "The Bible supports the key importance of light. Without light, it seems all life on earth would be impossible."

Shannon jerked to attention, raising her finger. "Not quite. We are still learning a lot about the possibilities of life. Bacteria-like organisms were very recently discovered living near super-heated volcanic vents in absolute darkness at the bottom of the ocean. They extract energy from the volcanic vents, not from the sun. Scientists were amazed that animals could live at extremely high pressures, at *very* high temperatures, and in total darkness."

"Yes, an exception," Dan said, "to the absolute reliance on photosynthesis. We do need exceptions, don't we? When scientists discovered that life form, they were stumped. Although they rely on DNA like all other life, naturalists had to introduce yet another whole branch on the descriptive tree of life, just for them. At first, scientists thought they were more ancient than modern eukaryotes, but DNA evidence refuted that concept."

"I'm sorry," objected John. "What is a *eukaryote*?" He stumbled over the word.

"I may have skipped that detail at the museum," Shannon said apologetically. "You see, until a few years ago scientists separated life into two major groups based on their cellular structure and how DNA is replicated. *Prokaryotes* are the common, simple, one-celled bacteria. They have no nucleus and no chromosomes. Instead, their DNA is attached to the side of the cell in continuous loops. Because their DNA does not have ends, prokaryotic cells don't suffer from telomeric deletions. They can replicate forever. Remember the examples we saw at the museum?"

"I only remember the chromosomes, those X-shaped things," John said, squinting.

"Sure, those are found in *eukaryotic* cells—cells of more complex life forms—with a well-defined nucleus containing DNA in the form of chromosomes with ends. We belong to that group. In 1996, scientists embraced the proposal from Wolfe and Woese that an entirely new branch of life was required to describe the *archaea* or *archaebacteria* that live in the dark at the bottom of the ocean. Like the prokaryotes, they don't have a well-defined nucleus, and yet, they have a genetic make-up more like eukaryotes. Scientists thought that perhaps the archaea were the most primitive of the three branches, but recent genetic evidence doesn't imply that one branch started before the others. All three branches seem to be equally ancient. It's quite a mystery."

"It's just like scientists to completely miss a whole different 'branch' of life," John said. "You can't trust science; it can't seem to make up its mind!"

"It's always being refined," Shannon said. "It's not that we were wrong before; we just didn't fully understand. True, scientists discovered another totally different branch of life—life remarkably different from the other two branches. But that doesn't mean the other forms of life are wrong. All three branches are still based on the same structures, the same DNA code, the same cellular mechanisms. There may be other forms we've been missing as well; that's true, but it doesn't refute the rest of our knowledge."

John finished his cookie in silence.

Dan said, "Read the next section, John."

"Okay. This is the end of this segment of the P-Account."

> *(Gen. 2:1) Thus the heavens and the earth were finished, and all the host of them. (2) And on the seventh day God ended his work which he had made; and he rested on the seventh day from all his work which he had made. (3) And God blessed the seventh day, and sanctified it: because that in it he had rested from all his work which God created and made. (4) These [are] the generations of the heavens and of the earth when they were created.*

"Bible scholars agree that the P-Account ends halfway through verse 2:4," John said.

"In the final verse, it uses the remarkable words *generations of the heavens and of the earth*," Dan said, looking out into the room. "As literally accepted, the word *generations* implies a much longer time frame that the word *day*. No wonder most people don't worry about the six-day issue."

"I don't see any hidden patterns of life here." Shannon seemed frustrated. "I'm afraid God didn't know about DNA, John. That blows your treasured stories right out of the water."

"Shannon, lighten up. We've only barely started," Dan said, before John could react. "And you're ready to conclude that your assumptions are true after covering only the first chapter of the first book. Patience, my dear girl!"

But Dan was a bit disappointed too. *Why would Walker suggest that they look here if they wouldn't find something?*

CHAPTER 23

John looked quite content to be talking about the Bible with his friends, regardless of whether they could find any connection with science. His tense facial expressions, obvious at the museum, were absent. Indeed, failing to find the pattern of DNA would not bother him at all, that was clear.

He said, "Let's move on. The J-Account of creation starts with the second half of Genesis, chapter two, verse four. It's the first time we see the name *YHWH,* shown as *LORD* in the King James Version. Remember, the P-Account never mentions *YHWH.*" He read the section out loud.

> (Gen. 2:4B) *In the day that the LORD God made the earth and the heavens,*
>
> (5) *And every plant of the field before it was in the earth, and every herb of the field before it grew: for the LORD God had not caused it to rain upon the earth, and [there was] not a man to till the ground.*
>
> (6) *But there went up a mist from the earth, and watered the whole face of the ground.*

"Can we try to read that literally?" Dan asked. "Essentially, it says that *every plant of the field* and *herb of the field* was created *before it grew* on the earth and then water was introduced. I can imagine that if you were faced with a lifeless planet, you would not be stupid enough to plant anything until after water was available. The first step then, would be to make sure enough water was around so the plants would have a fighting chance. But the plants were created *before* they were introduced to the planet and before water was added. To me, that implies that the plants were first created somewhere else. Earth was lifeless and dry until the mist *watered the whole face of the ground.* Only after that point would it be possible to introduce plants."

"Hmmm... I see," Shannon said. "You're saying that the plants existed first but not here on earth? Then water was added to the lifeless planet and only after that came the plants, right?"

"Exactly. It's a bit weird," said Dan.

"Maybe the next verse will help," John said.

> (Gen. 2:7) *And the LORD God formed man [of] the dust of the ground, and breathed into his nostrils the breath of life; and man became a living soul.*

"This, again, is the J-Account," John said. "The sequence of events here is not strictly described like the day-by-day P-Account. There's no day-by-day progression, no mention of how much time elapsed. Man is created from the dust of the ground, clay, as they say, but clearly before the animals."

Shannon said, "That sounds like one of those pesky inconsistencies between the two accounts, John. We just read in the P-Account that animals were created *before* man. Now in the J-Account, we read that man was created first. Talk about scientists. It seems God couldn't make up his mind either!"

John looked at Shannon. "It's no big deal. The J-Account doesn't emphasize the sequence of events, that's all. It's only a minor detail that has no real importance in the overall story."

Dan tapped his mouth with his pencil. "I'm going to quote you on this one, John. This inconsistency is really a good thing, an indication that a later editor didn't attempt to harmonize the stories and in the course of that work, stomp on details we might find useful. That's a bright side to the apparent inconsistency disaster. For our project, inconsistencies may indicate hidden meaning or the fact that our current interpretation is off the mark, not that the original text is wrong."

John nodded. "Of course, I would support the idea that the text is correct and our interpretation is wrong. That would authenticate the document even more." He thought for a moment and then turned back to the text. "This is the first mention of the *breath* of life. The breath was frequently tied to the life-spirit throughout the Bible. *Inspiration* literally means the taking in the spirit, that is, breathing in." As John talked, the others took a deep breath.

"I can imagine the mystical quality that the breath must have had, a mysterious invisible gas," Dan said. "It certainly wasn't understood to be many minute molecules bouncing around randomly. Instead, man could feel the breath going in and out and equate that with the mystical life force. Today, we know it isn't mystical at all."

"And God breathed life into the *man*. I wonder why the scripture doesn't use the name Adam." Shannon said.

"That section doesn't mention Adam by name, but it's even more general than that, I'm afraid," John admitted. "The Hebrew word for *man* is more like the more general term *mankind or humanity*. Again, it's plural rather than singular. If you want to be a strict literalist, that word would imply that several or many men were created at that time, not the conventional single person of Adam."

"I'm proud of you, John," Shannon said, smiling and nodding her head warmly. "I thought you'd be kicking and scratching to make sure everything matches the usual romantic story of Adam and Eve tending the small garden of Eden. You've admitted that Adam might be quite a large number of people and that even God might be plural. You're starting to surprise me."

"You can't argue with the text. I'm just reading along, and I think the points being made are perfectly reasonable. That's the power of scripture, it can mean different things to different people. Let's see what the next section looks like." John read.

> (Gen. 2:8) *And the LORD God planted a garden eastward in Eden; and there he put the man whom he had formed.*
>
> (9) *And out of the ground made the LORD God to grow every tree that is pleasant to the sight, and good for food; the tree of life also in the midst of the garden, and the tree of knowledge of good and evil.*

Dan jumped in. "Okay, John. This sequence of events continues the created-before-used pattern. We already read that plants are created first (Gen. 2:5) but not planted, then that mankind is created second (from Gen. 2:7) but not placed in the Garden, and third, that God finally plants the garden in Eden (Gen. 2:8), and fourth, that God finally places mankind in the garden (Gen. 2:15). This pattern is repeated over and over; it's more than something that could be written off as a translation error. Why not do it in the logical order? Was there a need to create man before he was placed in the garden? If so, then for how long? I imagine it'd be nice to have some time to let the garden grow, like the *generations* mentioned in verse Gen. 2:4."

"Yep, that created-before-used sequence is strange, all right," Shannon admitted.

"I'm not worried about those details," John said. "I just look at the larger picture of the general events; I don't pull them apart like a doctor dissecting an insect."

"Why not?" Shannon asked, raising her eyebrows. "If you dissect an insect, all the organs are in the right place, aren't they? You don't see the stomach before the intestines. God doesn't make any mistakes there. Why should God make a mistake in the sacred scriptural text?"

"Yeah, yeah," John said, giving in.

"Of course we have the special trees of Eden, the *Tree of*

Knowledge of Good and Evil and the *Tree of Life*. They've got to be important," Dan said. "And they're probably a mess too. I'm not sure how they will fit into our project, but I know they are mentioned again later, so let's wait till then to dissect them, okay?"

John's brow wrinkled. He said, "I think the next part might be easier. After describing a river that parted into four heads, it just repeats what was already said, that God took man and placed him in the garden:

> (Gen. 2:10) *And a river went out of Eden to water the garden; and from thence it was parted, and became into four heads.*
>
> (11) *The name of the first [is] Pison: that [is] it which compasseth the whole land of Havilah, where [there is] gold;* (12) *And the gold of that land [is] good: there [is] bdellium and the onyx stone.*
>
> (13) *And the name of the second river [is] Gihon: the same [is] it that compasseth the whole land of Ethiopia.*
>
> (14) *And the name of the third river [is] Hiddekel: that [is] it which goeth toward the east of Assyria. And the fourth river [is] Euphrates.*
>
> (15) *And the LORD God took the man, and put him into the garden of Eden to dress it and to keep it.*

John continued, "Although this J-Account doesn't deal with time sequences, it does deal with location quite clearly. This passage locates the *Garden of Eden* very clearly in the 'fertile crescent' between the Tigris and Euphrates rivers, a bit south of present-day Baghdad."

"I'm trying to understand this section," Dan said. "The easiest river is the Euphrates, since there's a river by that name in Iraq today. So, that's probably it. But what do you think about the others?"

Shannon moved her laptop in front of her and started working.

John leaned back in the green patio chair, which flexed under his weight. "Some say *Hiddekel* is an early Hebrew name of the river known today as the *Tigris*. It parallels the Euphrates, clearly marking Mesopotamia, the area constantly mentioned as the cradle of civilization. The *Pison* and the *Gihon* don't match present-day names, but I understand they're probably tributaries of the Tigris and the Euphrates. The Garden of Eden was next to these rivers, which simply have four major *heads*, or sources."

Dan leaned back too. "Sorry, John, I have a bit of trouble with that conclusion. The text clearly talks about Ethiopia. Ethiopia is not in the 'Fertile Crescent' at all, but in Africa, about 1,500 miles away; there's no doubt about that. The major river there is the Nile, the longest river on earth, running north from Ethiopia through Egypt, and creating one of the most fertile river valleys in the world. Are we forgetting the very successful Egyptian civilization and the enigma of the Pyramids under the protective watch of the ancient Great Sphinx? I would suggest that the *Gihon* is actually the *Nile*. It runs all through Ethiopia." He leaned forward and reread the verse from this computer screen.

> *And the name of the second river [is] Gihon: the same [is] it that compasseth the whole land of Ethiopia.*

Shannon clicked her mouse. "That theory matches very well, far better than the claim that the river was a tributary in Iraq. Now, if Gihon is really another name for the Nile way over in Ethiopia, I see no reason why the river identified as the *Pison* would need to be just a tributary of the Tigris and Euphrates. Why can't it also be a major river?" She looked over the top of her notebook computer. "In that same verse, it talks about *onyx*. I just did an Internet search on *onyx*, it says:

> *Onyx is a striped, semiprecious variety of agate, with white, black, brown or red alternating bands. The main sources of onyx are India and South America, but it is also found in China, Madagascar, Mexico and the U.S.A.*

"If we assume modern archeologists are correct, another important cradle of civilization was the Indus river valley, in western India. India is listed as the prime source of onyx," she said.

"You'd have to consider the Amazon River valley in South America as well," Dan said. "It was mentioned in that Internet article."

"True, but there's more. The other product mentioned in scripture for this area was *Bdellium*. An Internet search provides some corroborative information. First of all, we're pronouncing it wrong. It's pronounced *delm*. That's at least easier to pronounce. It says here it's '*a fragrant gum resin obtained from plants of the bursera (balsam) family and is similar to myrrh in color and shape but not smell.*'

"I'm scrolling down...yes, here is the location. This tree is found in Arabia and... *India*." She slapped her hand down on the table. "Yes, India would be a possibility, but not South America. Therefore, I claim that the Indus River valley correlates well with the river named *Pison* in the Genesis text."

Shannon was getting excited. "John, you say the name *Hiddekel* is the early Hebrew name of the Tigris River. But, it also says that it *goeth toward the east*."

"Right," he said. "Here is the verse again."

> *And the name of the third river [is] Hiddekel: that [is] it which*

goeth toward the east of Assyria...

"The problem here is that the Tigris River doesn't run toward the east, but mainly north to south. Sure, it runs a little to the east, but if you wanted to explain this river, you wouldn't say it runs to the east. It is a bit to the east of the Euphrates River, but including it in this list is obviously redundant. The Euphrates River itself clearly explains the Fertile Crescent. We don't need the Tigris to explain that again. I have an alternative explanation." Shannon was clearly enjoying this.

"What is it?"

"The better fit for this would be the Huang He or 'Yellow River' in China. It runs due east, taking a circuitous route over some 3,400 miles. Archaeologists agree that this was one of the main cradles of civilization. I could easily imagine the name *Huang He* could get mistranslated into *Hiddekel* by Hebrew scribes making sense of this story, not knowing Chinese and never having visited that river in China."

Shannon clicked a few more times. "It says here that the Yellow River valley is the cradle of the very successful Chinese civilization starting with the Xia—that is, 'Shaw'—dynasty, who were descendants of the Neolithic culture known as the *Longshan*, with artifacts dated at about 9,000 BC. It's clear that science supports the notion that the Yellow River should be linked to the mysterious river that 'runs to the east.'

"So, instead of one river with four forks, we've got four distinct rivers and their associated valleys suitable for the establishment of life. Indeed, these rivers connect in the oceans, as do all other rivers on earth. I think this is the reason you could say that the water splits into four forks. Scientists agree that the cradles of early human civilization were in the fertile Indus, Nile, Huang He, and Euphrates river valleys, an identical match to what is found in biblical literature! If this interpretation is correct, *garden* represents these garden-like river valleys, and *Eden* represents that they were where human civilizations would be established."

"There are four letters in the word EDEN too," John said, finger in the air. "Maybe each letter represents one of the four river valleys."

"Maybe if you spelled it I-H-E-N," Dan suggested. "Indus, Huang He, Euphrates, Nile. We just need a better name for the Yellow River that starts with the letter *D*, and we'd be in business."

"I give," John admitted.

"This idea certainly challenges the usual Middle-Eastern centric interpretation," Dan said. "Especially for Europeans, it would be almost unthinkable for mankind to have originated in Africa, India, or China. The Middle-East is hard enough!"

"This is amazing," Shannon said. "First, we read that 'God' is plural, perhaps a whole group of people, then that Adam is really *mankind*, another whole group, and now, that the single 'Garden of Eden' is more likely four separate birthplaces—not the single holy site near Babylon that's so often fought over. I like this. I like the way we are correlating what's known by science with the statements in the scripture. I wonder what else we'll find."

CHAPTER 24

R-R-Ring. Hall's cell phone rang while his car sat at a red light.

"Hello, Agent Hall speaking."

"*Hi,*" a woman's voice said meekly. "*Excuse me, sir, but are you the agent who visited the Pacific Institute of Theology?*"

"May I ask who's calling?"

"Rebecca Moreno. I'm Bishop Ward's executive assistant. Didn't you visit the PIT the other day?"

"Yes, that's right."

"I've wanted to talk to someone for a long time. I hope I won't get in any trouble."

"Everything is completely confidential. Do you have any information about the William Freeman disappearance?"

"*I really don't know very much. He was—*" Rebecca hesitated. There was background noise like the rumpling of fabric and perhaps some talking. "*Excuse me. This isn't a good time. Can I call you sometime on Monday?*"

"I can be reached at this same number at any time. Please call when you feel comfortable."

"*Thank you. I'll call later.*" Click.

Finally. Just as he had hoped, his contact with "worker bees" was paying off. And the Bishop's personal assistant would probably know a lot. You can't get much better than that. On the other hand, the Bishop may have put her up to this, to distract Hall from the truth of PITY and the whereabouts of William. Rebecca *seemed* harmless enough.

He watched some pedestrians walk across the four-lane highway in front of his car. This light was taking forever.

Hopefully, Rebecca would give him the breakthrough he needed.

CHAPTER 25

"Ready for more miraculous *seed juice*?" Dan brought in the rest of the coffee and split it up among the three mugs, not quite filling them. After starting another pot, he came back to the table.

"The four river valleys... that's an astounding match with scientific theory, if you read it right and have an openness to new ideas. Along these lines, there's been research into the history of mankind based on genetic changes. It's really an interesting way to look at things."

"Oh no, not more from the professor!" John sipped his hot coffee, eyes teasing.

Dan smirked. "In the 1990s a research group tracked human history through genetic mapping, primarily through mutations in the Y-chromosome and *mitochondrial DNA, mDNA.* I can't remember if we covered mDNA, Shannon. Do you want to explain it to John?"

John rolled his eyes.

"I guess the museum didn't cover that detail, or maybe we just missed it." She took a break from her computer to gather her thoughts, then spoke with a professorial demeanor. "*mDNA* or *mitochondrial DNA* is one of the most amazing parts of the cell, as is the whole structure of the mitochondria. Remember those purple blobs in the model of the cell at the museum?"

John nodded.

She said, "Those represented the mitochondria, key to the production of energy in the cell. They're really quite unusual because they have their own separate DNA. But their DNA is in a ring, much like the simple *prokaryotes*—the simple bacteria cells. Researchers suggest that early in the evolution of cells, primitive bacteria-like cells were incorporated symbiotically in the structure of eukaryotic cells. They replicate like bacteria, with no sexual crossing to mix the DNA of the father and mother.

"Your mitochondria are provided only by your mother in the egg. Except for nuclear DNA, you get nothing from your father. Therefore, you inherit your cellular energy production profile only from your mother. Any mutations that may exist can be tracked to your mother, to her mother, and so forth."

Dan took over, talking mostly to John. "If a mother has only sons, her mitochondrial DNA will not be passed on after that generation. Over time, more and more mDNA is lost until everyone alive can trace their mDNA to a single mother, the so-called *mitochondrial Eve*.

"Everyone alive today is related to a single distant mother from an mDNA standpoint. Yet, the mDNA around today is not totally identical. Occasionally, mutations occurred during the rollout of humankind around the planet. These mutations provide hints about the location and history of that rollout, providing an amazing record of our past. By studying at the mutations, it's possible to reverse the clock and determine where mankind originally developed."

"You should say *womankind*," Shannon said. "mDNA is provided only by the mother in the egg."

"Good point," laughed Dan. "*Womankind* is the better term."

John stayed serious.

Dan said, "Researchers took samples of mDNA from all around the world and mapped the migrations of humans over the millennia. According to their research, Mitochondrial Eve was from Africa, in the area of the upper Nile, in Ethiopia, and lived about 200,000 years ago. They also estimated the initial number of genetic variants at about 18,000, implying that there was a fairly large gene pool to start with—not just the single pattern of Adam and Eve."

"That seems to match the concept that the Nile valley was an important cradle of civilization, one of the four river valleys mentioned in Genesis," Shannon said. "The number 18,000... well, that supports the notion that the Hebrew for *mankind* was a plural word and that Adam represented the people from the four river valleys, about 4,500 in each one. You like numbers, John. You said *EDEN* might be an acronym of the four valleys. Well, if I can suggest something equally unsupported, *ADAM* could be an acronym as well, relating to the races of people in those four valleys."

"I'm not even going to try to figure out that acronym," John shook his head quickly, like a dog shaking water off its fur.

"Our mapping of the location of the rivers," Dan said, "makes more sense than the force-fit attempts I've read by Christian authors that—not surprisingly—conclude that all the rivers were in the Tigris/Euphrates valley. Given the world-view in ancient times, a relatively small, circular, flat world centered on Jerusalem, it's understandable that the Nile, Indus, and Huang He rivers would be missed. In fact, they probably were off the edge of those early maps, fallen off into space."

Shannon sipped her coffee. "I see no reason why theologians wouldn't easily accept that the garden might be in multiple locations. Why not?"

Dan answered. "That's easy. How could one man, Adam, tend more than just a small garden area? If it were four fertile river valleys, it would take more than one man. Period.

"In fact, in this J-Account, man has not been named Adam yet, and therefore an entire culture of people could have been the originators of the human species. The idea certainly fits the multiple-river theory better, and the Hebrew word for *man* being plural, *humanity*, as well. It would also allow the possibility of a larger initial gene pool, maybe the 18,000 members that I mentioned."

"I guess this theory solves the question about Cain's mysterious wife from Nod as well," Shannon said. "Nod could easily have been the Nile river valley. Our N-word match."

"Don't jump ahead! Let's focus on this section," Dan said.

"Sorry. You're right; I'm jumping way ahead on that one. But it has always bugged me anyway, and this would remove the difficulties of incest amongst the first family, wouldn't it? Okay... I'll stop. What's next?"

"One of the most unusual, most discussed, and most influential sections of the Bible. John, can you read the next verse?"

John read aloud:

> (Gen. 2:16) *And the LORD God commanded the man, saying, Of every tree of the garden thou mayest freely eat:* (17) *But of the tree of the knowledge of good and evil, thou shalt not eat of it: for in the day that thou eatest thereof thou shalt surely die.*

"Classic books and masterpieces of art describe the garden, these trees, and the Fall. The two trees were introduced in the prior chapter. Here, Yhwh notified the man that eating the *tree of knowledge of good and evil* would have immediate fatal consequences."

"I know you want to get into this, but let's wait on our discussion of these trees until they're mentioned again," Dan said. "We can note that here, Yhwh clearly states that eating of the Tree of Knowledge will cause immediate and certain death."

"Fair enough." John went on. "In the next paragraph, Yhwh creates the animals in an effort to find a *help meet* partner for Adam."

> (Gen. 2:18) *And the LORD God said, [It is] not good that the man should be alone; I will make him an help meet for him.* (19) *And out of the ground the LORD God formed every beast of the field, and every fowl of the air; and brought [them] unto Adam to see what he would call them: and whatsoever Adam called every living creature, that [was] the name thereof.* (20) *And Adam gave names to all cattle, and to the fowl of the air, and to every beast of the field; but for Adam there was not found an help meet for him.*

Dan said, "Naming *every living creature* would be quite a job.

Naturalists still haven't finished the work, even today. The systematic naming and classification of biological species was pioneered by Carolus Linnaeus in the early 1700s, the so-called *Linnaean* classification system."

"Kings play chess on folding glass seats," Shannon volunteered.

"What?"

"That's how you remember it. Kings Play Chess On Folding Glass Seats. The first letter of each word: *kingdom, phylum, class, order, family, genus*, and *species,* is the Linnaean system."

"Exactly, and thanks for the memory aid! That Linnean system did not utilize DNA relationships. It predated any knowledge of DNA. Instead, it used physical features such as having a vertebrae, being warm-blooded, having hoofs, feathers, and scales, or in the case of primates, whether or not they have moist noses. The branches of life in this system are strictly guesses and may have nothing at all to do with evolution.

"The wording, *after their kind,* indicates that evolution is incorrect, and that all species of animal life existed at the time of creation, the so-called *immutability of species* doctrine. From what we know today, we have about fifty thousand distinct species, and we are discovering more every year. If Adam had to name all fifty thousand animal species in one twenty-four-hour day, he would have let's see..." he worked his computer "...about 1.7 seconds to name each one—a very busy day to be sure, with no time to sleep. Obviously impossible!"

"You're way off track there, Dan," John said. "There are not fifty thousand animal groups if you group them at a less detailed level. I would say *birds* would be a good group, and Adam probably called them 'birds' or whatever Hebrew word was popular back then. How many species of birds are there? Naturalists probably list thousands. I doubt Adam named every species as science has named them today. This eliminates your ridiculous timing problem."

Dan squeezed his lips together and gave in without argument.

"How man first named the animals is not as critical as the fact that man *could* name them," Shannon said. "That means that symbolic language was available. The capacity to use symbolic language is the quintessential feature distinguishing modern humans from all other life on earth. Animals may use body language and sounds, but no other organism likes to slap a nametag on everything. No other organism has written symbolic language. No other organism has libraries or the Internet. Here, man was already capable of naming the animals, representing them by sounds. That means he had the advanced capacity for symbolic language."

"I don't mean to jump ahead, but we should make particular note that this capacity existed *prior* to the consumption of the fruit of the Tree of Knowledge of Good and Evil," Dan said. "The knowledge of language was not gained by eating that fruit."

"That is true," John said. "The fruit was eaten after naming the animals."

"Let me tell you what really bugs me about this section," Dan said, leaning back in his patio chair and setting his cup down so he could use his hands. "It's never clearly stated, but I assume *help meet* means *mate*. These words are strange choices, the only time they're used in the Bible. God was apparently searching for an animal that would be a suitable mate for Adam." Dan raised his voice slightly, and he leaned back up. "Why would God, who just created Adam, need to search or wonder about this question? It's as if God suddenly became quite limited in capability. No longer an infinite and omnipotent god, now he was a helpless experimenter. He used trial and error to determine if any of the animals would be an appropriate *help meet*. The Yhwh people experiment as if they were scientists, not gods, and somewhat helpless scientists at that. And surprisingly enough, they fail to find a mate. Does it make sense for Almighty God to fail?"

"An obvious boo-boo," Shannon said.

John's face reddened. "Are you sure *help meet* means mate? Maybe that means something else. I admit that it does clearly say that Adam's *help meet* wasn't found. Yet, I don't think you can conclude that God '*failed*.' It could be his intention to have Adam name all the animals and not find a mate. Not failure, intention."

"Uh, sure thing. I'm not certain I buy it, but I don't want to pursue it and take us farther off track. Let's continue," Dan said. "Here's the next section."

> (Gen. 2:21) *And the LORD God caused a deep sleep to fall upon Adam, and he slept: and he took one of his ribs, and closed up the flesh instead thereof;* (22) *And the rib, which the LORD God had taken from man, made he a woman, and brought her unto the man.* (23) *And Adam said, This [is] now bone of my bones, and flesh of my flesh: she shall be called Woman, because she was taken out of Man.*

Dan asked, "Don't you think that most people envision the act like this: God puts Adam to sleep; God cuts into his chest; God removes a rib and carefully heals the wound; then God waves his hand, and the rib sprouts arms and legs, becoming the first *Wo-man,* virtually identical to Adam, with the same bones and flesh?"

"Yeah, it's just like the medieval mind to treat women as nothing more than walking ribs. Hey, check this out," Shannon laughed from behind her notebook computer. "This web site says *men actually have one less rib than women*. Hah! How ridiculous! Sorry, men and women have exactly the same number of ribs. In fact, the overall anatomy of men and women is remarkably identical except for very minor details in the sexual and reproductive organs. The number of skeletal ribs is exactly the same. Men didn't inherit a ribcage with a rib missing due to the creation of Eve."

John instinctively felt his ribcage and counted each rib to make sure.

Dan said, "Whoever started that wrong-headed idea made a common mistake about inheritance, a mistake that scientists—even Darwin—made for years as well: *Lamarckian* inheritance. Originally, it was guessed that if an animal became very good at something, its abilities would be at least partially passed on to its offspring. For example, if a man worked hard and developed large muscles, would his children also have large muscles to be even more fit for that work? This theory was clearly refuted by Weismann in the early 1900s. He somewhat sadistically cut the tails off of twenty generations of rats, mating each generation of short tailed rats. The thought was that eventually rats would grow shorter tails in response to the environmental pressure of the carving knife. Needless to say, all the rats still were born with long tails."

"I guess you'll tell us there three rats, and they were also blind, right?" asked John with sarcasm in his voice. They chuckled uneasily.

"There's no evidence that offspring will inherit any *acquired* traits," Shannon said. "It would be very bad design for all men to inherit the acquired characteristic of one less rib from Adam. That would mean, by logical extension, that anyone with a broken leg might pass the broken leg to his offspring. Everyone would be handicapped in no time!

"Instead, the individuals with a genetic code that provides a particular trait might have a larger potential to survive and have more offspring than those individuals without that capacity. Over many generations, more of the population would have the genetic code and therefore the trait that favors survival. No *acquired* traits are transmitted from one generation to the next. This is the current understanding of the inheritance of traits. So guys, you don't have to worry that you've been shortchanged in the rib department, although that doesn't make up for your shortage in other departments, if you know what I mean." Shannon said, smirking.

"Very funny," John said with a straight face and then smiled when Shannon looked away.

"There's no doubt that the story of Eve's creation from a rib is very, very weird" Dan said. "The word *rib* has no particularly special significance anywhere else in the Bible. It's used a total of only five times, with the other four times explaining where a spear entered the body. God created Adam from the dust, why not do it again for Eve? And, if an insignificant piece of the anatomy such as a rib were used, why that instead of any other part of Adam's body? Why not something like a piece of hair or skin? Wouldn't that be easier?"

John shook his head the whole time Dan talked and then finally responded, motioning with his hands as he talked. "Tradition holds that God was defining the place of woman in the world. A rib is close to the heart. Close to the heart obviously means that men love women with all their hearts. Also, the location of the rib is commonly referenced in wedding ceremonies to refer to the place of the woman *beside* her husband. The wife should stand 'beside her husband' and not below or above him—this was the reason that God chose a rib and not a foot, thigh, or skull."

Shannon grimaced. "You're making me sick. Those explanations are just attempts to use the allegorical tale to support cultural norms. We really don't want to consider women as *walking ribs*—a mere afterthought. Men have been subjugating women for centuries. Your rationale does no better.

"First of all," she continued, "consider the saying *close to the heart*. We don't know which rib it was. Not all ribs are really that close to the heart. If you had to choose one, you would probably choose one of the loose ribs at the bottom front of the ribcage, to have perhaps the least impact on Adam when it was removed. However, God is viewed as all-powerful. He could have chosen any rib, including one from the back and right rib cage."

"Those are relatively far from the heart," Dan said. "But more than that, the heart is really not the source of our feelings. This is just a false cultural hand-me-down. Western culture starting with Aristotle teaches that the heart is the center of the person, where our feelings lie, where *we* are. The heart is simply a blood pump. Our feelings are in our brain. The cultural tradition of assuming our heart is so important probably started because people could feel the heart beating."

"And speed up and slow down based on our emotional state," Shannon continued the thought seamlessly. "It's firmly tied to symbols like the heart-shaped Valentine, phrases like *I love you with all my heart*, and songs like *I Left my Heart in San Francisco*. I don't want to give up those traditions, and I don't know anyone who does, so you're going to have an uphill battle changing them."

"And yet, we must admit that those traditions are far from accurate." Dan said. "So this concept that the rib was chosen because of this romantic idea is reasonable for our culture, but it's not universally satisfying from an allegorical standpoint." Dan noticed that he and Shannon were finishing each other's sentences while John looked on in silence.

Shannon said, "What I hate about this section is that, well... men are created *in God's image* while women are created from an insignificant *rib*. Men are seen as God-like creatures—women as an appendage or an afterthought. It's yet another maddening case of theologians justifying the subordination of women by men.

"Here's a web site with another theologian using the fact that men were created first and the rib story to support male dominance. He quotes Ephesians:" Shannon read from her computer, with a sappy singsong voice.

> (Ephe. 5:22) *Wives, submit yourselves unto your own husbands, as unto the Lord.* (23) *For the husband is the head of the wife, even as Christ is the head of the church: and he is the savior of the body.*
>
> (24) *Therefore as the church is subject unto Christ, so [let] the wives [be] to their own husbands in every thing.*

She simulated spitting. "It's sickening. I refuse to accept this tripe!"

"Shannon, you're going to have to start accepting your proper place if you expect to find a loving husband," John said, deadly serious. Shannon cringed and made a gagging sound as if she were going to vomit.

Dan changed the focus. "Let's assume the Yhwhists of the time had cloning technology. Then, it would be possible to remove a rib from Adam and use rib cells to clone Eve. I understand that some stem-cell researchers claim that bone marrow cells can divide indefinitely, with no fixed lifespan, and they can differentiate into other cell types. A bone such as a rib would be a dandy starting point for a clone. That would explain the *bones of my bones and flesh of my flesh* phrase. A clone would be identical. But, why a rib? God could use any starting point, including dust. Removing a rib and then healing that area of Adam's body was clearly more work than necessary. Cloning needs only a single cell, so why use an entire rib?"

"Let's face it. All these interpretations really do nothing to explain *why* God chooses a rib," Shannon said.

"That will have to remain a mystery, it seems," John said. "But however you slice it, man and woman are closely related and would be capable of reproduction. Here's the next verse:

> *Therefore shall a man leave his father and his mother, and shall cleave unto his wife: and they shall be one flesh. And they were both naked, the man and his wife, and were not ashamed.*

Dan said, "In the prior section, God could not find a *help meet* from among the animals, and so he created Eve. And apparently, Eve is the *help meet* for Adam—that is, his mate. Apparently, this is what *help meet* meant—woman, a sexually compatible mate for Adam, a wife. I note that these verses are quite general in nature. They talk about a man leaving his father and mother and finding a wife. But, how could this apply to Adam? Is he a man that could have left his father and mother?

"Wait a minute. I thought Adam was created from dust!"

CHAPTER 26

Hall answered his secure cell phone, using his hands-free headset. "Hello, Hall speaking." The freeway was at a near standstill, strange for a Saturday. He sat patiently in his car, continuing to consider recent events.

The visit to PITY was quite revealing. Hall firmly believed that visiting actual crime scenes and related sites was essential to solving cases. He particularly felt that "worker bees" can be the best investigative sources. They're out of the loop and don't know when to lie. Although PITY was a weird place and William's release was full of errors, it was not enough to implicate the PITY staff in his disappearance or in any wrong-doing. He hoped his latest contact with Rebecca might pay off eventually.

"*Hall, this is Fairchild.*" Hall knew voice of his superior, Special Supervising Agent Donald Fairchild, but Fairchild always identified himself in full, the habit of most agents. His cell phone had almost no static. "*I've received an urgent memo from the top brass. You're hereby off the William Freeman case. Sorry for jerking you around.*"

"They gave you no reason?"

"Probably organizational changes related to Homeland Security and the concentration on terrorist threats. They want us working on more important things. I wouldn't worry about it. Let's talk about it when you get to the office on Monday."

Of course, just as he was making some progress, he's pulled from the case. Rebecca took the risk to contact him—a breakthrough—but she said nothing of value so far. The sad truth is that any details he had uncovered would probably be lost in the shuffle, changing from one agent to another.

"I'll see you then."

Hall pressed the "Off" button on his cell phone. *I'm being jerked around, but it isn't the first time.* Off the case or not, it would be impossible to stop thinking about it.

The list of related disappearances told the story, and the name *George Stanfield* starting that list brought back memories from years ago, a case assigned to the neophyte agent, Russell Hall. Stanfield had worked at the PIT as a researcher and theologian. He, like William Freeman, disappeared, and there had been no full investigation. Hall remembered how irritated his supervising agent was, that day twenty-five years ago...

“Bill, what’s wrong? Something unusual happen on the Stanfield case?” asked Hall.

“You won’t believe this,” said Bill Platt, Hall’s supervisor.

“What?”

“They just wrapped up the Stanfield case with a pretty little wrapper. It’s closed.”

“Huh?”

“That’s right. Closed. Can you believe that? Suddenly they decided it was a car accident.”

“What car accident? We had no evidence of that! What the—”

“Look, I can’t believe it either. But, it’s probably best that we look the other way and move on to our other cases. We can’t get sidetracked on this one forever. Trust me. You’re still green; you’ve got a whole career ahead of you. Let me handle this. I’ll try to reopen the case. Otherwise, try to ignore it, okay?”

The case was never reopened. Now, he had promised Mrs. Freeman that he would do all he could. Hall hated to break promises, especially that one. And this string of missing persons implied something else was going on; other kids might be at risk. Over the years, Hall had admonished himself for not standing his ground and blowing the whistle on the cover-up of that earlier case. Now, it was happening again.

CHAPTER 27

"First, Adam was made from the dust of the earth. Then, we hear that Adam will leave his father and mother... Who? Mommy and Daddy Dustball, I suppose?" teased Shannon. "Like I said before, this story is simply contrived by those with power and money to keep the powerless in line. I'm not at all surprised to find this sort of mistake. Now, I'm even more convinced that we're wasting our time!" Her blood was clearly still hot from John's remark about the woman's proper place in the family.

"Shannon, don't get bent out of shape over the wording," John patted her on the hand. His gesture didn't seem to be helping Shannon. "That section is simply describing the general life cycle, where man will leave the father and mother and find a wife. Adam is the single exception to that rule."

Shannon didn't give up; she just glared silently.

"Folks, here is some more coffee. Care for a refill?" Dan offered to his friends. "Don't forget. We already made a good case for four river valleys and 18,000 people. It's not difficult if you keep that in mind." After filling the cups, Dan took the pot back to the kitchen and returned to an uneasy quietness. "John, what's next?"

"Okay, listen up, my friends. Experts agree that this next paragraph is one of the most critical passages in all religious literature and perhaps all literature of any type."

> (Gen. 3:1) *Now the serpent was more subtle than any beast of the field which the LORD God had made. And he said unto the woman, Yea, hath God said, Ye shall not eat of every tree of the garden?*
>
> (2) *And the woman said unto the serpent, We may eat of the fruit of the trees of the garden:* (3) *But of the fruit of the tree which [is] in the midst of the garden, God hath said, Ye shall not eat of it, neither shall ye touch it, lest ye die.*
>
> (4) *And the serpent said unto the woman, Ye shall not surely die:* (5) *For God doth know that in the day ye eat thereof, then your eyes shall be opened, and ye shall be as gods, knowing good and evil.*

> (6) *And when the woman saw that the tree [was] good for food, and that it [was] pleasant to the eyes, and a tree to be desired to make [one] wise, she took of the fruit thereof, and did eat, and gave also unto her husband with her; and he did eat.*

"As the story goes, the serpent—that is, Satan in the form of a snake—tempts Eve to eat the fruit of the Tree of Knowledge of Good and Evil. After he convinced her that the fruit was beautiful, tasted good, and created wisdom, Eve elected to eat the fruit, and Adam did the same." John read the next section too.

> (Gen. 3:7) *And the eyes of them both were opened, and they knew that they [were] naked; and they sewed fig leaves together, and made themselves aprons.*
>
> (8) *And they heard the voice of the LORD God walking in the garden in the cool of the day: and Adam and his wife hid themselves from the presence of the LORD God amongst the trees of the garden.*
>
> (9) *And the LORD God called unto Adam, and said unto him, Where [art] thou?*
>
> (10) *And he said, I heard thy voice in the garden, and I was afraid, because I [was] naked; and I hid myself.*
>
> (11) *And he said, Who told thee that thou [wast] naked? Hast thou eaten of the tree, whereof I commanded thee that thou shouldest not eat?*
>
> (12) *And the man said, The woman whom thou gavest [to be] with me, she gave me of the tree, and I did eat.*
>
> (13) *And the LORD God said unto the woman, What [is] this [that] thou hast done? And the woman said, The serpent beguiled me, and I did eat.*

"That short passage is perhaps one of the most well referenced portions of the Bible, with immense implications on the course of religious thought. It's key to the foundations of Christianity," John explained.

"Foundations aside," Dan said, "this whole section is quite inconsistent. Obviously, they ate the fruit of the *Tree of Knowledge of Good and Evil*, apparently anticipating instant death. That is what God clearly said would happen. Did we already forget the verses from the prior chapter? They were supposed to die *that day*!

"The problem is they didn't die that day. In fact, Adam lived another 930 years. Take a look at Genesis 5:5:

> *And all the days that Adam lived were nine hundred and thirty years: and he died.*

"Obviously, they did not die 'that day' as God clearly warned," Shannon said, using her fingers for quotes. "That's another big problem!"

"It must be devastating to literalists," Dan said. "Also, Adam and Eve didn't become super knowledgeable as you might expect after eating the *fruit of the Tree of Knowledge.*"

"Right. Adam had previously named all the animals, so symbolic language was something they already had," Shannon said.

"There was only one apparent change to Adam and Eve," Dan continued. "They gained the knowledge of their nakedness."

"It sounds like they also gained sexual desire and the capacity for reproduction," Shannon said. "It seems they jumped into the bushes and got busy!"

John and Dan both were a bit surprised at Shannon's somewhat graphic description. They both smiled at Shannon. There was an extra pause as the men attempted to focus on the subject matter and take their eyes off Shannon.

Dan recovered. "Right! That's what happened. According to this passage, to become *like the Gods* meant to understand sexual reproduction and desire, to notice nakedness and the difference of gender."

"Not so fast." John slapped the table. "This passage cannot be interpreted literally. It has clear allegorical meaning understood for centuries. The symbolic meaning is clear and strong. Given the heavy discussion of this section over the centuries, I doubt that we will be able to do much better."

"There's nothing inherently wrong with the allegorical approach," Dan said, "but the question is whether the correct interpretation of the symbols has been achieved. Let me show you what I mean. Let's start with the serpent. Verse 3:1 says:

> *Now the serpent was more subtle than any beast of the field which the LORD God had made.*

"Customarily, the serpent represents evil, and this evil is personified as Satan. Yet, if the story really was about the epitome of evil—Satan—why not be literal here? Why not say the serpent was more evil? Or, why not forget the distraction of the symbolic serpent and just say Satan, Lucifer, or Devil? Those names were available, weren't they? In fact, none of these names were used. Satan was never discussed per se in the original story. Why this point of view continues to persist is beyond me.

"It really bugged me, so I went ahead and did a bit of investigation. The concept of *Satan* did not enter into the Bible until the exile of the Jewish culture in Babylon; *Satan* is not explicitly mentioned until *I Chronicles*.

> (I Chron. 21:1) *And Satan stood up against Israel, and provoked David to number Israel.*(2) *And David said to Joab and to the rulers of the people, Go, number Israel from Beersheba even to Dan; and bring the number of them to me, that I may know [it].*

"But this same story was also told in the pre-Exilic version of the story in *II Samuel*, and it doesn't mention Satan. Almost all the other words are the same:"

> (II Sam 24:1) *And again the anger of the LORD was kindled against Israel, and he moved David against them to say, Go, number Israel and Judah.* (2) *For the king said to Joab the captain of the host, which [was] with him, Go now through all the tribes of Israel, from Dan even to Beersheba, and number ye the people, that I may know the number of the people.*

Dan continued. "Apparently, the *anger of the Lord* was retranslated into *Satan* during the 'Jewish Exile.' That Exile was a huge transition for the Jewish culture. The Assyrian empire attempted to obliterate the Jewish culture by moving them from their homeland and surrounding them with Babylonian culture. They forcibly moved the Jewish people away from Canaan on the coast of the Mediterranean near Jerusalem, over five hundred miles to the east to the area near Babylon. That's roughly where Baghdad is today. It's easy to imagine that the Jews were worried that they would forget their history, their roots, and their cultural heritage. Biblical scholars suggest that during their exile, the Jewish people preserved their culture and history in written form, preserved as the first books of the Old Testament.

"Because *Satan* first appears at this point in the text, it's reasonable to suggest that it was adopted from the pagan religions of Persia, religions that included gods that were the source of human sinfulness, much like our current concept of Satan.

"The bottom line is that the word *serpent* probably did *not* mean *Satan*. So let's drop back to a more literal interpretation and assume that when the Bible says *serpent,* it actually means an animal that we would consider a *snake*. Does this make sense in the story?

"You're going in the wrong direction," Shannon said, for once not supporting Dan. "I agree that the snake is quite *subtle* in that it slithers around quietly and stealthily. Most people don't like snakes and say that they're creepy, but creepy is not what the word *subtle* implies. My Bible uses the word *crafty* instead of *subtle*. Again, there is nothing really very crafty about a real snake. You could argue that the subtle nature of the snake is due to the fact that its bodily structure is one of the simplest of the vertebrates because it lacks any limbs. The reptilian brain is one of the simplest of the higher animals too. It's so simple that symbolic language—talking to Eve—makes no sense at all."

"In only one other place in the entire Bible does an animal converse with a human, and then it is an ass, an animal with a much, much more advanced brain, with a cerebellum large enough to understand higher concepts. But even an ass can't talk. But it's worse than that, Shannon. Figuring out the pieces is only part of the problem with this section." Dan rose from his seat and started pacing back and forth, waving his hands. "The larger concept of this story is utterly ridiculous. Why would God include the *Tree of Knowledge of Good and Evil* in the midst of the garden and then warn Adam and Eve not to eat it? Why not just omit the tree and let them live without death, thorns, thistles, and the rest of the implications of original sin? If indeed God is all-knowing, wouldn't he know that man would eventually eat the fruit after meeting the serpent? If God is all-good, why did he create evil? Worse yet, if God is all-good, is it possible to create such a evil temptation?"

"That's a good question," Shannon said. "How can any omnipotent God who is all-good create any evil? It's like asking if God can create a rock that he can't move. It's logically impossible. Plus it's something a loving god would never do. That's what I think."

Dan stopped and leaned over the place where he was sitting, bracing himself with his arms in a triangle. "The real inconsistency is clearly stated in the scripture. When God warned Adam, he said *in the day that thou eatest thereof thou shalt surely die*." Dan went back to pacing. "But they ate the fruit, and they did not die that day. And the scripture says they lived another 930 years. But God said they would surely die that day. What gives? Either die doesn't mean physical death, or *day* does not mean the twenty-four-hour day when they ate the fruit."

"Or God was just kidding around, or the whole thing is just a fabrication, as I said," Shannon said.

"Literalists have already pounded their fists over the twenty-four-hour day for the first story of creation," Dan said, pounding his own in his hand. "So they can't give in there: *Day* still must mean twenty-four hours in their book. Therefore, the only choice for literalists to solve this conflict is to say that the word *die* cannot be taken literally. Oh yes, that's the solution!" He stopped and looked at his friends. "It doesn't mean the literal 'physical death;' no, we don't want to be literal here! It means a *spiritual death*, whatever that means. Indeed, we could solve this problem the other way, by saying that *day* does not mean twenty-four hours. If *day* meant one million years, then they died that *day,* and it works that way too. In the end, the whole story is incredibly contrived. I really don't know how anyone can buy into this stuff!" Dan flopped back down into his chair. Shannon's emotions were clearly being reflected in Dan.

"Hold on, you guys," John said. He was clearly in the hot seat now to defend the story. "This story makes sense if you include how Satan originated. You see, God created the angels in heaven during the first days of creation. Satan was originally the angel Lucifer, who disagreed with God and revolted against him. God sentenced Satan to the pit of hell. But Satan wound up getting stronger, free to reign over the earth. The serpent was, in essence, Satan tempting Adam and Eve to disobey God's first commandment."

"John," Dan said, a bit sternly, "I know there is a lot of speculation about this section, but I really don't know where everyone gets this other story that includes *Lucifer*. It certainly isn't biblical in any sense. If so, where is it described? We didn't read that in the first chapters of Genesis—I'm sure we can agree about that!"

"That's true." John said. There was quietness.

Shannon looked up from her computer, apparently fresh with new information from the Internet. "The idea is probably from Milton's *Paradise Lost*, the epic poem telling the larger tale that John is bringing into play here. *Paradise Lost* was written much, much later, the mid-1600s. We can safely say that Milton was reading the same Genesis that we have today. He had no chance of interpreting it with our knowledge of the underlying pattern of life, but he took the liberty of including the religious lore and tales of the day to create a larger story that could make some sense. He went well beyond any strict literal interpretation."

"Milton's *Paradise Lost* describes a great many details that are not in any Bible I've ever read." Dan had already pulled up a copy of *Paradise Lost* on the Internet. "Listen to a few verses from this first page:"

Who first seduced them to that foul revolt?
Th' infernal Serpent; he it was whose guile,
Stirred up with envy and revenge, deceived
The mother of mankind, what time his pride
Had cast him out from Heaven, with all his host
Of rebel Angels, by whose aid, aspiring
To set himself in glory above his peers,
He trusted to have equaled the Most High,
If he opposed, and with ambitious aim
Against the throne and monarchy of God,
Raised impious war in Heaven and battle proud,
With vain attempt. Him the Almighty Power

Hurled headlong flaming from th' ethereal sky,
With hideous ruin and combustion, down
To bottomless perdition, there to dwell
In adamantine chains and penal fire,
Who durst defy th' Omnipotent to arms.

Dan continued without pausing, "Milton asserts that the Serpent is one of the rebel angels, who raised an *impious war in Heaven* and then was *hurled...down to bottomless perdition*. This matches your concept of the story almost exactly, John. But the question is, is this in the Bible, or did Milton just dream this stuff up?"

Dan was on a bit of a roll and his friends let him continue. He typed on his computer for a moment. "My Bible program finds the word *Lucifer* in only one place in the entire Bible, in Isaiah, chapter fourteen:

(Isaiah 14:12) *How art thou fallen from heaven, O Lucifer, son of the morning! [how] art thou cut down to the ground, which didst weaken the nations!*

"The larger context of these verses is talking about the king of Babylon. You might be tempted to say that the term *Lucifer* is a way to badmouth that king. However, an alternative translation considers it to mean *day star*, perhaps a reference to the planet Venus. The rest of the verse relates the meaning of its disappearance, an important event in astrological science. Indeed, Lucifer was commonly used in those days to name that planet. Certainly, this is not a reference to the *Fall of Adam*."

"Sure... I'll go along with that," John said.

"Okay, that's it for *Lucifer*. He's certainly no big biblical player. Let's look for *Satan*." He typed. "The term *Satan* is found in a grand total of forty-nine verses in the entire King James Bible. I already mentioned the first occurrence in I Chronicles, where *Satan* meant *anger of the LORD*. Then, in the book of *Job*, Satan resurfaces. There are side notes here stating that in Hebrew, *Satan* can be translated as *the adversary*."

"The book of Job is quite unusual in the Old Testament in that it has a different focus from the other books, away from the history of the Jewish culture and to a simple story of hardship," John said.

"Satan is the bad-guy trying to get Job to curse God to his face," Dan said. "Yet, amazingly enough, in Job 1:12, it was none other than God himself who asked Satan to attempt to shake Job from his convictions."

Shannon said, "It doesn't sound like Satan is acting independently. God asked Satan to challenge Job's beliefs. Satan was doing what God asked of him, that's all. Satan is not the omnipresent evil in charge of the world like you described, John."

"Exactly what I was going to say," Dan said. "That weak Satan is not the mighty deceiver implied by the Fall. Later in Job 2:4-6, God again asks Satan to try to shake Job's convictions, to do anything except to take his life. Satan is again mostly under God's control, released to do what he can to try to force Job to curse God. Apparently, Satan has no power except for that granted by God."

"Not an out-of-control renegade angel, by a long shot," Shannon said with a burst of air out her nose.

"The concept of an omnipotent God with a renegade angel who is out of control makes absolutely no logical sense. God would be able to put an end to any such evil if he wanted to. This passage in Job further buttresses the view that Satan reflects an abstraction of the evils of the world.

"I don't want to get sidetracked looking into every single mention of Satan in the Bible, even though there aren't too many. Let me scan this list... uh... There's one mention in Psalms, the footnote again says that the Hebrew is perhaps better interpreted as *adversary*.

"In Zechariah, *Satan* is a symbol of evil being cast out from the high priest."

"Typical," Shannon said. "It's like the TV-evangelists who've had been caught with their pants down or with porn in their back seat. Blame it on the Devil... It's always an easy way out. 'The Devil made me do it!' That's what they say!"

"That's it for the entire Old Testament. We can safely say that Satan was not a big player in that part of the Bible. The idea that Satan was a fallen angel is absolutely not scriptural."

"That's a nice Bible program you have on your computer," John said, who was the only one without a laptop. "You've made a good case that *Lucifer* and *Satan* are not big players in the Old Testament. Doesn't the New Testament explain this?"

"I'll look, but I want to eventually get back to Genesis. I'm just going to look for anything that seems interesting..." Dan clicked his mouse a few more times, proud of his technological edge. "In the New Testament, Satan is mentioned in thirty-four verses, over twice as many times as the fifteen verses in the Old Testament. By this evidence alone, we can say that Satan is more of a modern idea.

"Okay, Matthew 4:8 describes Jesus's forty-day trek in the wilderness, with Satan promising him all the kingdoms of the world. Sorry, but this doesn't clarify your story of Lucifer, the renegade angel.

"In Matthew 12:24-27, Jesus was brought before the Pharisees and was accused of working for Satan. Jesus used logic to confuse them."

"That's not about the *Fall*, Dan," Shannon said, stating the obvious. "It says nothing except that the logic of the Pharisees was bankrupt because it made no sense for Jesus to be working for the devil and then also cast out devils. What else do you find?"

"The next use of the term *Satan* is in Matthew, chapter sixteen, just after Jesus told his disciples that he must go into Jerusalem and face the elders and priests and be killed. Peter could not believe his ears and told Jesus that it could not happen, given that he was the Messiah. Jesus reprimanded Peter, saying '*Get thee behind me, Satan.*'

"Again, Jesus was not talking about a person known as Satan but instead about an idea of success in the world versus the true calling and plan for Jesus.

"So, that's not it... Let's move ahead to the book of Mark. It has the same wilderness episode, the argument with the Pharisees, and the reprimand of Peter. Mark 4:14 adds one new thing, the parable of the sower. After the word is sown in the heart, Satan comes to take it away—again the challenge of the world against the word of God."

"Satan symbolizes the distractions of the world, just like the use when Jesus was reprimanding Peter in Matthew," Shannon said. "It doesn't explain the Fall."

Dan continued. "The next mention is in Luke 10:17-19 after Jesus returns resurrected, gathers his original twelve disciples and an additional seventy disciples, and sends them out to minister to the world. The disciples returned saying that the devils and Satan are under their control, and Jesus says, '*I give unto you power to tread on serpents and scorpions, and over all the power of the enemy: and nothing shall by any means hurt you.*'"

John slapped the table. "There we are. Clearly a mention of Satan and serpents in that verse."

"That's not a very clear linkage, John," Shannon said. "It doesn't say that Satan is a serpent. It doesn't clarify how the Fall should be interpreted, that's clear. And it further refutes the concept that Satan is somehow acting independently. Jesus gives his disciples almost absolute power.

John didn't respond, instead reading the verse over again to himself from his Bible, mouthing the words.

"It's too bad that *Satan* is not tied to *serpent*, as you claim, John." Shannon patted him on the arm, returning his earlier gesture.

"Uh... It does seem you have a point." John started another organic cookie.

"Dan, let's not go over every instance. Just scan the search results and see if anything looks interesting." She picked up a cookie and leaned back in her plastic patio chair.

"Good idea. I'm skipping over a few uses here. They seem to use the term *Satan* to mean *sin* or *illness*." Dan used his finger to scan down the screen, reviewing each one as his friends waited and enjoyed their cookies.

Dan said, "Wait... Here it is."

John stopped chewing. "What...?"

CHAPTER 28

Hall slammed on the brakes, cursing under his breath. A rusty van swerved into the small space between his sedan and the SUV ahead of him. Brake lights glared; the five-lane freeway ground to a halt. His mobile phone signaled an incoming call, he pressed the switch to answer it. He didn't recognize the number.

"Hall speaking."

"Oh, Mr. Hall. This is Delia—Delia Freeman—you know, William's Momma?"

Just the person Hall didn't want to talk to, at least not until he was able to talk with his supervisor in detail about the unexpected change of assignment. "Oh, yes, yes. Hello, Ms. Freeman, I know who you are. How are you doing?"

"D'you find my William? Is 'e comin' home?"

"Just a moment, Ms. Freeman... Please hold a minute, okay?" Hall clicked the hold button. He wanted time to think about how he should handle the call. Why was he taken off the case? Hall tried to think of someone in the office who would want to change his assignment. Changing assignment wasn't that unusual, but he did promise he would do all he could to find William, and he really wanted to help out Ms. Freeman.

He pressed the talk button. "Ms. Freeman? I can't tell you much yet. Don't worry, we're making progress. But I'll be perfectly honest with you. We still don't know exactly what happened to William."

"Y'all haven't found 'im yet?"

"Ms. Freeman, I understand how anxious you are. I'll let you know as soon as we find out anything, fair enough?"

"Oh, call—call if you find anythin', one way or another. I can't get no sleep at night not knowin' 'bout my baby!"

"I'm sorry I don't have better news, Ms. Freeman. Please be patient a bit longer. I'm sure we'll track him down."

Hall didn't have the heart to tell Ms. Freeman that he had been pulled from the case and that the Bureau had essentially shelved it. At the same time, he was hoping the call from Rebecca would provide information sufficient to argue for continuing the investigation. If not, perhaps his supervisor would look the other way. Hall hated to leave cases just when he had started to make progress.

"I'll try to be patient. But please, Mr. Hall. Please call me, please."

"I will... I promise. Just relax and try to put it out of your mind as much as you can. Okay?"

"I don't know if I can... but, thank you, Mr. Hall."

"Good bye."

Hall was already thinking of how he would handle this situation with his boss. He was tired of being jerked around.

CHAPTER 29

The square of sunlight had moved across the floor as the day matured. Puffy clouds shuttled across the sky, visible through the Bower vine around the window. John and Shannon were startled when Dan suddenly said he had found the key connection proving the concept that the serpent was Satan. They both looked up and leaned forward to hear what Dan had to say. John chewed his cookie slowly.

"What do you mean, you found it?" asked Shannon.

"Revelation, chapter twelve, has an interesting passage. It describes a woman in heaven who is ready to give birth and *a great red dragon, having seven heads and ten horns, and seven crowns upon his heads*. It's interesting that this dragon appears in heaven. But it isn't really welcome there, as it is ready *to devour her child as soon as it was born*. Her child was apparently born without being devoured, and then the child *was caught up unto God, and [to] his throne*. The woman fled into the wilderness for 2,260 days. It sounds like a lot, but it's only a bit over six years.

"It goes on to describe a war in heaven, with Michael and the angels fighting against the dragon. The dragon loses. Then,

> *...the great dragon was cast out, that old serpent, called the Devil, and Satan, which deceiveth the whole world: he was cast out into the earth, and his angels were cast out with him.*

"That makes sense," John said, swallowing his cookie.

Both Dan and Shannon made faces like they had just eaten a lemon.

"You can clearly see that here, Satan is obviously described as a serpent—a great red dragon with seven heads, the Devil that deceived the world," John explained.

"Well, it does say that, but is this the same 'subtle' serpent from Genesis?" asked Dan.

"The text connects this vision of the *red dragon, having seven heads* to the serpent in the Fall, in that he *deceiveth the whole world.* Also, it connects the *blood of the Lamb,* meaning Christ, with the salvation against the power of the red dragon."

"It's interesting," Shannon said, "that the 'sacred' number seven is used to describe the red dragon. Does that mean that the deceiver is also sacred? Or maybe seven is not always sacred! And the dragon is allowed into heaven to have the battle. Why would God permit that? I'm having a hard time envisioning the dragon's ten horns on seven heads. Is there one on each head and three on his back—or maybe the center three heads have two horns each, while the outer four only have one horn?"

Dan said, "You'd think they would need either seven or fourteen horns. Or... maybe the horns are all on his back, like *stegosaurus*. I would almost be tempted to say this description might be describing a dinosaur. Unfortunately, no dinosaur or any real animal, for that matter, has seven heads. Maybe it's describing something completely different."

Shannon said, "I know. Maybe this is a description of some sort of molecule or virus. They might have a structure that looks like seven heads and ten horns. To find a match, we'd have to look over molecules or viruses to see if one looks like it has seven head-like structures and ten appendages that look like horns. Or it could be a simple story of a boy who perhaps sank into a coma or devastating illness during the first six years of his life, finally driving the illness out. In any case, this great red, seven-headed dragon doesn't match the simple, *most subtle of all creatures* serpent described in Genesis. He's certainly not subtle. This seven-headed dragon with seven crowns and ten horns simply is not the same 'serpent' described in the encounter with Eve. I don't buy it."

"Well, that's then end of my search for 'Satan' in the Bible. It looks like the idea that the story of a renegade angel, Lucifer, who rose up against God, is simply not biblical at all. I'm convinced that there is no biblical substantiation of the concept that the serpent is Satan. The 'whole-Bible' argument is a myth."

John sat silently for a moment, finishing his cookie and sipping his coffee. "Hmmm. You might be right. I just remember that story... I'm not giving up completely. I'm still going to try to find it."

Dan said, "If you find it, please let us know. That would really change the story. As it is, the concept that the serpent symbolized Satan is unsubstantiated."

"Okay. Let's go back to Genesis." John flipped back in his Bible. "Let's see... Right after Eve's encounter with the serpent, Genesis describes the aftermath of the *Fall*. Here the serpent is cursed, and Adam and Eve are booted out of the garden to suffer a life of toil and difficulty.

"God, sentences Adam and Eve to *thorns also and thistles*, and that man would *eat bread, till thou return unto the ground; for out of it wast thou taken: for dust thou art, and unto dust shalt thou return.*"

"Apparently, that just means that Adam and Eve would need to grow their food and eventually die or *return unto dust*," Shannon said.

"Right. Then God made clothing out of animal skins. This next part is interesting.

(22) *And the LORD God said, Behold, the man is become as one of us, to know good and evil: and now, lest he put forth his hand, and take also of the tree of life, and eat, and live for ever:*

(23) *Therefore the LORD God sent him forth from the garden of Eden, to till the ground from whence he was taken.*

(24) *So he drove out the man; and he placed at the east of the garden of Eden Cherubims, and a flaming sword which turned every way, to keep the way of the tree of life.*

"The *Tree of Life* is finally mentioned again," Dan said.

"It would allow man to live forever," John said. "So Adam and Eve were sent from the Garden of Eden, away from the *Tree of Life*. The whole garden area is guarded by the cherubim and a flaming sword that turns every way."

"There are several references in the Bible to the *Tree of Life*, but I can think of no real hints about what it might be, when I compare with science." Dan looked up from his computer. "Also, the *flaming sword* is never mentioned again. Those are certainly interesting images."

John stretched his arms up. "This section... it's extremely important because it explains the reason for Christ's sacrifice—to establish the new covenant and provide a mechanism to avoid the sin of Adam and start with a clean slate. Paul effectively tied this up in a nice package starting in Romans 5:12, where the sin of Adam is linked to the redemption of Christ.

"The Fall established the lock, and Jesus is the key to unlock the possibility of righteousness and avoid condemnation. The traditional story is still the best. Look guys, we're making almost no progress in finding DNA in this allegorical tale. What do you think?"

"I didn't see any DNA. Let's let this information ferment for a while," Dan said. "Remember, the advanced meaning is hidden. The Bible is a large document, but I feel we're looking in the right direction. This section is usually interpreted as very symbolic, a tale that is not to be taken literally but as an allegorical story with deeper meaning. The traditional interpretation is conflictive and inconsistent. We've thrown out the Satan connection for the most part, and if you do that, it still isn't clear about what it actually means."

"I'll admit that it's a passage that has caused a lot of head scratching over the centuries," John said.

"Just that fact alone may mean we are looking in the right place," Shannon interjected with an unexpectedly positive outlook.

"I just don't get any connections yet," Dan responded. "I need a few sleepless nights to come up with new ideas. You guys do the same, and we'll see if anything develops."

"I agree," Shannon said. "I need a break. It's looking pretty sad for the Bible. It's a mess."

John was clearly uneasy. "You've got to realize this is the sacred word of God, Shannon. I'll tell you what. You read this again and see if you don't feel it is absolutely from the mind of God. In trade, I'm going to get a biology text and review DNA and genetics, so I'm not such a numbskull. Deal?"

"Deal."

"Look, you two," Dan said. "Somehow, I'm sure we're looking at the right scripture. We just need to look at it the right way to see the pattern."

CHAPTER 30

Hall looked for a parking space in a nondescript industrial zone near the airport that included the prescribed landscaping, trees, and clean appearance. *There's a spot.* He pulled in and squeezed out of his door. The stall was a bit too small for the full-sized American sedans issued to field agents. Glints of sunlight flashed through the wind-rustled leaves of liquid amber trees. A small two-seat Cessna 150 buzzed overhead, likely on its way to the nearby local airport to practice incessant touch-and-go landings. Hall grabbed his leather briefcase and walked toward the building.

The local FBI office maintained a low profile. *Resident Agency* is all the sign would admit to. Adjacent commercial tenants were well aware that this was the FBI office, but it wasn't obvious to anyone else. The FBI didn't want public visitors blowing agents' cover.

Hall avoided the center whenever possible. He didn't like rampant politics that could poison a good day. To keep his nose out of office politics, he followed a simple strategy: Stay in the field, away from irritable, desk-bound agents of the Resident Agency.

Hall opened one of the two commercial glass doors and stepped into the lobby. Most businesses have a friendly and attractive receptionist at this location, greeting customers and vendors. Nothing of the kind was found here. Instead, the outer lobby was barren except for three little-used chairs around a small square table, placed to fill the vacant space. Hall walked directly across the lobby to a solitary door, took out his badge, and held it close to a black square piece of plastic on the wall as he placed his other hand on a beige panel with the outline of a hand on it. The black panel read information from his badge, and the beige panel measured the size of his hand and the minute ridges of his skin to confirm his identity. The latch on the door clicked. Hall pulled it open, grabbed his briefcase again, and entered the secure inner sanctum of the Resident Agency.

The interior of this building was one large open room with a sea of small cubicles. The perimeter had offices with doors for higher-ups, a bit of a reward for their stature, with the benefit of windows and some privacy. Hall walked past cubicles used by field agents, where he would normally set up shop if he were to stay here for any length of time, continuing directly down a corridor through the middle of the cubicles and all the way to the other side of the room and his superior's office. Hall wasn't happy, and he wanted Fairchild to know it.

Hall entered Fairchild's office without being invited in. Behind a desk piled high with manila folders sat the somewhat frazzled Supervising Agent Fairchild, a heavy-set man about five years younger than Hall. It was a bit of an advantage in this man's world to be a bit rotund; the extra weight implied authority and power. Hall was happy to be a field agent where he could see a bit more action, the light of day, and of course more exercise. Being confined to a desk inside a building was the ultimate in punishment, at least in his mind. Some agents must love it, he told himself.

Hall paced back and forth in the small area in front of Fairchild's desk, almost frothing at the mouth. "Don, what is going on here?"

"About what?"

Hall stopped pacing, waved his hands. "Don't act so bloody ignorant. You know damn well that the William Freeman case is only the tip of the iceberg. Please tell me exactly why this case should be shelved?"

"Hall, why does this case mean so much to you? We can't spend an unlimited amount of time on each and every little case. We have to move on to more important things. There's nothing new about that."

"Hey, look. We go back a long way, Don. What's going on here?"

"Have a seat," Fairchild said sternly.

Hall reluctantly sat in a chair immediately in front of Fairchild's desk. The chair was turned to one side so it could fit in the small size of the office.

Fairchild scribbled some notes on a scratch pad. "Look, Russ, we are at a heightened alert status due to the recent terrorist attacks." He continued to write. "You'll be working with DeVaney on DEA support. Sorry to have to change your work assignment without much notice." He gave Hall the note.

Can't talk here. Office is bugged.

Meet me at O'Sullivan's Thursday at noon.

There was a moment of silence. Hall realized things weren't as simple as he imagined. He changed his tune. "Well, the DEA does need help. And I guess I do enjoy working with DeVaney. I can see that there will need to be some shifting due to the heightened terrorist situation. It's drug interdiction from the border, isn't it? Oh well, you know best, as usual. Thanks, Don." Hall read the note again, winked, and then left the office.

This whole business has changed completely since the National Security Agency started calling the shots. Everything has become more politicized. The fact that they pulled me from the case means there is something they are protecting or hiding. I'm going to look into that old case; I don't care what office politics says!

CHAPTER 31

The three researchers avoided talk of the project for several days, although they met regularly for coffee and other conversation. Each tried to find the hidden patterns Walker said they might, thinking about the project and working on it in their free time, but nothing was coming together in terms of new interpretations.

Shannon was the first to break the ice. She sent an email to the others suggesting that they meet the next day for breakfast at the Pancake House on Ocean Drive.

The Pancake House, open 24 hours, could easily be seen from a busy freeway intersection. Travelers selected this restaurant mainly for its convenience, not for its gourmet fare. During the busy breakfast hour, with its din of conversation, dishes banging, and cash registers ringing, Shannon figured it would be a relatively safe place to talk. She arrived before the others and sat in one of the booths along one side of the main room where the window presented the awe-inspiring view of the parking lot.

Dan and John arrived, sat opposite Shannon, and exchanged greetings. The efficient waitress had coffee and menus in front of the newcomers before they settled completely into their seats. Shannon's composure would not be the envy of any poker player; the excitement of her "discovery" blared from her face, with her eyes wide open and eyebrows raised.

"I can't wait to hear what you have in store for us!" Dan jumped past typical small talk and pleasantries to the topic of Shannon's email.

"I guess you took me up on reading Genesis again, eh, Shannon?" John said.

"Well, I did promise, but I think this is a bit different than you expect, John." Her voice went up at the word think, with a tone of satisfaction that she had something new and exciting. "I was really bugged by the story, especially the part about the creation of Eve. Using a rib to create Eve just seemed to jab me the wrong way."

"Right in your ribs?" asked Dan, the joke not being worth a laugh.

John seemed apprehensive about what she was going to say; he kept sipping his coffee with an air of tension.

"I noticed we had success analyzing the four rivers of Eden, that was a tip-off to what would work. Taking scientific knowledge that we have today and making sense of the story using that information as a backdrop, that seemed to be the key to success, and that's what I tried to do here.

"I looked again at Genesis, chapter two, the section about the creation of Eve. We already concluded that man and woman don't differ at all in terms of the number of ribs. But how do they differ?"

"Look, Shannon," John said, "I'm sure you're about to tell us how different women and men are, that men are from Mars and women from Venus, and all that crap. I'm sure you'll work in the idea that women are actually superior, of course." He looked at her over his coffee cup, starting with an unusually confrontational tone.

"John... calm down. That's not the angle I'm thinking of. The question really is this: How do they differ from a *genetic* standpoint?"

"Oh, that's easy," Dan said. He straightened up in his seat like the star student. "From a genetic standpoint, I'd say the difference between genders is only in the twenty-third chromosome pair, there's no question about that. Females are XX and males are XY. That's it."

"Exactly," Shannon said. "That's what I was looking for."

"Hmmm... I think I see the direction you are taking," Dan said, hand pulling on his chin.

John still seemed to be trying to understand, his brow furrowed and eyes narrowed.

Shannon picked up speed. "In the female, the twenty-third chromosome pair looks like the other chromosomes in that they're a matched pair, the same size, designated XX." She wrote "XX" on a napkin. "In the male, the twenty-third chromosomes are the unmatched pair called XY. They're far different in size, with a large X-chromosome from the mother and a relatively tiny Y-chromosome donated from the father, not even one-sixth the size of the X." She wrote that as well.

"Sure, I remember that from the museum," John said.

"Each egg cell provided by the mother has a full half set of twenty-three chromosomes, with the twenty-third being the X-chromosome. The sperm of the father has matching pairs to the first twenty-two chromosomes and only a X or Y as the twenty-third. Depending on which sperm reaches the egg, that chromosome pair will be either XX—female—or XY—male.

"It's important to know that in the case of the female, only one of the X-chromosomes is chosen as the one used to produce the traits of the woman. The other is coiled up tightly into a *Barr Body* that is never used. In the male, the small Y-chromosome apparently acts as a switch to enable or disable genes in the partner X-chromosome, thereby creating a male. The default condition is female—that is, if no Y is included. It seems the special traits of the male is achieved only if the information in the X-chromosome is somehow perturbed by the few genetic instructions in the Y-chromosome."

The waitress returned, and they all submitted their orders from the breakfast menu.

"Granted, Shannon, that's all well and good. I guess that is the difference, from a genetic standpoint." John gave his menu to the waitress. "But that doesn't explain the story. I don't get it."

"Well, remember, the Bible won't use any modern terms, like *Y-Chromosome*. But another word might be used to represent that idea, a word that was available at that time."

"Go on." John was a blank. He looked around, searching her face for a hint and briefly looking at Dan.

"What was the difference between Adam and Eve in the story?"

"The rib. The rib was the difference," John said. "But we already said that men have the same number of ribs, so that takes us nowhere."

"I give up. I'm going to tell you." She hesitated for a moment and looked at her friends across the table. "I claim that the term *rib* is symbolic for *Y-chromosome*. It's that simple."

The din of the restaurant was continuous, but at their table, there was complete silence. The three friends looked at each other and at the notations on Shannon's napkin.

"Hmmm..." Dan said, nodding excitedly. "If you started with the full complement of chromosomes from the male, then removed the 'rib'—that is, the Y-chromosome—you would be left with only forty-five chromosomes instead of the full forty-six. That last chromosome pair would be only a single X-chromosome, but that's precisely the same situation as in other female cells if the other X is coiled up as the unused Barr Body. Only one X provides a sufficient genetic code for the woman. It's fantastic!"

John sat, quietly staring at the notations on Shannon's napkin.

Shannon said, "The technology of cloning is still in its infancy, but conceptually, if a cell were taken from the male and the Y-chromosome removed, that cell could, in theory, be used as the basis for cloning a female. Remember, the female uses only *one* of its two X-chromosomes. Assuming the cloning from this point would be possible, a female would result, as only the X-chromosome would remain in the twenty-third chromosome pair. There would be no Barr Body, but it's not used anyway. Before you challenge this too hard, I admit that there are some exceptions to this simplistic description. For example, the womb appears to have an important impact on how the fetus develops."

"So, *rib* means *chromosome*..." John thought out loud, still staring at the napkin.

"I'm proposing that this scriptural passage describes that Eve was cloned from Adam. To do so, it was necessary to remove the rib—that is, the Y-chromosome—in order to obtain a woman." Shannon showed them two pages she had marked from a college textbook, one showed a map of the Y-chromosome and the other, a picture of a rib.

"Oh my God!" exclaimed Dan, looking at the picture. "They look a lot alike, that's true!"

John took a huge gulp of air as the looked at the two pictures and the similarity sank in.

"If a man like Moses, without the scientific knowledge we have today, had viewed a magnified image of a chromosome, he certainly would not use the word *chromosome*, and he would not say *Y*," Shannon explained. "What would he say? From the looks of those pictures, magnified chromosomes look exactly like little tiny ribs."

"You are a genius!" Dan exclaimed. "Eve was an exact female clone of Adam, the identical she-twin. *Bones of my bones* equals *my chromosomes*. She would have the exact traits of the male but without the perturbation of the Y-chromosome."

"Twins don't normally occur like that," Shannon set her textbook down. "If you have twins that are male and female—that is, fraternal twins—they don't share the same genetic code, although they share the same womb. It would be interesting to meet a true identical twin of the opposite sex.

"That *would* be weird," John said. "If you met that person, I wonder what you would think. Maybe that he or she is very attractive, right?"

"John, you're an exception to that rule. I can't imagine a woman with your looks could be attractive." Dan scored, and John snapped his fingers, taking the hit.

Shannon said, "Let's complete the task by reworking the passage with new terms. The scriptural passage could be restated like this:

> *And Yhwh caused a deep sleep to fall upon Adam, and he slept: and he took one of his cells and removed the Y-chromosome;*
>
> *And from the cell lacking the Y-chromosome, which Yhwh had taken from man, cloned he a woman, and brought her unto the man.*
>
> *And Adam said 'This is now bone of my bones, and flesh of my flesh: she shall be called Woman', because she was an identical female clone of Adam.*

The waitress brought their order, set their plates on the table, and pointed at the condiments.

Dan doctored up his eggs with black pepper, ketchup, and salsa. "I like the direction this is going. Imagine for a moment that the genetic code for a woman were transported from a remote solar system to earth. Woman would exist first in that case, as it would be easiest to create the woman from that code. However, to create a man, you've got a problem.

You don't have the Y-chromosome at hand. You'd have to invent it out of thin air.

"Now, consider instead what would happen if the genetics for a male were transported from that distant solar system. In that case, the male would logically exist first. One of his cells could be used to create woman without *adding* the Y-chromosome. In other words, it's easier to start with a man and take out the rib-like Y-chromosome to make a female, than it would be to start with the female and *add* a new Y-chromosome, invented out of thin air."

"The biggest problem with this scenario," Shannon said, "is how a human can be cloned without a womb. The most successful cloning experiments thus far use quite a bit of the infrastructure of the cell and of the womb. For example, cloned sheep and cattle were created using an existing egg cell, sucking out the DNA and replacing it, and then implanted the egg into a ewe that would carry it to a normal birth. They used the entire complex infrastructure of the cell and womb and only transplanted the chromosomes. It would be more difficult to be sure, but certainly not impossible for Yhwh, the god of Genesis, to start without an egg or a womb."

"Well... I have no serious problem with your new interpretation," John said. "God certainly could have used cloning technology to create Eve, if he so desired. Indeed, I can see how this section makes more logical sense if it's interpreted that way. It doesn't change the overall story, so I'll go along, for now."

"What I like about this approach is that it eliminates the lore about the dominance of man over woman." Shannon sat up straight. "The 'default' form is woman. Man is just a perturbation, adjusted by the information in the tiny Y-chromosome. Man does not dominate woman, and woman does not dominate man. This finally levels the playing field, if you will."

"Ah-ha! Your ulterior motive is revealed," Dan said with a smile.

"Women are naturally at a lower position from men," John said, a bit condescendingly. "It's because Eve was first to be deceived to eat the fruit and then convinced Adam to eat with her. We should blame her failure to obey God's commandment on her female frailty. Women shouldn't be church leaders or even Sunday-school teachers, in my opinion."

Dan thought John was going over the top, but he decided to avoid a head-to-head exchange with him. "Shannon, your interpretation is very compelling. And, as John said, it doesn't adversely affect the rest of the story, so I don't think we should worry about any retaliation for this innocuous change. On the other hand, if it's accepted, it does grant women higher stature and at least partially flies in the face of intolerant male chauvinist church practices."

"If you ask me that will only be for the good," Shannon said.

"At least I think we're doing the right sort of thinking," Dan said. "I want to take a new look at the rest of this section to see if we can find further tie-ins."

The group finished their breakfast, threw around a few more ideas, and then proceeded to other topics. They split up with new energy and direction. They were beginning to see the pattern.

CHAPTER 32

Hall sat in a booth at O'Sullivan's, a mid-sized Irish pub, where apparently, it was safer to meet than at the Regional Center, despite all of its high security. Hall stirred his iced tea occasionally and played with the ice cubes and lemon slice while he waited for Fairchild. The pub was not just a drinking destination but also a restaurant, particularly during the day. Dark hardwood decorated the interior; each booth had high dividers, making them quite private. Even at noon, the restaurant was not well lit. It was obvious that a great deal of drinking and partying occurred here each night.

"Russ, there you are!" Fairchild squeezed into the seat across from Hall, his belly taking up the entire space between the back of the seat and the table.

"Don, how are you?" Russ extended his hand.

As Fairchild settled into his seat, the waitress arrived and asked if he wanted a drink. He ordered iced tea to match Hall's and then immediately ordered his usual club sandwich. Hall looked at the menu and ordered some soup; he wasn't really too hungry. The waitress departed, and there was some space for conversation.

"Don, look, you know I'm upset about my changed assignment. If you don't mind, can you just spill the beans so we can get that out of the way?"

"Just a second." Fairchild pulled a portable electronic device out of his jacket pocket, just smaller than a TV remote control. He pulled the antenna up, pressed a button on the top, and looked at the lights. He waved it around both sides of the booth, high and low. "It should be safe here. Uh, no hidden microphones. All clear."

Fairchild put his scanner away and leaned up to the table slightly, apparently to minimize the volume of his comments. He whispered, looking at Hall. "Russ, I'm sorry about the change of assignment; it surprised me as well. You know how bad it's gotten. I don't need to tell you that we have idiots running things mainly because of their loyalty to the President and their evangelical Christian beliefs. They seem to have no experience at all. They micromanage our affairs, looking at each and every case, demanding that we either pursue or ignore it based on the apparent loyalty of those being investigated. If they are in the fold, we ignore their case. If not, they get nailed—with trumped up charges if necessary. Believe me, if I had my way, you would be continuing on that case, particularly since there seems to be a string of cases that involve the PIT. But the people involved obviously have friends in the right places."

"Hmmm... I see." Hall took a drink of his tea. "Don, when I was in training, I was assigned to a case that involved the PIT. The investigation was aborted... aborted roughly the same way. That was about twenty-five years ago. I don't have any proof yet, but I can only imagine the string of PIT cases ignored over those twenty-five years."

"Hall, that is all well and good, but I don't want to risk my neck. My order for you to discontinue work on the Freeman case will stand. Any older case, do what you have to do, but keep me out of it. The old case you mentioned is probably off their radar screen, but it may not stay that way if you make any official requests for information. Be careful. This seems to be much larger than just a simple disappearance."

"Loud and clear, boss," Hall saluted, taking special note of the words "*do what you have to do*."

They ate the rest of their lunch, talking mostly about a recent fishing trip Fairchild had taken to Wyoming and the size of his largest catch. Nothing more was said about the PIT.

CHAPTER 33

"What's all the excitement about?" Shannon asked.

Dan had called a special "project meeting" at a table in the picnic grounds of Lake Azul Recreation Area. It seemed the here they could easily talk and not be in any danger of being overheard. It was Saturday, cool, clear, and dry. The picnic area overlooked a beautiful reservoir that had steep slopes on each side. It included a large, grassy open space mixed with tall trees and some dense bushes. So far, only a few people were trying their luck fishing, generally in boats on the lake. The friends sat at a picnic table with wooden top and seats, held together with a tubular steel structure. The top was etched with names, phrases, and some Valentines. Dan sat on one side so he could present to both John and Shannon equally.

"I'm not sure if I can stand it here with no coffee to drink!" Shannon pouted.

"Not to worry, my dear!" Dan reached into his backpack and pulled out a thermos of coffee and some cups. "I've got some Colombian right here!" They poured the hot coffee.

"Now, that's what I'm talking about!" she said with glee.

"I have to say, Shannon, your insight into the creation of Eve—that *rib* means *chromosome*—helped me refocus my attention on this. I may have some good stuff here. Unfortunately, it has more impact on the conventional view than the chromosome-rib connection."

"We're all ears," John said. "Go ahead and explain your story. Do your worst."

"I will, but I want you to reserve judgment until the end. You need to look at all the elements together. Plus, I've changed my views on some of the details. It takes looking at the entire story for it to sink in."

John and Shannon sipped their coffee and nodded their heads in agreement.

Dan had already set up his battery-powered laptop so he could refer to his notes. "Let's start with a fairly wide-angle camera lens and consider the implications of eating the fruit of the Tree of Knowledge of Good and Evil. What exactly happened at that time?"

Shannon spoke first. "Well, according to what's written in Genesis, not much happened at all. They already had symbolic language, so in terms of knowledge, they were way ahead of all other animals. Since Adam named all the animals long before that point, eating the fruit had nothing to do with that. They definitely became aware of their nakedness. It seems they became sexually aware at that point. That's about it."

"And what did they do?" John asked. "Oh yes, they jumped in the bushes and got busy, right?"

Shannon handled the question without even a small measure of embarrassment, although John's face reddened after he said it.

"Yep," Dan said. "That's exactly what I was looking for. Here's the verse." Dan moved his laptop to one side so they could both look at the screen. "It says: '*...and the eyes of both of them were opened, and they knew that they were naked.'*

"Their eyes being opened doesn't mean that they were blind up to that point; no one suggests that literal interpretation. You can't treat this literally. Opening the eyes has to do with their level of consciousness. Apparently, before that point, they didn't realize they were naked and didn't need aprons to cover their privates. This certainly implies that this tree has a whole lot to do with sexual awareness."

"We all know that sex is the result of original sin," John said. "Even today, the Catholic Church promotes the concept that priests are closer to God if they avoid sexual activities, and the result is the priestly vow of celibacy. Most Protestant churches have abandoned that practice, encouraging ministers to lead more balanced lives, with wives and families."

"Some even think *sex* is *original sin*," Shannon said. "These concepts are closely connected how ever you slice it.

John put his coffee down. "Traditionally, the *eyes being opened* means that man could choose between good and evil. At that point, sin entered the world. Does everyone directly inherit this sin? Or is it just the choice of good and evil, leaving it up to every man and free will to choose his course in life? Not everyone agrees."

Dan wanted to get to his point. "What is the meaning of the *Tree of Knowledge of Good and Evil* when compared with the pattern of life? I'll tell you, but first we need to understand the terms."

John and Shannon sipped their coffees.

"First, what does it mean *To Know* in the biblical sense?"

"That's easy," John said. "In the Bible, *To Know* means to conceive, to mate, to have sexual intercourse—carnal knowledge, if you will."

"Right. For example, consider the following verses in Genesis:

(Gen. 4:1) *And Adam knew Eve his wife; and she conceived, and bore Cain...*

(17) *And Cain knew his wife; and she conceived...*

(25) *And Adam knew his wife again; and she bare a son, and called his name Seth...*

"It's pretty clear. Although this use of the word *knew* is prevalent in Genesis, it's not widely used throughout the rest of the Bible. Usually the words *knew*, *know*, and *knowledge* mean what they do normally. But here, they mean just what you say, John—*sex*."

"I notice," Shannon said, "the interesting wording here. In each of the verses you read, Dan, first the man *knew* his wife, then she *conceived,* and then she *bore*, or gave birth to the child. If *conception* is becoming pregnant, *knowing* is certainly the sexual act itself. Also, the term *conceive* is commonly used today to mean to think or imagine something, again relating to the concept of knowledge."

"With this in mind," Dan said, "I claim we could rename the *Tree of Knowledge* the *Tree of Sex* or the *system of sexual reproduction*, taking the term *tree* to be a symbol for the idea of a *system*. Since good and evil are opposites, perhaps the notion of *good and evil* actually refers to the opposite sexes, male and female. John, please don't get sidetracked figuring out if male is good and female evil or vice versa. Good and evil are opposites and so are the two genders, from the standpoint of contributing genetic material leading to the offspring. Plus, I still have some other ideas on this I'll mention later. In any case, this tree should be restated as *the system of sexual reproduction using opposite sexes*.

"God warned Adam and Eve that they would *surely die* on the day that they ate the fruit of the tree of good and evil. Of course, there is a major problem for literalists when Adam and Eve don't die right away. However, if we interpret the *Tree of Knowledge of Good and Evil* to be the *System of Sexual Reproduction*, we have a much different situation, one that makes a lot of sense."

"I'm not sure I buy into this yet, Dan, but I don't have any problem with the Tree of Knowledge being related to carnal knowledge. It still doesn't change the meaning of the story," John said.

"Shannon, when we toured the Museum of Life, we reviewed the system of natural selection. For sexual reproduction to lead to adaptation through natural selection, it's necessary for the fittest individuals to produce more offspring than the less fit, with the less fit coming to an early death or at least not finding mates."

"Yes, that's vital to natural selection," she said. "After producing offspring and raising them to adults, the parents must eventually die or a huge population explosion would take place. And you can't have the benefits of adaptation through natural selection unless you have reproduction. Reproduction always produces more organisms; you definitely need a process that eliminates them at about the same rate. It follows that death is required, either by predators, accident, or simply a preprogrammed life span. In the end, if reproduction is included and if you want natural selection to have any hope of working, death is part of the system."

"Right. That's exactly my point. For natural selection to work, there must be death. The most fit must reproduce to spread their genes while the least fit must miss the opportunity. Reproduction means some of the population *must* die. This is not a choice. It won't work without it, period.

"Like we said at the museum, if people wanted to live forever, we'd have to stop having children or the population would grow without bound, and we'd start to die anyway due to lack of food, inability to eliminate waste, or rampant disease. Procreation would be severely restricted by necessity. Natural selection would cease."

"Okay, I think I get the picture. Let's say we all agree that you can't have everyone living forever and still let everyone have children," John said. "That's not too hard to understand. What does that have to do with this scripture?"

"Think of it this way," Dan said. "Perhaps Adam and Eve were faced with a simple statement of fact by God. Apparently, they weren't cognizant of sexual impulses before eating the fruit. At that time, it was perhaps possible for them to avoid a preprogrammed death. No death means natural selection would be defunct, like we said.

"If they elected to include sexual reproduction into the life cycle of humans—that is, eating the fruit—it would be impossible to live forever. Therefore, God warned them that eating the fruit and including sexual reproduction would also mean that physical death would be necessarily introduced into the human life cycle. This was a statement of the laws of nature in this area and not a commandment or a threat of punishment."

"Nice, Dan. This matches our concepts of natural laws we're all familiar with," Shannon said. "In other words, the laws of nature are not *threats of punishment*, although I guess you can twist them that way. You could say that gravity *threatens punishment* by forcing you to the ground. Water *threatens punishment* if you try to breathe it. It's ridiculous. That kind of thinking is a holdover from the pagan religions that felt that there was a god in each object and these gods were subject to emotions and impulses. The god of the ocean, Neptune, might get mad and punish you by drowning you.

"No, the world is not like that at all. The laws of nature are unemotional, unbreakable laws. No threats and no punishments. The laws exist without these concepts. Gravity is not a punishment. Neptune isn't poised to punish you if you make him mad. Our universe works without the concept of punishment in every other instance. It is consistent. And we should expect these laws to be the same in this case as well. No matter how you slice it, if you introduce sexual reproduction into the life cycle of humans, death will certainly result, either through a preprogrammed death or due to a scarcity of resources."

"Hold on," John said. "Let's say you're driving down the road, and you break one of the laws of physics. You'll crash and may die. So, nature *does* include threats and punishments, from this standpoint."

"John," Dan said, "you're making a simple but important mistake in your wording. You can't *break* a law of physics. If you're a lousy driver, you might crash. But in the process, you don't *break* any laws of physics. This isn't a cartoon. You follow *every last one*, including skidding across the road, hitting the guardrail, flying off the cliff, right up to and including the moment when your car is nothing but a crumpled ball of metal and you're being rescued by an EMT. These laws aren't breakable. If scientists ever find a way to circumvent one of the laws as we know it, they won't claim that the laws are suddenly flexible. The laws are hardcore. You can't break them. This is how the world works.

"In this case, if you reproduce, you must also die. It's like saying that if you drop a rock, it will hit the ground. There's no punishment here, just a statement of a law of nature. Death is not evil. Death is a requirement for this system to work."

A breeze blew suddenly through the park, swaying the oak trees and making them creak. Leaves made a sound reminiscent of water in a river. Boats on the lake bobbed on wind-driven waves.

"Remember the saying, 'The wages of sin is death'? I've got a new version: 'The wages of *sex* is death'," Shannon said. "If you include sexual reproduction, you must also include death. The wages of incorporating sex is that you must also include death."

"How true!" They laughed.

The laughter was a bit harder than normal as they fully realized the significance of these ideas. The pattern was beginning to crystallize.

CHAPTER 34

The air in the park was warming. The three friends left their picnic table and went for a stroll along the flat, paved roads of the park that wove through huge coastal live oak trees arching overhead. After making their way through gaps in the leaves, rays of sun marked the ground in irregular patterns. Scrub jays chattered high in the trees and an occasional gray squirrel scampered along the branches. Because Dan left his computer on the table, he didn't want to walk too far.

Dan said, "We spent quite a bit of time considering that DNA is the most minimal expression of a living creature. If we whittle 'you' down to the ultimate smallest, simplest expression, we have your complete DNA sequence and no less. Cutting DNA up into its constituent bases eliminates the order of those bases. The strand becomes worthless dust. All information about you is lost."

"Dan, you've gone over that point enough. We already firmly understand and believe that," Shannon said.

"I need to assert one more thing. DNA is common to all creatures."

"Yep, we agree on that too. Go ahead," encouraged Shannon.

"We already mentioned that the scripture in Genesis doesn't literally state that the serpent was Satan, and it makes little sense for the serpent to be a literal snake. So what is it?"

There was silence as Shannon and John spun this question in their heads. They didn't answer.

"Let me recite the verse again."

Now the serpent was more subtle than any beast of the field which LORD God had made.

"We've talked about two ways to interpret this statement. First, that the serpent is a real snake, and second, that the serpent is Satan, an idea that has really no support in the scripture."

"I wouldn't go that far, Dan," John said. There is that one reference in Revelation, remember?"

"Okay, but let's agree that it isn't supported very much, especially in the older texts."

"Fine. Go on," John said.

"I want to suggest that there is yet another way to take this statement about the serpent. Imagine examining all the *beasts of the field* to locate that one specific beast that is particularly *subtle*. According to tradition, that would be the serpent—the snake. Some translations use the word *crafty* as the correct interpretation of the original Hebrew instead of *subtle*. Line up all the creatures and look for the one that is the most crafty of all and pull out a writhing snake. But real snakes, as we mentioned, are not that subtle or crafty. Sorry, that interpretation doesn't fit very well at all.

"Instead, I would like to propose that we *slice the problem the other way*, so to speak. That is, consider all the beasts at once and focus on that one feature, of all features, that is the most subtle, but common amongst all beasts." Dan paused as if the others were going to finish the thought.

"I don't get it," John said.

"Try this. Visualize all the beasts lined up in a horizontal row. In the traditional interpretation, we would pick out one beast that fits our description—that is, that one which is the *most subtle*, or the most *crafty*. When we do it that way, they say we find the snake. Instead, slice across all beasts and select that one common feature of all beasts that is the most *subtle*." He paused again.

"I still don't get your point, Dan," John said.

"I don't want to give this away. I want you to make the connection yourself. The question is: What is the most subtle, the simplest expression of all the beasts of the field, that is all life?

"Dan, we already said that the most subtle expression was DNA," Shannon said.

"Do you get it yet?" Dan scanned their faces. John and Shannon were still blank.

"Oh, for heaven's sake!" Dan said, exasperated. "Listen. DNA is a serpentine or serpent-like molecule. It's the most subtle of all the beasts of the field, in other words, the simplest expression that's common to all the beasts that God had made." He looked at their faces. "The serpent is DNA."

Shannon and John were speechless as the truth of this interpretation started to sink in. John's mouth hung open; he stopped looking where he was walking, lost his footing, almost falling to the ground. His friends caught him and helped him stand.

A breeze could be heard blowing through the numerous trees, and leaves rustled nearby. A group of white egrets squawked in unison near the water's edge.

Dan continued. "We now understand the simplest expression of life, common to all life forms on earth. This simplest expression is the genetic code: DNA. You can't simplify further. If you have the DNA code and sufficient cloning technology, you could probably produce any corresponding life form, just like they did in *Jurassic Park*. Anything less than the full DNA sequence included in the chromosomes and you have only a bunch of worthless bases—household dust. We also know that it's common to all life forms on earth. There is no exception to that. None. DNA is definitely the most subtle form of all the beasts: you can't simplify further and still call it representative of a beast. To top it off, DNA is coiled about it self in a serpentine fashion. It looks like a serpent. Since the word DNA was not available, the Bible used this fairly cryptic description to represent DNA. And only in the last fifty years would we be able to understand this phrase with its true meaning."

A group of scrub jays chattered over their heads in a large branch of a nearby oak tree.

"Whoa. Stop right there. My head's spinning," begged Shannon. "The word *subtle* is sometimes translated as *crafty*. DNA is indeed the most crafty, serpent-like molecule common to all beasts of the field. It expresses exactly how any life form will be made. That's definitely the most crafty of all molecules. It is extremely crafty, being the basis of all life. And it can't be further simplified, so it's very subtle. Oooh! Dan, you're a genius!"

John was speechless and stood perfectly still. His breathing was short and choppy. Dan put his arm around John and helped him to continue walking the remaining distance back to the picnic table. By the time they got back to the table, John was recovering a bit more.

"Let's continue thinking along these lines," Dan said. "The first thing that happens is Eve's encounter with the serpent. The serpent asks Eve about the trees in the garden, and she tells the serpent that it's okay to eat of any tree except for the *Tree of Knowledge of Good and Evil*. This time, she says that God warned that they would instantly die if they even touched it.

"If the serpent represents DNA, this passage indicates that Eve was learning about sexual reproduction, natural selection, and the function of DNA. Although the story is told as if Eve were discussing this with the serpent, it's obviously not possible for chromosomes to talk with Eve. It's more likely that this meant that Eve was learning about DNA and genetics."

John, recovered enough to compose a sentence, said, "Dan, you say that Eve was learning all this stuff. How did she learn it? In other words, who told her? In the original story, the serpent talked to Eve and tempted her to eat the fruit. That's a pretty easy thing to visualize. Now, you're doing away with the serpent and assuming that Eve somehow is learning about DNA, but how?"

"That's a fair question, John." Dan thought for a moment. "I will grant that the text doesn't clearly explain how this happened, but it certainly is something that could happen in many ways, given the advanced sophistication of the Yhwh people. The video presentation on the darkness of a bush might be one way, such as in the burning bush scenario, to present the creation of the universe we talked about earlier."

"Yeah, okay. I guess that would be one way."

Dan continued, "The story says that the serpent explained to Eve that she would not die. I think this means that when a mother has a child, her genetic code is transferred to the child, and the child will preserve that code, mixed with the father's code, potentially producing an unlimited number of offspring after several generations. So, it's really true on a genetic level. Your genes don't die."

Shannon tapped Dan on the arm. "Dan, maybe this means that although you may physically die as a parent, your offspring will continue, and in them is your contribution to their genetic code. Eve was starting to understand the function of DNA and how it's preserved in subsequent generations."

"Sure. And another way to take it, Shannon, is to consider a race or species. Having offspring allows natural selection to occur, which improves the resistance of the race to environmental pressures, illnesses, and threats, thereby allowing the race to live forever. This also relates to the idea that Adam and Eve were not individual people, but a set of humans in those four fertile river valleys, and the species doesn't die, even when natural selection is included. It only improves the species over time.

"The next verse also mentions the eyes opening:"

> *For God doth know that in the day ye eat thereof, then your eyes shall be opened, and ye shall be as gods, knowing good and evil.*

"Here, *knowing good and evil* means incorporating sexual reproduction into the human life cycle, as mentioned earlier. Again, the word *know* is taken to mean *sex*.

> *And when the woman saw that the tree was good for food, and that it was pleasant to the eyes, and a tree desired to make one wise,*

"In this phrase, Eve is learning that sexual reproduction is pleasant and over time the process of natural selection would make the human race wise."

"I see," Shannon said. "This makes more sense to me. Sex is fun as well as being a means of reproduction. Kids can be fun too. With the action of natural selection—that is, keeping the genetic code for those who fare the best while allowing the others to be unsuccessful in finding a mate—will tend to improve the genetic sequence of the population, adapting it to more correctly fit the environment and therefore, achieving a form of wisdom. Gee, I like this... Sex doesn't seem evil to me. If it's evil, how can it feel so good? It just never made sense. Now it does."

"Now you see my point," Dan said. "Finally, Eve eats the fruit:"

she took of the fruit thereof, and did eat, and gave also unto her husband with her; and he did eat.

"Just think," Dan said. "Eve appreciated the tradeoff between a life with indefinite duration and one including sexual reproduction but also death. On the one hand, you have a limited set of adults that could live perpetually without any sexual reproduction, no need for any sex drives, sexual acts, or children. On the other hand, you have sexual reproduction, children, sex drives, and intercourse, along with natural selection and improvement of the species due to survival of the fittest and also, unfortunately, death. Eve chose the latter alternative, deciding to incorporate the system of sexual reproduction.

"Would you want to live in a world where a small set of humans lives without death, but where there are no—or few—children, sex drives don't exist or at least can't be acted upon due to overpopulation? Or, would you prefer a world where children's wonder exists, where sex and sex drives are useful, where a new generation can espouse new points of view and new ideas, but where there is preprogrammed death?"

"The choice is obvious," Shannon said. "This was not a failure of logic but an understanding of the basic pattern of life. The world would be a dull place without children, without sex and everything that follows. This was not a 'fall' or a failure at all.

"Eve chose wisely."

CHAPTER 35

Hall sat alone in the restaurant booth of a local sports bar, eating lunch and reading the *Los Angeles Times*. He suffered from the solitary life of an agent who had been frequently relocated to a new area in order to maintain his anonymity. Many agents have a hard time settling down and raising a family. Hall was no exception. It was only coincidence that he lived near the PIT again, where he had worked when he was an agent-in-training, twenty-five years ago.

Just as he was taking a swallow of beer, his cell phone rang. Hall finished swallowing, almost choking, set his glass on the table and pulled his phone off his belt. "Hall speaking," he answered, then wiped his mouth with a napkin.

"*Agent Hall?*" a woman's voice said.

"Yes, ma'am. How can I help you?"

"This is Rebecca from the Institute. You said I should call back later. I know I'm doing the right thing by calling, but I'm afraid."

"The best policy is to tell the truth. If you've done nothing wrong, there is nothing to worry about."

"I'm not afraid of that. I just don't want to lose my job."

"I understand."

"*You see, I don't really know about the boy you asked about. William Freeman. I can't remember that boy.*" She stopped.

"Is there anything you can tell me that can help me find out what happened to him?"

"Maybe. You see, many students go to another facility, and I never see them again. William may have gone there too."

"Where is the other facility?"

"*I've never been there. It's called the 'PITY Ranch,' but it can't be too far away. They're very restrictive. Almost no one goes there. I really don't want to say any more, Mr. Hall. I hope that helps you.*" Click.

Hall took another drink.

Hmmm. A secret facility. Now I'm getting somewhere.

CHAPTER 36

The sun was rising toward mid-day, but the picnic table was still comfortably in the shade. Dan wondered if John was quiet because he was trying to be fair to the new information without succumbing to his natural tendency to challenge it or throw it out. Or maybe he was still stunned. Either way, John was allowing Dan to proceed with this analysis without raising much objection, at least so far.

Dan continued. “The next section of Genesis details the immediate implications of eating the forbidden fruit. First, God learned that they ate the fruit and then, by the new interpretation, elected to include the system of sexual reproduction in the life cycle of man.”

> (Gen. 3:8) *And they heard the voice of the LORD God walking in the garden in the cool of the day: and Adam and his wife hid themselves from the presence of the LORD God amongst the trees of the garden.*
>
> (9) *And the LORD God called unto Adam, and said unto him, Where art thou?*
>
> (10) *And he said, I heard thy voice in the garden, and I was afraid, because I was naked; and I hid myself.*
>
> (11) *And he said, Who told thee that thou wast naked? Hast thou eaten of the tree, whereof I commanded thee that thou shouldest not eat?*
>
> (12) *And the man said, The woman whom thou gavest to be with me, she gave me of the tree, and I did eat.*
>
> (13) *And the LORD God said unto the woman, What is this that thou hast done? And the woman said, The serpent beguiled me, and I did eat.*

Dan said, “Here, Adam and Eve explain that they suddenly had sex drives and understood that they were naked."

Shannon seemed stern. "Why did God ask Adam if he had eaten the fruit and had to ask Eve how it happened? Wouldn't God already know what happened? Since he had to ask, the implication is that God is not all-knowing. It's just like the trial-and-error search for Adam's 'help meet,' Eve. Yhwh is described as a limited being, just like a human."

John shook his head. "Shannon, it could be that God just wanted Adam to have to incriminate himself. Just like when you know a child has done something wrong, you ask them to admit it. I really don't have any problem here."

"Of course not!" Shannon seemed disgusted with John's lack of curiosity. "Very well, John. Let's go on."

Dan continued to the next verse.

> (Gen. 3:14) *And the LORD God said unto the serpent, Because thou hast done this, thou art cursed above all cattle, and above every beast of the field; upon thy belly shalt thou go, and dust shalt thou eat all the days of thy life:*

"Here we learn about the fact that the serpent—DNA—is *cursed.* I had some trouble with this at first. It doesn't match the idea that it's not a punishment. Indeed, the idea that the Serpent is *cursed* doesn't make any sense under the view that the serpent represents *Satan* either. He was already cursed, even sent to the pit of hell by God. Why curse him again? If the serpent is just the snake animal, I understand that snakes are 'slimy' and give some people the creeps, but that's not what being *cursed* usually means. Plus, the words are *cursed above*, not below. What is the true meaning of being *cursed above all cattle and above every beast?*"

"I would guess," Shannon said, "that if something is *cursed*, it is *off-limits* and perhaps jailed or confined to an area where it cannot be accessed. Short of capital punishment, we imprison a person who violates our laws. That's how it's done today."

"God didn't eliminate the serpent; he just imprisoned it," Dan said.

"I see... I see what you're getting at." Shannon tapped her mouth with her index finger. Dan thought he could see the gears in Shannon's mind turning. "DNA... it's confined to the nucleus of each cell and never leaves, with messenger RNA delivering the instructions from the DNA strand to the ribosomes for protein production. Plus, the nucleus is in the center or *belly* of the cell."

"Right. Perhaps the term *belly* refers to the nucleus," Dan said. "That would be a great low-tech term for that cellular structure."

John remained quiet. Dan and Shannon were getting along very well in this discussion, and it seemed, once again, that John was being left out in the cold.

"It is clear: *Cursed above* is a way of describing the isolation of

DNA to the nucleus of the cell, which is a fact. It's not a negative comment but again, simply a statement of fact," Dan said. "God didn't get all emotional and smite the serpent with anger and force. That just isn't how the forces of nature work. They don't punish. They just are."

"You're stretching things here," John asserted, breaking his silence. "If we go along with the idea that the serpent represents DNA, the concept of being *cursed* could be a warning to mankind not to tamper with DNA through profit-motivated genetic engineering. I'm still worried about the fact that science immediately thinks it can start tampering with life as soon as it starts to barely understand it. I'm worried about cloning, stem-cell magic, and basically mucking with the code of life. Call me a dark-ages conservative if you want, I still think they're moving too fast here."

"That's a valid point," Dan said. "I worry about the immediate foray into genetic engineering in the 1970s as soon as scientists barely knew anything. The first thing they wanted to do was to change it, like taking a gene from an arctic fish that doesn't freeze and adding it to tomatoes. Now, we have frost-resistant tomatoes. Great job."

"But what if that fish also had big teeth?" asked John. "We might have to reissue the movie *Attack of the Killer Tomatoes* as a news clip!" They chuckled.

"Luckily, we haven't seen any huge problems from these first forays into this uncharted territory," Dan said. "Let's cross our fingers and keep a sharp eye for extreme science."

Shannon didn't seem to worry about this sort of genetic experimentation. She was a biotechnology major, after all. "It's simple. DNA is *cursed* by being carefully confined to the nucleus of the cell. It's an indication that it's very, very important to get the code right and preserve it from generation to generation and not to make any mistakes in the seventy trillion cells of the human body."

Dan said, "Let's try to make sense of the last phrase, *dust shalt thou eat all the days of thy life*. We encountered the term dust earlier: God made man from it. *Dust* likely meant the raw materials of the earth. Although you might consider *dust* to be a bad thing or a form of punishment, I don't think it's being used that way here. If you wanted to explain tiny particles to anyone without a microscope or other tools, you might show them the tiny dust particles floating in the rays of the sun."

"I know what you mean," John said. "Those little pieces of dust floating in the air. I'm always amazed how many there are. It almost makes you not want to breathe!"

"Pointing out those tiny particles of dust would be a good demonstration to explain very small particles," Shannon said.

"Also, most household dust—about seventy percent—is actually particles of human skin," Dan said. "Dead skin would probably be nutritious if we could stand to eat it. It's primarily proteins and their constituent amino acids. *Eating dust* probably means that DNA uses the basic elements and the basic twenty amino acids to construct proteins."

"*Eating dust* is a description about how the mechanisms of the cell are used to create proteins from amino-acids, or dust. That makes more sense than saying that a snake eats dust. Snakes don't eat dust. They eat mice, insects, and other animals, but not dust."

"Well, there is a snake-like animal that truly does eat dust," Dan said. "The asexual earthworm eats dust. It's an animal that's not much more than a section of intestine with the soil going in one end and out the other as it crawls."

"Oh yeah, I remember... it can be either sex or both at once—it's hard to forget that one!" John said.

"I don't see how it can be argued that *Satan* eats dust," Dan said, "at least not in any literal sense. Do angels—even fallen angels—need to eat? The serpent has already been cursed several times. Sentencing it to eating dust is no big deal. All that makes no sense at all. Having DNA *eat dust* by using the components of dust in the proteins it encodes is really much more literal.

"Shannon, what about this verse about the woman?" asked Dan, knowing Shannon would have an opinion:

> (3:15) *And I will put enmity between thee and the woman, and between thy seed and her seed;*

She supported her chin with her hand and stared into space, thinking. "Who is *thee* in this verse?" wondered Shannon. "Is God is still talking to the serpent?"

"Definitely," John said. "And, as Dan so carefully documented, *seed* means *bloodline* or *genetically related*."

"Well, under the interpretation that the serpent is a snake, *enmity*—hatred—makes no sense, except that snakes terrify many women," Shannon responded. "I'm not in that group, though. I've always liked snakes and even raised them as pets. Once you get to know them, there is no natural *enmity* between women and snakes, or for that matter, between the woman's *seed* or *offspring* and little baby snakes."

"What about under the interpretation that the serpent is Satan?" asked John.

"Okay, what would be the *seed of Satan*? We know that the offspring of Eve would represent the entire human race. You'll probably say, John, that we have enmity or a warlike situation between humanity and Satan. I don't know if Satan has offspring in the conventional sense, but perhaps the evil angels of Satan could be the *seed of Satan*.

"The interpretation of this is much simpler if we consider modern biotechnology knowledge and consider the serpent as nuclear DNA—that is, the DNA that we already said was *cursed above* and confined to the nucleus or belly of the cell. That would be the *seed* or *genetic pattern* of the serpent, DNA. But what is the *seed* of the woman?"

Shannon paused, waiting for Dan or John to come up with the answer. They both struggled to think of a genetic pattern that was the woman's and that had *enmity* with DNA. They looked this way and that, searching for an answer.

"Come on guys, you should know the answer to this!" They were starting to squirm, distracted by her challenge. Both drew a blank. Shannon gave up. "I'll tell you. I'm really disappointed, you guys!"

"Okay, smarty pants, please tell us!" John said.

"I already described what we know is the *seed of the woman:* mitochondrial DNA—mDNA—present in the mitochondria of every cell but originally only provided by the egg of the woman. Remember, the mitochondria have their own DNA, *mDNA*. It must be kept separate from the DNA in the nucleus so it doesn't get mixed up or accidentally combined. That separation is the *enmity* this verse speaks of."

"Bravo!" Dan clapped. "Enmity is finally clear!" John joined in and clapped weakly with Dan although the answer probably went beyond his immediate understanding.

Dan said, "We can move on to the next phrase:"

it shall bruise thy head, and thou shalt bruise his heel.

"You've been on a roll, Shannon. What do you think of this reference to bruising heads and heels? I don't think the conventional interpretation has any clue as to what this might mean, since Yhwh is apparently still talking to the serpent. If the serpent represents Satan, God would be saying that Satan's head would be bruised and that Satan would bruise *his* heel, but whose heel is *his heel*? Adam's?"

Shannon didn't answer. She looked up in the trees and closed her eyes for a moment.

"If Satan has already gone to hell, been cursed, and has eaten dust, there is little use in bruising his head, I know that much," Dan said.

"I've got it," Shannon said, snapping to attention. "Oh my!" She paused. "I can't believe this is here!"

CHAPTER 37

"How's your family these days?" asked Hall, leaning on the counter of the case records and evidence filing warehouse. Behind the counter was a huge room, walls lined with filing cabinets and in the center, eight workstations with clerks typing on computers, transcribing recordings from detectives and agents. At one end of the room stood a glass enclosed office with view of the records and evidence operation, perfect for the manager of the operation to keep a watchful eye over the incessant activity.

"My nerves are a wreck!" Bill Thoroski, manager of the records room, replied. "Our oldest son just started driving, and he's been driving us nuts! Between sports and homework, we haven't had much time for anything else. Plus, the amount of homework they give kids these days is ridiculous, and they expect us parents to understand it all."

"How's Judy?" Hall asked of Bill's wife. He filled out the official evidence request form.

"She's back to normal activity. Oh, and by the way, she wanted me to thank you for the get-well card. It's nice to have a wife again to help me with all these kids."

Hall handed the official records request form to Bill, which he accepted without really looking at it.

"Say, Bill. I need a small favor, if you don't mind. Hall tore a page from his small notepad and wrote the number of the *George Stanfield* case from years ago. "Can you dig up anything on this old case?"

Thoroski winked, acknowledging the unofficial request from his friend, with the understanding that he should keep the request quiet, and out of the tracking system.

"Well, let's see." Thoroski put the official form in the request basket and carried the small slip of paper back to the records area to search for the old file. He looked at the paper a couple of times and walked directly to the end of the long wall of filing cabinets and then around behind them to the next room. In another minute, he reappeared, empty handed. He walked all the way to the counter and then leaned toward Hall. He spoke quietly, "You've got a very old case there, but that isn't the problem. We have plenty of other cases in that time period, but that one is marked that it has been actively removed. Sorry, Russ, no cigar."

"Thanks Bill. That's what I needed to know."

"Hey, have you had any time to chase the little white ball?" asked Bill, straightening up.

"Not at all. My golf game was at rock bottom, but it's probably below the rocks now. I'm going to have to brush up on my skills before we waste time on the golf course. I was pathetic in our last game."

"I feel the same way. But I'm up for a game when you are."

"Thanks, Bill." They shook hands. Hall left the records room.

The file has been eliminated. That means they want to cover up all these cases for some reason. But why?

With the case file eliminated, he would have to go back to the area where Stanfield lived and see if he could find any clues. Every time he seemed to make progress, he got further from understanding what was going on.

CHAPTER 38

The three friends continued to sit at the picnic table, amazing themselves with the hidden secrets in Genesis.

“Hold on to your seats,” Shannon said. “I believe this verse

it shall bruise thy head, and thou shalt bruise his heel.

is a description of a very advanced process, one that scientists have only recently discovered.”

“You’re kidding. Another match?” John asked somewhat reluctantly.

“That’s right, and this one is perhaps the most astounding of them all. The more you read this literally, the more it corresponds to these advanced biological processes.” She paused, gaining their full attention. “I’m talking about telomeric shortening of the DNA strand. Let me refresh your memory about this very technical issue.”

```
5     3
A-T
T-A
G-C
C-G
 •••
A-T
T-A
G-C
C-G
3'    5'
```

“Please! And, remember, I’m way behind you and Dan on this biotechnology stuff!”

“Visualize that you have strands of DNA, each being a pair of ‘backbones’ with the four bases connecting them. It would look like a long ladder, sort of like this:” Shannon drew a ladder-like diagram.

“Remember, this is just a small section of a much, much longer string, and it would be twisted like a spiral staircase. Hard to draw, so I didn’t try. I’m only showing the ends. Those three dots in the middle mean this continues for another say, seventy million ladder-rungs. At this scale, it would probably extend across the continental United States. Fortunately, in the nucleus, our DNA is wound onto supporting structures to keep it organized.”

“Right,” John said. “I still remember the five hundred miles of hair.”

“Yeah, that would be about as much hair as forty people with hair averaging a foot long and with a thousand hairs per square inch.”

"Can we get off of your hair obsession please! I thought I was bad."

"Sure, go on please, Shannon."

"Now, each half of each DNA strand has ends. Science calls these the *five*, *three*, *five-prime*, and *three-prime* ends. The numbers refer to the actual structure of these ends, normally called the *head* and *tail* ends. The two strands always pair up with the head of one being aligned with the tail of the other. When the DNA is replicated, there is a zipper-head like molecule, *polymerase*, which builds a new mate to each side, resulting in exact replication. Those zipper-head molecules always work in the same direction, although it's possible to have several zipper heads working in the same direction but in different places on the strand. They work fast too, lining up millions of bases per second.

"The problem is that at the ends, dubbed the *telomeres*, the zipper head stops a bit early each time. It can't duplicate the last few bases in that region, thus a bit of DNA is lost in each replication. You probably remember this from the museum. Natural death may be one possible result of this shortening. The bases in the telomeres are not needed for the generation of proteins, but once the zipper head starts to delete bases used to encode something essential to the organism, the resulting protein will be corrupted and, according to this theory, natural cellular death would occur. I hope I'm not going too fast."

"I'm hanging on just fine. Go ahead," John said.

"Relating this to the verse in question, the *head* is the head end telomeric region of the DNA strand and the *heel* relates to the tail telomeric region. That is quite literal, indeed. *Bruising*, well, that relates to the base deletions that occur during replication."

A gust of wind could be heard in the distance making its way down the canyon. The sound increased until it reached them and blew leaves over the table. The flock of white egrets took off in the distance, squawking as they did so.

Dan clapped. "You're right! This passage describes the leading theory of natural death. The shortening or bruising of the ends of the DNA would mean cells could divide only a fixed number of times. This is lining up really well. You may as well go ahead and tell us what the next verse means, although I do have something to contribute. Here it is:"

> (Gen 3:16) *Unto the woman he said, I will greatly multiply thy sorrow and thy conception; in sorrow thou shalt bring forth children;*

"That's simple," Shannon said. "An obvious difference between female and male is that women bear the children, and we do undergo a great deal of pain during childbirth, more than any other known animal. Our births are almost always difficult. The baby's head is so large that the mother's pelvis must expand to allow the head through and at the same time, the baby's head is composed of a number of plates that can compress to become narrower during childbirth. It's no secret that Caesarean sections account for nearly a quarter of all births performed in the U.S. What other animal needs a surgical operation just to give birth?

"That handles the second part, *in sorrow thou shalt bring forth children*. But if conception means the actual unifying of sperm and egg, I don't agree that the word *sorrow* makes any sense for *conception*. Normal lovemaking doesn't require epidurals!"

"I've got a twist on that analysis," Dan said. "I looked up the translation of the word *sorrow* in Hebrew, and it has several meanings. One is the obvious: painful emotion. Another meaning may have more application."

"What is the other meaning?" asked John.

"*Womb*. A woman's uterus, where the fertilized egg develops."

"Oh, that's a nice change," Shannon said smoothly. "It makes sense that the woman's uterus would be increased in size during pregnancy and indeed, in the uterus, she brings forth children. My, that's interesting that the word for *sorrow* is the same for *womb* in Hebrew. This may also relate to the woman's menstrual cycle, a necessary addition if she is to have children. I don't know any woman who is happy about having a period!"

"What do you think about the next phrase, Shannon," asked John. Dan didn't want to touch this one, but it seemed John was still rubbing Shannon's nose in this.

and thy desire shall be to thy husband, and he shall rule over thee.

Shannon jumped on it, as expected. "Certainly, with sexual reproduction included in the life cycle, it's normal for the wife to be attracted to her husband. That settles the first part. Then I would say that it is a fact that the male of the species is physically larger and stronger; it's natural for men to have the upper hand, at least physically. Today, work requiring large muscles is easily avoided, and women should do just as well as men, even in high-tech combat situations."

The men fidgeted uncomfortably.

"I've got it." She snapped her fingers. "This is better."

The men looked up.

"The male decides the gender of the offspring, while the female doesn't have any say in the matter. Remember, mothers can contribute only an X, while the father can contribute either X or Y, in this way, *he shall rule over thee* means that the man will make the decision with regard to the gender of the baby by contributing either the X or Y version of the twenty-third chromosome."

A family started to set up their picnic at a table nearby but not so close that they would be able to hear.

Dan turned back to their conversation. "I like that better. It gets to the heart of the matter, and it's a simple fact that the male does decide the sex. It also explains the other misguided tradition suggesting that men should dominate in all decision making.

"Let's go on to the next verse."

> (Gen. 3:17) *And unto Adam he said, Because thou hast hearkened unto the voice of thy wife, and hast eaten of the tree, of which I commanded thee, saying, Thou shalt not eat of it: cursed is the ground for thy sake; in sorrow shalt thou eat of it all the days of thy life;*

"Most of this verse is simply repeating what had actually occurred. Except for the last phrase: *in sorrow shalt thou eat of it all the days of thy life.* The fact that the term *sorrow* means *womb* might be useful here. It makes sense to me that man, as symbolized by Adam, will be subject to the sex drive—that is, *eat of it* with woman near the womb *all the days of his life*. The *it* in this phrase relates to the fruit of the *Tree of Knowledge of Good and Evil*, interpreted as the *system of sexual reproduction*."

"It's a plain fact that men seem to always have sex on their mind!" Shannon said. Dan and John laughed uneasily. All this talk of sex and reproduction made the topic even more tantalizing.

Dan got back on track. "How about the next verses:"

> (Gen. 3:18) *Thorns also and thistles shall it bring forth to thee; and thou shalt eat the herb of the field; In the sweat of thy face shalt thou eat bread,*

Shannon was sure of the answer. "Here, natural selection is explained. For natural selection to work, it's necessary for humans to live in a challenging situation, as clearly described by *thorns and thistles* and *sweat of thy face*. Darwinian natural selection is understood to be beneficial for the human species, a necessary natural system for humanity to adapt to the ever-changing earthly environment. If natural selection is to be an active system, it's necessary for humanity to struggle to decide who the fittest really are, followed by natural death of those who are not as fit, and finally, sexual reproduction among the fittest. When Eve chose to go down this path and not continue to be childless, stagnant tenders of the Garden of Eden, She and Adam were ejected from that protective laboratory to the struggles of the world."

"You're scoring well today, Shannon," Dan said. "The next section also explains the necessity of death, the returning to the *dust*—the natural elements on earth:"

> *till thou return unto the ground; for out of it wast thou taken: for*

dust thou art, and unto dust shalt thou return.

"This is the physical death that is a logical requirement for natural selection to work. It's not a *punishment* for violating a commandment, but a natural consequence of sexual reproduction, natural selection, and adaptation to the environment."

Dan said, "Listen to this:"

> (Gen. 3:20) *And Adam called his wife's name Eve; because she was the mother of all living. Unto Adam also and to his wife did the LORD God make coats of skins, and clothed them.*

"They were about to be ejected from the Garden of Eden, a protected genetic laboratory. They needed some clothing for protection from the elements outside the safety of the Garden," Dan said. "Humans are somewhat maladapted for the environment outside the Garden. No other animal needs clothing. I guess it's fair to ask the question to intelligent design advocates: Why did God design us to need clothing when all other animals are adequately protected with fur? What an obvious design defect! Why should we need to get dressed every day? Is there a reason God couldn't have been a bit more intelligent about this?"

"Humans are quite a bit different from the other animals in many ways," Shannon said. "I already mentioned the difficulty in giving birth. Indeed, the need for clothing is another of those big problems in our design. I, for one, would not want to be furless, naked, and cold. If we all had fur, we wouldn't need clothing, would we? Our fashion industry would be defunct. John, I think I really understand the concept of intelligent design! Needing clothes was obviously by design because God is a *fashion designer*!"

"You killed that one before it ever came to life!" John said.

Everyone chuckled courteously even though the joke didn't deserve it. They were aware of their clothing. Dan noticed the slightly unbuttoned top of Shannon's blouse.

Dan said, "Consider this verse:

> (Gen. 3:22) *And the LORD God said, Behold, the man is become as one of us, to know good and evil: and now, lest he put forth his hand, and take also of the tree of life, and eat, and live for ever:*

"Since the first humans elected to incorporate sexual reproduction and natural selection, they moved beyond the laboratory curiosities and will take on a life on par with the creators—that is, *become as one of us*. This verse implies that the Yhwh people were very much like the humans they germinated here on earth. Otherwise, how could the early humans become one of them? They continually speak of themselves in the plural sense, as *us*, and the Hebrew word for man used here is more like humanity—a collective noun implying more than one entity.

"Now, let's consider the *Tree of Life.* If we accept that the *Tree of Knowledge of Good and Evil* is about sexual reproduction and its implications, what is the *Tree of Life?* Well, here's what I think: Apparently, there is another way to organize the life cycle of humanity such that we can live forever. This alternative or additional system is what the scripture is calling the *Tree of Life*. If we continue to define *tree* to mean *system*, it's not clear what this system is, but perhaps it's related to the idea that the telomeric shortening and natural death would be avoided. I don't have a good pattern match for the *Tree of Life*. Can you think of anything, Shannon?"

She paused for a moment. "Not right now, Dan. You may have a good point about telomeric shortening, though. I'll have to think about the mystery of the *Tree of Life*. We may not have that knowledge yet. If God has effectively hidden this information from us, perhaps we won't know what it is. If we can't determine the answer for this, it actually further solidifies our interpretation."

"Okay," Dan responded. "We'll have to wait on that one. How about this verse?

> (Gen. 3:23) *Therefore the LORD God sent him forth from the garden of Eden, to till the ground from whence he was taken. So he drove out the man;*

"Man would have to get along on his own devices outside the protection of the genetic laboratory of the Garden of Eden. The words *till the ground* imply that man would farm to obtain the food required for life.

> *and he placed at the east of the garden of Eden Cherubims, and a flaming sword which turned every way, to keep the way of the tree of life."*

"This description," Shannon said, "of *a flaming sword that turns every way* reminds me of the image of a radioactive object, such as uranium, that emits high-velocity particles in all directions, particles that fly right through your body and will break down DNA. Even a light dose of radioactivity can induce cancer, making it very difficult to obtain anything close to eternal life.

"I can envision that," Dan said. "But in addition to the flaming sword, we also have *Cherubim*. They're frequently mentioned in the Bible, envisioned as mutated winged beasts, a cross between a man, a lion, and an eagle. This could be the warning about dangers of genetic mutation from the use of radioactive elements. It could even be a warning about the possibility of obliteration through nuclear war. God has not hidden the *Tree of Life* from us but has protected it somehow. We may be able to find a match for the *Tree of Life* and yet realize that it would be impossible to achieve due to natural genetic mutations that occur from exposure to radiation, radioactivity, or cosmic rays."

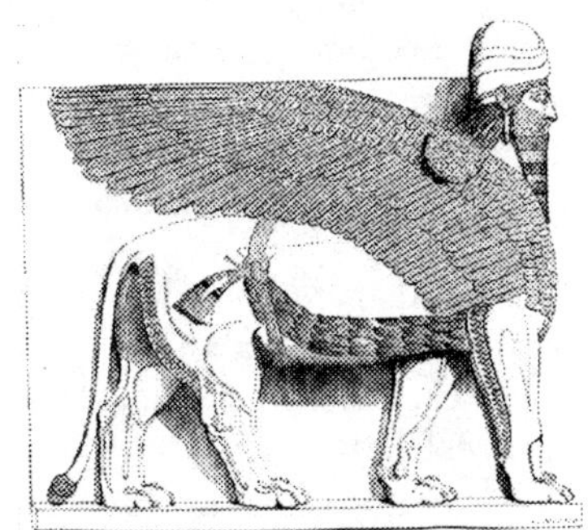

Typical of Cherubim from Ancient Mesopotamia

"That image of Cherubim is quite different from the cherry-cheeked angel flying around with a bow and arrow like Cupid," Shannon said. "Could the reference in Genesis actually be to the most famous of the ancient and enigmatic lion-man creatures?"

"What do you mean?"

"The Great Sphinx. The Nile River Valley was probably one of the four rivers of Eden. If the Great Sphinx is the Cherubim guarding the Tree of Life, this may be the key to unlock the mysteries of the ancient Sphinx and the amazing Pyramids of Egypt."

The egrets launched into flight in unison from the water's edge, squawking as they flew away from a child chasing them.

"Wow, good thought, Shannon," Dan said, leaning back a bit. "The Great Sphinx is one of the most mysterious objects on earth, the largest three-dimensional sculpture ever made. And it faces exactly east, just like the scripture says. I must say you surprised me with that connection. The famous Sphinx might be guarding the way to Eden and the Tree of Life. The Sphinx is apparently guarding the pyramids, which lie just behind it, just to the west of its protective influence. This matches the verse exactly. Are the Great Pyramids related to the *Tree of Life* and the entrance to Eden?"

The sun was shining off the lake creating a blinding stripe of light, interrupted by the fluctuations of waves. A group of fishermen floated near the shoreline, casting their lines.

"Whoa, Dan. Whoa. You are jumping to conclusions." John wasn't ready for these sudden leaps.

"Okay, but, let's keep that idea in mind. We might be able to link that more tightly to our pattern later."

"Fair enough. But, just stop going crazy on me!"

"Dan, that's the end of chapter three of Genesis," Shannon said, standing up and stretching to the side. "We've done enough damage for one day. Let's sleep on what we have done so far and see if the match seems correct or just a sham."

"It is very impressive," John said. "I'm going to do you and myself a favor and not rip your ideas apart just yet. It's an amazing match. But, you've reduced a commandment, threat, Fall, and punishment to a statement of fact followed by a wise choice and natural implications. When we get back together, I'm sure I'll be able to tell you where you went wrong."

"Sounds reasonable to me," Shannon said. "Throw rocks at it, that's what science is all about!"

Dan checked the people around their area and could see no reason to be concerned about surveillance. The group realized they had spent a bit more time than originally intended, so they spent no more time talking, said goodbye, and walked to their separate cars. On the way out, Dan noticed Shannon and John spending some time holding hands by her car. *They seem to fight all the time, and now they're holding hands. I don't get it.* Feelings of jealousy surprised him. Dan always knew that John had a thing for her. But John and Shannon seemed to be on different wavelengths. *Shannon and I do well together, but I don't want to intrude on their relationship. I'm happy having both John and Shannon as friends.* Dan didn't really know what to do. He wasn't even sure what he wanted. But he did want to get closer to Shannon.

He drove out onto the road, the image of the Sphinx guarding the Tree of Life and entrance to the garden, somehow related to the ancient and enigmatic Great Pyramids of Egypt, continued to persist in his mind. *Somehow, these must all be related.*

Dan pulled around the corner and onto his street. He noticed a plain sedan in front of his house. *I wonder whose car that is.* He parked his car and walked up the front rock steps. A man stood on his porch.

CHAPTER 39

Dan finished walking up his steps and approached the stranger on his porch. "Can I help you with something?"

"Good afternoon. I'm Special Agent Hall with the FBI." Hall showed his badge to Dan. "I'm looking for a... uh, Daniel Stanfield."

"I'm Dan Stanfield. Is there a problem?"

"If you don't mind, I'd like to ask you a few questions."

"Sure, come on in." Dan unlocked the door and pushed it open. Hall followed him in. Dan turned on the lights and set his canvas backpack down. "Would you like a glass of water or perhaps a soda?"

"Actually, I'm fine. I've been drinking water in the car. But, thanks for offering."

Dan obviously wasn't prepared for company. His living room, if it can be called that, was, as usual, stacked with piles of books and papers, leaving only several narrow pathways to get through.

Hall glanced toward the end of the room where, instead of the typical TV, an array of computer screens looked like the control center of a spaceship, the screens being updated with graphical computer output. "You're into computers?"

"I do fiddle around a bit." Dan moved ahead of Hall to clear some stacks of information, freeing up a chair for the agent.

"Here, have a seat." They sat in Dan's green plastic patio chairs at the end of the dining table. Dan's mind raced to formulate a reason that the FBI would want to talk to him. *We've gone too far in our discussions. The FBI was ready to put a stop to it... No, that couldn't be it... That's just insane. Well, if it was not about our project, what could it be?* Dan decided to wait and see what the agent had to say.

"Dan, I'm working on a case, and I'm hoping that you will be able to shed some light on it." Hall fished out a small notepad and pen.

"I doubt I can help, but I will if I can."

"What was your father's name?

"My father... uh, George. George Stanfield."

"And his current address?"

"Sorry, he's no longer alive. He died in a car accident when I was ten."

Since the accident, Dan had rarely had anyone ask him about his father. He and his mother had moved just after his father's death, so no one asked him about it much. But this was getting strange. In the span of only a few days, his father had been mentioned both by Walker and now by this FBI agent. *I wonder if Hall is after Walker. He told me to be careful. This is probably what he was worried about.*

"Your father worked at the Pacific Institute of Theology, right?"

"That's right, the 'PIT.' He was a theologian, a researcher and writer, but I was pretty young then. I didn't really know what he worked on. I guess some sort of religious stuff."

"Did you see your father's body after the accident?"

"Well, no. They said it was too far gone for any open-casket display. We had a small memorial service with our immediate family. My mother was very protective. She didn't want me to be adversely affected. Geez, I was only ten. It was hard enough for me to lose my father. Seeing a mangled dead body, that would have probably scarred me for life."

"That makes sense. Did you have any further encounters with the PIT?"

"We moved away immediately." Dan fiddled with a bottle cap from the table. "I was so young." Dan was starting to get worried about all these personal questions.

"You may be surprised to hear that I worked on your father's case when I was still in training."

"No kidding? It's been twenty-five years. I'm impressed. Still working on it are you?"

"Well, not exactly. It was closed long ago. Prematurely, at least in my opinion. I was just working on a new case that also involved the PIT, and it's been closed suddenly as well."

That other case was probably all about Walker, I suppose.

"I don't want to get your hopes up, but there may be some connection between these two cases. It may shed some light on the exact details of your father's death."

"Really." Dan continued to fiddle with the bottle cap. *My father died in a car accident.* Dan had come to terms with this many years ago, but these questions were stirring up new emotions that he didn't understand. He felt like he was ten all over again.

"Daniel Benjamin Stanfield, get over here and sit down!" his mother, who was dressed all in black, said sternly. She motioned to the small, white folding chair next to hers under a temporary shade structure. Danny reluctantly took his seat, knowing that she meant business when she used his full name. He watched the birds and squirrels that were active nearby, but his tears seemed to be never-ending. His mother handed him another tissue. The full reality of his father's sudden demise was a concept beyond his youthful age, but it was still a huge shock; he resisted even sitting with the group seated in the rows of white folding chairs. A large casket sat in the front of the shaded area, flowers in stands on each side. The casket was closed. Only a few people were there. Danny knew only Aunt May.

He now remembered how his mother had looked and acted in those days after his father's untimely death. *Was she overcome with grief of the loss over her husband?* Dan had a realization. He recalled the answer with a slight extra pump of adrenaline. No, she was not. She was more afraid than sorrowful, afraid like a helpless small animal being pursued by a large and hungry predator. Was her fear just part of the fact that she was suddenly a single-parent mom who would need to fend for herself, without her loving partner? There was more behind it. But that was as far as his speculation could take him.

A friend of Dan's father, a theologian and minister, but not someone from the PIT presided at the funeral. *That's another interesting twist*, Dan thought of his recollections. *No one at all was there from the PIT.* Was Walker there? *No, he could not recall Walker.* After the words of the minister reading of the Twenty-Third Psalm, the group split up quietly and walked to their cars. Dan remembered looking back at the coffin as they walked out of the burial area.—Mom, when do they put the coffin in the ground? —Oh, they do that later, she said.

"Mr. Stanfield... Mr. Stanfield," Hall said, raising his voice. "I said, is there anything at all you can remember about the situation with your father?"

Dan's mind snapped back to the present. He dropped the bottle cap on the table. "Sorry. Uh, no... nothing." Dan really didn't know much. He wasn't just acting ignorant. It seemed the best memories of his father's face were from pictures his mother gave him. For once, Dan was short on answers. Sure, Walker had mentioned his father, but Dan didn't want to reveal that conversation, at least not yet.

"Here's my card. Please call if you remember anything."

"I'll do that. Thanks."

Hall stood up and Dan escorted him out to the porch. He then watched him descend the steps and head for his car.

It was almost two weeks since first meeting Walker. Now, Dan was looking forward to seeing him again. *He may know something more about my father.* Dan turned into his house and sat in front of his computer array in his wheeled task chair.

* * *

After Dan entered his house, Hall turned back, walked to the rear of Dan's car, reached under, and attached a small cigarette-pack-sized device to the undercarriage. Then he left.

CHAPTER 40

John flopped into his chair. "You've ruined the story... You've turned it on its head!" Their coffees were fresh, and the crowd at the coffee shop was still light. "Sorry, my friends, I just don't buy it. You say the *Fall* is a *wise choice*, *Satan* is now *DNA*, and *original sin* is nothing more than *sex!* I'm afraid you've turned the sacred Holy Bible into a big joke."

"Having a good morning, John?" Dan said, smiling. "Look, I realize it's certainly a new way to look at things. It's different, but what's wrong with it?"

"Well, for one, the *Tree of Knowledge of Good and Evil*. You say it represents the *System of Sexual Reproduction between the two sexes*. That's a huge stretch. I looked at the original Hebrew for the word *knew* that you claim this means *sexual relations*. Well, that may be how it is used in the phrase 'Adam *knew* Eve.' But it's not the same word as the Hebrew for *knowledge* as used in the *Tree of Knowledge*. The level of consciousness of Adam and Eve seems to have changed, since it says their *eyes were opened*."

"Hang on to your chair, John, I actually agree with you."

"Huh?"

"I've got an alternative way to think about this, but first I need to build a picture in your mind," Dan said.

Shannon seemed amused that the two men were sparring over a single word meaning sex.

"Fine... go on," John said, noticeably calming down.

"The question I want to ask is this: What is *knowledge* with regard to life? We live in a world where we can gain knowledge not just through first-hand experience but hopefully from other people, books, and the general culture. *Culture* is the preservation of certain information from one generation to the next."

"Sure. Stories, songs, dance. What of it?" John asked.

"It's more than that," Dan said. "Humanity is blessed with the unique capacity for symbolic language. The written word is now the principal means to transmit culture from one generation to the next. And the first material to be written down in past centuries was religious culture, always the most carefully preserved and transmitted. In AD1455, Gutenberg invented movable type, and the first volume produced was, of course, the Bible. In 1904, the offset printer was designed, ushering in the age of production printing and books that everyone could own. Today, there are more than fifty thousand new book titles published every year, with millions of copies printed. The Internet has further accelerated the explosion of information and, hopefully, of knowledge."

Shannon swallowed hard. "Some would argue that point. Remember the quote from Einstein: '*Information is not knowledge.*' Having a wealth of information does not mean you know any more. The Internet is nice, but there's so much trash!"

Dan said, finger in the air to make his point, "Focus on truth. The scientific method and peer-reviewed journals are a formalized approach for the transmission of culture and knowledge; they attempt to avoid bad information and move from information to knowledge. Before new theories are accepted as scientific fact, other scientists must replicate the experiments to validate the theory."

"Right, Dan. That testing is key because it ensures the reliability of the knowledge and helps people to avoid mindless beliefs and wrongheaded ideas," Shannon said. "Constant testing through experiment is undoubtedly the most reliable way to formulate knowledge. Without it, we would still think the world is flat and everything was made of earth, wind, fire, and water."

"And to be able to communicate these ideas and theories, you need symbolic language," Dan said without any gap. "Humans are unique in their use of symbolic language to transmit culture and knowledge from one generation to the next. Animals may teach their offspring a thing or two, but they rely on *instinct* to bestow behaviors necessary for survival. Only in humans is knowledge transmitted using symbolic language. Animals in nature automatically know how to hunt, raise and nurture their young, and how to behave in social groups. And they do a great job of it, even if separated from their parents at birth. That's the knowledge I'm talking about."

Dan paused, expecting Shannon to finish the thought.

John looked like he had missed the train. "Okay, Dan. But how does this relate?"

"Well, the important question is this: How is instinctive knowledge transmitted?"

"Yes, that's it," Shannon said, getting back in sync. "Well, instinctive knowledge could be propagated by one thing and one thing only—nature's program: none other than DNA!"

"Well done, Shannon! Life uses DNA to remember and transmit knowledge. It records how to build the organism, how the organism is to behave as an individual, and how it is to behave in higher level social structures. And, DNA is formulated and refined through natural selection. Each generation acts as an experimental scientist, testing minute variations on the theme, keeping the best and throwing out the rest. Each generation is mated with the best of that generation, the best traits and behaviors kept for the next set of mating, the bad results thrown out without reproducing."

Shannon said, "In essence, within each species, the set of DNA variations encodes the knowledge of what works in the environment, the good ideas."

"Perfect, Shannon. Now, with that foundation, I can make my point. I believe that's what's meant by the *Tree of Knowledge of Good and Evil*," Dan said. "The miracle of the genetic code combined with natural selection. Survival of the fittest is a learning machine of the largest order. DNA is the means to keep track of the knowledge. *Good and Evil* is the success and death, the good and bad, that natural selection chooses and refines."

"DNA is all about information and knowledge nature's knowledge," Shannon said. "The amazing thing to me is that we are able to understand these underpinnings of life—nature's scorekeeping mechanism. Life as we know it is all about knowledge. DNA is the means to record that knowledge. Sexual reproduction provides variation by combining the traits of the parents. Natural selection chooses the best, the *good*, and discards the worst, the *evil*. All these functions are intimately related. What gets me is that all this is clearly outlined in this ancient scriptural passage."

"The *Tree of Knowledge of Good and Evil*," Shannon said, "still relates to the system of sexual reproduction, heredity of traits, and natural selection, as you first suggested, Dan. I like the new way of looking at it." She turned to John. "Does this settle your concern about the word *knew*, John?"

John was quiet for a moment. His confrontational energy had abated. "Okay, I'll accept this concept of knowledge. It's clear that DNA can encode a great deal of information, and certainly it could be what is described here."

Dan and Shannon smiled at each other as if they had been on the same team and had conquered a determined adversary.

"I've got another issue though," John said.

Shannon and Dan both groaned playfully. "What?"

"Well, the concept that Eve made a wise choice. It's clearly refuted by later scripture. Paul writes about it in First Timothy. Here, let me read this."

> (I Tim. 2:11) *Let the woman learn in silence with all subjection. But I suffer not a woman to teach, nor to usurp authority over the man, but to be in silence. For Adam was first formed, then Eve. And Adam was not deceived, but the woman being deceived was in the*

transgression.

John was adamant. “There’s no question. This passage clearly supports the traditional version of the story. Obviously, Eve’s choice was not wise. She was deceived to violate God’s commandment. This relegated woman to a second tier, both in the church and in society. And rightly so. Women are the lesser sex and are out of place trying to act like priests and pastors.”

Shannon let out a puff of air and shook her head in disbelief.

Dan tried to rescue the situation. “At first glance, John, I would say you have a good point. However, on second thought...” Dan paused for a moment, tapped his mouth with a pencil. He said, “Yes, yes. Listen to this.

“First of all, we’d have to agree with the part that says Adam was created first. In our new interpretation, the fact that genetically, the man has both X and Y components of the twenty-third chromosome pair explains the authority of man over woman. Man is certainly dominant in that important respect: The father controls the gender of the baby. Of course, it is still a matter of chance which sperm will fertilize the egg, but the sperm is of both kinds, either X or Y. The mother’s egg has no say in the matter. This maps into the part about the woman learning in silence.”

“Yes, I see what you’re saying,” Shannon said. “The woman will *learn in silence* because the egg does not make the determination of the baby’s gender. The sperm does that.”

“Right.”

John said, “You’re still left with the last part which clearly says that Eve was *deceived.* Deception does not imply a *wise choice.* Explain that!”

“You have me in a corner, John, but there is a way out. First, the word *deceived* may have changed in it’s meaning since those ancient times. We use the word *conceived* to mean both that a person thinks of something and in another sense that that the egg is fertilized and is successfully developing in the uterus. Perhaps the word *deceived* could also mean two things, the usual sense when a person reaches a false conclusion based on misleading information and second, perhaps also something to do with life. The word *deception* is similar to *conception* and could be a way to refer to the process of moving from the protective environment of the genetic laboratory of the Yhwh race and placed into the reality of the terrestrial world, thorns and thistles to boot. Or it could be another name for death, which was introduced as a inescapable part of the life cycle of mankind. *Conception* means life; *deception* means death.

“If you accept the hidden interpretation, Eve was clearly choosing between two alternatives. One choice is conception, sexual reproduction, children, and therefore, and unfortunately, death—that is, *deception*. The other choice requires limiting the population to a small number of people with unlimited life spans, no children, no conception, and no deception. In other words, no sex. If you favor new life, you also have to allow death. How could this be anything but a wise choice?"

Shannon was still perturbed. "This section is typical of excuses the church uses to subjugate women, keeping only men in positions of power. Eve clearly made a wise choice, turning the tables. Eve took the action, and man has had to follow her lead. I'm sorry, but the church has had this one completely upside down!"

"Shannon, you're just going to have to accept your place in the world," John said. "Men are in charge here, and we'll always be in charge. The church was only reflecting this fact of human nature."

"Oh, John. You are so ridiculous you make me laugh, or cry, I'm not sure which!"

Dan couldn't help but think, *their relationship, whatever it is, is doomed.*

CHAPTER 41

Dan sat in front of his computer array, thinking.

No matter when it happens, one of the most traumatic events in anyone's life is the death of a parent. But it's not supposed to happen when you're only ten. The agent asked me about my father, but I know almost nothing. It's embarrassing.

Dan had never visited his father's grave. For that matter, he didn't even know where it was. Strange, now that he thought about it. Sure, he understood that it would devastate a ten-year-old to see the mangled body of his father. But you wouldn't see the body by just visiting a cemetery grave site somewhere. Why hadn't he and his mother ever visited the grave? It was a question that he could only recently start to consider. Maybe his mother thought that would be difficult for a young boy to process that death, or perhaps she was in denial. And whenever he did bring it up, it seemed his mother had always answered only vaguely, never really answering his questions.

With the Internet, I should be able to find where my father is buried without too much difficulty, Dan thought. He opened another browser window to view lists of the deceased in likely cemeteries. The Internet had grown from a Defense Department prototype to worldwide ubiquity in just over a decade. Dan's generation was fortunate; it had grown up with computers and had ridden the wave of the dot-com bubble. Dan was a perfect example of an adept surfer on that wave, the ride finally paying off with a house near the coast and time for interests in sailing, cycling, and various technical issues. Of course, he also maintained his love of history and science. And now, he couldn't stop thinking about religious matters and this crazy project.

Dan was adept at using the Internet to find what he needed. But today, he was getting nowhere. His intensity only increased with each failed attempt. Like a dog looking for a bone buried long ago, his focus increased as he found no bone under any rock. Finally, he got up from his computer, walked to the window, and looked out.

Nothing! I can't believe that my father's name isn't even listed! Perhaps, he reasoned, *many of the cemeteries had only recently opened their web sites. Maybe the shortage of information was not so hard to understand after all.* Dan struggled to remember any unique details about his father's funeral. He recalled walking to the parking lot with his mother and looking back at the entrance to the cemetery. *There must have been a sign...*

Dan closed his eyes and held the bridge of his nose with his fingers. The image of the sign formed in his mind. What did it say? Dan looked into the darkness of his memory. He tried to make out the words...

Green Lawn Memorial Park

Dan snapped his fingers. "That's it!" He trotted back to his desk and started a search for the name. Several possible matches were listed, and he clicked the one that seemed right. However, after reviewing the web site, he could find only contact information and no way to directly search for the deceased. He dialed the telephone number.

"*Green Lawn Memorial Park. Welcome!*" the recording said. There were some announcements that these days are always part of any call to a business. Dan pressed the button to speak to a real person. Some moments elapsed. He clicked his mouse and fiddled with his computer while he waited.

"Customer Service, Crystal speaking. May I help you?"

"Thank you. I'm looking for information about my father, George Stanfield. He died about twenty-five years ago, but I have only vague memories. I recall that we had a memorial service at your cemetery. Is he buried there?"

"*Uh, sure, I can look that up for you, Sir. We have everything on computers, you know, so, like, this should be easy. I say 'should' 'cause I'm still just learning how to use these silly programs, you know.*" There was some background noise on the line, as if she were moving around and getting situated. "*What was the guy's name again?*"

"Stanfield, George Stanfield."

"Hmmm. Yeah..." She seemed to be working. *"I like typed it to search for anyone buried here by that name."* A short pause was followed by an explanation. *"Oh wait, I got it."* And after another longer pause, *"Is it S-T-A-N-F-I-E-L-D?"*

"Yes, that's right."

"Sorry, but..." she paused. *"There's no record of that name."*

"Did you check for *anyone* with that last name?"

"I already tried looking through the list for names that were, you know, about the same. Are you sure it's like THIS cemetery?"

"It's been a long time, but I do recall seeing your sign after my father's memorial service."

"*Memorial service? Hey, I have an idea. I can check on memorial services. Just a minute.*" There was a short delay and more background noise. "*They don't put those in the computer, you know. I... I guess I'll have to look into the, you know, old scheduling books. I don't even know if they still have those from like twenty-five years ago.*" Dan could hear shuffling of paper and opening and closing of books. Finally, she came back on the line. "*Yeah. Here it is.*" Dan's heart beat faster. "*George Stanfield. Yep. A memorial service was held here. You were right about that.*"

"You mean there was a memorial service but no burial?"

"*That seems right. Not uncommon, you know, 'specially if the body's going to be like cremated, or something like that. I can check.*" Another pause was filled with similar sounds. "*Sorry. Gee, that's weird. There's no cremation... or, you know, at least we didn't handle it. And, it doesn't say the body was moved to like anywhere else, but I'm sure that's probably, what happened, you know.*"

"You mean you had the memorial service and then lost track of the body?" Dan could feel himself getting angry. *Calm down; anger will get you nowhere. She's obviously just a kid.*

"I'm like sure we didn't, you know, lose track!" She paused, her voice a bit flustered. *"These records are like incomplete; a simple, you know, oversight, I'm sure. We'd like never do that. The laws are, you know, like strict."*

"Is there any thing else you can tell me?"

"Not really, sir. That's the only information I have."

"Thank you. Thank you very much. Uh, you've really helped me out."

"Thank you for calling Green Lawn Memorial Park."

Dan placed the phone in the cradle and sat back in his chair, stunned by the conversation. That memorial park was probably in violation of more than one law regulating the handling of dead bodies. Or perhaps it was due to the clerk's confusion or plain ineptitude. *I should probably visit the cemetery myself to see if I can find his grave.*

Dan was feeling many emotions; he couldn't understand why all this was happening. The recent multiple inquiries about his father were all too weird and coincidental. With both his parents now gone, an intense sense of loneliness swept over him like a tsunami decimating a coast. Then a surprising thought came to him: He desperately wanted to talk—talk with someone to fill this sense of emptiness. Shannon.

CHAPTER 42

"Well, Shannon, you might as well throw in the towel on your silly story of evolution," John said, folding his arms. It was Wednesday morning at the coffee house. A couple of days had passed since they last spoke, and John was taking the offensive. His cutting tone and words were in distinct opposition to the forced half-smile on his face.

Dan looked over his coffee cup and waited to see how Shannon would handle the challenge. It seemed that as a creationist, John couldn't resist challenging Shannon's evolutionist beliefs, despite any desire he may have had for a deeper relationship with her.

"Sorry, John, that's only wishful thinking." John's attack didn't seem to ruffle her feathers much at all. Her eyes and smile registered that she understood the friendly jab, while at the same time accepting the challenge to spar. But there was a change in the tone of the conversation. Dan knew she didn't like the male domination slant John had been endorsing in the past few days.

"Shannon, you're ridiculous." John leaned across the table and waved his hands, his face getting redder with each word, the veins almost popping from his forehead. "How can you believe that we started from nothing, with only chance as our guide? We agree that the book of Genesis describes advanced facts of biology, right?"

"I'm sure I don't need to answer that, John," she replied calmly. "Have you suddenly forgotten our talks over the past two weeks?"

"Shannon, discovering biological information described in ancient literature doesn't fit with your cherished beliefs that we arose by a fluke of nature. Sorry, evolution can't explain how advanced technical information—the structure of DNA, natural selection, even information about, what are they?... Oh yes, *telomeric deletions*—you can't explain how that information could've been known in ancient times... how it could be described clearly in these ancient biblical stories. There was a guide—divine inspiration, the Lord God, the Yhwh of Genesis." John slapped his hand on the table with each word. "God must have revealed that advanced information to Moses so he could describe it in Genesis. Here, we have indisputable proof that, indeed, God created our world. Face it, Shannon, evolution is a hoax!" John sat back and crossed his arms, but he really didn't settle down very much.

Dan held his cup to his lips partially as a shield. John's words were sharp. And even worse, he had a valid point. Dan knew that Shannon agreed that the linkage they had found in Genesis was very convincing and could not be written off as a simple coincidence. At the same time, Dan was surprised by John's attack, especially after seeing his two friends together in the park holding hands. It didn't make sense.

Shannon leaned into the conversation. "I'll grant that technical information about biology is hidden in the stories of Genesis. It seems we agree on that. But you're the one with the problem, my dogmatic friend."

John kept his arms crossed. "I've got no problem. I like the connection; it only more clearly authenticates the Bible as a sacred document."

"John, you're too much. From our interpretation, Eve understood the positive role of DNA and natural selection in the life cycle of humanity. She chose the wise course—not unlimited life spans, but life spans limited to what we see today, about a hundred years. She chose children who would learn and develop and fill us with new ideas, goals, and outlooks. She chose love, relationship, and indeed sex. And she chose natural death as a necessary and unavoidable component of the system, not as a punishment.

"The result was just what Yhwh said it would be. Yhwh warned that death would be included in our life cycle... and it was. There was no commandment of God to be disobeyed. Yhwh stated only the facts of the system of natural selection to Eve. There was no threat of *punishment,* no *Fall,* and your worst nightmare: Since there was no Fall, there was no..." Shannon used her fingers to put quotes in the air, "'*original sin.*' What Eve chose was not a sin. No, it was just the opposite. It was a wise choice—a choice offered freely and accepted with wisdom and understanding.

"Now, here's the kicker: How can you say that Christ had anything to die for, if there is no original sin? Face it, John, all your beliefs are based on nothing."

John's face flushed. Dan could see John's jaw muscles flexing near his temples as his teeth clenched rhythmically.

Shannon continued her attack. "How does the story of Jesus dying on the cross to cleanse us of our original sin make any sense? Without original sin, how can it? I'll tell you. It makes no sense, none at all. Christ is obviously nothing more than a myth! A fabrication! A lie!"

After Shannon stopped talking, an uneasy quietness seemed to settle into every nook and cranny of the coffee house. Other patrons had stopped talking and were now discretely listening in. The ticking of the clock on the wall suddenly seemed to be the loudest sound in the room. Dan could tell that even for Shannon, saying those words out loud was painful.

Those biblical stories seemed to be part of the fabric of society, familiar to nearly everyone. Like rumors repeated enough times, they seemed absolutely factual. But Shannon's words came from her dominant analytical and rational side, a side that left no room for believing such stories.

Yet John had a point, and for Shannon the sting of John's verbal sword would be hard to ignore. The theory of evolution did not mesh with the new interpretation of the ancient stories in Genesis. Indeed, it didn't make sense for DNA to have been understood in the days of Moses, especially in sufficient detail to outline it in Genesis with such clarity.

Dan looked at his friends. He could see that Shannon's remarks impacted John deeply. His eyes were red and puffy. He looked one way, then another, searching for something to conceptually hold on to. It seemed that Shannon had just ripped everything out from under him and he was in a free-fall.

Dan wanted to stop the duel from escalating, spilling more metaphorical blood and inflicting permanent wounds. Like a referee at a hockey game, he jumped in to separate the duelists. "Okay, okay, you guys. You both bring up good points, and we should certainly look at some of these implications." He struggled to keep a very relaxed tone of voice to help his friends recover their composure. Even he had been struck by Shannon's last comment.

"I've had enough." John left his coffee half full, jerked to his feet, and stomped toward the door of the coffee house as he threw on his jacket.

Shannon sat red faced. She knew she had crossed the line. "I'm sorry, John." But, she said it a bit too quietly for John to hear.

John left without looking back or saying another word. The silence was a harder blow than anything he could have said.

Shannon sighed. "It looks like... I... I went too far."

"He did start it," Dan said, clumsily.

"I know. That's what bothers me." There was a short pause as Shannon recovered her composure. "Look, I've got to get going, Dan. I've already done enough damage for one day. I'll see you later." Shannon rose, took her cup as well as John's to the counter, and left the coffee house.

Dan worried about his friends. *I'm sure they'll patch this up.* But after the thought drifted through his mind, he wasn't really sure what he wanted.

* * *

Dan refilled his coffee as he waited alone at the small round table, the same table where he and his friends had first dabbled with this "project." It had been two weeks, and Dan wondered if the stranger would return as promised. Walker had warned Dan that this project could involve more than they bargained for, that even talking about it could be dangerous. But he didn't say their friendship would be ruined.

CHAPTER 43

Dan wondered about Walker, his prompting to start the project, and his paranoid warnings. It seemed his whole world had changed in only two weeks, and now it was time to meet the vagabond again.

Finishing his coffee, Dan looked at his watch. *Maybe Agent Hall had already gotten to Walker.* His mind continued to roll over the pattern match, the difficulties with his friends, and the challenges each was probably facing as they attempted to square the new interpretation with their beliefs regarding evolution, creation, and original sin.

Lost in thought, Dan broke his concentration when the barista spoke his name into the telephone behind the counter. "Dan? Uh... Yes, he's here... One moment please." He put the phone on hold and brought the cordless receiver to the table where Dan was sitting. "Dan, it's for you." The barista's voice had an extra note in it, indicating his surprise of receiving a call for Dan on the shop's telephone.

"Hello?"

"Dan, please don't mention my name." Dan instantly recognized Walker's distinctive voice. "*Calmly leave the coffee house in a few minutes and walk down to the corner of Ocean Boulevard and Third Avenue. Wait by the large pine tree in the small park there. I'll explain everything later. Make sure you're not being followed. Say 'Go ahead with the repairs' like you're talking to the auto repair shop.*" The silence of disconnection and dial tone replaced Walker's voice.

"Go ahead with the repairs. Yes... Thank you." Dan uneasily played the role of talking to the repair shop.

With the handset still up to his ear, he casually glanced around to see if anyone was listening in. There was only a couple on the other side of the shop and they seemed to be minding their own business. They were clean-cut and well-dressed—nothing like Walker. Dan didn't understand why this level of paranoia was warranted, but he figured he would play along.

He left the shop and ambled down the street, looking in store windows and maintaining an easy-going pace. He had no practice at losing a tail, but he did his best, using the technique he'd seen on action movies and TV shows. To be safe, he decided to walk down a block, over one, and then back up, rather than just walking straight down the street. That way, he could discretely look over his shoulder to assess the situation. No one seemed to be tailing him, so he approached the tree mentioned by Walker. He looked around.

No one was there.

This guy is just playing with me!

Dan stood for a while and then noticed a small note lodged under the bark on the tree's far side.

Walk north on the beach. — W

CHAPTER 44

The finance committee meeting brought John back to his church, and again he passed his pastor's office. John looked in the window and saw Monty waving him in. John wondered what his pastor would think about the difficult question of original sin, a question he had made no real progress considering since the argument with Shannon. Having a few minutes to spare, he entered Monty's office.

"Good morning, John!"

"Got a minute?"

"Sure. Come on in and make yourself comfortable. Here, have a seat."

John let go of the door and walked to the blue sofa next to the chair where Monty was sitting. The sofa and chair were set in an "L" shape. Several other comfortable chairs were arranged on the other side of a coffee table. It was an area specifically suited to informal groups and prayer meetings. Monty set a book and notepad down on the table at the end of the sofa, stood up, and shook John's hand. John leaned back and relaxed into the cushions.

"Have time for a 'Question of Faith'?" John asked.

"Great, my favorite. What is it?"

"Original sin."

"What about it?"

"Well, is it necessary? Do you believe it?"

"Absolutely! Christ depends on it."

"How's that?"

"Here's the thing, John. Christ's suffering on the cross and resurrection are the basis of our beliefs as Christians, right?"

"Of course," John said. "Like it says in John 3:16:

For God so loved the world, that he gave his only begotten Son, that whosoever believeth in him should not perish, but have everlasting life."

"Exactly. Now, how is it that God's son perishing on the cross can provide everlasting life?"

"Well, I understand that Jesus represented the sin of the world and actually became that sin when he was crucified. That opened the door for sinners to find a path to God."

"Now, where did the sin of the world come from?"

"Right, original sin. Sure, I already know that. But, Monty, what if there was no original sin?"

"In that case, sin never would have entered the world. Adam and Eve lived without sin in the Garden of Eden before they violated God's commandment. When they committed that act, the original sin, violating the clear commandment of God not to eat of the Tree of Knowledge of Good and Evil, they were cast out of Eden. They died spiritually at that instant, becoming sinful creatures. They made a choice, a choice to have sin in the world—sin that we all inherit. You, me, everyone, we all are naturally sinful, and as a result, we face death. However, Christ gave us that single path to heaven—to everlasting life."

"So without original sin, there would have been no need for Christ's sacrifice?" John asked.

"That's the inevitable truth. If original sin were ever proven to be a myth, I would probably have to give up my belief in Christ too. That is how important it is."

John sat still, completely stunned by Monty's absolute dependence on this one concept. He noticed the numerous certificates of completion and recognition covering the wall across the room, behind Monty's desk. The ceiling fan slowly rotated in the middle of the room.

"Now, John, are we going to see you sitting with those friends of yours at a service pretty soon?"

John fidgeted. "Uh... maybe. I just don't know." He twirled his pen in his fingers. "Monty, the thing is that our project has gotten really strange. I lost it with Shannon. She said just what you did that Christ's sacrifice is based on the concept of original sin, and that if there is no original sin, then there is no reason for Christ's sacrifice, no reason for the cross."

"Good! You're definitely making progress with your friends now, John. She seems to understand the concepts perfectly!"

John wasn't sure if he should continue, but he did anyway. "The trouble is this: What we've found is really amazing. We found that in Genesis, the Fall was a description of DNA, natural selection, and the workings of biology. And if you accept this new interpretation, you have to give up on original sin. It's hard."

"John, the Bible is not a science book. Looking for something like DNA in the sacred scriptures is nothing but a joke! And giving up on original sin... it's obviously the work of Satan, infiltrating your mind with doubt! I'm sure that this ridiculous interpretation is just a big mistake."

"Maybe."

Monty scooted to the edge of his seat. "Here's what I want you to do. Get back with your friends and see where this all leads. But keep me in the loop. I may be able to give you some more suggestions after I bounce this off some of my colleagues."

"Are you sure that's a good idea? Some people may get upset over this."

"Don't worry! We don't live in the Dark Ages. Christians today are sure of their beliefs; they aren't going to blow a cork just because someone has some other way to interpret a verse here and there. Just look around you. We're the most powerful, most wealthy nation on earth. Why? It's because we have God on our side. Keep the faith!"

"I'd rather keep this between just you and me."

"Nonsense! I just want to run this by my good friend, the Bishop. He's an expert in this very area."

"Well... the Bishop? I guess that'll be okay, but don't spread it farther than that, okay?"

"Of course! You can trust me, John." Monty patted John on the knee. "I'll call you later about this."

"Thanks, Monty." John looked at his watch. "Oh my, I'm almost late." He got up, and Monty followed suit, shaking John's hand. "Thanks again."

As John walked out of the office, he noticed Monty picking up the phone.

CHAPTER 45

Straight down from the small park, Dan followed a narrow public access road to the beach. The beach in this area was sandy, with a hundred-foot vertical cliff about twenty-five feet back from the high point of the waves. Above, located impossibly close to the edge of the cliff, expensive homes challenged the erosive power of the ocean. A pile of smooth, rounded rocks eased the transition from the vertical eroding wall to the horizontal sand. Piles of seaweed were randomly and yet evenly distributed here and there on the sand.

Dan looked around for Walker but could see only about a dozen other people enjoying the brisk air and scenery of the shore. Conversations were private here, masked by the sound of the waves violently crashing onto the sand and the banging of rocks shifting occasionally. And today the waves were large and had excellent form, prompting Dan to think about the possibility of surfing. *Nice waves,* he thought, surveying the surfers already on the water to see if he knew anyone. Dan saved the thought for another time and turned north as the note suggested.

Looking at the numerous strata in the cliff face, Dan thought of the thousands of years represented by each layer, the entire series probably encompassing millions of years. *The earth is extremely ancient. That is certainly obvious by simply examining this one eroded cliff.*

After about a quarter of a mile, the homes disappeared from the brink of the cliff. The area became more remote and difficult to view from any vantage point. Here, there was only the ocean, the shore, and the cliff—the natural world virtually untouched by human activity.

Suddenly, Dan felt a hand on his shoulder. He turned with a jerk to find Walker by his side.

"Good morning, my friend," he said. "Let's walk." They continued up the beach between the rocks at the base of the cliff and the crashing waves.

Dan said, "Thanks for meeting me. I don't understand all this secrecy, but I didn't see any tails."

"Thanks for taking precautions. I'll explain all this later. How are you doing on the question of DNA?"

"Well, we surprised ourselves with some astounding pattern matches. I'm really excited about our progress."

"What about your friends?"

"Well, they're a bit upset right now, but they'll come around. It seems our project is challenging everybody's point of view."

"Hmmm. Interesting. I figured it would. Now, how can I help you?" Although Walker was still only barely more than an acquaintance, Dan felt an unusual calmness about him. Almost as tall as Dan, he was probably in his mid-sixties and in great shape for his age.

"I'm not sure yet. I need to build some confidence in you. We've only really just met. And yet, our short interaction at the coffee shop has prompted quite a large change in my view of the world. It's certainly affected my friends."

"I'm happy that you decided to take the risk. In the end, you'll be glad that you did." They continued to walk side-by-side down the beach, dodging the piles of seaweed and moving up to the rocks when a larger breaker threatened to drench them. They would move back toward the waves during a low spell.

"Years ago, I was working at the Pacific Institute of Theology." Walker still looked more like a homeless man than someone who could be from such a prestigious institution. Dan had spent his early childhood in that area, and he remembered the PIT as ominous white buildings on the top of the hill.

They continued walking next to the din of the waves crashing on the beach. Walker painted a picture of his past. "I was happy with my job there, intensively researching the early years of Christianity. We were unraveling the history of the time of Jesus, his teaching, and the likely scenarios for the formation of the Christian movement and the Christian church. Our results were both startling and at the same time oddly reassuring."

This sounded familiar to Dan. Their project was proving to be a mix of the same feelings, although he wasn't completely certain about the reassuring part, at least not yet.

"Unfortunately, my work was in sharp contrast to the conservative and changeless views of the Institute. Although not officially part of the PIT, extreme fundamentalist groups influenced its policy and outlook. Those groups had a very hard time with the work I was doing and were determined to stop me. I received both personal death threats and threats to my family if I continued working and, in particular, if I published any of my findings. Trust me, those whackos will do almost anything to protect their precious story.

"I decided to stop fighting them. To keep my family safe, I made a deal with the extremists, promising not to publish my work, and I had to leave the Institute. I moved to Colorado and changed careers, eventually finding work in real estate. I avoided my family to ensure their safety."

Walker looked at Dan again. “You can probably imagine, I wondered how they were doing over the years.” He looked back out to the ocean. “I would sometimes return incognito to see them, but I never had the guts to let them know who I was or to reveal the secret about my life. In time, I let my wife in on the secret. She would visit me, and we maintained our love for each other.”

“Did you ever get the nerve to actually contact the rest of your family?”

“Not really. I didn’t risk talking to my son until just the other day.” Walker stopped and looked directly at Dan. “You see, Dan, you’re talking to George Stanfield, your father.”

A large wave struck the rocks nearby and shot up into the air directly behind Walker. Seagulls flew overhead, squawked, and hovered on the wind off the ocean. Dan felt cool spray of the ocean on his face.

Dan looked closely at Walker. As if a huge jigsaw puzzle had been instantly completed, the picture of his past could now be clearly seen. The many trips his mother made for “business” purposes now made sense as did the negative impression his mother gave him about the PIT. It all fit cleanly into the scenario Walker described.

Memories of time with his father, although fragmentary, had always been pleasant. As he looked at Walker’s face under his thick beard, he could see his own genetic similarities. It had been twenty-five years since he had seen his father—a father he had assumed was killed in a car accident and lost forever. Now, his father, seemingly resurrected, stood in front of him.

Alive.

CHAPTER 46

Dan put his hands on his father's shoulders and looked deeply at his face and eyes to see if he could discern the truth of what Walker had just said. Dan felt a sudden welling up of emotion that he never fully experienced when he lost his father as a child combined with the joy of finding a parent assumed to be long lost. But there was something else. Anger. Anger that his father simply walked away from the family. Anger that Walker apparently felt he could not trust Dan with the secret. But the positive feelings won the internal battle. Dan briefly hugged his father and felt a release of emotion.

Dan and his father walked down the beach. They encountered an area where the cliffs protruded into the surf. A narrow pathway led to higher levels to avoid the deeper water crashing on the rocks. They found a private dip in the rocks where they could sit, talk, and enjoy the beauty of the ocean. Walker explained the car accident cover story and his identity change.

They discussed just about everything—his mother, school, work, and even some politics. Walker described his home in the mountains in Colorado. Over the years after his change of identity, he had been quite successful in real estate investments. After their conversation, Dan was certain that this was his father, a blood relative who could be trusted.

All hesitation about sharing the results of their project disappeared. Dan went ahead and briefly described the incredible correlation between the pattern of DNA, natural selection, and biotechnology in the J-Account in Genesis.

Dan explained the challenges his friends were struggling with and asked for advice.

"I can see that you've inherited my inquisitive nature! I think I can help with your project. My work from the Institute is actually perfectly suited to help sort out the questions of original sin and the life of Christ. I don't think I'll be able to help with Shannon's questions on the reliability of evolution, so count me out of that one, but I'm still interested in what she comes up with; she seems very bright." He winked.

They laughed.

"What do you think about getting your friends together so we can talk this over."

"I'm not used to all this secrecy. Where can we meet?"

"A friend of mine has a place in the back country. It should be safe, at least for a while."

Walker wrote some details on a sheet of paper and handed it to Dan. They worked out a possible time on the weekend. Dan and his father walked toward the access road of the beach. Then Walker headed the opposite way and disappeared from sight.

Dan took a minute to gather his thoughts, looking out over the ocean. His emotions were truly mixed. He could sense the joy of meeting his father again, after twenty-five years believing he was dead. Yet, at the same time, he felt abandonment and anger that his father had never visited him all these years, even waiting until long after his mother had died before looking him up. Why wait? At this point, he could only assume that his father had very good reasons for keeping his distance. As his father, Walker was due the benefit of the doubt.

CHAPTER 47

From a bird's-eye-view, the buildings of the university campus looked like toys sprawled on the floor of a child's room with student ants crawling between them. Near the center of the colony, a particular ant worked its way along a well-trodden path. Shannon's flat leather shoes had low heels that clicked on the patterned walkway. The additional weight of her backpack with her usual collection of books and notebooks intensified the sound of her steps. Taking the route she had walked many times before, she ignored the intervening trees, landscaping, and anonymous students who walked nearby. Instead, she remembered only her recent argument with John. She regretted plunging the sword so deeply. But his challenge was what haunted her. The wound had festered. She thought of his most trenchant remark:

> *Evolution can't explain how this advanced technical information... could've been known in ancient times.*

Shannon was not a creationist. Quite the contrary, she had studied Darwin's *Origin of the Species,* Mendel's laws of heredity, and was a good student in her courses on these topics. The startling conclusions of the project had not been good to her model of the world. *I admit that the ancient biblical scriptures contain advanced technical information about DNA and the biological facts of life.* Shannon knew that the intricacies of the actual mechanisms of life were so complex that encoding these in an ancient story would be virtually impossible. But, a high-level overview could be preserved in a simple story, and indeed, the key points were. The correlation went beyond mere chance or luck.

It was Thursday, 10:25 A.M., and Shannon was only five minutes ahead of an appointment with Dr. Houserman, a leading expert on evolutionary theory. The rhythmic clicking of her heals helped her mind work on the issue ahead of her.

Shannon rarely shrank from a challenge. She didn't want to fully admit it, but she allowed some possibility that a god beyond our understanding created humans and our world, but probably not strictly along the lines of what was described in Genesis chapter one. She had long ago abandoned that biblical story, but it was not an easy transition. Shannon's mind drifted to a scene from her past.

* * *

"Dad, I'm not going to Mass today." The words fell flat, like a dead fish on the floor that Sunday morning. Shannon walked down the stairs to the kitchen table. The kitchen in the Pointer household was the center of her family's life, where family and friends could nearly always be found. On the far side of the table, Philip, her father, sat quietly. He was dressed in one of his two suits, ready for church.

Shannon's father was a practicing Catholic, serious about his commitments to the church. He rarely missed Mass. Even when on business trips and vacations, he would find a suitable place of worship. Philip was also a natural poker player. He could restrain the display of his emotions. Even a small change in his mouth could be interpreted as a smile or a frown. His callused left hand played nervously with one of the coasters on the table. Today, the ends of his mouth were flat.

"I'm sorry, Shannon. I don't understand at all! You didn't go to Saturday Mass, so you have to go this morning."

"I don't enjoy church anymore, Dad. It's too old-fashioned for me."

"Enjoyment? It's not about 'enjoyment,' Shannon. You don't have to enjoy every part of your life. It's your duty to the church to attend. And, yes, it is old-fashioned. But it's *supposed* to be old-fashioned. The customs of the church date back to the time of Christ. It's the house of God, and those customs must be respected. You must go. That's all there is to it."

Shannon's mother, Beverly, continued working in the kitchen and only reluctantly listened to the exchange. She opened the refrigerator door as a shield.

A university sophomore, Shannon was home for the summer. Her new experiences as an undergraduate were in sharp distinction to the simple and uncomplicated life in her Ohio home town. She wanted to respect the ancient customs of the church, but the detailed scientific theories of the world had become much more believable than the simplistic stories of the Old Testament. In addition, she had grown to resent the male-centricity of the church, the prohibition on birth control, the doctrine of priest celibacy, and the disgusting tolerance of pedophilia by the priesthood. She planned to hold the church accountable, not so much for the numerous reports of child abuse by priests, but more for the inaction by the church hierarchy even after irrefutable evidence and admissions of guilt.

"I'm sorry, Dad. I just don't think I can honestly go to church and claim to be a believer when I don't believe anymore. The customs of the church are just that, customs, and nothing more."

His hand stopped rotating the coaster; his heartbeat could be seen in his hand, the coaster moving slightly with each beat. "That's not true. The Bible and the church are the best guide for life."

"Maybe, but scientific fact does not always support the Bible. The story of creation isn't even close to being supported by science. Evolution is a far better model, and it's widely supported by experimental science."

"Your mind has been corrupted by the leftist-atheist professors at your school!" His pace quickened and the veins in his forehead protruded. "Don't go down that path too far. You'll go straight to hell! This evolution talk shouldn't keep you from going to church. You can't judge Christianity by the Old Testament. What will our neighbors think? I won't take no for an answer. Our church is based on the teachings of Jesus Christ. Don't you believe in Jesus?" He seemed to be spouting off disjointed sentences searching for the right counterargument, a bit like a children making noise outside a caged zoo animal, trying to get a reaction.

"Sure, I believe that Jesus was a great teacher. I do consider myself a follower of Jesus—I've no problem leading my life as a moral citizen according to what he taught."

Philip's voice grew sterner. "Jesus is the *Son of God*. You're saying that you don't believe in the Son of God? He was more than just a good man. He died on the cross for your sins so you could be saved. You can't ignore that fact. Without Christ, you're doomed to an eternity in hell. Do you want to spend eternity in hell?"

"Dad, you and Mom are wonderful and loving parents. I'll always treasure your model of living great lives." Shannon's sincerity was disarming. "I just don't think that attending Mass will help me in my search for truth."

"Shannon, don't mislead yourself. There's no ultimate truth in the textbooks of your classes or in that Darwin crap."

"You might be right, Dad. But, I'm not going to church; I'm sorry."

Nothing more was said, and they avoided the topic in her subsequent visits back home. In the intervening years, Shannon had taken classes that emphasized the strength of science in revealing the truth and an underlying assumption that natural causes can be found for our universe. Scientists had long ago dismissed the idea that spirits were running things. And this view had never been violated in Shannon's experience.

* * *

Shannon rounded the corner of the humanities building and entered the doors to the internal hallway that extended the length of the building. It was her usual shortcut to the life sciences area.

She knew that John was right in one respect. Modern evolutionary theory does not support the concept that humans could have understood DNA and the fabric of life when the Bible was written. Instead, it paints a much different picture. Earth is a very ancient planet, about 4.5 billion years old. That's 4,500,000,000 years and not the roughly 6,000 years as proposed by Bishop Usher, who claimed creation occurred on October 23, 4004 B.C. at 9:00 A.M. Shannon recalled the classic movie, *Inherit the Wind,* a fictional account of the Scopes Monkey Trial, during which the defense attorney Clarence Darrow drew laughter in the courtroom when he asked if that was 9:00 A.M. Eastern, Central, or Pacific Time. She smiled and sighed with satisfaction.

Shannon knew that modern scientific theory asserts that after earth cooled significantly, molecules capable of replication arose and populated the oceans. After several billion years, life took a huge step to form larger and more stable replicating molecules and eventually, the simplest single-celled organisms. The next big step in evolution was from these single-celled creatures to organisms with numerous cells working cooperatively for the whole. The cells differentiated to perform different functions, such as to form muscle, skin, skeleton, blood, and guts. Eventually fish swam in the oceans, and some would encounter the shoreline. Developing lungs and legs, the fish started to walk about and gradually evolved into amphibians, reptiles, mammals, and finally humans.

Evidence of this sort of progression can be seen in the layers of rock. Fossils of certain life forms exist in some layers but not others. Geologists have been able to accurately map the layers and which life forms are in each one. Using modern dating techniques, they can also accurately determine the time period when these layers were deposited.

Most of this work requires not complex scientific theory but rather simple common sense. A rock layer higher in the strata was deposited after the one below. Indeed, sometimes the layers will be upset or even inverted due to catastrophic events such as floods, volcanic eruptions, and severe weather. But such inversions are relatively rare. The overall scene is one of gradual change over many millions of years. Fossils found in lower strata and not in higher strata are forms that thrived during earlier years and not during later ones. The existence of ancient fossils of extinct animals and plants stands in stark contrast to the fixed-species-created-by-God viewpoint Shannon learned in Sunday school. *Creationists never could explain the dinosaurs; they're certainly not described in Genesis. The millions of years when the dinosaurs thrived can't fit into the 6,000-year biblical history.*

Shannon reached the end of the hallway and resumed her route to the life sciences building.

Scientists tend to regard evolution, a theory that permeated Shannon's science education, as not just a theory to be tested, but as a factual template into which everything must surely fit. It certainly seemed that evolution is well beyond just the concept proposed by Darwin in the *Origin of the Species* in 1859. *Scientists have been buttressing Darwin's theory with experimental data for over a century.* She thought, *Today, it is simply incontrovertible.*

Shannon reasoned that since the theory of evolution was bulletproof, the perception that there was a clear correlation in Genesis with biological facts of life must therefore be discarded as either self-deception or perhaps interaction with another life form that had evolved separately.

Indeed, based on the discussions with her friends, she could discern a clear correlation between biology, DNA, and the J-Account. But was this correlation real, or was it just their minds finding a match where one did not exist? There were many linkages between the patterns—too much for it to be a simple case of coincidence.

Shannon continued to try to make sense of their findings. If evolution is fact, the correlation could still be true under other scenarios. For example, life could have evolved separately on other planets. If those life forms visited earth, they might bestow their advanced knowledge on us. With that said, it's quite impossible to imagine that a separately evolved life form would in any way correspond with that on earth, particularly in the exact formulation of DNA, amino acids, and in the detailed processes of life. The statement *In Our Image* seemed to shut this option down. It is likely that we are very much like any original extraterrestrial visitor. Our ancient precursors likely had a DNA *image* very much like ours.

Shannon stopped thinking along this latter thread and decided to focus on the question of the factual basis for evolutionary theory. If there were severe holes in the theory, Shannon felt she could entertain the possibility that the pattern they found in Genesis was more than self-deception.

Shannon entered a large greenhouse that extended out from the life sciences building. The highly oxygenated damp air was a pleasure to breathe. She dodged puddles of water and ducked under an occasional low-hanging vine and fern branch as she stepped gingerly up wide concrete stairs to the building entrance. She turned for a moment and looked at the tangled mass of life. "I love life," she said quietly to herself. The full spectrum of the intricacies of life filled her mind, from the vast number of animals, plants, and organisms filling every conceivable niche in the environment to the complexities of the cell and the challenge of DNA. Her attention turned to her own body, a colony of trillions of individual cells. *We are a part of this matrix of life, and yet we've been able to understand a great many of its secrets. It's truly amazing.*

After taking the scene in for another moment, she turned and entered the building, then walked down a set of stairs to the basement level of the building where professors had their windowless offices. Overhead, there were many exposed pipes and ducts, labeled with colorful vinyl labels: oxygen, nitrogen, vacuum, vent, and water. Ducking her head at times, she walked to the door reading

A. M. Houserman, Ph.D.

The door was slightly ajar, but she couldn't see in. Shannon checked her watch—it was 10:30 on the button. She knocked on the heavy wooden door. The solid wood minimized the sound of her knock. She knocked again, this time a bit harder, about as much as her knuckles could stand.

"Yes, come in," a voice with a pleasant singsong quality called from inside.

Shannon could push the door only partially open. It was blocked by a large stack of papers that extended far out into the room. Dr. Houserman was seated at his desk facing the left wall. He didn't look up immediately but continued to read and mark papers, apparently grading students' attempts at mathematical symbols and expressions.

The filing method used by this professor was clearly the "pile and forget" technique. Save the walkway and his sitting area, nearly every square inch of floor had piles of papers, some recent, some obviously not too recent. His bookshelves were packed. Books were placed into every available slot, regardless of orientation. Shannon noticed the several dusty humanoid skulls at the top of the bookcase, supported by silver metal stands. *At one time, this office was probably nicely decorated,* she thought. The wall behind the door had photographs of dinosaur skeletons with a much younger Houserman proudly standing next to each of them.

"Good morning, Shannon, please have a seat, I'm just about finished here." After making a few marks on the paper, he looked up to Shannon, removed his reading glasses, and pushed the last few dark brown hairs over his balding head. He always seemed happy to discuss nearly any topic with Shannon. His kind eyes were set in his largely uneven sun-damaged face, which testified to his many years of work in the field.

"You said you'd like to chat about evolutionary theory?"

"That's right. That is, if you don't mind."

"That's somewhat of a tall order, but you're asking me about my favorite topic, so that can be dangerous. Perhaps knowing why you're interested would help prune the tree of possible answers and keep me from talking all day."

Shannon resisted divulging the details of the project, especially since it involved religion. She thought that might significantly change his response. Or he might kick her out, unwilling to spend any time at all. "I'm working on a related research project, and I wanted to find out just how solid evolutionary theory is today."

"Oh, good! I have only a few minutes, and you ask me a question that can take a whole lifetime to answer correctly!" He chuckled. "Well, I can give you a short overview of the key points, a sense of the weak areas and the points that are not in dispute. I can at least give you a basis for further research in those areas that fit with your project. If you want a more in-depth treatment, I'd like to see you in my *Evolutionary Genetics* class."

"Sure, I would really appreciate that. I might be able to take that class; that's a good idea. I really appreciate your time on this." She smiled and any resistance Houserman may have had melted into her smile.

He leaned back in his chair, placing his elbows on the armrests so his arms formed a triangle shape with spread fingertips touching and index fingers resting on his mouth. He looked almost as if he were praying. His eyes looked ahead, his mind apparently working to bring relevant facts together into a neat nutshell that he could present to Shannon.

"As is usually the case, we have a bunch of facts that are known with a high level of certainty and overarching theories that attempt to put these facts into a natural, logical, and simple arrangement.

"Now, if we look at the facts side of the ledger, we have the fossil record as deposited in ancient rocks and our knowledge of how things seem to work today, in terms of Mendelian inheritance, DNA, and genetic theory."

"Doesn't that pretty much prove evolution?" Shannon already had some paper out to take notes.

"There is great truth to any concept of evolution. We are subject to the march of time. Human culture and knowledge evolve over time. Today we are faced with realities—nuclear war, population explosion, climate change, and the like—things that were not even on the radar screen in early times. And they didn't have radar screens either. No one can object to the concept of evolution at this level."

"Right. Of course not."

"Darwin proposed a very specific theory based on natural selection and survival of the fittest. He saw clear evidence of adaptation in species of animals on his trip aboard *The Beagle*. The finches on the Galapagos Islands were obviously related and yet were significantly different from each other."

"Sure, I've read much of what Darwin wrote."

"In Darwin's day, although animal breeders had long known the power of breeding methods using artificial selection, Mendelian genetics had not yet been discovered. And indeed, DNA and the details we know today were unknown. The popular theory of inheritance postulated that each organism would develop traits during its life and pass those traits to its offspring, but the exact details were not at all understood."

" Lamarkian inheritance—right, I've heard of that."

"Their guesses were wrong in this area. Everyone knew they were working with limited knowledge about those details."

"But those things are settled. Doesn't that put Darwin's theory to bed?"

"Not exactly. The concept of variation *within* a species due to sexual recombination of traits is not disputed at all. And it's not disputed that some animals will fare better than others. Some will be more successful in propagating their genetic pattern. This within-species evolution is called *microevolution*, and it's heavily documented by experimental evidence. Darwin took the liberty of extrapolating his observations on microevolution to support the notion that all life was derived from a distant ancestor. With gradual minute changes in these forms, coupled with the effects of natural selection—survival of the fittest—one species of organism would gradually change into another similar species. Over millions of years, we have the set of animals we have today, in a number of distinct groups."

"Sure. That's the normal concept of evolution."

"The key to this theory is the vast amount of time available for the job, only partially accepted during Darwin's era. With additional research, these large expanses of time are absolutely supported today."

"With large expanses of time a settled fact, that seems to support Darwin's conjecture, right?"

"Well, yes. But, unfortunately, that wasn't the only concern. Darwin knew his theory was not fully supported by fossil evidence. He proposed that minute variations were responsible for the change from one form to the next and that natural selection was the sole agent for selecting among the alternatives. Variation was strictly by chance. Selection was by the law of survival of the fittest.

"To progress in minute variations from one form to another, intermediate forms would be expected, a lot of them. If a fish were to turn into a reptile, or more accurately, if these two animal types had a common ancestor, we would expect to see many intermediate forms along the way between that ancestor and the modern animal. Between reptiles and mammals, many intermediate animals representing the minute, gradual changes suggested by Darwin would be expected."

"Sure, of course."

"At that time, they had no evidence of the gradual change proposed by Darwin's theory. I'll quote Darwin himself on this." Dr. Houserman looked up at a small piece of paper on his wall with the quote from Darwin and read it out loud.

Why does not every collection of fossil remains afford plain evidence of the gradation and mutation of the forms of life? We meet with no such evidence, and this is the most obvious and forcible of the many objections which may be urged against my theory.

—Darwin: On the Origin of Species by Means of Natural Selection

"But in the 1850s, the fossil record was only just starting to be revealed," Shannon said.

"It was easy to blame this on the inadequacy of the fossil record. It's only a matter of luck if an animal becomes a fossil and again, only luck if anyone happens to find them. To top it off, the person finding them must also be a scientist who could interpret them. But that's not all. Many animals produce lousy fossils. If they have only a fleshy body, they don't fossilize well. Thus, it was easy to accept the concept that intermediate forms may have existed but were simply not available as fossils. Even if you do find the fossils, changes in organisms that do not affect the skeleton or shell would not be reflected in the record."

"Yeah, but with over a century and a half of research, they've probably filled in the fossil record to support Darwin's theory, right?"

Houserman paused before he answered. He held his fingertips again against his lips. "It's a bit of a secret amongst researchers in this area, but the answer is basically a resounding no. Over the last 150 years, scientists have been facing the challenge of supporting Darwin's assertions or refuting them. During this time, the fossil record has been carefully studied, Mendelian genetics defined, DNA discovered, and the genome sequenced. Fossils of essentially all modern animals can be found in geologic strata. Yet those missing links are still missing. The gradualism as proposed by Darwin has not been experimentally supported. Period."

Shannon was quiet. She noticed a current of air blowing out of an air conditioning duct. The ducts and other pipes were left exposed in the space where an acoustic ceiling might normally be installed.

"Researchers, in their attempts to experimentally support Darwin's assertion, chose animals that fossilize easily, such as shellfish, and they found sometimes millions of years of stasis—relatively little change—punctuated by a rapid, burst of change. The burst usually occurs in a single layer of rock, perhaps forty thousand years thick. Indeed, a long time in human terms, but quite rapid when compared to the millions of years of stability. Stephen Jay Gould popularized this concept with the term *punctuated equilibrium*."

"Oh, yes, I've heard of that."

"Even if you allow for this burst of change, there are huge gaps in the fossil record between the major groups. Science books today teach a linear progression from simple to more complex types. The classic chain—bacteria-colonies-sponges-fish-lungfish-amphibians-reptiles-mammals-humans—is the progression of these organisms in the geologic record. Yet, as I mentioned, if Darwin's gradualism is to hold, you would need to have intermediate forms. Moving from reptiles to mammals, for example, you would expect a large number of fossils over a very long time span when these animals gradually evolved from some common ancestor. The two groups have remarkably different physiology, with different heart structures, different nervous system arrangements, and the like. The two animal types are vastly different. Darwin said they would evolve slowly, moving through all the intermediate forms. The problem is, those intermediate types are missing." He hesitated. "Look, over the last 150 years, top scientists worldwide really tried to find the links, analyzing animals that easily fossilize. Those *missing links* still exist in the fossil record, and as a result, experimental support of Darwin's theory is still lacking."

"What about our understanding of genetics, DNA, and inheritance. It probably supports Darwin's theory, right?" Her background in biotechnology did not consider evolution directly, but it was a common assumption of the framework in her textbooks and among researchers. Scientists could claim to be evolutionists without fear of condemnation. A belief in creationism was intellectual suicide.

Houserman paused and tapped his lips with his pointed index fingers. "Actually, it's unfortunately the case that recent developments in this area have moved us further away from support of Darwin's gradualism. It's a point that is rarely openly admitted in the scientific community, and further research is not heavily funded. Researchers used to be more interested in evolutionary theory. We see it as an assumed backdrop, but research in this area has been relegated to a lower priority."

Shannon was silent again, feeling stunned by his response. She had taken almost no notes at all.

"Today, it's assumed that DNA mutations are the driving force behind variation. Change of one base or accidental duplication or inversion of a section of DNA may affect the organism that will improve its chance of survival. But almost all of these sorts of changes do not. Most—almost all—are only detrimental.

"Here's the problem. Let's assume you have a sequence of DNA bases that encode a protein or enzyme." He wrote on his notepad. "Consider this sentence:"

HERE IS A SEQUENCE THAT HAS MEANING

"Can you make single character changes and still maintain a syntactically and semantically correct sentence? That is, can you make single changes to that sentence and get other sentences that also have meaning, even if that meaning is different?"

"Well, not really. I don't see any real changes that can be made to keep it as an understandable sentence, except perhaps to change from HAS to HAD," Shannon said.

"You'll have better luck with very short sequences, like changing CAT into DOG and having an understandable word at every step:

CAT -> HAT -> HOT -> HOG -> DOG

"In a single short word, it's possible to have mutations that change the sequences, while still retaining meaning. But in the longer sentence, it's rarely possible. And if you consider the typical 10,000 unit length of a typical gene, it's incomprehensible that viable forms could be found by random mutation."

"Wait. I thought mutation was the driving force behind evolution. Random mutation supplies the new ideas for natural selection, right?"

"Today, researchers admit that random mutation is unlikely that driving force. *Coding theory* and *finite field theory* heavily support this conclusion. You'll want to look those up on your own, but basically we're talking about the mathematics behind error detection and correction. Let me give you a feeling for this. In the CAT to DOG progression above, you could make a single character change and still wind up with a valid word. Make a single mistake, and you can't tell. In the longer sentence, you can make a mistake and you won't move to another valid sequence. You'll notice the mistake and be able to correct it. In fact, the errors can be numerous and still the sentence is readable.

Houserman wrote another example on his notepad.

ELNXCELET STNTEUDS CTEPLOME TIEHR HRWOMEOK DLIAY

"That's a total jumble, but I can still read it!" Shannon said. "And, I have done my homework!"

"With only first and last letters correct, your mind does an amazingly good job of extracting the intended sentence. This illustrates the fact that there is a long distance between valid sequences, a trait called *redundancy*. It's used in computer technology to create self-correcting codes, since the redundancy establishes distance between valid words. Depending on how much redundancy is introduced, one or more characters can be self-corrected. With proteins consisting of thousands of amino acid 'letters,' the likelihood that random changes will result in another valid sequence is nearly zero.

"And DeVries proved in the early 1900s that single-base pair mutations will almost never result in a beneficial change in the organism. Single mutations will never cause evolution."

"I find it hard to believe that evolutionary theory is not supported by our modern understanding of genetics. I assumed that the final dotting of i's and crossing of t's had been completed years ago."

"Sorry, it's definitely not put to bed yet. At least, Darwin's view of gradualism is hard to support."

"If Darwin's theory isn't supported by our modern genetics, what is?"

"One of the current interesting theories is called the *null theory*. In essence, it claims that natural selection's primary utility is to exclude deleterious mutated forms, not to move to wholly new forms. It winds up being more of a weeding-out process than one that generates new forms. Given Darwin's theory, it was guessed that we would see most evolutionary change, driven by mutations, in the most heavily used parts of the genetic code. However, just the opposite was found. The 'junk' DNA that's seemingly not used for any purpose includes more mutations than the critical parts of the code. The thought is that mutations occurred at the same rate in all parts of the genome, and mutations in useful regions were most often rejected. Natural selection seems most useful for eliminating errors in the code, rather than as the building blocks of variation."

"So natural selection only helps eliminate errors?"

"In a way. Let me explain this in a slightly different way. It was originally proposed by Darwin that species vary over time, gaining variations through recombination of their traits. You can see this in the finches that Darwin studied on the Galapagos Islands. When Darwin proposed his theory, remember that Mendelian Genetics and the mechanisms of DNA weren't yet discovered. He assumed that somehow the advantageous traits of the individuals were passed on to their offspring. Everyone knew the understanding of those mechanisms was deficient at that time, but today we don't have an excuse. We accept that the mechanism is the genetic code and the only means of determining which traits are advantageous is by survival of those animals with traits that best suit the environment. All Darwin's actual observations can be explained with these mechanisms. Again, there is no dispute that you can achieve reasonable variation through sexual recombination of traits and occasional mutation. Those are the sort of changes that Darwin actually witnessed in his observations.

"But extrapolating this theory is where Darwin gets into trouble. Over very long periods of time, will these subtle changes gradually add up to cause dramatic changes in the organism? That question has never been supported by experiment or by any genetic-level theory. In fact, many of Darwin's assumptions have been found to be false."

"Like what?"

"Well, a good example would be his claim that evolution would occur most rapidly in animals living in a harsh environment, when resources are scarce and the mortality rate is high."

"Right. That's reasonable."

"The selection of one variant over another would occur more

rapidly in that harsh environment than when the going was good and almost every animal survived and had equal offspring. In times when resources are plentiful, when life was easy for these organisms, that would be the time of relative stasis—that is, slow evolution. That's what Darwin thought, and as you said, it seems perfectly reasonable. In fact, the opposite was clearly found to be the case. When life was relatively easy, the fossil record showed *more* variation and therefore faster evolution within that life form. When life was difficult, relative stasis was the rule."

"Gee, that does seem to be quite startling, completely derailing that part of Darwin's theory. Dr. Houserman, I'm really surprised by your answers. I've been learning about evolutionary theory throughout my science career. Darwin's theory is heavily touted in science books, and if you asked me before our conversation, I would have argued that it is fact—a done deal."

"You're right. There's a huge misconception by the public about the scientific acceptance of Darwin's theory. His original theory is not supported by experimental evidence. It sounds good, but it is wrong."

"Wrong? Evolution is completely bankrupt?"

"Not at all. The understanding of our geological past is very strong, and dating methods continue to be refined and enhanced. We have unassailable evidence of vast time periods for evolution of life to occur, a fact not clear at Darwin's time. Different types of animals exist in the various geologic layers, each seemingly branching from simpler life in lower layers and contributing to more complex forms in those above. Animals that have long been extinct, such as the dinosaurs, provide strong testimony to the possibility of the evolution of life. However, those in the field know the facts—experimental evidence—simply do not support the gradualism originally proposed by Darwin. The experimental evidence doesn't support the idea that the simple theory of natural selection should be extrapolated to govern all evolution. Darwin had it right in many areas, and his actual observations were excellent and thorough. Yet the extension of within-species natural selection to evolution of all life falls short."

"I see. Although the principle of evolution appears solid, the details remain an open question, right?"

"That's a good way to put it. The overall concept of evolution is still sound."

"What about the origin of life?"

"There's only grand speculation on that. It's suggested that life originated from a primordial soup of elements on earth, with the heat of the earth and lightning contributing energy to encourage chemical reactions basic to life. The first 'life' was perhaps a simple replicating molecule, such as RNA. Replication is an essential capability of life. It's not difficult to imagine such simple molecules duplicating themselves—

in essence, the first primitive form of life."

"Right. RNA could be considered a precursor to our form of life."

"If you neglect some troublesome details, it follows that self-replicating sequences of RNA could be the result of random combinations of primordial soup. Getting to DNA is another matter. You see, RNA is relatively simple and unstable when compared to DNA. It's only a single-stranded molecule, and the bonds are not as strong as those in DNA, which is a robust, double-strand molecule. To get RNA to replicate reliably, it's necessary to limit the length of the sequence, or it falls apart before it completes replication. In contrast, DNA is much more difficult to replicate because it is much more stable. That stability means it can be much longer than the longest stable RNA sequence. But the downside of that stability is that DNA requires the helper protein, *polymerase*, to replicate. But that helper protein itself is quite large and would not be possible to create with RNA. RNA always falls apart before it can reliably create the helper protein. You must have DNA to make the helper protein, but you need the helper protein to be able to use DNA."

"Yes, the chicken-and-egg problem at the lowest possible level: DNA will not replicate without DNA already available to make polymerase, right?"

"Some theories try to explain how it could happen in a much more roundabout way. One thing is really clear, however. Life is much more difficult to get started than we originally thought."

"I can't believe it... theories of the origin of life being very sketchy. I've always regarded evolution as fact... Darwin's theory as foolproof... I don't know what to say."

"This is the current state of affairs, but I wouldn't write it off for all time. We may find a way to get to DNA using strictly naturalistic processes, but the exact route isn't clear yet. The path from primordial soup to life is not simple or straightforward. Life may be much rarer in the universe than we assumed."

Houserman sat quietly for a moment and then jerked to attention. "I'm sorry, but I'm out of time. Let me recommend two books that look at the gaps you seem to be interested in. John Maynard Smith, a noted evolutionist, compiled an excellent work called *The Major Transitions in Evolutionary Theory,* which covers the various difficult changes in life required if evolution is to be factual. It's written at a level you might appreciate, given that you're a student in this area. It's not an easy book for people without at least some biology courses under their belt. The book *Crisis in Darwinism* is a more popular treatment of the key challenges to evolution. Both of these books are scientific discussions and not based on arguments in favor of religious creationism or so-called intelligent design."

Shannon made her notes. "Okay, thanks. I'll definitely look those up."

"I hope I've been helpful to your research. Just let me know if you want to chat again." Houserman looked at Shannon with a kind smile and tapped her on the forearm. Shannon was surprised that he spent so much time with her, but she always suspected he had a bit of a crush on her. He gathered his material as she grabbed her notepad, and they both exited to the hallway. Houserman stood for a moment in uncomfortable silence and then shook Shannon's hand lightly, said goodbye again, and strode off.

She stood alone in the dingy basement hallway of the life sciences building outside Houserman's closed office door, a bit dazed. She had assumed that Darwin's theory was simply fact. With the theory of evolution under question, she was really sorry that she had been so hard on John. And the wound from John was opening into a larger crack in her view of the world.

CHAPTER 48

Did I hear something? The ceiling and walls of Hall's bedroom reached a partial focus. Hall squeezed his eyes shut to clear them and then stretched them open.

R-R-Ring.

Oh, that's what I heard... my cell phone. The distinctive ring signified that the caller's number was restricted. Hall looked at the clock. 5:45 A.M. *It better be an important call.* He reached for his cell phone, which was being recharged by his bed and squinted at the display. Hall rotated around and sat up on the side of the bed, squeezing and stretching his eyes to try to wake up. A sprinkling of light only slightly disturbed the darkness outside. Hall cleared his throat and opened his phone.

"G'morning... Uh... Hall here." His voice was still filled with sleep.

Silence mixed with a tiny bit of background noise.

"Hello!" Hall said again, slightly louder.

After another few seconds of silence, Hall heard a voice, modified by electronics to avoid recognition. "*I am calling to warn you.*" It sounded like a robot but with pauses and pacing reflective of a human voice.

"Who is this?"

"You don't need to know who I am. Just listen."

Hall's mind raced, jumping ahead to who and why he was getting this call early on Friday morning. Normally, as an FBI agent, he could access the number of any caller. But, if the caller was sophisticated enough to use that sort of voice concealing equipment, the number would be suppressed as well. Hall was working on several cases, but which one...

"Go ahead, I'm listening."

"*Stay away from the PIT. If you continue your investigation, you will be sorry. You've been warned.*"

"Why are you telling me this? Who are you?"

"*Let's just say I'm a friend. You're being watched. I'm sure this call is monitored. Just do as I say.*" Click.

Hall looked at the display of his phone, still working the sleep out of his eyes. It blinked the duration of the call and then returned to the time. The voice on the line, despite being intentionally distorted by electronics was still strangely familiar, but still unrecognizable. He got up, threw on some sweats and walked to the balcony at the front of his condo. The sliding-glass door opened easily, and the ocean breeze greeted him, fresh off the Pacific Ocean wilderness. His body reacted, springing awake as the moist chill dampened his skin.

The beach. Hall had always been drawn to the life and action there, even though he came from a small-town in Illinois, far from the coast. Hall walked out to the edge of the balcony and peered over the rail, looking down the two stories to the concrete sidewalk and seawall below. Even at this hour, several joggers could be seen working their way up and down the shoreline walkway.

The FBI position had been great, but it had its shortcomings, including the need to move from place to place on a regular basis, allowing Hall to blend in with his targets, usually high-rolling drug importers. This current stint was a good one; the life and action of the beach area appealed to Hall, and there was no shortage of toned California babes to choose from. Yet, with all that promise, Hall had missed finding his sole mate and any lifelong commitment. Oh, sure, he had a lot of laughs with very attractive women. But, his biggest regret was that he had no children, no tight-knit family or role as a father.

And now he was receiving anonymous calls warning him of a threat. Clearly, doing his job was somehow a threat to someone. The unexpected removal from the case was certainly more than just an administrative move. Somehow, the PIT was able to shake the huge FBI organization to have its way.

No one is going to threaten me. My only real lead is Daniel Stanfield. If they're threatening me, Stanfield is probably in danger too.

CHAPTER 49

John threw on a light windbreaker, gathered his Bible and notepad, and walked toward the door of his townhouse. Dan had invited him and Shannon to a meeting at a house somewhere in the mountains, John didn't exactly know where.

R-R-Ring.

John stopped in response to the sound and went back to the table where his cordless phone sat, next to the newspaper opened to the stock market pages from the day before.

R-R-Ring

John almost lived on his phone. But business calls on Saturday mornings were unusual as most financial markets were closed on weekends. John picked up the phone and pressed the talk button.

"Good morning, John speaking."

"*Good morning John, this is Pastor Monty.*"

"Hi, Monty. I'd love to talk, but I'm on my way out. I have only a minute."

"*That's fine. I won't hold you for long. I just wanted to let you know that I contacted my friend about your questions on original sin. He said he wants to talk to you about it.*"

"Can't do it today, Monty. I'm on my way to meet my friends."

"*The atheists?*"

John's face reacted with disgust. "Huh? Well, I guess you might call them that, but I don't think they are that far gone, Monty."

"*Look, John, it may be best for you to avoid them. Remember, if you put a clean pig in with a bunch of muddy hogs, they don't all come out clean. You're more likely to get muddy in the process.*"

"I thought you said it was a good idea to try to show them the way back to the truth of Christ. We are reading the Bible. What's the harm in that?"

"*Why question the truth of our beliefs? We know in our hearts we are right, don't we?*"

"Absolutely. And that's why I'm not worried. Look, I've got to get going."

"*Just be careful that you don't start believing some scientism atheist crap. Call me when you get back, okay? I'm worried about you."*

John was surprised in Monty's choice of words. "Sure, I'll call you, Monty. But, I really don't think there's anything to worry about."

"*Okay. But, call me. Bye.*"

"Bye."

John pressed the "off" button on the telephone handset, set it down, and stared blankly at the financial section of the paper. *Monty certainly changed his tune since our last conversation. Maybe he's troubled about original sin. I wonder what the Bishop had to say.*

CHAPTER 50

Dan steered his car off the hilly mountain road and into a driveway, stopping in front of a heavy wooden gate with rustic horizontal rails. The property was well fenced, the driveway well maintained. No house or building could be seen from the road. "We followed the directions Walker gave us, and the address matches, so this must be it," Dan said to his friends.

They had been driving for about forty-five minutes due east into the mountains on a winding road. After some reluctance, John and Shannon agreed to get back together for a skull session with Dan and Walker. They were clearly still uneasy about their recent argument, but neither of them seemed to want to start anything on the trip. Dan had reassured his friends that Walker was trustworthy, that Walker knew Dan's father long ago. But, following Walker's suggestion, Dan stopped short of revealing their shocking relationship.

"Here, use my cell phone to dial this number." Dan handed the phone to Shannon in the front seat.

Shannon dialed the number. "It's ringing... It beeped and... that's it—silence."

"Good. Enter the code that I wrote below it... right there."

Shannon entered the four-digit number. After a brief moment, the gate jerked slightly and rolled back to one side, pulled by a chain along a track in the ground. Dan drove past the gate and onto the one-lane paved driveway, noticing the gate closing in the rearview mirror.

They drove for about a quarter mile around an intervening steep, grassy knoll, eventually up to a house with a barn-like garage. Dan parked his car in the front of the house, and the three friends got out, stretched their legs, and followed Dan up the stairs to a large, wrap-around porch surrounded by numerous trees. The shade from the trees intensified the coolness of the overcast skies.

Walker greeted them as they got to the door. "Welcome, friends! Please come in."

"You clean up nicely!" John complemented Walker, who looked completely different from their initial impression at the coffee house, his clothing changed to newer, cleaner attire, his long gray hair combed and tied back.

The house was quite airy inside. The high-vaulted, open-beam ceiling and knotty-pine walls smelled of a rustic wooden building. Along one wall stood a huge library of books with a rolling library ladder to access the top shelves. Gentle classical music played in the background. A small fire burned brightly in a large fireplace at the end of the room.

Another man about Walker's age entered the room from what looked like the kitchen. Walker said, "My friends, this is a very dear colleague of mine, Edgar Milton, a physics professor from the university." Everyone shook hands and exchanged names. "Make yourself at home; look around if you wish. I'll get drinks for everyone."

As he went to the kitchen to fetch the order, the three friends walked around, each attracted to a different area. John went outside to tour the porch and look at the view. Shannon looked at the overall floor plan, kitchen and living areas. Dan was drawn to the library. They converged on the table at one end of the living area where Walker brought their drinks on a tray.

They settled into seats around a heavy wooden table with uneven edges, the natural surface of a tree with a knot here and there, but the surface was remarkably smooth from years of use.

Walker wanted to get started as they sipped their drinks. "First, thanks for being careful and not attracting attention. We've noticed strange events lately and we've caught people apparently spying on us. Edgar's been a big help over the years, allowing me to stay in his house when I was in the area."

For the next couple of hours, Dan, Shannon, and John described the results of project they had stumbled on—a pattern match that was indisputable, clear, and yet upsetting. A match that could agitate the thoughts of both theologians and evolutionists alike, yet one that was so significant that the group felt it was their duty to continue to pursue their research. Edgar and Walker asked questions occasionally but mainly allowed the group to make the presentation.

Finally, and somewhat reluctantly, Shannon and John admitted they had pushed each other's buttons. Each apologized again.

Shannon explained her dilemma. "My family was Catholic, especially my father. He was a steady member of the church and a huge influence on me. But my university career in biology pushed me away from the creation story and toward evolution. Biology today has an underlying assumption of evolution: that we evolved strictly by chance over eons of time. Our project provides amazing evidence that the ancient story of Genesis encoded details about DNA, natural selection, the subtle differences between man and woman, and even the wisdom of incorporating sexual reproduction and childbirth into the life cycle of humanity. Where could this information come from? Evolutionary theory, as I understand it, doesn't support the concept that ancient humans would have known these advanced facts. John, you were right to challenge me on this."

John nodded with appreciation.

"I went to see one of my professors, Dr. Houserman, who is an expert on evolutionary theory." Shannon described her encounter with Houserman, as well as some additional reading she had done on evolution.

"The bottom line is that Darwinian Theory—the idea that a single primordial ancestor coupled with gradual, imperceptible change over many millions of years could result in the various species—is simply not supported by experimental and fossil evidence. In other words, these theories are still only tentative and are not resolved to the level of 'fact' as I had assumed.

"On an intra-species basis—that is, within a given order of animals—natural selection and variation have been proven. Take dogs, for example. They certainly vary substantially to adapt to their environmental niche. What is clearly *not* supported is the customary progression from simple species to more complex, from bacteria, to multi-celled colonies, to fish, to amphibians, to reptiles, to mammals, and finally to humans.

"I have to admit, I was surprised. I accepted evolution, like a good little schoolgirl, without any question at all. I assumed that Darwin's theory had been buttressed over the years with reams of experimental evidence. If that were the case, it would be appropriate to accept it as fact, just as factual and reliable as the theory that earth is a sphere. But it simply isn't. It may still be the best theory we have, but that doesn't mean it's absolutely correct. Many people who have rejected six-day creationism assume that Darwinian evolution is the only alternative. Sorry, it's not necessarily the case."

"Shannon, I'm impressed... All this from my outburst, eh?" John said. "Sounds like you may have to embrace the concept that God created us!" Dan got the feeling that John was hoping that Shannon would come around to his male-dominant point of view, to the imagined idyllic family, the one praying together at the steepled church and returning to the white picket-fenced home with children joyfully playing in the yard and subservient wife toiling in the kitchen.

Shannon said, "Don't get carried away, John. Microevolution has been proven by experiment clearly enough. Macroevolution may still be true, even though we don't currently have sufficient proof. My point is that at this time, it still has a few loose ends. And more than that, some important assumptions have been proven incorrect. Science doesn't start accepting theories as fact until all these issues are resolved. And, since it's not hard-core fact, we have to be open to the possibility that our Genesis revelation might be more than just a figment of our collective imagination."

"You'll have to embrace the only viable alternative theory, Shannon: intelligent design. It's the only obvious alternative."

"Sorry, if there are two theories and one is not holding water, that doesn't mean that the other one is automatically true. Each may be partly true, or more likely, both are false with some completely different theory representing the truth," Shannon responded.

Dan said, "If there are two light switches on the wall and you happen to see a plane fly overhead, if you flip one switch and it doesn't control the plane, that doesn't mean the other switch will control it. The facts surrounding the plane flying over are far more complex than either of the switches on the wall. Science has uncovered many secrets about our world, and almost without exception, the facts of nature are much more refined and detailed than we ever could imagine or conceive.

"For example, the Greek philosopher Empedocles imagined a world with four key elements—earth, wind, fire, and water. It turns out that there are three components to all matter—protons, neutrons, and electrons. They form the hundreds of elemental atoms of the periodic table and the innumerable combinations of inorganic and organic molecules."

Shannon took the ball. "Was the first concept of four elements false? Absolutely. But the concept that all matter is made of simple constituents is absolutely true, and the actual theory about how those simple elemental particles combine to form all types of matter is much more complex than implied by the four-elements concept."

Shannon turned back to John. "This same pattern can be applied to the theory of evolution. Darwin's initial theory is like the four element model of nature. It's not exactly right, but the general idea is. We just need to understand the complexities of the details. We certainly should not scrap the whole idea of evolution and replace it with non-evolving intelligent design, especially if we have to conform to the ridiculous six-day theory."

Dan said, "I'm really surprised by your new position on this, Shannon. You've been our resident evolutionist, and I've usually been on your side. I never thought you'd reverse course. Although it's a bit of a shock, it's a good one in one respect: Your new point of view supports the validity of our new interpretation of Genesis."

The expression on John's face flipped quickly from satisfied to worried.

CHAPTER 51

"Let's have some lunch, shall we?" Edgar said. "There are bits and pieces in the kitchen we can throw together to make sandwiches." Time seemed to vanish when the group discussed this material, transcending the requirements of the daily routine. They took a break, prepared some sandwiches, and then milled around and chatted about inconsequential topics.

Looking out the front window of Edgar's house, Dan enjoyed the view down to a meadow and beyond to a valley far below. The rays of sunlight beaming through a hole in the clouds and onto the verdant hillside across the valley.

The group returned to the rustic table while Walker fiddled with the fireplace at the far end of the room.

John spoke up. "Shannon, you seem open to the possibility that evolution may be still be just a theory with a few problem areas. And as we know, you've challenged me to address the issue of original sin. That puts me in the hot seat, so perhaps we can discuss that."

"That sounds good, John. But will you be able to keep your cool this time?"

"Shannon, give me a break, will you? Our new interpretation of Genesis implies that Eve made a wise choice, not a mistake and therefore, not a sin. If it wasn't a sin, then it follows that there was no original sin. With no original sin, the idea that sin was released into the world at that point is false, and the default state of mankind is good, not evil. I like that idea, except for one minor detail: How do you explain the obvious sinful nature of mankind? Our prisons are filled to the brim with murderers, rapists, and felons. If man's nature is essentially good, why are prisons necessary? The morality of mankind would be seriously bankrupt if not for the redemption of Christ from our natural, sinful state. The story in Genesis and its link with Christ is explained by this simple observation of human nature."

Walker was standing by the fireplace after inserting another piece of wood. He walked back to the table as he spoke. "Yes, my friends, now that definitely is the question. Are the core beliefs of Christianity true, even if we might bicker on the details? It comes down to the question of whether humans are essentially evil or essentially good. Over the years, various cultures have weighed in on opposite sides of this question. Indeed, humans do seem to have a tendency to get off track."

John sat with his arms folded and he nodded in agreement.

Walker stood next to his empty chair. He used his hands to make his points in the air. "If we assume that the inherited sin from Adam is not the reason for this apparent evil, and if we discount bad behavior of people who are obviously mentally deranged, why is it that there is so much war, disagreement, and strife? I believe this is the central question you're asking."

"To me it proves that sin does exist," John said.

"Well, I have my own opinion of the answer to this question. I can relate it to you fairly easily, if you're game," Walker said.

"Sure," John said. The others nodded.

"It's been a question that has dogged theologians for centuries. As David Hume reasoned about God:

> *Is he willing to prevent evil, but not able? Then is he impotent. Is he able, but not willing? Then is he malevolent. Is he both able and willing: whence then is evil?*

"It's a difficult question, to be sure. In essence, why is there evil? Or is there?"

The group didn't try to answer these rhetorical questions and waited for Walker to continue.

"First, I want to dispense with the notion that the forces of nature represent evil. I'm sure you've seen National Geographic specials featuring a lioness chasing a gazelle through the grassland of Africa and eventually eating it. The gazelle flees for its life with terror in its eyes. Is this evil?"

"Not from the viewpoint of the lioness!" Dan answered.

"Right! The lioness is only getting her next meal—there's nothing evil about eating! If you could ask the gazelle, it would probably say the lion is evil. Yet, we must admit that there's nothing evil about animals eating their prey in the natural circle of life."

Dan said, "In fact, in balanced ecosystems, predators fill an important role, weeding out the infirm and weak from the herd. What seems evil at first is actually quite good when viewed from that angle."

They looked back to Walker, still standing. "Let's try another one." He stroked his beard. "In 2004, earth's tectonic plates moved, resulting in the Sumatra earthquake and the devastating tsunami disaster. 275,000 fatalities were tallied, more than from any other earthquake in recorded history. This disaster was obviously devastating and horrible, but was it evil?"

"It was a sad situation, I have to admit that," John said. "But earth was created by God, and the tectonic plates moved according to the laws of nature. I don't think earth is evil. Yes, I see your point. That probably wasn't the that was brought into the world by Adam's sin."

"Good," Walker said. "My point is that *nature* is not sinful. Sin is strictly a human issue."

"Okay, I'll accept the idea that nature is not sinful," John said. The others nodded.

Walker said, "Now, let's move to my next point. I sincerely believe that most, if not all, problems in this world—human sin—can be traced to a simple limitation of the human as a thinking entity. I'm not certain, but I believe the philosopher Kant first detailed it. L. Ron Hubbard mentions it in his book *Dianetics*, the foundation for the biofeedback-based discipline of Scientology. Even the billionaire investor George Soros incorporates this limitation as a keystone in his philosophy for predicting the behavior of investors, very successfully, I might add."

"Limitation? I don't feel limited. What is this limitation?" John asked.

"Have you noticed that friends with various points of view have no trouble having friendly conversations on safe topics like the weather, sports, home improvement, gardening, fishing, or even new car models? As soon as you venture into 'touchy' topics like religion or politics, you may lose a friend from a simple conversation."

John and Shannon traded glances and let out puffs of air.

Walker continued. "Etiquette experts insist that in polite conversation, we treat these topics as taboo. How can it be that people with very similar backgrounds and current interests will frequently differ on these topics and take the difference very personally? This fact is a symptom of the problem I'm speaking of."

"Sure, I'll certainly agree that some topics are difficult to discuss. What do you think, Shannon?" John asked, his head cocked to one side.

Shannon chuckled.

Walker walked slowly around the table as he talked. "Your knowledge of the world is in essence a model. You use that model of the world to predict what will happen if you do something. Your job is to create as accurate and as complete a mental model as possible. If your model is very accurate, it will predict the future well, and you may be very wealthy or at least comfortable in your position in the world. If you have trouble making a good model, you may be a homeless derelict."

Dan felt this last statement seemed a bit ironic coming from Walker, whom he first assumed to be just that.

"Even if you're considered an expert in a given field of knowledge, you'll know your knowledge is limited. Plus, a person can't be an expert in every field. This fact is truly driven home if you browse the Internet or visit the Library of Congress. You'll instantly learn that there is far more information than you can possibly process in your lifetime. But the capacity of our minds is quite impressive, nonetheless."

"The complexity of the world is far greater than can be encompassed by any mental model," Edgar said, making a rare contribution. "Even if the complexity of the world *could* be captured for a given moment in time, for a given subset of topics, your model would be out of date as the world progressed to a new state. It's an interesting question only recently tackled in a general way. *Complexity theory.* It's one of my favorite topics, may I?"

"We'd love it!" Dan said quickly; the others nodded, except for John who continued to sit quietly with his arms folded.

Walker leaned against the back of the leather couch that was next to the table, half-sitting on it.

Edgar said, "We are faced with reality that's extremely complex, to the point that even if a model were possible, it would probably still not generate reasonable conclusions. It's difficult if not impossible to get the model set up so it has the correct initial conditions."

"You'd better give us an example," Dan said.

"Consider the weather. Predicting the weather has been a goal of humanity since storms wreaked havoc on villages or drought devastated crops. Recently, mathematicians built models of the atmosphere on supercomputers, attempting to fully predict future weather conditions. The problem was that the models were so complex that even a minor change in the initial conditions would produce a dramatic change in the future weather, to the point that the predictions were sometimes dead wrong.

"This category of problems is in an amazing area of research called *chaos theory*, initially discovered by meteorologist Edward Lorenz."

"I've heard of that," Dan said. "The butterfly effect: A butterfly flapping its wings in one part of the world might cause a huge storm in another."

"Precisely. This effect, exemplified as *fractals,* appears to guide much of the variation in life, such as the structure of plants and your fingerprints. Chaos theory provides a mathematical understanding that not all systems are predictable. They're not deterministic. You can't predict the exact outcome, no matter how good your model is!"

Walker said, "Modeling every aspect of reality is indeed impossible. Our minds can deal with only so much complexity. We have to admit that our model of the world is incomplete and frequently incorrect.

"But my point, my dear Walker, is that the world is so complex that even the most accurate model is still inadequate. Everything is interdependent, and it's impossible to predict exact outcomes. But chaos theory was a breath of fresh air in one respect. It became acceptable to admit that science would never model the world exactly. Scientists are certain about only one thing: uncertainty."

CHAPTER 52

Walker waited for everyone's full attention. "Even though we know that our model of reality is not absolutely accurate, our mind understands only one thing: In the present, we are always right. We admit error only in the past. If you can recall a time that you were wrong, you're still 'right' at this moment. I claim that this simple fact may be responsible for all conflict, war, and disagreement in the human condition."

"That's quite a statement, Walker. Is this your replacement for sin?" asked John.

"To a large extent, yes."

"A large extent? You're definitely going overboard here," John said. "I don't feel that I'm right all the time. I've been wrong many, many times. Anyone who's married knows they're wrong, almost all the time!" The group chuckled lightly.

"You're missing the point, John. Just because you think you're right doesn't mean you really are. We already agreed that your model of the world is incomplete. You can't accurately model every detail of reality. Yet, you still *think* and completely *believe* that you are right, NOW."

"It seems I'm still wrong much of the time."

"John, I have a challenge for you," Walker said.

"A challenge? What is it?"

"If you are so sure you are wrong most of the time, just demonstrate. Be wrong, right now."

"That's easy." John thought for a moment. "I say: two plus two equals five. That's wrong, isn't it?"

"You make a great straight-man, John. Indeed, that was an incorrect *answer*. Your mind wanted to come up with an answer that would technically be wrong, so you could answer the question and be right, making me wrong. Unfortunately, that makes you *right* again: Your answer was wrong!"

"Hmmm. I see," John said. John thought for a moment, apparently trying to think of a situation where his mind could be wrong at the present. "How about this: I see your point now, and I was actually wrong when I tried to meet your challenge by being wrong. Therefore, when I tried to be wrong by being literally wrong, I was right in that regard, but I was actually proving that I could be wrong by trying to be right another way."

"John, give it up!" Shannon wasn't the only one who couldn't follow that difficult logic. Everyone but John laughed at the absurdity of his attempt to be right.

Walker answered. "I'm not sure of your logic, John, but I do know that you think you are right again! We can only be absolutely 'right' in the present. You can't be knowingly wrong now. This is the problematic thought pattern I was referring to. Again, we know our model is incomplete, inaccurate, and biased. We know we can never comprehend every detail of the world. We know that the world is a chaotic system, and even if we did have complete information, the future would still be unpredictable. We know we 'fall short of the glory of God.' Yet, we are right, one hundred percent of the time. We are right that we can't comprehend every detail. We are right that our model is inaccurate. Our mind continues to feel that it's right in spite of the fact that it cannot be right. If you find you don't agree with something I say, you'll be right about that. Even if you disagree with this very point, if you're right about your disagreement that proves the point again."

John asked, "What if you're in a situation where you're doing something that you know is wrong? Maybe you just realized the implications of what you're doing, and the results are clearly wrong. Aren't you wrong then?"

"You're *right*, it is wrong. And you may be able to devise sufficient rationale for why it's still reasonable for you to proceed with the act, wrong under other circumstances, but perhaps not under the current circumstances. If a crook steals something, if a businessman fraudulently utilizes 'creative' accounting practices, if someone exceeds the speed limit on the freeway, if the politician decides that lying to the public is ethically correct when the end justifies the means—we know that their minds are always right at the time.

"Even acknowledging that the practice may be illegal, they still are right about that. Being right doesn't necessarily mean being legal, rational, ethical, or even consistent. Being right means that in your mind, *your model* is one hundred percent right, including the parts of the model that say you're unethical or acting illegally."

"Your definition of *right* means being consistent with your mental model—not necessarily 'true' or even moral. Right?" John said.

Walker seemed to take on the mannerisms and gestures of a preacher; the pacing of his comments could have come from a television evangelist.

"The ability to confess that your act or position was indeed wrong is actually quite good for your mind. It allows you to clearly be right with no conflict or psychological denial. As a general rule, it's probably wise to admit your wrong-headed thinking as soon as you can and change your behavior accordingly. This keeps your mind right, and that's healthy.

"People, especially politicians, have a very hard time admitting that they are wrong. Wars have raged for years after the public realized that any pretext was based on wrong-headed thinking, if not outright deceit. Thousands of people died as a result. Bribes are accepted everyday by authorities all over the world knowing that they are illegal, but standard operating procedure, nevertheless. All are examples of an inability to admit being wrong.

"But there is a bright side. One of the paths to life transformation taught by many churches is the possibility of change, that old thinking patterns were wrong and new patterns can be adopted."

"Absolutely," John perked up. "To change, it's necessary to get to a point where it's possible to admit that current state of affairs is wrong. I understand that—I've been through it."

"Is seems it would be hard to realize that your model is wrong," Dan said. "As people consider events, statements or ideas, they will evaluate the truthfulness of any new information by comparing it with their model, sometimes called their frame. If the information disagrees with the frame, it is accepted, otherwise it is thrown out as lies. The model would seem to persist much longer than it would if they could more objectively evaluate the information."

"That's right," Walker said. "People tend to simplify as much as possible, using rules of thumb, simple slogans, and statements by pundits to decide whether to adopt new information to the model. Theologians have understood this phenomenon for years. They call your model your *presupposition*."

"It sounds like your *bias* would be the difference between your presupposition and reality."

"Bravo, my son," Walker said, clapping lightly.

Son? The word startled Dan. *Does he want to reveal our relationship, to eliminate the inaccurate perception the others must have?*

CHAPTER 53

Rebecca pushed a lunch cart into the conference room and began transferring sandwiches, salads, and finger foods onto a table at the back of the room. The group of fifteen men sat around a large walnut conference room table. The man standing at one end used a computer projector to present slides onto a large screen. She listened discreetly as she worked.

"As you can see, church attendance is down to about twenty-percent of the population," said the energetic and trim man, pointing to the down-turned graph projected on the screen.

A man of medium to heavy build slouching in his seat along the right side of the square interrupted the speaker. "But, Tom, hasn't it been well established that church attendance has been stable at about forty-percent? The results of the Gallup poll are very reliable. Your twenty-percent figure is way off."

Tom didn't get the least bit rattled, almost as if he was happy for the interruption. "Gary, you're right about those poll figures. They've been widely reported for years, and Gallup is well respected for using great sampling techniques. Unfortunately, they used telephone polls that asked respondents to describe their own church-going habits. Actually counting heads or cars in parking lots gave us the right figure, about twenty-percent."

"Are you saying that the other twenty-percent lied about attending church?" Gary said defensively.

Tom said. "Let's just say they 'misrepresented' their actual attendance. Such misrepresentation is most prevalent in the Deep South, where Christian culture is strongest."

"I wouldn't call it lying," said a dark-haired man with a distinctive mustache seated across from Gary. "It's normal for people to over-report desired behavior and underreport undesired behavior. That's just human nature. The twenty-percent figure is probably correct, as sad as it seems. Go on, Tom."

Tom clicked to the next slide. "After the terrorist attacks of 9/11, attendance spiked, at least for a few months. This red line shows the level of giving. It spiked as well." He clicked to the next slide. "Each time the threat level was raised to Orange or Red, we received small but significant spikes in attendance and giving. But, if the threat level remained unchanged, attendance and giving returned to normal levels." Tom looked at his audience to let that fact sink in. "And, as you can see in this slide, personal reminders of the threat, such as personal searches and the presence of armed security officers, further increased church attendance." He scanned the group. "Fred?" He called on the man with the mustache.

"I guess we could conclude that to maximize church attendance and giving, a frequently changing threat level, including constant reminders of our tenuous situation, is definitely our best strategy!"

"Exactly," Tom said. "And during those threats, the public more fully embraced conservative values. Even if they didn't make it to church, they voted our way and contributed to conservative causes. If the world continues to be unstable and unsafe, we'll have our best chance to return our country to its Christian roots, a nation will support the Christian values we all believe in. We will finally achieve the goal we've been working on for years."

"Now is the time to make our move," Fred interjected from under his mustache.

Tom flipped to the next slide. "But we've got a larger problem. Islam. As you can see in this chart, the Islamic world has higher birth rates and has a population that is growing faster every year. We've got to keep the Christian birth rates up if we're going to have a chance. It's a numbers game in the end."

Gary said, "Right, Tom. We've already got a lot of traction against abortion rights. We've got to keep the birth rate up as high as possible. This idea that women should be able to plan their families has got to go. And we need to deny access to the 'morning after' pill and other birth control."

At that point, Bishop Ward entered the room. The group rose from their seats in unison and dipped their heads in humble acknowledgment of his stature. He took a seat at the rear of the table, and the others returned to their seats.

"Continue," he said quietly as he gestured like a king with a limply held hand.

"Your Honor," Tom said, "we just reviewed the overall impact of reports of terrorist threats on church attendance and the level of giving. A regular change in the threat level was the best for our overall performance in that area, and we're all grateful for the impact you've had in making sure the threat level is heavily promoted in the media. And finally, we were reviewing the challenge of keeping our birthrates up in the Christian world since we're rapidly falling behind."

"Yes, I know," the Bishop said.

"Let's review our strategy for the upcoming local elections. Monty, you have a report on that?" asked Tom.

Monty was seated to the left of the Bishop. He rose from his chair and walked to the front, while at the same time, Tom took his seat toward the front of the table.

Monty spoke without using the projector. "As you know, we have three of the five City Council members. We've got to unseat John Taylor, and we'll have full control."

Rebecca pushed the emptied cart out of the meeting room and went back to her desk near the entryway of the executive office building of the PIT.

I'm sure that the public would be astonished. Much of local government is controlled from this tiny private meeting room, Rebecca thought.

CHAPTER 54

Dan's face flushed; he tried to take a sip of water, but his glass was empty. *Walker just called me "son." I wonder if he intends to reveal his true identity.* No one else seemed to react, apparently accepting this as an older master talking to his student, so Dan decided to let it go.

"The best approach is to start without any presupposition," Walker said. "Although it may not seem viable, it's actually a very powerful strategy. You need to start from an assumption of uncertainty." He counted on his fingers in the air. "First, we know from our knowledge of the complexity of the world that our model is incomplete, inaccurate, and biased. We know that our mind is always 'right' in spite of the fact that we are inherently fallible in our thinking and frequently wrong. We know we 'fall short of the glory of God.' We know that it can be difficult to accept new information if it conflicts with our current model that we are certain is correct. It doesn't sound like we should trust any presupposition we may have.

"Even though it is difficult, the only way to fairly evaluate new information is to avoid a rigid presupposition and start from the standpoint of uncertainty."

"That sounds like... are you talking about *faith*?" asked John.

Walker said, "If *faith* to you means your model is absolutely correct and any changes are attempts by the devil to put you on the wrong course, then you are *certain*, not *faithful*. Any new ideas will be thrown out as lies. If you're certain that you know who God is and have him defined specifically in your mind, you have no need for faith. Being *certain* is not being *faithful*."

John readjusted his sitting position.

"Isn't it true that being faithful is important only if there is uncertainty?" Walker asked rhetorically. "Would we need the concept of faith if we were absolutely certain of everything? I don't think so. Uncertainty is a requirement for faith to exist. If someone says *have faith,* this also must mean *be uncertain*."

John nodded his head in reluctant agreement.

"Our mind has a tendency to be ultra faithful because it's absolutely sure that it's always right. That's why strong religious beliefs are so satisfying. The mind loves to have something to believe in as perfectly true."

"I heard that our minds are wired up to believe in something," John said. "There is a measure of comfort in knowing God and his plan."

"That's probably true. But let's get back to the underlying question," Walker said. "It's my contention that wrong-headed thinking is due to the incapacity of the human mind to correctly model everything and yet each person is utterly convinced that his model is right. If man had the capacity to acknowledge being wrong and to change direction without a second thought, we would probably avoid wars, fights, and many disagreements."

"If I understand your point, Walker," John said, "you say the sinful nature of the world is not due to the Fall, to the deception of Satan, or to the weakness of Eve but can instead be traced to how our mind works. Is that what you are getting to?"

"Yes, that's my point. It's simple, but it's powerful, and once you get the point, you will realize the truth in it."

John said, "I agree that our minds can't comprehend every detail of the world. I'm certainly way behind on most information, especially computers, biotechnology, and other high-tech stuff. Yet, I have a hard time believing that this limitation is responsible for all the 'sinful' nature of the world."

"You're right, John," Walker said. John blinked with surprise. Walker continued, "I don't think it's the *only* reason for the so-called sinful nature of man. I brought this up for two reasons. First, your religious views are very close to mine, at least when I started my research years ago. I know how hard it is to embrace a change in long-held beliefs. Knowing how my mind works helped me to consider that perhaps I should entertain the factual evidence I was seeing and allow myself to have been wrong in the past and change my position in the present. Believe me, I understand completely what you're going through."

"Yes... I'm struggling with the new interpretation, especially because it challenges the substance of original sin and as a consequence, Christ. In fact, I don't know if I'll ever be able to change my beliefs."

"You're doing a pretty good job, John. Even entertaining these ideas is more than many people can do. My second reason for bringing up the 'always-right' phenomenon is that it can explain human conflict and disagreement. Otherwise, why would politics and religion be considered improper for polite conversation? The same evidence, yet different conclusions. Those topics are avoided because each person has built a model based on incomplete information and will protect that model rather than allow it to be proven wrong. It's easier to believe that the other guy is obviously wrong than to entertain the possibility that you're wrong. Since two conflicting views can't both be right, this can blow up into major confrontations, feuds, skirmishes, and major wars."

"That certainly sounds right!" John said, incorporating the key words as a subtle joke. The others nodded in agreement. John and Shannon met eyes for a moment.

"The recent and continuing conflict between the Islamic world and the primarily Christian and Jewish western world can be traced to fundamentally different viewpoints. Each thinks that they're obviously right and that the other side is confused. Muslims view America as the *Great Satan,* and America believes that Muslims just don't get how 'moral and right' Americans are. Is there a common ground of reality between these two groups? If each side could honestly consider the other side and build an accurate model, you would think that a peaceful result could be found. Yet, the nature of the mind will work against this logical result."

"That makes sense," John said. "It seems like many disagreements could be traced to that same fact. But I still don't think it's the basis for all sin. What about something like rape or adultery? Those don't seem to be due to the 'always right' condition. How is that explained?"

"Indeed, there are many so-called 'sinful' activities that can be traced not to the always-right phenomenon, but instead directly to the sex drive and the related hormones of physical existence. The competitive spirit is linked to herd domination, creating conditions where the genes of the dominant male will become more prevalent in the population.

"Throughout history, as the old leader was overthrown, the new leader killed not only the old leader and his generals, lieutenants, and advisors but also all his wives, mistresses, and offspring—limited genocide. The new leader lived in a world of sexual promiscuity so that he could spread his genes as rapidly as possible. Even revered biblical leaders had many wives, mistresses, and concubines.

"For example, in the book of Judges, we learn that:"

> (Judges 12:8) *And after him Ibzan of Bethlehem judged Israel. And he had thirty sons, and thirty daughters, [whom] he sent abroad, and took in thirty daughters from abroad for his sons. And he judged Israel seven years.*

Dan was fast with his analysis. "It seems that Ibzan had sixty children in only seven years. Let's see, if each wife was as productive as possible, I would think that at least ten women would be necessary, but perhaps more like twenty or thirty wives and concubines, especially if you factor in the high rate of infant mortality that was the rule in those days. Anyone would admire this king's virility if he produced sixty children in only seven years. He was obviously a very busy man!"

"Freud linked virtually everything to the sex drive," Walker added. "He may have gone overboard on some things, but with regard to sin, he may have had a point. I would be willing to bet that most crimes, most 'sins,' can be linked to the sex drive, especially when additionally linked with the 'always right' phenomenon."

"Walker, you're making the sex drive sound terrible," Shannon said, frowning. "You could probably look at statistics the other way and show that culture, family, music, and the arts are also due to the *positive* consequences of the sex drive. I for one would not want a world without it."

"I do like one thing about considering that *sin* is linked to *sex*," Dan said. "It makes good sense with our new interpretation of the story in Genesis. Eating the fruit of the *Tree of Knowledge of Good and Evil* resulted in the eyes of Adam and Eve being 'opened' and an acknowledgment of their nakedness, their engaging in sex, and the eventual birth of Cain, Abel, and Seth, as well as untold other children. If, indeed, the consumption of this fruit introduced the possibility of sexual reproduction into the life cycle of humanity, we did, in essence, inherit this 'sinful'—that is, 'sexual'—nature from Adam. This assumption goes a long way toward harmonizing how that story is accepted today with our high-tech interpretation. If Adam and Eve did in fact introduce the possibility of sexual reproduction, we inherited our sexual nature from that choice. But a key point remains: Sexuality isn't evil. What it doesn't do is explain how the crucifixion of Christ would redeem us from our sexually aware state."

The group nodded.

Walker held up his hand to make sure he had the floor next. "Did Jesus have sexual desire and related 'family values?' In his day, it was very unusual for Jewish men to be unmarried. Some writers have proposed that Mary Magdalene was the wife of Jesus. Da Vinci's famous painting *The Last Supper* shows a figure to Jesus's right who has customarily been taken to be John, but after recent restoration of the painting, the figure appears to be a woman, perhaps Mary Magdalene, his wife.

"According to some sources, Jesus's wife and children were exiled to France, and the whole issue was suppressed by the church. The Knights Templar supposedly protected and preserved the truth, referred to as the Holy Grail. The idea that Jesus had a wife and family would mean also that Jesus had 'sinful' sexuality, and this thought was more than the church could stand. Since then, they've been afraid of sexuality and any contribution woman has had, blaming Eve—incorrectly—for the sinful nature of all humanity."

CHAPTER 55

"We might be more comfortable closer to the fireplace," Walker said.

They moved to a leather sofa and matching stuffed chairs in front of the large rock fireplace at the end of the main room. Walker hovered over the fire for a few minutes, tending and poking it, while the others took their seats. John sat by Shannon on the sofa directly in front of the fireplace while Dan sat in a chair on one side, leaving the remaining chair for Walker. Edgar excused himself to do other work and left the room.

Dan felt it was time to pull things together. "I'm wondering if we could take all the information we've piled up and assemble it into a big picture—a sensible theory of our origins and where we are today. I like to think that everyone has some measure of truth to contribute, scientists as well as theologians. We have the biblical story of Genesis remarkably authenticated by our new interpretation. We have holes in the theory of evolution, although much of it has been proven to be true on a within-species level, and the overall picture of evolution seems sound. Is there a way to put both religious history and science into one common theory? Can we build a model including our origins and the reality of our spiritual lives? Is it possible that everyone is a little bit right here?"

Shannon reacted quickly. "Dan, that is our ultimate challenge—to make sense of this crazy world. But I find it difficult to think that we'll ever be in command of enough information to meld all these different specialties—specialties that can take a lifetime to fully understand. The bottom line is that we can try to put together such a model, but although we may be right in some respects, we'll certainly be wrong in others."

Dan noticed that Shannon's foot and ankle were close to his leg. He imagined they were touching, and maybe they were. "If everyone waited until there were no doubts, we would have no theories at all," he said, "only known facts, and we would have very few of those. We'll never have absolutely complete information. To have a theory means you look for the most logical solution as you can while you simultaneously acknowledge that you have only partial information. But we're in pretty good shape. Today, we have a better chance than at any other time in history. Our scientific culture sits on top of centuries of development and thousands of contributors. Only recently—since the early 1800s—have we had any sense of the pattern of life and genetics. Now, we are saddled with the responsibility of describing our discovery of this connection between the scripture in Genesis and the pattern of life. The world needs to know about this. We need a model that incorporates this new revelation."

"Let's get started," Shannon said. She scooted forward in her seat, sitting upright. She was obviously much more interested in this line of thought.

"Great. Where should we start?" asked Dan.

"I'm most concerned with how this new story affects the theory of our origins. The fact that our interpretation eliminates the concept of original sin doesn't really concern me too much." Shannon turned her head to look at John more than at Dan. "Those issues will obviously be of highest concern to a strict Christian—like you, John," she teased in a tone dripping with playful scorn.

"Lighten up, Shannon. I'm not a 'strict' Christian. I'm open to some change, within reason. I understand your description about changing your mind, Walker. I'm ready to try."

Dan looked over to Walker, then back to Shannon and John. "Fine. Let's first look back in time from Genesis to form a new model of our origins. After that, we can look forward from the time of Genesis to sum up how this affects our present-day beliefs. Shannon, you know about this. What about our origins compared with evolution?"

Shannon rested her arm on the armrest next to Dan's chair and tapped her mouth with her finger for a moment. "The key disconnect between the present theory of evolution and our discovery of the secrets of DNA in Genesis is simple. If we evolved on this planet with no assistance from any outside force or intelligence, it would be very unlikely that the Genesis story-tellers would have known about DNA. Those secrets were unknown for at least another five thousand years."

Walker sat on the hearth and poked at the fire. "Would it be possible for the general concept of evolution to be correct *and* for the discovery of secrets in Genesis also true? I think that's the issue you're wrestling with."

"Yes, that is a valid question," Shannon said. "Could an advanced civilization—one approaching the sophistication of our own—have existed prior to the writing of the book of Genesis?" Shannon asked the group, but looked mainly at Dan.

"Sophisticated civilizations come and go, leaving only a few traces," Dan said. "For example, the Great Pyramids in Egypt represent a civilization that some researchers claim flourished thousands of years prior to the strict literalist biblical creation in 4004 BC. Some researchers claim that those pyramids were built long before that time, even 10,000 or 20,000 years earlier, yet are amazing feats of engineering, difficult to construct even today. Their exact purpose is mysterious. Researchers guess they were simply tombs, built during the Egyptian Old Kingdom at about the time when Moses first told his stories. But no sarcophagi were ever found in the Great Pyramids. Either they were long since plundered or maybe they were never there. Egyptian kings dug their tombs into the limestone rock of the *Valley of the Kings*. Caves, not pyramids."

Dan continued one of his technical binges. "The Great Pyramid of Cheops has amazingly exact dimensions, differing only 7.9 inches between the longest and shortest sides out of 756 feet, less than one tenth of one percent off. Each face is oriented precisely toward each of the compass directions, with a side off less than one tenth of one degree. As a result, each corner is almost exactly a right angle.

"That's not all. The location of those pyramids is absolutely unique. They needed a firm foundation of bedrock to support the massive load over 13 acres without sinking for 10,000 years. When viewed from far above the earth, the continents are distributed evenly around the pyramids, almost as if the earth could be balanced at that point. All those details are unnecessary for a simple tomb. The Pyramids represent a serious wrinkle in the history of the world, that's for sure."

"I'll say! They've always boggled my mind," Shannon said.

"Did the creators of the pyramids also understand DNA technology and bestow this information on the writers of the J-Account? The square-based pyramids have four sides, and each side has three edges. That's the magic four and three we mentioned earlier, related to the four bases in DNA grouped into three character words; add it up and you get seven."

"Relating to the seven seals in Revelation," John said.

"Also," Shannon said, "Genesis says that *Cherubim* guarded the entrance to Eden. We've already connected the similarity of this reference of that lion-eagle-man creature to the famous Great Sphinx near the Pyramids. Is the Sphinx guarding the entrance to Eden? Are the enigmatic Pyramids part of the gateway to Eden?"

"We would still be left with the question of whether the Egyptian civilization was the natural result of evolutionary and natural scientific progression, obtaining the secrets of nature at that early date, or was that civilization and possession of those secrets the mark of an advanced visitor?" Dan asked rhetorically.

"The Great Sphinx is truly a mind-blower," he continued. "No one really knows when the Great Sphinx was created. There are no inscriptions or hints on the artifact itself. Most archeologists assume it was created about 4,500 years ago, along with the Pyramids of the Old Kingdom. But, it is very difficult to date the Sphinx. The builders didn't mine rocks in one area and use them to build the Sphinx in another. The rock around the figure was removed, leaving the original rock of the sculpture, making accurate dating of the Sphinx virtually impossible."

Dan looked at some notes he had made. "In 1991, Dr. Robert

Schoch, a geologist from Boston University examined the unique weathering patterns on the Sphinx and its enclosure. He concluded that those patterns were not caused by the wind, as had previously been thought, but by water—torrential rains pouring down in sheets.

"This revelation convulsed the world of archeology: The Pyramids and other structures showed no similar vertical weathering patterns. They wondered, was the Great Sphinx much older than previously assumed, created during a period when rains were more common and long before the other monuments were built? This evidence suggests that the Great Sphinx is much, much older than the Pyramids. Indeed, it might be the Cherubim left to guard the Tree of Life."

"Unfortunately, if the Great Sphinx is the Cherubim from the scripture," Walker said, "this does nothing to explain how the knowledge of DNA could have been developed independently at that time. The hand-carved Sphinx is not representative of the ultra-high technology required to break the DNA structure, code, and operation."

Dan nodded. "Not high enough, I agree."

There was a moment of complete silence.

"What about the Greek culture?" Walker asked.

"You mean, you think it could be a source of the DNA knowledge in the scripture?" Shannon asked.

"I don't really think so, it was a bit too late," Dan said. "But it is an example of a peak of knowledge that was subsequently lost. Democritus was one of the most prolific writers of the Ionian age. He outlined all scientific knowledge available in about 500 BC. Instead of the bickering Greek gods that were popular at the time, he modeled the world with understandable natural laws and was very close to the mark in many ways. Unfortunately, of the seventy-three books he wrote, not a single work remains, all destroyed in the destruction of the great library of Alexandria in Egypt."

"How about the Antikythera Mechanism?" Walker asked. "Have you considered that?"

"I'm not really familiar with that..." Dan jumped out of his seat and trotted back to his laptop, still on the table. "Let me look that up." Dan clicked and typed for a moment. "Yes, here it a description of the Mechanism. Let's see... found in AD 1901 in the wreck of a Roman ship off the coast of the island of Antikythera..., about halfway between Crete and Greece. The date... yes, scientists estimate the date of the device to around 150 BC. It's a box of hand-cut bronze gears with inscriptions. Scientists guess from reproductions of the device that it could track the heavens and would have correctly predicted an eclipse ninety-nine percent of the time. More than a thousand years elapsed before instruments of such complexity emerged in Baghdad around the year 900. Wow."

"It sounds like a difficult jump in the steady march of engineering science," Shannon said. "If nothing else, it shows how a peak of knowledge was lost, and not too long ago. Especially when you consider thousands of millions of years, we could have had thousands of peaks. There may indeed have been some advanced civilization that understood DNA, I would think."

The fire cracked and popped.

"We've always heard of the lost continent of Atlantis. That may have been just such a peak." Shannon said.

"Atlantis... Yes, Atlantis. That is an interesting old story, isn't it?" Dan responded. "I know it's mentioned by Plato, in his famous dialogs. Give me just a second. I can probably search for that fairly easily also." Dan typed and clicked again, taking only a minute to find the passage. "Here is the section from Critias, part of the Works of Plato:"

> *Let me begin by observing first of all, that nine thousand was the sum of years which had elapsed since the war which was said to have taken place between those who dwelt outside the Pillars of Heracles and all who dwelt within them; this war I am going to describe. Of the combatants on the one side, the city of Athens was reported to have been the leader and to have fought out the war; the combatants on the other side were commanded by the kings of Atlantis, which, as was saying, was an island greater in extent than Libya and Asia, and when afterwards sunk by an earthquake, became an impassable barrier of mud to voyagers sailing from hence to any part of the ocean.*

"I don't know how Plato got this idea for Atlantis, whether it was based on some actual evidence of lost continent or if it was completely contrived. We are told that Atlantis existed some nine thousand years earlier. That would have placed it at about 10,000 BC. Could that culture have been sufficiently advanced to know about DNA?"

"I doubt it," Walker said, "but it's something we can't completely disprove either. The story of Atlantis is probably complete fiction. Have you ever heard of any real evidence of such a civilization?"

"If an ancient culture existed," Shannon said, "all traces of it could have been destroyed by the changes in the earth's tectonic plates. There is abundant evidence in geologic strata. But in all the evidence from millions of years, there is no clear evidence of any significant human civilizations until the relatively recent cultures in the river valleys we mentioned. Stories are one thing, but evidence is something else.

"Dan, you mentioned the mapping of human history as suggested by our Mitochondrial DNA and Y-chromosomes, tracing back to the *Mitochondrial Eve* and *Y-Adam* in Africa about 200,000 years ago. Did those studies imply any very ancient civilization, a civilization that could have evolved on its own and independently discover the hidden secrets of life?"

"Well, 200,000 years is a very long time. It might be possible for one or more civilizations to have advanced to our level and then been lost. The time from the creation in Genesis to today is only about six thousand years. You could have had civilizations like ours develop at least thirty times in that span and then have been completely lost, only to start again. Yet, in the mDNA mapping, there were no serious discontinuities in the progress—no evidence to support that notion." He thought again. "It's possible, but we have no real evidence to support it.

"I honestly think we can throw out this possibility. If there were such a civilization, it would have needed about the same amount of time as ours to develop the sophistication to independently discover the secrets of DNA and the pattern of life. Archaeologists would have long ago identified that civilization from the wealth of artifacts that would have been available."

"It seems our conclusion is clear," Shannon said. "We find no obvious evidence that another very ancient civilization evolved on earth, developed sophisticated scientific knowledge to independently discover DNA and the pattern of life and then provided this to the early writers of Genesis. There would be tons of archaeological evidence—fossils of cars, houses, planes. Sorry, no one has found that. I vote to disregard that possibility. Is everyone with me?"

Grunts of agreement filled the room.

"Hah! Again, you've been backed into a corner," John said with joy. "Now, you'll have to admit that God is reality!"

CHAPTER 56

Rebecca re-entered the meeting room and stood by the Bishop. The strategy meeting was still in process. They were now discussing the control of the school district and going over which teachers should be terminated due to their religious or political leanings. Rebecca whispered in the Bishop's ear, keeping her head down. "Sir, Commander Jackson is in the foyer. He says it can't wait."

Rebecca turned and quietly walked out of the room, keeping her shoes from clicking on the marble floor as well as she could. She pushed the door open and walked down the hallway to the foyer. Commander Jackson wore digital camo gear and a fatigue hat, firearm strapped to one leg. He paced the floor with deliberate steps, his head tilted down. As Rebecca neared, he looked up.

"The Bishop will be out in a moment."

He dipped his head to thank her, steely gray eyes piercing. She walked back to her reception desk.

A few minutes passed. Jackson continued to pace as he waited; he displayed a nervousness that seemed to contradict his soldier persona.

Finally, Bishop Ward emerged from the meeting room and walked over to greet the commander.

"Sir!" the commander said. He didn't salute, but doing so would have easily matched his tone.

"Jackson, why are you here? I told you not to come to the PIT. What's so important that it can't wait until I get back to the Ranch?"

Jackson stared into his eyes. "I just need to talk to you for a few minutes, sir."

The two walked into the Bishop's office for their private conversation.

Rebecca wondered what was going on at the Ranch. *Was this about the boy?*

CHAPTER 57

"Would you care for a spot of tea?" asked Edgar in his slight Welsh accent, joining the group from his work elsewhere in the house.

They accepted the offer, and Edgar poured for them. He also offered milk for their tea, the English custom.

As they fiddled with their cups, Dan spoke. "John, you're using the usual 'creationist' argument. That is—if evolution can't explain everything, then biblical creation must therefore be true. Sorry, there are many other alternatives that will fit our interpretation of the J-Account and yet depart from the young-universe concept of creationists."

"The creation theory is an obvious alternative because creation is clearly described in the Bible. You don't have to be a scientist to understand the truth of that description."

"Let me explain another alternative," Dan said. "It's based on the idea of *anthropocentrism.* Have you heard of that?"

"Well, I'm not sure... What does it mean again?

"Human-centered," Shannon answered.

"Okay, but so what?"

"Well, we naturally assume that we're in the center of everything. For example, what did people think the world was like in biblical days?"

"Flat, right?"

"Exactly. A flat circular disk with the clouds of heaven above and the fire and brimstone of hell below. Right in the middle of that disk was Jerusalem, of course."

"Sounds right."

"Eventually, they realized the model was wrong. 'Oops, not quite right,' they said. Earth isn't flat after all... It's a sphere. And, Jerusalem can't be in the center. In fact, there is no 'center' on the surface of a spherical planet such as earth. Oh, well, all is not lost. Earth is obviously still in the center of the universe, with the sun, moon, planets, and stars rotating around the primary focus of God's creation, with hell buried within the sphere and heaven somewhere else. The popular concept traded a flat earth with Jerusalem in the center for a spherical earth that was still in the center of God's creation.

"Oops, wrong again! Earth is not in the center the solar system.

Instead, earth is a relatively tiny third planet orbiting a massive sun. No big deal. The solar system is at least in the center of the universe.

"Oops, we missed that one! Our sun is a fairly insignificant star in one of the outer arms of a massive spiral galaxy, the Milky Way, that is at least eighty thousand light years across with two hundred billion stars like our sun. We now know there are billions of other stars and galaxies in a universe that's of indeterminate size. Is the Milky Way in the center? Not even close. We still don't know how you might locate such a center if there are no real boundaries."

"I see what you mean, Dan. It seems it's human nature to assume we are the center of attention," Shannon said.

"But the truth is, we're not," finished Dan. We've made the same mistake over and over and over again."

"The 'always right' phenomenon and anthropocentrism seem highly related. Not only do we think we are right all the time but we also think the universe revolves around our mind," Walker said.

"Scientists have the same shortcomings," Dan continued. "Evolutionists assert that life independently evolved here, the center of the start of life. We probably should start with 'oops,' since we've been wrong on that one so many times before. From our record of missing this point, it seems inevitable."

"Are you saying that we didn't evolve?" asked Shannon.

"No... not exactly."

"We've already covered the fact that the layers of development in the fossil record are quite substantial," Shannon said. "You seem to be saying on one hand that life didn't evolve here and then on the other, that it did. What do you mean?"

"Sorry. I mean to say that life may have primarily evolved somewhere else in the universe. It may have been actively seeded here on earth—*directed panspermia*. That would explain the existence of the embedded information about DNA in Genesis. And it might explain away some of the sticky points in the current body of knowledge about evolution."

Dan noticed that Shannon and John were sitting a bit apart, each repelled by the thoughts of the other.

"Hmmm." Shannon looked to the side and squinted. "There are certain observations that seem to support that theory. One is the uniqueness of humanity. I realize it's not scientifically supported; it's just an observation. But isn't it obvious that humans are remarkably different from other animals? Humans just don't seem to fit into the natural order on earth. Animals tend to fit within their niche with just enough of what they need, not more than enough to upset the balance.

"For example, the rabbit usually can outrun the wolf, although from time to time an injured rabbit will become a wolf meal. If the rabbit were much faster, the wolf would rarely eat. And if the wolf were much faster, it would always catch the rabbit, and the wolf population would grow rapidly but then reach a crisis when all the rabbits are gone. The wolf and rabbits fit their niche perfectly, like a key in a lock."

"Ecological systems are truly amazing," Dan said. "Tightly integrated and finely balanced. It seems there is a predator for every type of prey, a limit to population for every animal."

"It's not really the same for humans," Shannon continued. "We've been blessed with a brain far more sophisticated than other animals, the ability to use spoken and written language, the ability to grasp and manipulate objects and use tools. Do we really need this level of intelligence to survive? I think not. It's much more than necessary, like a wolf that can outrun all its prey.

"Humans are so much different from other life forms on earth, we get the distinct impression that we may not have evolved directly from the lower animals on this planet, just by chance."

Walker nodded.

"Physically, we are made of the same building blocks as all other life, the same DNA code, the same twenty amino acids, and the same cellular structure," said Dan. "At that level, we fit the natural order. Our genetic code is almost exactly the same as the chimpanzee, with over ninety-seven percent of the genome match—"

Shannon interrupted. "That can be deceiving, Dan. Ninety-seven percent suggests almost no differences when the actual difference is substantial indeed, in about forty million specific DNA changes. Forty million. Our intelligence, our ability to utilize symbolic language, and our obvious domination of earth clearly sets us apart. I don't think this notion is at all new."

"I think everyone here has a sense of that idea. Indeed, it's not scientifically provable, but that doesn't mean it's not true," Dan said.

"With all that said, I imagine your suggestion could be possible, Dan. Perhaps life evolved elsewhere, somewhat along the lines of what Darwin had in mind. That ancient race could have intentionally seeded life on earth. That would explain how the secrets of DNA and the pattern of life could have been available to the early writers of Genesis, why evolutionary links are still missing from the fossil record, and why humanity is so remarkably different from the 'lower' animals."

"Are you suggesting that green men in UFOs visit earth every so often to plant the next stage of life, directing evolution every step of the way?" asked Walker, speaking to Dan.

"Oh, come on!" John said, thrusting his arms into a tight lock.

Dan jumped up and walked around the group as he talked. "Wait. It sounds crazy, but it's possible. DNA-based life may have been *seeded* on earth. Genesis chapter three refers to four cradles of civilization, the Euphrates, Nile, Huang He, and Indus river valleys. It describes the establishment of human cultures in these valleys and the introduction of sexual reproduction in the life cycle of those humans, based on the serpentine structure of DNA. You could make the case that the story in Genesis describes just such a seeding of life."

Shannon continued the thought. "An ancient and advanced race was simply looking for a suitable planet to establish life on, sending a 'seed' of humanity to see if it would take hold."

Dan paused by his computer, referred to it, and then continued. "In Genesis chapter one, it says

> *And God said, Let there be light: and there was light. And God saw the light, that [it was] good...*

"God saw that the light was good. Does this make any sense at all? Just think: How can an omnipotent god create something that's anything but *good*? Certainly, God would never make any mistakes, never create anything bad or wrong. Does he ever say 'Oops'? That would be impossible, right? Why include a verse saying that the light was good? It only makes sense if the 'gods'—the plural *Elohim* in Hebrew—actually were imperfect beings that could make mistakes. Isn't it more likely that these beings needed to find a suitable star, one about the right size, the right age, and have planets that could possibly support life? We could rephrase these verses to be:

> *The ancient Elohim people searched for a suitable star, and they found one, and it was good.*

"Hey, this is fun. I like your idea, Dan," Shannon said. "Keep going. What about these verses:"

> (Gen. 1:6) *And God said, Let there be a firmament in the midst of the waters, and let it divide the waters from the waters.*
>
> (7) *And God made the firmament, and divided the waters which [were] under the firmament from the waters which [were] above the firmament: and it was so.*
>
> (8) *And God called the firmament Heaven. And the evening and the morning were the second day.*
>
> (9) *And God said, Let the waters under the heaven be gathered together unto one place, and let the dry [land] appear: and it was so.*
>
> (10) *And God called the dry [land] Earth; and the gathering together of the waters called he Seas: and God saw that [it was]*

good.

"Well, let's see. That follows directly with the concept that life was established—seeded—by ancient, non-omnipotent beings. The first step in the establishment of life is to form water on the planet. If you were an ancient race trying to establish life, you would first find a good star, as described in verses three and four. Then, on a suitable planet, it's apparently necessary to produce water, at least for our type of life. The ancients probably tried this on other planets and for one reason or another, failed. Too cold or too hot and the water would freeze or evaporate, never condensing into life-sustaining oceans and rivers. In other words, it was a trial-and-error activity. When it worked correctly, it was *good.*"

Shannon said, "Mars looks like it could have had water at one time, with eroded river valleys and reports of canals seen even with crude telescopes. Early astronomers thought that those canals marked Martian civilizations, civilizations that could be either friendly or bent on the merciless destruction of earth."

"War of the Worlds!" John used a menacing voice inside cupped hands to make an ominous echo.

"Martians aren't ready to invade earth!" Dan chuckled. "Recent space probes and robot rovers eliminated that idea. The question is: Did life ever exist on Mars? At this point, there is still no definitive proof, but if there was, it wasn't much. Data from the surface and images of river-like channels imply that liquid water may have existed on the planet long ago.

"Mars may have been an early failed attempt by the ancients to establish a suitable environment on a planet in our solar system. Listen, if you were a DNA-based ancient race attempting to seed yourself in a new solar system that had some chance of being suitable for life, you would try to produce a life-sustaining water environment on all planets that are a close match to a known profile. Many would fail, but once in a while, there would be a success, and such a success would be called *good.* The scripture doesn't describe all the failures, like Mars."

"Let's go on," Shannon said excitedly. "The next statement in Genesis that *it was good* occurs when God establishes the sun and moon in the sky for timekeeping and light."

> (Gen. 1:14) *And God said, Let there be lights in the firmament of the heaven to divide the day from the night; and let them be for signs, and for seasons, and for days, and years:*
>
> (15) *And let them be for lights in the firmament of the heaven to give light upon the earth: and it was so.*

(16) *And God made two great lights; the greater light to rule the day, and the lesser light to rule the night: [he made] the stars also.*

(17) *And God set them in the firmament of the heaven to give light upon the earth,*

(18) *And to rule over the day and over the night, and to divide the light from the darkness: and God saw that [it was] good.*

(19) *And the evening and the morning were the fourth day.*

"That shoots a huge hole in your theory, Dan," John said. "You said the sun and solar system were the first thing found, why find these again?"

"That's what I thought at first, John. Indeed, it doesn't match the 'literal' view of creation either. If God created light as his first act, why would he need to create the sun? However, it can be reasoned to make some sense."

"How?"

"Let's assume that the ancients first located a star and suitable solar system and found an appropriate planet that could sustain liquid water. It may have been the case that this planet had a bad rotational rate. It could have been like Mercury, where it takes 176 earth-days for to complete one solar day, and the temperature swings from -300°F to 800°F in the process. Or like Venus, with a 224-day year but a 243-day rotation. On Venus, the sun moves backwards in the sky, taking ten earth-days for the sun to move the distance we see on earth in only an hour. But the atmosphere is so thick on Venus that the heat is kept in, and it has very uniform and even higher temperatures, reaching 900°F. If we had either of those scenarios on earth, our climate would be very, very different, and would probably be terribly unsuitable for life."

"Yes, that would certainly be true," Shannon said.

"Instead, adopting a reasonably fast, but not overly fast rotation rate is important to the stability of the weather and climate on earth and therefore to viability of life. If the ancients established the twenty-four-hour rotational period, this would clarify the meaning of that verse."

"I see," Shannon said. "The verse is simply talking about a change to a reasonable rotation rate. That fits with your theory of ancients seeding earth. You said that Mars might have been a failed attempt. Does it have a reasonable rotational rate?"

"Almost the same as what we have here, 24 hours and 39 minutes."

The fire continued to crack and sputter behind Walker. Dan sat down.

"Amazing. Go on," she said.

"God finds that the fifth-day resulted in something good as well:

(Gen. 1:20) *And God said, Let the waters bring forth abundantly the moving creature that hath life, and fowl [that] may fly above the earth in the open firmament of heaven.*

(21) *And God created great whales, and every living creature that moveth, which the waters brought forth abundantly, after their kind, and every winged fowl after his kind: and God saw that it was good.*

(22) *And God blessed them, saying, Be fruitful, and multiply, and fill the waters in the seas, and let fowl multiply in the earth.*

(23) *And the evening and the morning were the fifth day.*

"If the ancients could find a star and solar system that met their criteria, a planet that accepted the establishment of water, a rotation rate that was suitable or could be adjusted to be suitable, they could proceed to try to establish life," Dan said. "If they attempted to seed life, it may have been that something about the environment would not be quite right for life, resulting in a failure. The fact that everything was going well in this tiny niche of the Milky Way galaxy meant that the ancients could say that it was *good*—the seeding of DNA-based life was proceeding well."

"At least on earth," Shannon said. "As you said, if Mars was a failed attempt at seeding life, it obviously would never be recounted, unless you could find a Martian Bible. Of course, such a Bible would never be written because no human cultures were ever successful there. You never hear about the failed attempts."

Dan turned to face Shannon more squarely. "Regarding seeding life, the J-Account of creation describes that the plants were introduced first. Animals need plant life for food and oxygen. Only long after the plants had stabilized could animals and then humans be introduced."

"All this sounds so very wonderful," John said. "But it's really a joke—just a stretch of the imagination. You haven't solved the mystery of our origins, only pushed it back to another more ancient race. Sure, I can see that it could possibly fit the scripture for ancients to have seeded earth. It may answer how life originated here and how the secrets of DNA could have been encoded in Genesis. Big deal. Then you have a new question: Where did those ancients come from?"

"Yep, that is a stumbling block." Dan hesitated and then said, "You're asking: 'If life needed a helping hand to evolve here, how could it evolve anywhere else without a helping hand?' Right?"

"A big problem, isn't it?" John wielded the question like a tiger playing with his prey. "Were the ancients seeded by an even more ancient race? And was that race seeded by a very, very ancient race? Eventually you get to the race that was not actively seeded, and you have to tackle the actual origin question. Hah! You're backed into a corner again! You've admitted that the fossil record doesn't support Darwin's theory. Even if ancients seeded DNA life on earth, your only way out will be to admit that God had a hand in this!"

John cracked his knuckles to express his joy at making such a strong point. But his joy had its limits. Shannon's sword regarding original sin and the truth of Christ was still in his side. And the wound was festering.

CHAPTER 58

"Regarding the idea of seeding life here, have you heard of the Raelians?" asked Walker.

"I'm not sure." They all shook their heads and squinted, brows furrowed.

Walker rose from his seat on the hearth. "Originally founded by Claude Vorilhon, from Quebec, Canada. He claims that in 1973, he encountered an alien spaceship and the beings he met were in fact 'ancients,' much like those postulated by your seeding scenario, Dan."

"Oh, really?"

"He wrote a book describing his encounter, changed his name to Rael, and developed a cult-like following. His followers, the 'Raelians' want to establish an embassy for the Elohim extraterrestrials in Jerusalem. Lately, you may have heard of this group with regard to cloning experiments."

"Their story sounds like it correlates well with our theory that our planet was seeded by these ancients. Right?" asked Shannon.

"Not completely," Walker said. "A careful reading of Rael's book reveals a problem. We know that the serpent represents the *most subtle* form of all creatures: DNA. But that meaning is in conflict with his book. Rael says that he had a personal encounter with extraterrestrial spacemen and that they supposedly told him exactly how to interpret Genesis. Yet, even with the details from his 'close encounters of the third kind,' his interpretation of the Fall was more like the conventional interpretation. Adam and Eve were still breaking a commandment. The clincher is this: The serpent represented a group of snake-like renegade scientists and not DNA."

"It looks like we can throw out that cult as a hoax. The spacemen did not explain the hidden meaning of the serpent as DNA!" Shannon said.

"A litmus test..." Dan said, a bit of excitement in his voice. "The serpent is our litmus test. Any supposedly sacred or inspired document can be tested to see if the serpent is taken to symbolize DNA. In this case, the spacemen should have known the true hidden meaning, but they didn't."

"Litmus test?" John asked.

"I imagine it would be fun to see if other supposedly sacred or inspired texts that mention this story can be refuted by the same litmus test. I'm talking about the Islamic *Al-Qur'an*, the *Book of Mormon*, and even the prophetic writings of Ellen G. White of the Seventh-Day Adventist Church. If they conflict with this single important point, that would mean they are contrived by humans—false-prophecy, so to speak."

"Of course, that litmus test works only if you accept that the pattern we found in Genesis is legitimate," John said.

"And, those sort of tests can be dangerous." Walker leaned toward the group. "Extremists of those groups you mentioned are not unheard of, and they may not take a liking to your comparisons." The fire sputtered and cracked. "Yet, I found this exact question intriguing, and I tested all of those documents you mentioned."

"What did you find?"

"They fail the litmus test. Every one. You can see why it makes me a bit worried. Let's try not to focus on that point, if you don't mind. I really don't want to give those groups any ammunition."

Dan looked at his father. He felt angry that thinking about something could be so dangerous, that voicing an idea could be so offensive. But it still may be wise to avoid offending those groups. Doing so could be a huge mistake.

CHAPTER 59

The Saturday morning beach skies were overcast and the temperatures cool. Later, as the morning matured and the shoreline beckoned, tourists would flock to this popular area, crowding the streets and parking areas. It was simply part of the diurnal rhythm of any beach area near a large city. Although Hall hated the constant battle with the crowds, he loved the ocean. His strategy was to leave his condo early to avoid the onslaught of those impolite masses. Today, his morning ritual included a trip to the laundry service to drop off his shirts and suits for cleaning and pressing. Hall didn't stray far from his weekly habits, a system he had refined over the years, a system that ran like clockwork.

But systems that run like clockwork can also become predictable, and such predictability can be a risk. In war, the more your enemy knows about your regular movements, the easier it is to design an effective attack. Regular, repeating movements are the easiest to understand and predict. A random, irregular pattern is almost impossible to predict. But people usually don't run their life like that.

People find themselves repeating the same movements from one day to the next. The same roads, the same route to work, the same stop for coffee, and even the same donut. Not only that, they rush along, never exploring alternate routes, rarely changing from a lunch selection that is already known to be satisfying.

Hall was a professional investigator. Although he relied on the patterns and regular movements of the people he investigated, he was also aware that from time to time, his own habits would have to change to avoid becoming an easy target for the criminal enemy. The FBI would force changes to the mundane repetitive life style of their agents by regularly moving them to different locations. However, it doesn't take long for those regular patterns to resurface.

And that was the case today.

The laundry service Hall used was in a small "L"-shaped plaza, with only a half-dozen stores. He pulled into the parking lot and selected an empty parking stall across from the laundry service, got out of the vehicle, opened the door to the back seat, and pulled out his laundry basket filled with shirts and slacks that needed cleaning and especially pressing. Hall hated to iron his own shirts.

He then hoisted the basket to his shoulder and proceeded to walk across the lot. Halfway to the building, he heard the roar of an engine. His field of view was blocked to the right by the basket. He continued walking toward the laundry service, neglecting to turn his head toward the sound. *Probably it's just some teenager just revving his engine*, he thought.

The sound was too close—much too close.

Hall finally turned to look for the source of the sound. A black car was within a few feet, then in contact with Hall's right leg. Being over six feet tall, Hall toppled over, his legs knocked out from under him like a catcher tripped by a runner sliding into home plate. He hurled his laundry basket to the side and then tumbled over the hood of the car, striking his right eyebrow on the windshield. While his face was pointed toward the car, he attempted to look in, but the windshield was heavily tinted; he could see nothing of any consequence. His body rolled off the driver's side of the car, and he fell to his knees, facing the other way, with blood from the cut over his eye beginning to flow.

Hall jumped to his feet, but the car had already exited the small parking lot. He pulled his gun from his concealed holster. The time it took for Hall to run to the street allowed the car to speed to the next corner and turn right. *Damn! I missed the license!* It didn't matter. He was sure it would lead nowhere.

Hall felt the pain of the cut on his brow. He checked it with his hand and discovered the blood. *I need to apply pressure to stop the blood flow.* He held his right hand to the wound while he collected his laundry from the parking lot asphalt. *I'm sure this attempt to put me out of commission has to do with the warning about the PIT.*

Under these obviously dangerous circumstances, many people would resolve to avoid the issues of the PIT, William Freeman, and the missing George Stanfield. But not Hall. This attempt on his life only further solidified his resolve to continue his investigation, to continue even if his defiance of orders from above put his upcoming retirement in jeopardy.

CHAPTER 60

"Even if you accept the idea of seeding our planet with DNA-based life, that only pushes the question of origins back to an earlier civilization. You still have no real resolution to the question of our origins," John said with the smile of a triumphant competitor.

"True. We might never be able to learn the history of these ancients who we assume might have seeded life here," Walker responded as he moved back to the hearth.

"Well, there is one chance," Dan said. "If this theory is true, we might eventually expose a record from the ancients with significantly more detail than the brief story in Genesis."

"That would be great, if it were possible." Walker picked up the black wrought-iron poker. "There are other ancient documents that we could review to see if we could find an even larger description. We already mentioned the idea that there is a special connection to the Great Sphinx in Egypt. Egyptian religious inscriptions might include information about DNA."

"Oh gawd! That sounds like another huge project," John said, with a sigh. "We already have our hands full with our current project. If you're suggesting that we look for links in all the Egyptian inscriptions, this project will obviously never end! I would suggest that we turn back to the Bible; we're not close to being done even with that one volume."

"Fair enough. We can reserve the analysis of all the inscriptions in Egypt for next week, if that's okay with you!" Dan said.

"Good idea, yes, next weekend it is." Everyone chuckled.

"Let's look back at the Bible." John reopened his black leather Bible on the edge of the coffee table. "Some religious scholars are adamant that the J-Account in Genesis is older than the P-Account, even though the P-Account is presented first. But is there any record of earlier versions of those accounts? I've never heard of any."

"Remarkable parallels can be seen in the ancient cuneiform documents from the cultures that existed in Babylon during and prior to the time of the Jewish exile." Walker turned from the fireplace. "The idea is that some of the myths and legends from that area may have been incorporated in the Genesis accounts or perhaps even are the source of those stories. Remember, historians say that during this exile the Bible was likely penned to preserve the threatened Jewish culture, so it makes sense that perhaps the stories from that area might have also been included."

"You say *cuneiform* documents?" asked Shannon.

"'Documents' is a bit of a misnomer. They're actually *tablets* of clay, with indentations created by a stylus pressed into the clay." Walker punched the fireplace poker in the air to illustrate how it might have been done. "They are remarkably robust, just the type of written material loved by archaeologists. The problem was that for centuries, we didn't know how to decrypt the tablets."

"How did they ever figure it out? I would think it would be almost impossible to discover what some cryptic depressions in clay would mean without some stake in the ground, some idea to get started."

"No kidding," Walker continued. "The thousands of tablets discovered in the Babylon area were gibberish until the breakthrough made possible by the *Behistun Inscription*—the 'Rosetta Stone' of the cuneiform language, if you will, decoded in 1851. That famous inscription is engraved high on a stone face along a well-traveled road. It had been admired by travelers since about 500 BC. Luckily, it's quite high up on the cliff, about a hundred yards off the ground, virtually impossible to reach and deface. It describes the military victories of the Persian king Darius-I in three languages, cuneiform text in Old Persian, Babylonian, and finally Elamite. The actual text on this inscription doesn't seem important to our work. But it was crucial to allow us to decode the cuneiform tablets."

"So once they were decoded, what did they say?" Shannon asked.

"Most unearthed cuneiform tablets recount money exchanges—financial records of little interest to theologians and philosophers. However, tablets written in about 1150 BC recount the creation myth *Enuma Elish*. It's not an exact precursor to the Genesis P-Account but it does have some similar phrasing." Walker picked up a book from a few that he had stacked nearby in preparation for their discussion. He turned to a marked page. "Here is the section from the fifth and sixth tablets that's most interesting:

He [Marduk] made the stations for the great gods;
The stars, their images, as the stars of the Zodiac, he fixed.
He ordained the year and into sections he divided it;
For the twelve months he fixed three stars.
After he had [...] the days of the year [...] images,
He founded the station of Nibir to determine their bounds;
That none might err or go astray,
He set the station of Bêl and Ea along with him.
He opened great gates on both sides,
He made strong the bolt on the left and on the right.

In the midst thereof he fixed the zenith;
The Moon-god he caused to shine forth, the night he entrusted to him.
He appointed him, a being of the night, to determine the days;
Every month without ceasing with the crown he covered(?) him, (saying):
"At the beginning of the month, when thou shinest upon the land,
Thou commandest the horns to determine six days,
And on the seventh day to [divide] the crown.
On the fourteenth day thou shalt stand opposite...

"My blood will I take and bone will I [fashion],
I will create man who shall inhabit [the earth],
That the service of the gods may be established, and that [their] shrines [may be built]."

"I didn't read every verse, since some have big gaps. Even though this has a similar flavor to Genesis, chapter one, you will agree that it doesn't seem like a direct precursor. This passage simply describes the sun, moon, and stars and further describes the phases of the moon, so that each quarter phase represents the seven-day week.

"Christians today assume the week was defined by the seven days of creation described in Genesis, the sacred number seven. Not even close. The seven days of the week are simply one-quarter phase of the moon. The features described in the cuneiform tablets are aspects of our world that would be obvious to any observer and could be incorporated in any creation myth. Just because they're found in other poetry and scripture doesn't mean that poetry is somehow divinely inspired."

Shannon looked stunned. "I have to admit, I always assumed Genesis defined the seven-day week, and that was that. The relation to the phases of the moon is a very obvious source and probably also the source for your sacred number seven, John.

"Sorry, there isn't much there to sink our teeth into." Walker admitted. "Even if we found evidence of more ancient documents, we would still be faced with limited terminology and would not be able to understand their history. It would be quite a problem, unless we could also find another Behistun Inscription to decode it. The fact is, theologians have been searching for the precursor to Genesis for centuries. The new advances in this area are encouraging, but it may take more archeological discoveries before we get much further. For now, this is a dead end.

CHAPTER 61

"I've listened long enough," John said. "Although the connection between the J-Account and all that biology stuff is appealing, it's probably nothing more than a matter of coincidence—a figment of hopeful imagination."

"We should be happy that John is willing to ask these questions," Walker said. "We need a thorn in our side to help us consider every angle." Everyone except John chuckled; he remained deadly serious.

"Let's give John the benefit of the doubt," Dan said as he stood. "He is asking a simple but important question: Is finding the pattern in Genesis total coincidence, a simple result of DNA-based life looking for such a pattern and being perhaps over-eager to find it? Are we just looking at a cloud in the sky and imagining that it represents a rabbit, looking at the moon and imagining that we see a man? Are we looking at a rock that looks like the Virgin Mary and falling to our knees because water is seeping from the rock near her eyes?"

"Exactly my point," John said, snapping his fingers.

"We should ask this question: Is the pattern match beyond a simple coincidence? If it is, then it will have more in common than a simple *one-point coincidence.*" Dan returned to his seat.

"What do you mean by a one-point coincidence?" Walker asked.

"Well, if the two patterns coincide—that is, match—in only one way, this would be a one-point coincidence. The more points in common, the more the two patterns are connected, and the less likely it could be an accident or a contrivance. It's a geometric relation. If two details are in common, you have to multiply their probability of occurring alone. If many details are aligned, it's almost impossible for it to be coincidence."

"I think I understand. Let's start with a simple coincidence... the one point coincidence. What would be an example?

"Here's one: Consider the pattern match between the codons in DNA with the patterns of the *I Ching*, the ancient Chinese tradition. Indeed, the number of unique codons—sixty-four—matches exactly the number of patterns of the *I Ching*, but the match stops there. The *I Ching* does not discuss the principles of biology, natural selection, or the serpentine structure of DNA. The connection is interesting but not persuasive."

"There are also sixty-four squares on the chessboard, but I doubt that people are saying that the game of chess is linked to DNA or to the sacred *I Ching,*" Shannon said.

"Exactly. These cases exhibit a single-point match, a match based on the fact that the number sixty-four is involved—two to the power of six. Multiply two together six times, you get: two, four, eight, sixteen, thirty-two, sixty-four. Just because that extremely round number is an important part of the patterns doesn't mean that they're linked."

Walker said, "Clearly, in the DNA and Genesis correlation, we have a multi-point match, with details that go far beyond any sort of simple coincidence. But there may be another explanation."

"Like what?" Dan asked.

"Just this. We're all based on DNA. It's true, even though we didn't know it until this last century. Now, here is the question: Is it possible that we would 'accidentally' come up with a story, such as that in Genesis, that includes many of the elements about DNA and the pattern of life, the accident ever more likely because we are based upon DNA ourselves? For example, what is the popular symbol for the medical profession?"

Shannon spoke up. "Isn't it the two snakes climbing a staff, with wings at the top? It does look sort of like DNA!"

"That's right," Walker said. "The caduceus. When people see it, they probably think it was originally based on the serpentine structure of DNA, but it was actually designed long before the 1950s. The ancient Greek culture used this symbol for Hermes—'Mercury' in Roman translation—messenger of the gods, inventor of magical incantations, conductor of the dead, and protector of merchants and thieves. In the AD 600s, alchemists were referred to as Hermeticists and as *practitioners of the hermetic arts*. The Indian branch of alchemy, the Nagayuna, uses the naga symbol—two intertwined serpents—to symbolize the unification of the body's energies. So it is indeed intimately related to the medical profession.

"In Greek times, however, the primary symbol for the medical profession was a staff with a single climbing serpent, the *Asclepius wand*. It dates to antiquity, a symbol of the Greek god of healing. There were many stories of healing that were attributed to Asclepius, probably exaggerations to be sure."

"I see your point," Shannon said. "Both of those symbols were used back in the ancient Greek culture, long before we knew the structure of DNA. It makes you ask the question: Was selection of this symbol total coincidence, or is there an inherent tendency for humanity to choose DNA-like symbols and stories? If so, our finding of the pattern of DNA in Genesis could be another result of that tendency."

"Another explanation is more likely," Dan said. "You see, *Dracunculus medinensis,* a parasite worm common in ancient times, was often referred to as the *fiery serpent* because of the pain it induces. Up to six feet long, this pencil-lead-diameter worm lives just under the skin of its human host. To remove it, the ancient physician would make an incision just in front of the head of the worm and pull it out by slowly winding it on a staff. In those days, the worm problem was so widespread that the symbol of the worm-on-a-stick denoted a physician who could help remove it. Obviously, it has nothing at all to do with DNA, but it's an example of yet another single-point coincidence of no true importance.

"The biblical book of Numbers mentions the parasitic worm:

> (Num 21:8) *And the LORD said unto Moses, Make thee a fiery serpent, and set it upon a pole: and it shall come to pass, that every one that is bitten, when he looketh upon it, shall live.*
>
> (9) *And Moses made a serpent of brass, and put it upon a pole, and it came to pass, that if a serpent had bitten any man, when he beheld the serpent of brass, he lived.*

"If you read this verse with the understanding of the prevalence of the parasitic worm, it can be interpreted as a description of how to remove the worm by twisting it onto a brass pole, a bit cobbled up over time."

"Yes, that's quite clear," Walker said. "How about the primordial mythic symbol of the *uroboros*, the serpent eating his own tail, symbolizing the infinite, forming a circle or the figure-eight. It was popular goddess symbol even in ancient Egyptian culture."

"If the caduceus relates to the snake-like double helix of DNA, perhaps the uroboros relates to the circular structure of mitochondrial DNA and to the immortal prokaryotic bacteria," said Dan. "It's indeed interesting that we have these symbols from ancient times that relate to the structural forms of DNA in all life."

"Yet, those examples illustrate single-point coincidences," Shannon said. "Just like the coincidence of sixty-four—sixty-four codons in the DNA encoding scheme, sixty-four *I Ching* symbols, and sixty-four squares on the chess board—the number is the same, but there is nothing else to tie it together.

"With these, we have the coincidence of the climbing serpent: the serpentine structure of DNA, the caduceus of Hermes, and the staff of Asclepius. Finally, the coincidence of the circular uroboros."

"We can compare these single-point coincidences with the multiple-point pattern match we are dealing with," Walker said.

"To start with, the serpent being the most subtle of all creatures—DNA—is certainly central to the pattern match. With Adam's rib representing the Y-chromosome, we have a two-point match. The explanation of the consequences of incorporating sexual reproduction in the life cycle, the subsequent description of the menstrual cycle, discussion of telomeric shortening, separation between mitochondrial and nuclear DNA, and other details—we have a multiple-point pattern match that goes well beyond coincidence."

"I see what you mean," John said. "With all those connections in common, I can see that it'd hard to come up with all those connections at random or by chance."

The group sat quietly without talking for a few moments, all looking at the fire. Walker poked the logs, causing the fire to crackle and throw out sparks. The significance of the match—a match far beyond any simple coincidence—was truly sinking in.

CHAPTER 62

Hall left the laundry service and limped back to his car. It had taken a while to gather up all his laundry. Only one shirt was run over by the car, and the laundry service said they could probably save it. He opened the door of his car and got in, rubbing the side of his leg where the car had hit it. For a moment, Hall reflected on what had just happened and on other recent events.

Why would someone assault me, he wondered. *Did this have to do with the William Freeman case?* It was just one of a number of similar missing persons cases. The PIT was central to all these cases, a theological institution claiming to rescue distressed youth, an institution that sparked memories of old cases in Hall's mind, and one with a secret "Ranch" facility somewhere. The FBI was generally independent from politics, prosecuting crooks across party lines regardless of their affiliation. But recently something had changed, not only within the government as a whole but also within the normally independent FBI as well.

This attack in the parking lot implied that someone wanted to distract Hall from the trail leading to the PIT. Some people might find a telephone warning and drive-by assault enough to prompt a move to safer activities and to ignore that line of investigation. Not Hall. These events only hardened his resolve.

Now, Hall's only real lead was Daniel Stanfield, a man who barely even knew his father, a father who is one of the series of missing persons. And if Hall was being threatened, it made sense that Dan would be as well.

Hall started his engine and drove toward Dan's house.

CHAPTER 63

John stood up and paced back and forth in front of the fire. He was quiet, but to Dan, his body language spoke volumes. John was wrestling with the wound from Shannon and perhaps was now ready to confront the questions emanating from the Fall. He kept pacing slowly as he spoke. "The match we see between the ancient story of the Tree of Knowledge, the serpent, God's warning, death, and the modern knowledge of biology... well, I admit that this match goes far beyond the level of coincidence. I have no real problem when I consider only the story in Genesis." John stopped at one side of the room and looked out the window. "The trouble is, this part of the Bible is not an isolated part of the story. You can't just change it without some serious implications. It's essential to Christianity."

There was an uncomfortable quietness. Walker sat on the hearth near the steadily burning fire, ready to care for it at any moment.

Finally, Walker spoke up. "Your question, John, is very important, but you need to ask yourself if you really want to know the answer." He turned from the fire to look at John. "As with Shannon's question about evolution, the answer to your question may not be what you expect."

John looked out the window, still listening.

"Dan probably already told you that I studied similar material years ago when I was at the PIT. I can tell you that my results were astounding, and they were certainly not well received. I hoped that these questions would be substantially safer by now, but that's simply not yet the case."

John turned from the window, Walker continued. "Since the mid 1980s, there's been resurgence in the evangelical Christian churches and an associated intolerance of competing ideas. They believe they already have the story straight and everyone should fall into line, right behind their lead."

"That isn't surprising," Dan said, sitting in the chair near Shannon. "It's the case in any strongly religious culture, isn't it?"

"True, it's not new, not at all. But it's still a fact we must acknowledge. Now... before we continue, we must consider the risk. Should we explore these topics and be exposed to answers that may contradict traditions and stories that have been accepted as fact for centuries? Are we willing to be the modern-day Copernicus and suggest that earth is not in the middle of the universe? Do you really want to know the truth, even if it's disturbing, uncomfortable, and perhaps dangerous?" Walker directed his voice to John, who wrinkled his brow and raised his eyebrows at the same time, pressed his lips together as he listened. "If not, I'm happy to stop and leave you to your beliefs. I respect your faith and beliefs and have no agenda to replace them with anything else. This must be your choice."

John ambled from the window and took his seat, but he kept shifting positions, finally settling in with arms crossed. "I have a strong faith that will never be lost. I'm ready. Please go on. Tell me the truth as you see it."

"Are you sure?" asked Walker.

"I'm sure."

Dan and Shannon nodded their heads. "Go on," Dan said.

"Edgar!" Walker shouted into the other room. "The screen and projector, can you help me set them up?"

Edgar, who could be heard from the other room, walked in as he talked. "Oh yes... no problem, no problem at all!" He walked to the other side of the room, pulled out a foldable screen from the corner, set it up on one side of the fireplace, and then set up a conventional slide projector on the table directly behind the couch. Dan assisted when he could, always available when it came to technology. Walker pulled the curtains where John had been standing.

Positioning himself in front of his "class," Walker returned to his role of professor at the Institute. He held the slide projector controller in one hand, and he used the shadow of the fireplace poker to occasionally point to details on the slides as if it were a presenter's pointer. He looked up at the screen to get things adjusted.

"I pulled out one of my presentations on this topic from years ago. Although it's a subject near and dear to my heart, the opportunity to publish anything has likely passed me by." He turned to face the others, his expression darkened. "It remains a very dangerous topic. You won't find this information in most Bible-book stores or being taught from pulpits—those only support the mainstream view. Critical treatment of religious views is rarely found in popular literature or in churches today. Where can it be found? Only in out-of-print books or back-eddy archives, by diligent searchers willing to seek out buried information, willing to risk any consequence in pursuit of the truth." Walker turned to the fireplace and poked the logs again, delaying the start of his presentation for at least a minute or two. Dan figured the delay was probably to process some latent emotion connected with his experience with the PIT and his lost identity.

"I'm ready, Walker," John said, reasserting his willingness to continue. Books, laptops, and notepads were scattered over the rustic coffee table near the fireplace. There was still just enough light in the room for the group to easily see each other.

Walker turned from the fireplace, his composure changing back to the confident professor as he addressed the subject matter. "The first step in this process is to separate the questions as clearly as possible." Walker pressed the projector control to move past the title slide, to display a photograph of the "Fall and Expulsion," a portion of Michelangelo's work on the ceiling of the Vatican's Sistine Chapel. Here, the great master depicted Eve accepting the forbidden fruit from the serpent—having the torso and head of a female—coiled around the tree. Also shown is an angel ejecting the couple from the garden of Eden.

"Your assertion regarding Genesis is quite appealing. If we can explain the creation of Eve, and more importantly, the Fall and Expulsion, in terms of the laws of biology, facts of DNA, heredity, natural selection, and natural death, I would think this explanation would be embraced by even the most dogmatic of theologians. Indeed, it authenticates these early chapters of the Bible like no other approach. Fictional storytellers of that age, no matter how ingenious, could never have contrived the story so that it so completely describes those hidden truths."

The group nodded. John sat with his arms firmly crossed but nodded as well.

"But there is a glitch." Walker's voice in the darkened room took on a quality of a spiritualist at a séance mixed with volume and pacing characteristic of a preacher gesticulating from a church lectern to his enraptured congregation. "We're not talking about some unknown section in the tiny and rarely-used book of Zechariah with little if any impact upon the structure of Christianity. No, we're talking about the keystone, the most referenced part of the Old Testament, perhaps the most critical passage of all known literature—the tie between Jesus and Adam, his original sin and the resulting corruption of humankind to become inherently evil. And more significantly," he scanned the eyes of everyone listening, "justification for Christ's crucifixion and the redeeming power of his resurrection."

Walker stood in the light of the projector, the scene from Michelangelo falling on his face, in a way that he seemed included in the masterpiece.

"If the keystone of original sin is removed, does the archway of Christianity fall? And if it does fall, what is the truth of Jesus the Christ? Ah yes, those are the questions, my friends." Walker stroked his beard. "These questions—difficult questions—go to the heart of religious beliefs. Most believers rarely consider such difficult questions. Yet, this is what we must do here. We must ask: Are these traditions based in fundamental truth, or are they just conveniences of the church? And perhaps more importantly, we must also ask if these myths can be ignored, or must they be understood and dealt with fairly and completely."

The group looked up at Walker as if he had recovered his place at the PIT.

"Answer this," Walker said. "What is *original sin*?"

"Eating the forbidden fruit," Shannon volunteered quickly.

"Not exactly. It's true that Adam and Eve ate the fruit. But the sin was violating God's commandment not to eat it. That was the sin, the first sin of humanity." Walker stepped to the other side of the screen.

"Sure, you've answered the obvious question, but that's not really a complete answer. You must ask: What were the implications of that action? Aye, now, that's the question I'm talking about, a question debated and fought over for centuries.

"So original sin isn't directly related to the act of sex, right?" asked Shannon.

"Sex was only the implied result of eating the fruit. The Federalist Doctrine of original sin—perhaps the most strict formulation—focuses on the act of violating God's commandment; eating the fruit was only incidental, and sex wasn't even part of the picture. Breaking the commandment, aye now, that was the sin. Everything that followed was simply the natural consequence of that act."

"Good. I just don't see sex as being 'sinful.' It is part of life, required for procreation and children. We are all the products of that act. It can't be a sin!"

"Shannon, put yourself in the position of ancient man and look through his eyes," Walker continued. "He had no idea of the laws of nature or the underlying principles of life. He didn't know about cells, genetics, or how sex worked. Yet, he conceived that the world should be governed by a set of fixed and unchanging laws and rules. That was an important conceptual leap, a leap made possible by the idea of a single creator who might establish those fixed laws. The Greek Pagans had no such luxury with their plethora of bickering gods without any underlying rules of the road."

"Science would not exist otherwise," Shannon said. "The notion that experiments are repeatable by anyone and should provide the same results is absolutely essential to science, and it is a notion that has produced astounding results."

"Even though we agree that God works with a set of fixed laws of nature, we must consider if the tradition of original sin is part of those laws. Does it make any sense? Throughout history, those who disagreed with powerful leaders would be charged with heresy and threatened with execution, suppressing their contrary views. Reconstructing the history of the views of the church is quite difficult because they actively destroyed evidence of any contrary opinions. The perception that these religious questions are settled is desired by the established churches, but they are far from put to bed. The man on the street will tell you that original sin is a biblical fact, a fundamental foundation to the structure of Christianity. The truth is really far different. The debate was simply forgotten; it was never really solved."

"I'm wondering why we need the notion of original sin at all," Shannon commented.

"Original sin is just an attempt to make sense of the world," Walker answered, "a world that included the catastrophe of death. If you accept the concept of a single, all-powerful god, a god who is 'good' by definition, how can you explain the horrible notion of death?"

Walker paused for a moment but no one tried to answer that difficult question.

"Somehow, they had to imagine a world where God was good, so good that he would not introduce death to the life cycle of man himself. Man was the bad-guy in the story, introducing death by violating the commandment, thereby adding this evil construct to the life cycle of mankind."

"No, that's not right." Shannon caught their attention. "Man was not blamed for the wicked transgression against God." They wrinkled their brows. "Oh, no. The blame for death was not put on the shoulders of either God or man. It was the fault of the weaker sex, as usual: woman. The church has relied on women to shoulder this blame for centuries. It makes me sick!"

John fidgeted under the naked truth of Shannon's remarks.

"I'm sure it was hard to imagine death as a integral part of the life cycle, a cycle relying on natural selection for adaptation to the environment, and therefore death, to improve the species," Dan said. "Hard to imagine that Eve—woman—should not be blamed, but instead, praised for her wise choice. The traditional meaning of the story explained how the most evil construct—death—could be introduced. Science, in contrast, sees death not as an evil, but as an essential, positive ingredient. With our new understanding, the tradition of original sin is simply obsolete."

"I doubt your conclusions will be adopted by most theologians," Walker said. "Various flavors of original sin have been postulated and discussed over the past two thousand years, a continuum from weak to very strong forms. In the weakest form, original sin was the act that introduced death into the life cycle of humanity. You argue also that it is intimately related to the introduction of the system of sexual reproduction. I doubt many would disagree with that. You argue that it was not a sin at all but simply the introduction of sex that was chosen by Eve. Under this weakest form, it was the 'original choice' that was made available by God or the ancients, as you propose. Do we inherit the tendency to be sexual beings? Yes. Do we inherit the fact of death as a result? Yes. This weakest concept of original sin, if recast as the 'original choice,' is supported by our new interpretation of Genesis."

"Bravo!" Dan said.

John seemed to relax. He said, "In this weakest form, if the act of eating the fruit simply added the possibility of death, changing humans from immortal beings to mortal beings with a finite life span, I don't hear the concept of sin in that definition."

"The stronger forms include a stronger concept of sin. First, sin can be passed to the descendants of Adam and Eve. An even stronger form is understood as a general 'condition' of sin as a backdrop to the nature of humanity. These stronger concepts of original sin are vital to the rationale behind the larger and very coercive doctrines central to the rise of the Christian churches."

"It's strange. It's such an important part of Christianity, but the term *original sin* never even appears in the Bible," Dan said

"What? Of course it does!" John said, pulling his head back, like a cobra ready to strike.

"Sorry, I can search the Bible in an instant with my computer. It's not there. It's a term that may have been added later by theologians to describe that concept, I guess." Dan said. "Even if it's referred to with other terms, it's certainly not mentioned very much. You would think it would be found all over. It isn't."

"When did this all get started?" asked John.

Walker pressed the control to the slide projector, causing it to move to the next slide. It had both a picture of Augustine of Hippo and a map of the northern section of Africa. "Historians tend to agree that Augustine coined the term. He was the Bishop in Hippo, an African city in present-day Tunisia at the northernmost tip of Africa, due south of Italy and Rome. He wrote lengthy religious discourses, both to cast doubt on practices of paganism and to clarify Christian doctrine."

Another press of the button displayed the next slide, showing a section of text. "Take a look at this short section from Augustine's *City of God*, written in about AD 430. Here he is explaining how it can be that Adam's sin is propagated to everyone." Walker read it to the group.

> *In the first man, therefore, there existed the whole human nature, which was to be transmitted by the woman to posterity, when that conjugal union received the divine sentence of its own condemnation; and what man was made, not when created, but when he sinned and was punished, this he propagated, so far as the origin of sin and death are concerned.*

"As I said, Augustine and other early church leaders had to explain how God could allow death. They did it by hoisting the blame firmly on the first parents and went on to implicate all humanity. The stroke of genius behind this doctrine is that it fully integrates the story of Christ into the ancient Fall and eliminates the concept that the good deeds of man are sufficient for admission into heaven. As the pinnacle of his masterwork, it became necessary to appeal to the redeemer, that is, Jesus, to gain freedom from the burden of Adam's sin—even for infants. You can't do it yourself. Now, you need the church, or you are toast—banished to hell for an eternity."

Shannon said, "That was one of the hardest things about my Catholic upbringing to accept. I just can't imagine that a newborn baby can be considered sinful, to fry in the pit of hell for eternity. Why? And a sprinkling of some water by a priest will solve this? How does that make any sense at all?"

John squirmed in his seat, seemingly tempted to start in with Shannon, but he bit his lip.

"So, if you obliterate original sin, why have a redeemer?" asked Walker. "Why have the cross, the resurrection, Christ, and the New Testament at all? This will be the most difficult question to address."

The room was quiet except for the cooling fan in the slide projector. Walker flipped past several slides and stopped on an image of the painting *Jesus Driving the Merchants from the Temple*, by Jacob Jordaens.

"Break the story of Jesus into two parts. First, we have the reality of the person of Jesus, who walked the earth and taught important life principles. I show here Jesus when he drove the merchants from the temple, but you will find very few works of art depicting Jesus teaching and interacting with his early followers. Most art concentrates on the birth and death of Jesus, but little else. Yet, Jews, Muslims, and even atheists rarely dispute the fact that Jesus existed. Our first challenge is to determine if there is any conflict with our new interpretation in Genesis with the history of Jesus and his accepted teachings.

"If we make it past the first part, a larger challenge will be the story of Jesus that's more important to most Christians. Jesus is not just a great teacher but also the Son of God, who takes the sin of the world and essentially becomes sin, is crucified, and resurrected so that man can be redeemed from this sin of the world, sin that was introduced through the actions of Adam and Eve in the exact passage you're working with. Can we rectify this with the new interpretation? That's the second challenge."

"I... I won't argue yet. Go on," John said. It seemed at times that Walker and John were the only ones in this religious class situation, with John at the front of the class and the other "students" listening carefully, the energy of the conversation centered mostly between Walker and John.

"The first question can be restated more succinctly as follows: Do any records of Jesus's teachings conflict with our new interpretation of Genesis? We can put this to bed fairly easily for those who believe the Bible reflects an accurate description of the life of Jesus. All we need do is read over a red-letter edition of the New Testament to see if Jesus ever refutes the hidden meaning of the Genesis story." Walker clicked the projector to show *The Wedding Feast at Cana* by Véronèse, a huge and stunning work displayed at the Louvre, one of the very few works depicting a scene from the life of Jesus, a scene where Jesus performs the miracle of producing adequate wine for the party.

"It turns out that Dan is right," Walker continued. "The exact term *original sin* never occurs anywhere in the Bible. But beyond that, Jesus never mentions the Fall, the serpent, the Tree of Knowledge, or anything in Genesis at all. It would be different if Jesus said *Satan tempted Adam and Eve*. It would be different if Jesus had mentioned the Fall. He didn't. There are simply no comments by Jesus related to this question. Also, if Jesus had said, *I'm here to redeem you from the original sin of Adam,* we would really have something. Nothing of the kind was ever mentioned or even implied by Jesus."

"I'll have to take your word for that," John said. "But I can easily verify that for myself by reading over my red-letter edition of the New Testament, and believe me, I will."

"Are you comfortable," Dan asked Walker, "in accepting our interpretation based on this first part of the story of Jesus? You found no conflict, right?"

"I see no conflict at all with the traditional history of Jesus and this first part of Christianity. Jesus passes the litmus test because he never even mentions that material. Remember, the litmus test is simply the fact that the serpent represents DNA. This single fact is something that would not be decipherable until 1953, when the structure of DNA was discovered—a serpentine molecule, the *most subtle* expression of all creatures. We can use this connection alone to separate divinely inspired from concocted. If any text asserts that the serpent represents Satan, that text is suspect and likely fictional. No truly inspired document would make the terrible mistake of upsetting the hidden meaning of that section."

"Right. That is a great way to separate the wheat from the chaff," Dan offered.

"If you also assume that the words of Jesus in the New Testament are accurate and if Jesus clearly asserted that the *serpent* represents *Satan*, it would be difficult to also assert that Jesus was 'in the know' about the hidden secrets in Genesis. Would the Son of God know about these secrets? You bet, unless Jesus was kept deliberately in the dark about this question, and the inspired writers were also allowed to spoil the hidden secrets of Genesis.

"Luckily, we don't have to pursue that line of thought at all. Jesus doesn't spoil the hidden secrets by falsely asserting that the *serpent* represents *Satan*. And, as you mentioned, Dan, the New Testament never does either. For those people who wish to accept the new interpretation *and* continue to believe in Jesus, this *is* good news."

"Good news, yes. I see what you mean," John said. "In essence, you're saying that nothing in the New Testament refutes our new interpretation of Genesis chapter three. That's what I was thinking!" A wrinkle of concern disappeared from John's face as he relaxed to the support Walker gave to his beliefs. He finally uncrossed his arms. Dan and Shannon sighed with relaxation as well.

So far, only the first part of the question had been addressed. Without stopping, Walker launched into an area much hotter than they had imagined, clicking the projector to show a painting from 1525 by Joos van Cleve, *The Crucifixion.*

CHAPTER 64

Hall parked on the street below Dan's house. He gingerly trotted up the steps to the porch and was surprised to find the door was open about a foot.

"Mr. Stanfield?" He stood on the threshold, looking in through the opening in the door. It was dark inside, and Hall couldn't see much as his eyes struggled to adapt to the darkness. "Mr. Stanfield!" he repeated in a louder voice.

Silence.

Hall pushed the door open and walked in. Computers were pulled down; computer screens were bashed, and papers and books were evenly and randomly distributed across the room. Someone had trashed Dan's house. *Probably someone from the PIT,* Hall thought.

"Dan!" Hall yelled in case Dan was injured somewhere in the house. He listened carefully.

Hall pulled out his pistol, holding it in front of him as he entered each room, much like a commando might infiltrate an enemy compound. After he covered the last room, he put his weapon down and inserted it into his concealed holster. Hall relaxed into the reality that Dan was not at home.

Hall thought about the fact that Dan was the only real lead that he had.

One thing was clear—Dan was in danger.

CHAPTER 65

Walker continued his oration. "We're not done yet. We've explored only the first part of the story of Jesus. Indeed, the New Testament and the words of Jesus do not conflict with the new interpretation. Jesus passed our litmus test. That part was easy. Now we have to deal with the second component of Christianity, a component that is much more challenging."

John sat with his arms crossed; Shannon sat next to John on the couch, and Dan sat in the sofa chair positioned at the end of the couch. Walker stood in front of the screen, the image of the crucified Christ sometimes directly superimposed over his own figure.

"If the amazing correlation between biotechnology and Genesis chapter three is correct, we have to reinterpret the true meaning of that scripture. The story, an exceedingly important one, changes dramatically. Humanity does not inherit sin from Adam. Because there is no original sin, the default nature of humans is not sinful and evil. In many ways, our new interpretation is a more literal than the one we learned during our childhood lessons in Sunday school.

"With all that said, we must consider perhaps the most difficult questions we could ask: *What are the true teachings of Jesus, and do they rely upon the evil nature of humans, or is this a contrivance by the church?*"

"This... this is the exact area I am having trouble with," John said, hesitantly. "Instead of the serpent symbolizing evil, it symbolizes DNA, the most subtle form of all creatures. There was no Fall, just 'choice' between two undeniable alternatives. Then what?"

"Exactly. That is the question." Walker paused, apparently so he could index his mind into the volumes of material ready for dissemination. "Scholars in theology have been asking that question for thousands of years. Only with recent archeological finds and careful critical analysis of the scriptures has any realistic answer surfaced. Shannon, you mentioned how lucky we are to be at a point in history when we can finally understand some of the underpinnings of life: DNA, genetics, and natural selection. Theology is in a similar situation. We finally have a clearer picture of the underpinnings of Christianity: the life of Jesus, the formation of the Christian church, and the history of church doctrine. Yet asking such questions can be difficult and sometimes dangerous, particularly if the question impacts accepted beliefs of groups whose power and influence are anchored in those beliefs."

Shannon looked up with interest. Dan thought she was well aware of their close physical contact, but she didn't seem to mind at all.

Walker clicked the projector controller, and Leonardo da Vinci's *The Last Supper,* undoubtedly the most famous image of Jesus with the apostles, appeared on the screen. "One clear hint that something was amiss is the fact that even staunch evangelicals have admitted that the gospels could not have been actually written by the apostles Matthew, Mark, Luke, and John. In fact, the Gospel of John was one of the last New Testament books to appear. When it was written—in about AD 90—John had been probably long dead. Unless, of course, John was only about fifteen when he was found fishing the Sea of Galilee and remembered details from sixty years earlier when he wrote his gospel at the age of seventy-five."

Dan spoke up. "The typical life expectancy of men of that age was probably about forty years, if they were lucky. If your dates are correct, two or three generations had passed before that book was written."

"Exactly. Writing was not uncommon during this era though there was a great deal of illiteracy. If they could write, the apostles could have easily written their own books, and if not, they certainly could have found someone to help. The exact author is unknown, but scholars do generally agree he was not Matthew, Mark, Luke, or John."

"Why not assume that the apostles simply recited their stories orally and that those stories were transcribed later, after being handed down by the Oral Tradition?" John asked.

"These were important stories—the most important in their lives and in the lives of the human race. It's hard to believe that they waited one or two or three generations to write them down or for that matter, until the age of seventy-five. Anyway, as soon as researchers realized that the names on these books were probably incorrect, they wanted to dig deeper to discover what else was fudged. Scholars looking only at the books of the Bible made little headway until archeologists found other very important ancient documents, including the *Gospel of Thomas* and *The Sayings Gospel Q.* These books provided key insights into both the contemporaneous thoughts of the followers of Jesus and the subsequent rise of the Christ cult and the Christian church."

The group was starting to understand why Walker's research was considered dangerous. Dan noticed that the word "cult" induced a negative body reaction in his friends, even though he knew the word did not necessarily have a negative connotation. It certainly did have that impact.

"I've never heard of those books. What are they?" asked John. "Are they part of the *Dead Sea Scrolls*?"

"Well, no. You'll recall perhaps that those scrolls, discovered in caves near the Dead Sea, were written primarily the time of Jesus by a Jewish fundamentalist sect called the *Essenes*. They substantiated many parts of the Old Testament, but they didn't help New Testament researchers at all except that some researchers believe Jesus may have been an Essene. In all the scrolls, there is no mention of anyone in the New Testament.

"No, I'm not talking about the *Dead Sea Scrolls*. I'm talking about the *Nag Hammadi Library*, written at the time of Jesus and lost until 1945, when they were discovered in an earthen jar in Egypt."

Walker clicked to show a map of the area around Cairo, with the town of Nag Hammadi highlighted and the location of the discovery marked. "This was an important find indeed, for it contained original documents from the time of Jesus. One of those documents, *The Gospel of Thomas,* is a valuable document indeed, the earliest known written document during the time of Jesus. It even quotes Jesus and his disciples.

"However, you don't find this book in the 'official' New Testament. In a way, we're fortunate that it was lost and not controlled by the church. It wasn't subject to any 'tweaking' by church officials." Walker clicked to the image of the earthen jar that had contained *The Gospel of Thomas.* "Remember, the Christian Bible was not reduced to its final canonical form until three hundred years after Jesus, so there was plenty of time for tweaking. The *Gospel of Thomas* provides a clear and simple picture of the actual events and thoughts of the followers of Jesus.

"The other document is called the *Lost Sayings Gospel Q*. It's not really a separate artifact but is derived from the common portions of the synoptic gospels—that is, Matthew, Mark, and Luke. Researchers consider the synoptic gospels too similar to be the result of simple coincidence. Instead, it's more likely that they were derived from a common source document. This common source is the invaluable *Lost Sayings Gospel Q*. The term *Q* is from the German word *Quelle,* meaning *source*."

Walker continued to fill the part of the learned theologian, his face revealing the passion that he felt for this area of knowledge.

"It's not going to be practical for me to try to cover all the aspects of these documents in a quick overview, but I can recommend that you read both the actual books and the scholarly writings that discuss them. They are available in spite of heavy resistance by the established churches. In fact, *The Gospel of Thomas* is a pleasantly short book. What I would like to do instead is to cover what is probably the true story of Jesus, as implied by these recently uncovered documents."

John and Shannon sat in rapt attention while Dan clicked his mouse on his laptop perched on the edge of the coffee table, the light of the screen flashing on his face in the darkened room. Even though Edgar's home was rustic in appearance, it was outfitted with wireless networking that allowed Dan's laptop to effortlessly access the informational wealth of the Internet, something Dan appreciated, and at present, he was accessing a full-text version of the *Gospel of Thomas*.

Walker continued his ad hoc lecture, recounting the early history of Jesus and Christianity as formulated in the latest scholarly studies, pointing out that historians and researchers split up the development of the New Testament into a number of phases, based on organizational movements and books that were written.

He clicked to an map of the Roman Empire as it existed during the time of Christ. "The picture of life in those times has been painted by various contemporary sources, from the biblical records of Palestine to the records of the Roman Empire. The Jewish holy land was ruled by a primarily secular culture vastly different from that of the Jews: the Romans." Walker pointed out the extent of the Roman empire on the map. "They were attempting to control a massive empire, stretching for thousands of miles."

Walker turned to face his audience. "About sixty years before Jesus was born, the Romans took over the *Second Temple* kingdom—a theocratic form of Jewish government—but the conquerors kept the temple system alive for more than a century. The temple-based puppet government provided a basis for economic and political control in Palestine. Jewish leaders, subject to the whim of the Roman government, were permitted to maintain their positions of power only to ensure ultimate Roman control. Eventually, however, that temple-based government provided little use to the powerful Roman Empire. The Romans marched on Jerusalem and destroyed the temple in about AD 70."

Walker paused for a moment before continuing, moving out of the light of the projector.

"At that time, most religious and philosophical thought arose from the *mystery cults,* which were centered on such figures as Osiris, Serapis, Attis, Adonis, Mithra, the 'Great Mother,' and the Syrian Goddess." Another click and the slide changed, now showing a list of the cults with an image next to each that had been taken from ancient artwork. "Curiously enough, many of these legends surrounded figures that fit the story of Jesus, including a miraculous birth in humble surroundings, noble lineage with stars or other cosmological events marking the birth, 'wise men' visiting from afar, and gifts of frankincense, gold, and myrrh bestowed. At least twenty of these mystery cults included an untimely death, marked by an eclipse or other event, and some even included a crucifixion. Acknowledgment that these cults included many of the features in the story of Christ is not new. Yet, this truth may still surprise Christians who assume that the Bible is the first expression of these elements."

Walker stopped for a breath.

"So, parts of the story of Christ were simply adopted from the mystery cults, is that what you're suggesting?" Shannon asked.

"It's likely." Walker clicked again. A rock bust of Homer shared the screen with an etching of Moses holding stone tablets of the Ten Commandments. "The main epics, the works of the Greek *Homer* and the Jewish *Torah*, greatly influenced thought at that time. The bickering gods of Homer's work stood in distinction to the concepts of a righteous god and divine law that are central to the Jewish Torah. But both supported social justice, rituals for celebration, and promotion of a peaceful, family-centered life"

The Virgin of the Rocks, by Leonardo da Vinci, filled the screen after another click. "There are plenty of masterpieces depicting Jesus as a child, but his life before meeting the apostles is really quite mysterious. We're told that Jesus grew up in Galilee and apparently had some education, but almost nothing is recorded about him as a person, and virtually no artwork exists depicting the bulk of his life. A thorough biography is absolutely impossible. Historians describe him as a sensitive man but not the constructive, systematic thinker necessary to logically formulate consistent philosophies or theologies. He didn't create a social program for others to follow or a refined religion that invited others to see him as a god. He talked, and his followers listened. When he talked about life, he simply made sense. The 'Kingdom of God,' he taught, is inside each of us. He promoted the socialistic view that we should contribute what we can and take only what we need.

"At the pinnacle of his influence, followers united around his notions of a perfect society. They conceptualized this society as a kingdom. Any individual was fit for this kingdom, regardless of bloodline or *seed*. Obviously, this new concept meant that a mixture of people would be found in that future utopian kingdom. In contrast, the Jewish philosophy made ethnic distinctions extremely important and made induction of converts impossible if they weren't ethnically pure.

Walker continued with images of art and maps, illustrating each comment he made to his students. "No early group thought of Jesus as 'The Christ,' and none had a concept of a larger Christian church. This fact is quite startling to today's Christians. The word *Christ* originated from the Greek *khristos*, a translation of Hebrew *Messiah*. In those early years, Jesus was not thought of as a Messiah or Christ but rather as a Jewish teacher who founded some schools of thought.

"Oral lore and memories of Jesus are all they had at first, and they were reshaped as the generations passed. The *Lost Sayings Gospel Q* is the earliest written record of a group of Jesus people and spans about fifty years, from about the AD 20s until after the Roman-Jewish war in the 70s. The habits of these Jesus people were similar to those of the Cynics. You might recall that the Cynics were a group founded by

Antisthenes—a follower of Socrates—in about 400 BC. The Cynics believed that living a virtuous life—that is, living according to nature—is all that is necessary to attain happiness. They disdained conventional values, such as wealth and social status. The early Jesus people also followed this general philosophy.

"During the next few decades, the truth of Jesus faded and his followers enhanced his divinity. Jesus became a divine being talking to God his Father and debating with Satan his tempter, a prophet who knew both past and future events. His followers were linked with God's great plan for Israel, ready to take their places by his side on judgment day.

"First, they added pronouncement stories where someone questions what Jesus says or does, and he gives a sharp response. They follow the Greek *chreiai* form, similar to the Socratic, Cyrenaic, and Cynic traditions. Mack makes the case that these pronouncement stories were an attempt to harmonize the early Jesus movements with the Jewish tradition, as they're usually about those questions."

Walker's audience didn't recognize every name mentioned by this obvious master of the information, but they realized that they could delve into the details later. Nevertheless, they sat in rapt attention, amazed in a way that this researcher of Christian theology admitted that the story of Jesus was far different from what mainstream churches taught.

Walker continued, displaying an image of the tablets discovered in the Nag Hammadi library. "The *Gospel of Thomas* was written in Coptic, the last stage of the written Egyptian language. This Gospel consists only of the sayings of Jesus, with a very short narrative to set the stage. The *Thomas People*, like the *Q People* were interested only in the sayings of Jesus. Their gospel contains only 113 verses, each describing a quote from Jesus. For example, here is the start and end of the *Gospel of Thomas*." Walker read from the slide, skipping through to the end.

> *These are the secret sayings that the living Jesus spoke and Didymos Judas Thomas recorded.*
>
> (1) *And he said, "Whoever discovers the interpretation of these sayings will not taste death."*
>
> (2) *Jesus said, "Those who seek should not stop seeking until they find. When they find, they will be disturbed. When they are disturbed, they will marvel, and will reign over all. [And after they have reigned they will rest.]"*
>
> (3) *Jesus said, "If your leaders say to you, 'Look, the (Father's) kingdom is in the sky,' then the birds of the sky will precede you. If they say to you, 'It is in the sea,' then the fish will precede you. Rather, the kingdom is within you and it is outside you. When you*

know yourselves, then you will be known, and you will understand that you are children of the living Father. But if you do not know yourselves, then you live in poverty, and you are the poverty."

(4) *Jesus said, "The person old in days won't hesitate to ask a little child seven days old about the place of life, and that person will live. For many of the first will be last, and will become a single one."*

...

(112) *Jesus said, "Damn the flesh that depends on the soul. Damn the soul that depends on the flesh."*

(113) *His disciples said to him, "When will the kingdom come?"*

"It will not come by watching for it. It will not be said, 'Look, here!' or 'Look, there!' Rather, the Father's kingdom is spread out upon the earth, and people don't see it."

"The entire *Gospel of Thomas* is the sayings of Jesus, nothing more. Many consider it as the best uncorrupted view of the followers of the living Jesus. They viewed themselves to be Jesus's true disciples—members the 'Kingdom of Light.' Amazingly enough, there's no description of the last supper, no miracle stories, and perhaps most troubling, no mention of the crucifixion."

"Sounds bogus to me!" John said. "How can we believe an account that doesn't even mention the crucifixion!"

"The crucifixion is under question from other analysts as well," Walker said, grabbing a book from his pile and opening it at a marker. "Let me read this section of the Islamic *Al'Quran*, translated by Yusfali:

(004.157) That they said (in boast), "We killed Christ Jesus the son of Mary, the Messenger of Allah";- but they killed him not, nor crucified him, but so it was made to appear to them, and those who differ therein are full of doubts, with no (certain) knowledge, but only conjecture to follow, for of a surety they killed him not:

"The *Al Qur'an* was written in the AD 600s, and even then, not everyone agreed about the reality of the crucifixion."

"Hmmm," John said, cocking his head to one side.

Walker then described the next stage of the enhancement of Jesus to divinity, introducing the miracle stories from the *Gospel of Mark*, which create the impression of a divine power dramatically entering human history in the person of Jesus. "These Christian miracle stories read like the hundreds of reports of miracles, like those of Asclepius, in the Greco-Roman age.

"You say that no miracles are described in the *Gospel of Thomas*, is that right?" John asked.

"It makes you think," Walker continued. "Why would the Gospel of Thomas omit such amazing miracles? Archeologists who discovered that ancient document were struck by the realization that the miracle stories were missing, and logically, those stories must have been added later, probably adopted from the many commonly told miracle stories of the day. Jesus's miracles vary between the gospels as well, hinting of their later inclusion and apocryphal nature.

"During the first generation or so after his death, Jesus was elevated to divinity, and his teachings were de-emphasized. Followers were preoccupied with notions of martyrdom, resurrection, and the transformation of Jesus into a divine, spiritual presence. This change in focus in the Jesus movements did not happen overnight. The change actually took about twenty-five years—about a generation—enough time for the truth to be forgotten."

An image of *The Conversion of St. Paul* by Benozzo Gozzoli followed. "Evidence of the Christ Cult comes mainly from the letters that Paul wrote during the 50s. This stage of Christian theology can be clearly identified by the use of the term *Christ*, by the characterization of the community as sinners, and by appeals to the ancient scriptures. The basis of the cult was two common and powerful components—the Greek myth of the noble death and the Jewish myth of the persecuted sage. The final story of Jesus includes both story elements. But that's not all. Paul had a stroke of genius—called *kergyma*—which linked the death of Christ to the Old Testament, authenticated Christ's divinity, and treated the Old Testament as nothing more than a prequel."

Walker continued by explaining that Jesus's death allowed the inclusion of gentiles in the religious order. "Even without a Jewish bloodline and without adherence to the Jewish laws, gentiles could be welcomed into the fold, a very important move for the propagation of the new religion. Be faithful and follow the model of Jesus. No painful circumcision is required, and there is no need to follow difficult Jewish law. Jesus's death on the cross was sufficient to expiate all sins.

"Since Mark contains the first reference to the death of Jesus as a crucifixion and since that story is dependent on the martyr myth of the larger *kergyma*, we really have no way of knowing anything about the historical circumstances of Jesus's death. All historical evidence cited by those wishing to support this story dates from long after Mark's gospel was written. In other words, the entire story of the crucifixion may be simply an extension of the *Mystery Cults,* many of which already had this powerful element."

John sat with his arms folded. He was quiet, but Dan noticed his irregular breathing when Walker mentioned these particularly challenging ideas. It seemed he was getting red in the face, but Dan wasn't sure.

Walker's dissertation finally arrived at Paul's letters. "Written in about the 50s, his letters to the Thessalonians and Galatians are the first Christian writings for which we have manuscript documentation. Remember, although Paul never met Jesus, his writings dominate the New Testament. These earliest letters provide a snapshot of an early Jesus movement. Paul introduced the concept of eternal life, which could be attained only at the end of time.

"Paul paired Adam and Christ as the representative figures of the two epochs, instead of the earlier use of Abraham. He described Adam as human and Christ as divine. He interpreted the 'Old Covenant' into a story of the Christ, using verses chosen here and there to prove that Jesus was the Messiah, but really these connections are weak at best. For example, they interpret that Christ was the 'rock' from which the children of Israel drank in the wilderness and that Christ was the 'sacrificial lamb.' Unless you really wanted to believe it, you would throw these prophetic connections out as inconsequential and far-fetched.

"Paul's *Letter to the Romans* is clearly the most mature statement we have of Paul's religious ideas, providing the first systematic rationale for Christian myth and ritual. It's often regarded as the most influential text in the New Testament. Paul, for the first time, alludes to the idea that human beings are inherently sinful because of the Fall. This concept is apparently his own invention, and its implications, as we have seen, have been enormous in the overall story of Christianity.

"Although this development was significant, the largest step from the earlier Jesus people toward the story of Christianity we have today was provided in the *Gospel of Mark*." Walker flipped to an image of St. Mark, the Patron of Venice. "The author of Mark is unknown. It seems the author, whoever that was, took the many little sayings and stories of Jesus from earlier traditions and combined them to develop an image of Jesus, his power, the plot to have him killed, and the conflict between Jesus with the establishment. The author dared to imagine how the crucifixion and resurrection might have looked if played out as a historical event, something the earlier stories had resisted. This obvious fiction was apparently composed by one of the great novelists of history. It became the accepted story, creating an incomparable figure of Jesus the Christ and Son of God. Without this story, Christianity as we know it today would have never emerged."

John moved forward several times as if he wanted to argue each point, finger sometimes in the air, but he stayed remarkably quiet as Walker continued this heretical blasphemy.

Walker continued without inviting John to argue the points. "The *Gospel of Matthew* appeared next. No, it was not written first, as is implied by its placement in the New Testament, but in the late 80s by a 'scribe trained for the kingdom.' It's a document of Jewish Christianity, interweaving the teachings of Jesus from the book of the *Lost Sayings Gospel Q* into Mark's story of Jesus and adding some sayings and stories of his own, although it reproduced the *Gospel of Mark* pretty much as it was written. Jesus's birth is described, as well as suggesting that Jesus must have had spectacular Jewish credentials, with an unbroken genealogy from Abraham, David, through the exile and restoration to end with Joseph and Mary."

"I find it curious," Dan said, "that they chose to illustrate Jesus's Jewish bloodline through Joseph. If Jesus was born to a virgin, Joseph's genetics would have obviously been inconsequential."

"You're right, but the Jewish culture required these credentials to support Jesus's divinity. Yet, as we already pointed out, the whole topic is a bit out of place since Jewish bloodline was no longer essential to gain admission to the Jesus movements anyway."

"This only further supports your assertions, Walker," Shannon said. "Again, these supposedly inspired and sacred documents shouldn't have an error of that magnitude. Jesus was totally unrelated to Joseph, according to the story of the Virgin Mary. Jesus's Jewish bloodline should have been traced through Mary, not Joseph. Of course, it would be difficult—no, I'd say impossible—to trace a divine bloodline through a woman, wouldn't it?"

CHAPTER 66

Walker, having completed his presentation, walked to the windows and drew back the drapes. The sun finally broke through gaps in the overcast sky, its light now entering those west-facing windows, shooting through the house and shining onto the floor near their meeting area by the fireplace. There would perhaps be another hour of sunlight.

The group finally understood why the authorities of the church seriously wanted to oppose any success Walker might have in publishing his research. John, who had been good at keeping himself quiet during Walker's "lesson," was the first to speak out.

"Walker, are you honestly saying that the story of Christ, the Son of God and savior of our world, is simply a big myth, a complete fiction? And that the crucifixion might not ever have happened? It's hard to believe that the story is not well documented from other sources. The Roman Empire was good at keeping records, weren't they? How about reports by Pilate?" John did a good job of keeping his voice calm, but his face was highly distressed.

"If you can find those reports, I would love to see them! We have only statements made decades or centuries after the fact. You would think there would be hundreds of independent contemporaneous reports. Are there? No, not a one. We really have nothing of the sort."

"I'm sure there is some record of Jesus!" John exclaimed.

"Christians sometimes point to the writings of Josephus, who lived from AD 37 to 100 and wrote a 1,200-page volume of history. Unfortunately, in all those pages, only two paragraphs refer to Jesus. And worse yet, researchers regard those paragraphs as highly suspect. It seems from the evidence that Christian followers intent on supporting their religious views added those paragraphs much later. We are left with really no proof at all, certainly nothing of contemporaneous nature such as records of executions, minutes of hearings, and the like.

"The *Lost Sayings Gospel Q* and especially *The Gospel of Thomas* are particularly important. They predated both the writings of Paul, who never met Jesus, and the contrived gospels, written generations later. In all early material, no reference to any crucifixion is made. And, as I mentioned, other 'sacred' documents, such as the Islamic *Al'Quran*, explicitly state the opposite.

"I warned you. The sad truth is that the teachings of Jesus are really far from the overarching structure of Christianity taught today. But the good news is this: We agreed that our new interpretation of the story in Genesis refutes the importance of original sin. It seems Jesus didn't care about original sin either. Tying Genesis to DNA authenticates that story like no other proof ever offered. Yet, it has the opposite effect on the story of Christianity accepted by most churches today, even though Genesis is only lightly touched on in the New Testament. The bottom line is that the new interpretation you propose not only exposes the true meaning of Genesis but also forces the adoption of the true life of Jesus and a reassessment of the most coercive elements of Christianity. Indeed, the accuracy of the theory of evolution is brought into question as well. I think you've hit a kernel of truth here, but I think it's a kernel that will get stuck in the teeth of almost everyone!"

"Sorry, John, you lose! All your treasured beliefs are just concoctions!" Shannon plunged the sword again. Dan couldn't believe it.

John's face reddened, and tears welled up in his eyes. Dan was worried he might do something he might later regret—strike back at Shannon or Walker. Dan really didn't know John very well. What is he capable of? Outright violence? John stood up headed briskly for the door. "I'm going for a walk. Just leave me alone!" No one followed him.

"We should give John some space to think on his own. I'll bet he's feeling threatened," Dan said. "Let's all take a break until he comes back."

Dan thought John's behavior looked like a repeat of the events at the coffee house, probably something John had replayed many times in his life, like a tape being playing on a mindless tape recorder. It was time for a break. Dan and Shannon were not immune to the upsetting nature of this unassailable analysis by Walker. They needed some time as well.

Walker ambled into the kitchen. Dan found himself alone with Shannon.

CHAPTER 67

John walked around Edgar's house to the top of the hill, hiking around the centuries-old coastal live oaks indigenous to the area. The skies were still overcast, but the air was clear under the flat cloud ceiling. John could see over the next few hills but not all the way to the ocean. The short hike up the hill let the blood flow and settled his emotions.

Walker may be a knowledgeable theologian in command of this information... Walker must be wrong! Or am I? Right now, I wish I could have a cigarette... Why did Monty act so strange...? Walker's analysis is clear and understandable...I keep losing control... Sure, the followers of Jesus probably enhanced the story of Jesus over time... I miss my family... If Walker is right, it only supports the new interpretation of Genesis... That's what makes it worse... Shannon!

Tears came to John's eyes as he relived some of the grief of his former life that had been changed so dramatically by Christianity. The beauty of the view before him, the wonders of earth, and the purpose of his life were clearly not something he could understand, but Christianity was much larger than his tiny life or these ideas.

"Dear God, please help me understand this challenge to my faith," John prayed out loud. "I'll never turn back to my old life, no matter what happens. Show me the way."

He recalled that the *Gospel of Thomas* said that those who found the truth would be disturbed. That certainly felt true right now.

John spent another few minutes piecing together his thoughts, taking in the beauty of the view before him. The green rolling hillsides soothed his mind. From this vantage point, he could see the driveway winding out to the gate where it entered the property and joined the road beyond. If he looked the other way, he could see Edgar's house down below.

John was lost in thought, looking at the view, but he suddenly straightened to attention. A plain sedan pulled up to the gate, paused, traveled farther down the road, and parked behind some bushes.

CHAPTER 68

"Shannon, you're hitting John too hard. You've got to lighten up! He's having enough difficulty as it is."

Shannon looked directly at Dan and then down, making eye contact only occasionally. "You're right. I went too far again." She sighed gently and had some difficulty swallowing. Shannon looked at Dan, touched his hand and said, "I feel close to you, Dan, but I'm afraid. I don't want to hurt John."

Dan was ecstatic to hear how Shannon felt about him. He felt the same way about the situation with John but was happy that at least the ice had been broken. *I've been trying for days to think of a way to make my feelings known...*

Shannon got up. Dan expected her to walk the other way. Instead, she turned toward him, moving closer. His heart leaped, pounding with intensity. She stopped by his chair and leaned over. She moved closer. Her lips were within a fraction of an inch from Dan's. He could feel their heat, but she was waiting—waiting for Dan to confirm. He leaned forward and made contact, a bit more than a peck but still restrained. She leaned into it harder, then disengaged.

"Would you care for another drink?" She smiled and seemed to dance into the kitchen.

Dan's heart beat wildly. He followed her.

A large butcher-block island stood in the center of the kitchen and light streamed through a set of windows high above. Pots, skillets, and pans hung from a rectangular stainless steel hanger. Walker poured lemonade over ice cubes, turned to face the butcher-block, and leaned against the counter. Dan and Shannon leaned against the island side-by-side opposite Walker. Dan could feel the warmth of Shannon as he stood next to her. Her breathing was still fast, and he automatically matched his breathing with hers.

Walker said, "I have an interesting idea."

"What is it?" He was tempted to say "Dad," but didn't.

"I know there are many stories in the Bible that could be

reconsidered with our new understanding of biological principles. I was thinking about the story of Noah's Ark."

Dan was having some trouble focusing on the question, "I doubt there is much truth in that story. It's been clearly documented that Noah's worldwide flood could never have occurred. The Great Pyramids in Egypt were built almost four hundred years before Noah's time. The Egyptian culture never mentioned any worldwide flood."

Walker took a drink and swallowed with satisfaction. "That's true. By the time of the Flood, civilization had spread widely. Stonehenge in England was built eight hundred years before, and the Mayan civilization originated five hundred years earlier. No flood is mentioned by those cultures either."

"I have to admit," Shannon said, "the concept of the flood has always bothered me. How could an omnipotent god make such a huge mistake in his creation, a mistake that required wiping the slate clean and starting over? Why not get it right the first time?"

"Yeah." Dan chuckled.

Walker took another sip. "Not only that. Why would God need the Ark? God shouldn't need living animals on a boat to repopulate the earth! He created them to begin with, why not do it again? An omnipotent god could have repopulated the earth with a snap of his fingers! Even in the traditional creation story, it took only a day. Why flood the earth and wait 150 days?"

"It's crazy," Dan said.

"Instead, think of this. Maybe this was yet another description of the seeding of life on earth that you postulated, Dan. The ancients involved were not omnipotent, just advanced and sophisticated. They wouldn't need a huge Ark to hold all the living animals. Only the tiny genetic code would need to be preserved. A small genetics laboratory would be sufficient. Perhaps the Ark was an interstellar craft used to transport life from the dying planet of the ancients. The genetic pattern of life was housed on this spaceship, along with Noah and his family. The forty days of rain, that could be interpreted as simply a cover story to keep Noah and his family from fearing the trip. Noah may be simply another name for Adam, the initial set of humans used to seed the earth."

"Hmmm. You're certainly concocting a story from—"

They heard the door slam in the other room.

John blinked his eyes clear of tears and looked more closely at the sedan. A man in a business suit walked down the fence line and climbed over. John thought he could see a firearm glisten under his jacket. The man walked to the driveway and turned toward the house.

John scurried back down the hill to warn the others.

"There's a man walking up the driveway. I think he has a gun!" John said as darted into the house, out of breath from the run down the hillside. Walker, Dan, and Shannon ran in from the kitchen.

Edgar met them in the front room, adrenaline in his eyes. "Walker, you stay here. I'll be outside." Dan could hear Edgar open a cabinet in the adjacent room and slam a door in the rear of the house.

Walker waited just inside the front door as the man approached the front steps.

"Stop right there!" Edgar shouted. "This is private property!"

Dan looked through the window. He could see a rifle sitting on the top of the rock wall at the corner of the house with Edgar behind it, the rifle trained on the man.

The man stopped in his tracks and put up his hands.

"Damn!" reacted Walker, whispering to Dan as they witnessed the scene through the window. "I was afraid of this. He's probably one of Bishop Ward's stooges. Be careful!"

CHAPTER 69

"Who are you? Why are you here?" Edgar yelled over his pointed rifle.

The man yelled back. "Don't shoot! I just want to talk."

"Who are you?"

"Agent Hall, FBI. I'm just going to pull out my identification, okay?" Hall cautiously reached into his jacket and pulled out his folded leather badge holder, careful not to make any sudden moves. He held it up, opening it with one hand.

Dan whispered as he looked out the window. "That guy came to my house just before I met you on the beach. He asked about... *my father...* and the PIT. I didn't think much of it at the time."

Hall kept his arms in the air. "Look, I'm here just to ask a couple of questions. I understand your hesitation, believe me."

Edgar apparently wasn't buying it. His rifle was still trained on Hall.

The agent yelled back to the house, "I may have some information about George Stanfield, Dan's father. Is Dan here? If he's interested in information about his father, I might be able to help."

Edgar shouted back. "Don't make any sudden moves! Remove your firearm and put it on the ground."

Hall slowly pulled his handgun from his jacket holster and laid it on the ground.

Edgar approached and walked behind Hall, picking up the handgun as he stepped over it. "Walk inside, and no sudden moves." He said, keeping his rifle trained on Hall, who walked with his hands up, FBI badge holder in one hand. As Hall entered the house, he gave his badge to Walker, who took a close look at it.

"He looks legitimate, Edgar. *Special Agent Russell G. Hall, FBI.*"

"So sorry, Agent Hall. I'm not used to unannounced visitors round here. Do come in." Edgar lowered his rifle.

"Thank you. I'm sorry to visit like this, but I had little choice. I have a difficult problem, and I'm hoping you can help me." Hall turned so his vision also included Dan. "Dan... Oh, hello again. I was hoping you'd be here."

"Is it the standard operating procedure of the FBI to stalk a citizen and violate his privacy rights? I told you I would contact you if I had any information. You have no right to follow me here!" Dan was right, but he was still going a bit too far. After all, this was a legitimate, badge-carrying FBI agent.

"Now, now, Dan." Walker wanted to defuse the situation. "We don't want to ruffle the feathers of the friendly FBI agent, do we? Maybe we can help him out. We've done nothing wrong."

"Agent Hall, can we get you something to drink? Come on over and have a seat. How can we help you?" Walker was extending a huge olive branch. "Edgar, give him back his gun." Edgar hesitated, then complied, still ready to aim his weapon.

Hall pulled the ammunition cartridge from the gun, making sure everyone noticed. Then he tucked his firearm into his concealed holster and sat down. Edgar finally relaxed fully when Hall put his gun away. At least the visitor hadn't grabbed the gun and started shooting.

"Agent Hall, I'm Walker. This is Edgar, Shannon, and John. I guess you've already met Dan. How can we help you?"

"I'm sorry to have to approach you this way, but I was out of options. Dan, when I visited your house, I mentioned that I was working on a case that involved the Pacific Institute of Theology. Several students are missing from their youth rescue school, the Pacific Institute of Theology for Youth, or 'PITY,' as they call it. I was just an FBI agent in training when I first had a run-in with this PIT place. Dan, back then it was your father, George Stanfield, who disappeared while working at the PIT. We were prematurely pulled off the case. Later, newspapers explained the disappearance as an auto accident. I knew better; there was no accident. I didn't understand what was involved back then.

"Now, I was assigned to another case involving the PIT, one of a whole string of disappearances. I interviewed Bishop Ward and connected the dots with your father's old case. The Bishop's assistant contacted me and told me that students at PITY receive training at some secret 'Ranch.' She didn't elaborate. Either she didn't know the details, or she wasn't willing to tell me, I'm not sure.

"Anyway, I'm sharing this information because that case basically exploded in my face. The NSA, Homeland Security, the FBI, and the CIA have become highly politicized. They cater to whomever's in power at the time and put cronies in positions where they don't belong. Dan, I've never been happy with the results of your father's case. I have a feeling he was forced to leave the institution. Others are also disappearing without a trace. I'm just not comfortable dropping my investigation.

"Not only that, I went by your house earlier today. It's been ransacked, probably by the same people who have been threatening me."

"Ransacked? What do you mean? Did they take my computers?"

"Stuff was just thrown around. I don't know how much damage you'll find to your computers, but it looked pretty bad."

"Damn!" Dan was having difficulty thinking about anything else while he processed this shocking news.

Walker jumped in. "You were saying something about Dan's father?"

"My house was ransacked?" Dan repeated again.

"I was hoping Dan could help me with the question about his father. He might have been murdered and the whole thing covered up as a car accident. Or, he may still be working for the PIT, or even the Pentagon, in a covert role of some kind. I just don't know."

"My computers..." Dan finally gathered himself and reengaged. "You said my father... If we could find him, exactly what did you have in mind?"

"Well, it may be a long shot, but if he's alive, he might be able to help us figure this out. I'm not sure what our next step would be. Maybe he could infiltrate the PIT, perhaps by reestablishing his relationship with the Bishop."

"I don't think... you don't know the sort of people you're dealing with," Walker volunteered, fumbling for words. "If Dan's father is indeed alive, he has suffered enough at the hands of that scum-bag Bishop. Why would he want to help you with this?"

"To tell you the truth, I shouldn't even be working on this case, but I'm worried that the Bureau and the Department of Homeland Security are being controlled by political concerns and powerful churches. But that's not all. According to my informant, PITY is getting millions of dollars in faith-based initiative dollars, far more than necessary for the operation of their small facility. If we can locate your father and convince him to help us, he will have little to lose that he has not already lost."

Dan was starting to see it Hall's way. He was surprised that the agent was revealing so much of the information behind the case, but it certainly helped to reassure the group that he was on their side. It was up to his father to step forward.

Hall took a closer look at Walker. "Your name is Walker, right?" Walker nodded, his face flushing with the awareness that he may have said too much to this agent. He hoped Hall knew his name just because he was introduced. "Have I met you before?"

"No, no... I don't think so."

"How do you know the Bishop?"

There was an extended pause during which Walker apparently sized up his options. Dan wondered if he would reveal his identity or attempt to formulate a string of lies.

"Dammit, Agent Hall," Walker rose and started to pace. Everyone was quiet. "I can't go on. I'm... I'm George Stanfield... I'm Dan's father." The group froze with disbelief and then slowly began to see the marked resemblance between Dan and his father—Walker—George Stanfield. "Look. My life has been ruined by the Bishop. Recently, several business deals went sour for no reason. I think the Bishop discovered where I was living and has been pulling strings to destroy my business. I decided to find out if I was right, if the Bishop is to blame for my recent 'bad luck.'

"I've secured a position at the PIT as a groundskeeper, and I might have access to much of the facility. I'm not sure if I'm doing the right thing, but I've had enough. Tell me how I can help you. Nothing would make me happier than bringing the Bishop to his knees and closing the PIT for good."

CHAPTER 70

Walker shifted down to first gear to slow for the next speed bump on the steep grade. The narrow two-lane road wound its way up the hill toward the outcropping of white plaster buildings at the top. The PIT buildings on one side of the hill went back at least a century or two, and for the most part they looked as they had when Walker worked there years ago. The ones on the other side were quite new, having been added in the last several years and probably, he thought, paid for by government funding. Even the older ones were well maintained. This was not a poor nonprofit barely able to pay its bills.

Walker approached the closed wrought-iron gates and the guardhouse in front of the gates and leaned out the window of his small, rust-spotted truck.

"May I help you?" questioned the guard.

"Uh, yes. My name is Walker, the uh, new groundskeeper. I'm supposed to ask for Carlos."

"Oh, yeah, that's right. He said I should expect you. You'll have to park down the hill, you know, in the employee parking area since there's no employee parking inside. Just drive back down and turn right at the bottom. See that parking lot down there? Then walk back up. I'll try to find Carlos for you." He reached for the phone.

"Okay, thanks." Walker put the truck in reverse and backed down the hill, parked as instructed, and then walked toward the guardhouse. From this elevated vantage point, he could see the buildings of the PITY school, laid out below much like a big letter "E," but with five rows of buildings instead of three and a large sanctuary connected to the upright of the "E."

Walker had almost arrived at the guardhouse when a black limousine with heavily tinted windows pulled up. The brown license plate had "US GOVT" printed above the number. Walker slowed his pace so as to be out of sight to the driver while remaining within earshot.

The driver leaned out of his window slightly as he spoke with the guard; the visor of his blue officer's hat shaded his eyes. Walker noticed the driver wore a blue Class-A Army uniform and shoulder insignia. "Good morning, sir," he said. "The Bishop should be expecting us."

"Yes, sir! Yes... the General... the Bishop is expecting the General! Please drive up and park in front of the executive office building." A steady hum of electric motors accompanied the swinging of the double wrought-iron gates decorated with dual crosses. The limousine driver raised his automatic window, drove through the gates and up the winding road, disappearing behind the first set of buildings.

Walker completed the last few steps to the guardhouse and waved to the guard.

"Got your truck parked? Go on up to the top. Carlos will meet you there."

Walker was dressed in work clothes and a baseball cap. With his full beard, his appearance fit the role of a gardener and building maintenance worker perfectly. *Well, the Bishop obviously has some business with the military. I'm sure recruiters have a field day with this organization. Especially since they've been missing their quotas lately.* Walker rounded the corner and entered the central courtyard of the facility. A stout Mexican man dismounted his electric cart and walked over.

"Buenos días," he said, shaking Walker's hand.

"Sí, buenos días," Walker said. *I hope he also speaks English—my Spanish is limited.*

"I'm Carlos. You name Walker, true?"

Good, he speaks English. "Yes, thank you—Uh, *gracias*"

"No time for a tour now. You go to work first, and I give a tour later. Here is the room of tools," Carlos motioned to a small, dark room near the entrance to the courtyard. Although his sentences followed the construction of Spanish rather than English and he pronounced all th's as d's, his accent was really not too heavy. "Come, first easy work for you. Here's the hoe."

Carlos handed a hoe to Walker and mentioned that the day was nice for working since it was still cool. Walker agreed. He led Walker toward the executive office building, walking along the right side of the courtyard. Walker looked at the black limousine parked in front of the steps and large wooden doors leading to the Bishop's office. Leaning on the car just behind the driver-side door, the driver puffed on a cigarette and tapped his foot to the beat of a country-western station.

Walker followed Carlos down a shady hallway, out a wooden door with semicircular top, and finally to a small rose garden area on the other side of the building. "Pull weeds here." Carlos pointed to the rose bushes just outside the Bishop's office and in front of the large convex windows. The work was light, just some small weeds here and there to take care of. Gardening had always been something Walker enjoyed. It allowed his mind to settle and wander over the events of the day. He started working, pulling the weeds and turning the soil with the hoe. "I return in thirty minutos. I give you a full tour later, okay?" Carlos walked away.

Walker found himself positioned just outside the windows of the Bishop's office. He could not believe how well this was working out! *Carlos said he wouldn't be back for about half an hour. That should give me enough time to find out what's going on.* He looked at the innocuous belt buckle provided by Hall with its wireless listening device and GPS tracking electronics. He pulled a few weeds and lifted his head to look into the Bishop's office.

Unfortunately, because the bottom of the windows was a bit over his head, his view was primarily of the ceiling and far walls of the office. When he stood up tall, he could just barely see the top of the Bishop's head. *I can't see his visitor at all. If I could only get a little bit closer, I might be able to hear what they're talking about.* Walker moved through the rose bushes to a position next to the white walls of the Bishop's office, just under the large protruding windowsills. *I can't hear anything and can't quite see what's going on. I need to find something to stand on!* Walker pulled a few more weeds as he searched for a way to climb up a bit higher. He moved along the wall, hunting like a hound in pursuit of a fox. There was nothing to stand on here.

At the end of the building to the far right of the windows, he turned the corner. There, some boxes and crates were stored, apparently from recent gardening projects. He grabbed an empty black plastic pot, the kind used by nurseries for growing plants, and dusted it off. It was the fifteen-gallon size, perfect for an ad-hoc step stool. Walker positioned the plastic pot upside-down just under and at the far right of the windows. He looked around briefly to make sure no one was watching. *If anyone sees me, I'll be toast. Carlos won't be back for twenty minutes at least.*

"Dan, hold this GPS Tracker. All we have to do is follow the little red dot on the screen."

Dan took the electronic device, about the size of a thin paperback book. It had a backlit LCD screen that displayed a map dynamically with the red dot always in the center. "I imagine you used this to track me to Edgar's house?"

"Hey, I'm a good guy. Trust me." Dan really didn't mind. During their conversations on the way up the coast to the PIT, he had grown to respect and admire Hall. Their car was parked so they could see the PIT facility on the hill in the distance.

"I'm starting to understand this display. Yes, I see..."

"Those devices are pretty sensitive, down to a few feet. Here, click the center button to zoom in." The red dot appeared over a satellite image of the region, detailed enough to show the buildings in the complex. "Walker is near that building on the west side of the facility."

* * *

Stepping up on the pot, Walker stayed in a crouching position, his head just below the level of the window. He took off his baseball cap and then carefully raised his head up, peering into the Bishop's office but ready to lower himself back down if his position was in their line of sight.

This is a good vantage point. The Bishop and the General were now clearly in view. Because the windows curved out and at the end, Walker was able to see the sides of the two men seated across the room. The Bishop sat behind his desk while the General sat in a low-flung sofa-like chair facing the back of the desk.

The General had the upright posture typical of a military man, yet the chair the Bishop provided for guests was very low indeed. As a result, the General was at least a full head below the Bishop. This low-chair strategy was typical of a person who wishes to maintain a dominant position in his office. It reminded Walker of the scene in *It's a Wonderful Life* when Mr. Potter invited George Bailey to his office to offer him a job and take over the ailing Building and Loan. George sat in a ridiculously low chair, sinking far below the usual level as he reluctantly accepted a cigar from the evil Potter.

But despite the level of the seats, the General took the superior position in terms of body language. The Bishop, although physically higher, groveled before him. The General gestured strongly with his hands. He was far from touching the Bishop, but his words had the same effect as slapping a prisoner in an interrogation. Walker could hear only garbled hints of speech through the dual panes of modern windows fitted into the ancient sills, a surprising feature of these old buildings. Walker couldn't forget the drafty old windows of his office in the building on the other side of the courtyard. The upgraded windows was proof of the level of funding now available to this operation—probably from the General. Yet, although Walker could not hear their conversation, their body language spoke volumes.

The Bishop seemed to be explaining his way out of something. The General continued to put pressure on him. Suddenly, the General stood up, moved closer to the desk, leaned over, and stared directly into the seated Bishop's eyes. The General's outstretched finger stabbed the top of the desk, and the Bishop jolted with every forceful stab as if the General were poking holes in his chest. The Bishop lowered his gaze in a sign of submission, his lips only barely moving, almost trembling. The General stared at him for one more moment, turned quickly, and strutted out of the office. The Bishop sat limply at his desk, staring at the empty surface. Walker enjoyed seeing the Bishop grovel for once, but it concerned him that the Bishop was dealing with the Pentagon and apparently marching to their tune. *Rubbing these guys the wrong way could get me into serious trouble. I think I've had enough of this!*

Walker lowered himself from the plant bucket, stood on the ground, and returned his baseball cap to his head. He faced the building as he looked down at the belt buckle so Hall and Dan would hear him. "The Bishop met with some sort of military general. I'm leaving. This is too hot for me!" Walker turned around and stopped in his tracks.

Carlos stood before him holding the sharp tip of a shovel at Walker's neck.

CHAPTER 71

Carlos pushed the shovel tip into Walker's neck, but he didn't break the skin. "Oh, no you're not—you'll have to explain yourself to the Bishop! Come with me!"

The shovel remained positioned beneath Walker's chin as the Mexican led the eavesdropper through the rose garden, through the wooden door, the shaded hallway, and back into the central courtyard. The General's limousine was just leaving the central courtyard, turning down the winding road toward the guardhouse as Walker entered the courtyard. He tried to make a run for it, but Carlos was too strong. Walker could feel years of manual labor in Carlos's grip. He was destined to confront the Bishop, a confrontation he had avoided for twenty-five years.

The two men entered the reception area of the building and Rebecca jumped up and moved away from her desk, backing up to the wall. "Call the guards!" Carlos yelled. Walker struggled. Rebecca moved back to her desk and dialed the phone.

Carlos and Walker walked through the gallery-like hallway toward the Bishop's office, pausing outside the large doors. Here, Carlos confronted a small problem. The doors opened out, and he had both hands already in use, his right hand holding Walker's wrists behind him and his left hand holding the shovel to Walker's throat. "Open the door!" he commanded. Carlos released Walker's right arm, applying even more pressure with the shovel. Walker complied, and they stumbled into the ostentatious office.

Carlos breathed heavily, adrenaline obviously flowing. He said, "Your Honor, this man look in your windows from the garden of roses. He's a new worker." Carlos backed Walker up to the wall, holding him there with the shovel at his throat. The Bishop rose from his desk, apparently a bit concerned that this soiled individual might dirty his clean white walls. He walked toward Walker as Carlos jabbed him with the shovel.

"Well, well, well, what do we have here? Looking for trouble, are you? Who are you?"

"Talk!" yelled the gardener, stabbing his neck harder, almost breaking the skin.

"Uh... I... can't... talk..."

"This shovel is sharp—like a knife. Don't move! I'll use it if I have to!" Carlos reduced the pressure.

Walker nodded slightly. "My name... my name is Walker."

"That's it? Walker?" The Bishop laughed. "I don't believe you. What's your real name? Sneaking around spying in windows? Why?"

"Honest, I mean no harm. I decided I don't want the job after all. I'll be on my way now!"

"I know that voice. I can't quite place it... It seems like a voice from the past..." The Bishop looked around. "I think I know... Yes, I know who you are! Your beard can't conceal your real identity, you fool!"

"I swear... I've never been here before. Please let me go!"

"Don't lie, Stanfield. Oh yes, I know who you are... my good friend George Stanfield, coming back to visit the Institute and your good friend Bishop Ward, is it?

"I don't know what you're talking about. I don't know any George Stanfield."

"Oh, that's right. You're *Walker* now. Don't worry, I know who you are. You can't fool me."

"Fine. It's no pleasure to see you again, Bishop. Uh... You've taken twenty-five years of my life." Walker just about spat as he looked at the gold rings on the Bishops manicured hands. A feeling of disgust rolled through him as he thought of how the Bishop had repeatedly manipulated his life.

"Bishop, it looks like you've been quite successful in growing your operation, probably sucking up to anyone who will give you money."

"George, you haven't changed a bit, have you? I'm sorry to say that you just don't know a good opportunity when you see it. You're forever blinded by your idiotic idealism. I'm sure you haven't returned here to patch everything up and get back into the fold. No, you're too far gone. Sorry, my good friend, you wasted your life by perpetuating those destructive lies. And you've learned too much already."

The Bishop put his hand to his chin, thinking. "I think I know what we'll do with you... Yes, yes... I know. We'll have you take a visit to the Ranch and learn first-hand how well our methods work. "Rebecca! Where are the guards?" the Bishop projected his voice out the door.

Walker was desperate. "Look, I'm willing to help you out. I realize I'm a sinner, and I want a second chance."

"I don't believe you, Stanfield." Saliva dripped out of the Bishop's mouth, spitting the name as he said it. "Did you ever abandon your heretical research? I'm sure you're still convinced you must spout off to the world. Oh, and yes, we've been keeping track of your pathetic life." The Bishop stared into space, not focusing on anything in particular. "Between you and me, I actually agree with many of your conclusions.

But what I really believe is really quite immaterial. I keep my doubts to myself, and I stay with tradition. Without the cross, we have no power to influence the minds of men. I know I must settle for a less-than-perfect situation in the near-term as long as the long-term situation promotes Christianity. That's all I care about."

Walker wasn't sure what that all meant. Was there any way out of this situation? Silence seemed the safest course of action.

The Bishop's bodyguards entered wearing camouflage fatigues with pistols strapped to their legs. "Tony. Carl. Take our friend to the Ranch, and introduce him to the humility of the cross."

"Yes, sir!" the bodyguards answered in unison, bowing slightly. They seemed like zombies to Walker. *Can't they think for themselves?* They pulled Walker's arms behind him and put a heavy-duty zip tie around his wrists, pinching his skin. They shoved him forward, making Walker stumble, almost losing his footing. He caught himself before he hit the floor.

CHAPTER 72

Hall and Dan had listened to the entire conversation between Walker and the Bishop through the belt-buckle bug.

"They are going to take him to that 'Ranch' you mentioned." Dan said.

"Right"

"*Humility of the Cross*—they're probably going to a prayer meeting. Or, maybe it's some sort of new movie."

"I was hoping it wouldn't come to this," Hall said. "I was hoping that Walker could extract details from the Bishop without getting himself captured. At least we gave him that bug so we can track him. That should lead us to that Ranch."

Dan looked at the display of the GPS device. "Walker appears to be moving out of the facility somehow."

Hall looked through binoculars to the main gate of the PIT facility. "The gates are closed. Uh, where's the red dot now?"

"There must be another way out, because the dot is on—what's this—101 North. We'd better get moving if we are going to keep up!"

"Relax, Dan. That's the beauty of these GPS systems! It doesn't matter where they go as long as they're within reach of a cell-phone tower. We don't have to 'tail' them like the old days. I'll just get on 101 North, no problem. We risk losing Walker only if they drive out of cell-phone range or if they confiscate his belt. Hear the engine and road sounds? By the sound of it, he's still wearing the belt buckle. I wonder why he isn't saying anything."

"Maybe he's gagged... or knocked out."

"He probably still has the belt on. See, the dot is moving. If they confiscated his belt, the dot would probably be motionless, and we wouldn't be hearing vehicle sounds. If that happens, we could lose track of Walker."

This didn't make Dan feel much better. Hall drove as Dan watched the GPS tracker device, and gave Hall information on Walker's current location. After they drove north for about twenty miles, they turned east, continuing for about forty-five minutes along a winding road into a sparsely populated area of rolling hills, occasional dry creeks, and wooded dells. During the drive, Dan hinted about the project interpreting Genesis. Hall didn't react, being used to a purely secular career and avoiding talk of religion during his contacts with the public.

"My family is from Ireland," Hall said, "and of course, we were raised Roman Catholic, as is about eighty-five percent of Ireland. During the '60s and '70s, North Ireland was a battlefield between the Protestants and the Catholics. Many Irish rejected the violent church and instead embraced secular traditions, an important choice that led to the final peace agreement in 1998, brokered by President Clinton, one of his proudest moments. Believe me, I followed it closely."

"I don't notice any accent in your voice, but you do have the ruddy complexion of the Irish, I can see that."

"I've been in this country too long, but I haven't lost all my roots. I do still enjoy a pint of Guinness at the pub when I'm off duty."

Dan was feeling more comfortable with Hall all the time. He smiled, but his smile quickly turned into a frown as he looked at the display of the GSP device. "They're a bit north of the road here, but the display doesn't show any roads. It's just a big blank area, and there is no satellite image at all. How can they be out in space with no road?"

"Hmm... They must be on an uncharted road of some kind. Here, press that button to display our position."

A blue dot appeared on the display at their current location. "We should see a turn off but no road is shown on the map—look for a side road to the left."

Hall slowed down a bit to look for the unpublished road. "I don't see any road... Wait..." In a dell where the main road made a hairpin turn, the density of the trees effectively hid the start of a dirt road. "This looks like it might be it." Hall turned the steering wheel sharply hand-over-hand. He veered off the road and rolled to the start of the uncharted dirt road. "How does it look on the tracker?"

"Not sure, but it must be the right one."

"Hey, there's a sign up ahead." The sign was old and rusty with a few bullet holes, one corner heavily bent over, and the whole thing leaned to one side.

NO TRESPASSING - KEEP OUT
AMERICAN POWER NETWORK
MAINTENANCE ACCESS ONLY

Hall ignored the sign and kept driving up the ascending, winding dirt road, proceeding carefully around each corner. The road was well traveled, somewhat surprising for a utility maintenance road. It rose in elevation to a relatively flat plain with occasional rapid dips into dry streambeds. Here, the hills were covered with low olive-colored scrub brush that had seen many years of dryness. Yellow-red rocky dirt dominated gaps in the bushes.

A string of high-power transmission line towers ran east to west and disappeared into the distance to the right and left. As Hall and Dan approached the towers, they steadily increased in apparent height until they were directly overhead. The access road teed onto a dirt service road running east-west under the towers which looked like huge gray aliens with four legs, wide shoulders, and three arms hanging down on each side, holding the six huge, drooping high-voltage lines.

Hall stopped his car at the intersection of the access and the east-west service roads. "Which way should we turn?"

"The dirt road to the right is well traveled," Dan said. "The other way is full of weeds... seldom used. Turn right."

"Aye, right it is. We'll stay on the well-traveled road." Hall turned right and followed the tower service road. "Can you see their position on the GPS tracker?"

"No. I can see our dot but it's not picking them up at all—it went blank—it's flashing *Out of Range*!"

"Don't worry, that means only that they're out of cell-phone range. We'll have to go by feel from here on out."

The sedan Hall was driving was absolutely the wrong choice for this rugged terrain. In some places the heavily eroded dirt road had deep channels cut to one side. The utility towers had obviously been placed to achieve the lowest-cost straight transmission line route without consideration of the best route for the service road. As a result, the service road went up and down over grades normally avoided by any sane road designer. Hall was pushing his sedan to its limits.

At the bottom of one of these dips between hilltops, another road joined the service road on the left and continued north. "Look, all the traffic appears to turn that way," Dan said. Hall turned the sedan to follow the new road north.

Over the next crest, Hall stopped suddenly. A small cloud of dust from behind their car blew past them. "I see something up ahead. Hand me those binoculars."

Hall peered through the binoculars and adjusted the focus. "I see a fenced area and a secure entry and... ah, yes, some video cameras, the all-weather security type... one on each side. That's probably the entry... the PITY Ranch. I'll bet that's where they took Walker." Hall handed the binoculars back to Dan and shifted his car into reverse. He backed up carefully to avoid another dust cloud. "We can't go right up to the gate, or we might be captured ourselves."

"Russ, you're an agent of the US Government. Can't you just go up to the gate and demand Walker's return?"

"Not this time. The whole Bureau seems to be marching to the orders of the tainted Department of Homeland Security and the National Security Agency. If we attempt a direct assault, I'm sure we'll be captured ourselves. I'm not even supposed to be working on this case."

"Then what are we doing here? I'm not used to working outside the law like this, Russ."

Hall didn't say anything. Their activities didn't seem to bother him at all.

After getting back over the crest of the hill, Hall turned the car around and returned to the tower service road. "Let's try going a bit farther on this utility road. We need to find a way to approach the Ranch without being detected."

Hall turned left onto the seldom-used tower service road. This part of the road was even more of a challenge to Hall's sedan. Over the next hill and down into the next water-hewn valley, the high-voltage transmission lines soared overhead, the two towers on each side of this expanse remained behind the hills. The small valley had what looked like a road but was actually a sandy, dry streambed. Hall pulled into the streambed, parking behind a bush that was about eight feet tall.

"We'll need to walk in from here. If we drive any farther, we'll probably get hopelessly stuck in the sand." They got out of the car; Hall opened the trunk, grabbed some gear, and put it into a small backpack. "Here, put on this camo gear I had for hunting." Hall gave Dan camouflage outer clothing. "I'm not sure what we'll be getting into, but we may as well use it since it's here." They put on the outfits.

I'm starting to worry about what Hall might have in mind, but it looks like I have no choice but to try to rescue my father. It seems remarkable that he just happens to have this camouflage gear in his trunk.

Hall threw the backpack over his shoulder. "If we walk up this dry streambed, we should run into the same fenced area. Fairly lively, now!" Hall strutted off and Dan jogged up behind him, pushing to keep pace with the healthy agent.

They walked until they reached a steep embankment that rose to a chain link fence. In the distance, they could hear regular pops of gunfire inside the facility.

"Before it went blank, the GPS signal showed Walker somewhere inside this fence," Hall said. The two men crouched near the twelve foot chain link fence topped with three strands of barbed wire that slanted in.

"That's funny," Dan said. "I would expect the barbed wire to slant out if they wanted to keep people out of the facility. The fact that it slants in means they're more interested in keeping people in, not out. It's more like a *prison* than a Ranch!"

Dan looked at the tall fence and heavy-gauge chain-link fabric that had holes too small to allow a foot to get any traction. "The last time I saw a fence made of this sort of stuff was at the San Diego Zoo around an animal enclosure. It looks like it will be nearly impossible to climb. They spared no expense. It looks like we'll have to use the main gate."

"Don't worry, I have other plans," Hall said. He pulled some compact wire cutters out of his backpack and positioned them to cut a hole in the fence.

"Are you sure this is okay?" Cutting through the fence was definitely going further than he expected.

"Look, we don't have any choice at this point. We have to find Walker."

"Shouldn't we get a warrant or something like that?"

"Dan, this whole thing is being covered up by the Feds. At this point, we won't get anywhere going through official channels. Plus, with the Patriot Act, you can get away with almost anything. Relax."

"I thought you said you were off the case. If you're off the case, the Patriot Act isn't going to cover you. I can't believe you asked Walker to get involved. We don't know what they are going to do to him. He may be killed."

"Look, Dan, I didn't expect the Bishop to do anything this extreme."

"Of course you did! Why did you give Walker the GPS belt-buckle? You said the main reason you wanted to infiltrate PITY was to find the second off-site facility, this Ranch."

"That's true, I wanted him to get that information, and I gave him the belt-buckle with GPS just in case. But I was hoping it wouldn't come to this. We have no choice but to go through with it. Dan, it'll be dark in no time. Let's go in and see what we can find out before we lose daylight. At least we know where he is."

"That's not quite right. You said we only know where his belt-buckle is. They may have anticipated that we would be tracking Walker and simply transported his belt-buckle to lead us to this facility. Once we go in, we'll be trapped and won't be able to leave."

Hall didn't respond. He finished cutting the wire mesh and pulled the section open, creating a hole just large enough to crawl through. He pulled off his backpack, pushed it through and then followed it, staying on his hands and feet.

Dan looked at the hole, realizing it was a one-way trip to a future he never would have been involved in if he hadn't met Walker just over two weeks ago. But, he did agree with Hall. There was really no choice. They had to try to rescue his father.

Dan got down on all fours and squeezed through the hole. After he rose to his feet, Hall pulled the fence closed so the hole would be hard to see from a distance. Hall was smart. Dan noticed he cut the hole behind bushes on both sides of the fence so it would be obscured from view.

"Dan, don't move. We need to look for a trip wire." He looked carefully near the ground. "Usually, near the fence... as a security measure. Stay behind me."

Hall looked like a Native American tracker, checking for all signs as they walked. After about ten yards, Hall found a thin wire near the ground that could be easily broken by an intruder or escapee. "Step carefully over this wire. If it's broken, it will alert security. Watch for additional wires like this one on our way in."

They stepped over the wire and made their way up a slope between sparse sagebrush and an occasional red-barked manzanita. At the top of the slope, they peered cautiously over the ridge, half expecting to be seen by some security guards. A small valley stretched beyond the hill with a narrow path at the bottom in another sandy dry streambed. They squeezed through increasingly dense brush down the hill toward the streambed until they burst out into the path. From here, the crackling of gunfire was louder.

Hall carefully placed two rocks side by side. "These rocks will mark our route back to the fence."

Dan was starting to get very worried. He had thought he trusted Hall, but now, he was having some doubts. Was he just a stooge from the Bishop who was trying to get him into this prison? *I'm not going to worry about that! At least Hall expects us to be leaving. If he was on their side, he wouldn't spend his time with those rocks.*

"This looks like the right direction." Hall pointed down the path, which they followed west, toward the main entrance road. Dan could see footprints in the sand left by others, perhaps a large group. After several hundred yards, the small path teed onto a much wider road. They kept their heads below the height of the brush and looked out carefully onto the road before entering.

"Dan, stay back," Hall said with a soft voice. He motioned with his hands.

"What is it?"

"See that dust cloud over the ridge? Hurry, climb up to those rocks. Duck under those bushes." They both got under laurel sumac bushes next to rocks that were slightly above the level of the road. They could easily see the road from here without being seen, as long as they were still.

The dust cloud grew closer, and they could hear a drill sergeant's commands above the rhythmic sound of marching boots. The squad appeared over the hill and passed in front of the two intruders.

One of the soldiers chanted, and then the group responded in unison to each verse:

Christ he died to save our soul!
To hell we'll go to pay our toll!
We fight the devil with all our might!
We'll kill the bastards, we are right!

The verses continued with the same sickening combination of Christian doctrine and battle cries put to the typical foot soldier marching tune. Dan had been concerned when they opened the fence, but now, his stomach turned over as he was hit by the full realization of what might be going on at this "Ranch." Normally, soldiers are trained to defend their country, almost as if the country were a deity. But that's not good enough—not anymore. Now, they are defending God. *You can't consistently get the ultimate sacrifice unless you move it to this level,* he thought. They watched the helmeted and camouflaged soldiers pass, carrying their M16 weapons and heavy backpacks, marching behind three tall red Christian crosses carried by the leaders, boots kicking up a steady cloud of dust.

Except for the modern-day M16 automatic assault rifles and body armor, the scene reminded Dan of the largely unsuccessful Crusades of the medieval period, a period of ruthless campaigns by both the Islamic culture and Christian Europe. Dan, half hypnotized, reviewed that unfortunately history in his mind.

In the first hundred years or so after Mohammed's death, the Islamic faith spread rapidly putting intense pressure on the Christian church. Islam teaches that nonbelievers are always given the option to convert; otherwise the Islamic holy book, the *Qur'an,* commands *jihad* or holy war. The migration of Islam proceeded from Saudi Arabia, north through Damascus, Jerusalem, and up through Syria, conquering all of the Persian empire within fifteen years. Then the conquering Muslims swept through North Africa, entering southern Spain about sixty years later.

Although they were ruthless, they allowed Christians and Jews to continue to practice their faith, albeit only discreetly. The three cultures lived in relative peace, tolerating and fading into each other. But this nominal truce only lasted so long.

Christian leaders hated the idea that Muslims held the Holy Land of Jerusalem. Even worse, the Christian church and the powerful Pope did not control the Holy Sepulcher: Jesus's sacred tomb. How could God allow that!

Pope Urban II kicked off the first Crusade with a rousing speech in Clermont, France, in AD 1095, about four hundred years after the Muslim takeover. He said that every Christian should march on Jerusalem and free the Holy Sepulcher from the grip of the wicked Islamic infidels. Of course, the commandment "Thou shalt not kill" posed a bit of a problem, but only a small one. The Pope simply declared that killing non-Christians infidels was not just allowed; it was encouraged. Any soldier doing so would gain eternal penance for his sins, basking for an eternity in heaven.

Bloody and difficult, the first Crusade was the only one even moderately successful in "freeing" Jerusalem. For the most part, crusaders were composed not of military troops but rather of peasants and farmers. Loosely coordinated campaigns by the hungry and weak

Christian believers were no match for the Muslim strongholds. The defending Turks easily slaughtered them in repeated ambushes and sallies. As usual, more died from exposure and disease than from battle losses. But they still made progress.

After four years of struggle, the Christians approached Jerusalem, eventually capturing it. Then they began an orgy of killing—men, women, and children. Muslim refugees took shelter in the Dome of the Rock Mosque with a promise of sanctuary. But the Crusaders executed everyone inside anyway. They then turned to the Jewish synagogue, set it afire, and killed everyone who took shelter there. Innocents were slaughtered and sacred shrines plundered. Finally, the rampage of Jerusalem ended because no one was left to kill. The streets flowed ankle-deep with blood. It was an event that would be forever etched in the minds of the Islamic world, linked with the ruthless character of the Christian culture and the symbol of the torturing cross.

Jerusalem was held only for about four-score and seven years, a small island of European Christians amid a sea of hostile Islamic adherents. Finally, Saladin, the Muslim King of Egypt, recaptured Jerusalem. He offered the European Christian residents a safe departure with their possessions once they paid a ransom tax, and he allowed the orthodox Jewish synagogue to reopen. Downright compassionate when compared with the ruthless Christians.

Multiple Crusades and conflicts followed over the next several hundred years, all of them largely unsuccessful. Today, we remember these times and its heroes such as Peter the Hermit and Richard the Lion-Hearted and ruthless Christians, such as Vlad Tepes "The Impaler," who killed thousands of Muslims by impaling them on sharpened stakes set vertically in the ground, with the poor victim struggling to be free as the spike penetrating their abdomen, the impalement quickening with more struggle. The legend of Dracula is based on Tepes, known to wear the black and red cape of the Order of the Dragon. The myth surrounding bloodthirsty Dracula is perhaps based on an effort to explain the incredible behavior of Crusaders of that period.

Three red crosses disappeared as the road veered to the left. Dan watched the Crusader-like contingent march farther down the road, as his mind returned to their situation in the Ranch. He noticed that the steady and uneven sounds of gunfire had stopped, perhaps due to the late hour.

"Now... it looks safe," Hall whispered.

Dan could still hear the soldiers' chants in the distance even if the words were unclear.

"Try to stay out of sight." Hall moved along the side of the road and looked carefully around each turn to avoid any sudden confrontation. He also looked back from time to time to check on anyone who might be approaching from the rear. Dan felt comfortable in one respect: Hall was with a pro, someone who really understood how to penetrate a facility like this. He could see that Hall was probably enjoying himself, adrenaline up and eyes sharp.

This dirt road ran roughly due north, probably the same road that entered the front gate that they had seen earlier, and descended gradually into a gently sloped valley. The bushes grew steadily taller in size, and an occasional eucalyptus tree towered overhead. The density of the trees increased until the road opened out into a large cleared area around a compound of about a dozen clustered buildings. Hall stepped off the road into the organic litter of the eucalyptus forest, staying behind some thick bushes just on the edge of the open area, a great place to hide while observing the compound. "We'll survey the situation from here for a few minutes."

The sun had already set, and dusk was setting in. They had only a few minutes to memorize the layout of the compound before full darkness descended. To the left of the compound, a fitness course, one of the largest Dan had seen, complete with ropes, climbing walls, and tall posts filled an area of unknown extent. Past that was what looked like a series of shooting ranges with targets set in the distance on raised berms.

"Look over there," Dan whispered, pointing to the right. On a small hill that was even with the compound, the outline of a number of wooden structures was barely visible. "Those things up on the hill... They're some sort of pole or something." It was dark in that direction.

"Here, we're going to need these." Hall pulled out a pair of night-vision binoculars. "These will let us see in the dark."

"I've seen these in movies, but I've never used them before." Dan was always curious about any new technology. The binoculars had two eyepieces that converged to a single, large protruding lens.

"Just look through them like any other binocs, but these amplify any light available." Hall turned the unit on and handed it to Dan.

The unit was heavy and dense. Dan could hear a slight high-pitched whine from the instrument. When he held it to his eyes, a green display of the scene filled his field of view, lighted like the full light of day. He scanned the compound, and saw people walking around and a panel delivery-type truck that was probably the vehicle that had been used to transport Walker. Just past the panel truck, a half dozen military Humvees were parked, each with desert camouflage paint and a large machine gun bolted to the roof.

He scanned over to the large poles on the hill. "Oh, my God! Those are not just poles... they're crosses and..." He shuddered and said in a horrified whisper, "People are hanging on them!"

CHAPTER 73

"You're kidding. Let me take a look." Hall had to pull the night-vision binoculars from Dan's hands. Hall raised the binoculars to his eyes as Dan sat frozen in shock with his mouth gaping open.

"Damn. You're right. They're learning firsthand about the sacrifice of Christ, I guess. That must be the 'humility of the cross' that the Bishop was talking about."

"You can't be serious. Do they drive spikes through their hands and feet?" Dan said.

"I can't see that far. Wait, I should be able to zoom-in... Nope, no spikes, just rope. They must hope that the whole practice is kept secret. Rope's bad enough. This place is sick."

"Let me see again," Dan said. He put out his hand and waited for Hall to hand him the night-vision binoculars.

After Hall finished surveying the rest of the compound, he handed the instrument to Dan. "This looks like the training camp you were talking about, maybe for some deal the Bishop has with the General. I would imagine Walker is somewhere inside. Can you hear anything from the bug device?"

"No... Remember? It doesn't work here. We're out of cell phone range. We're not going to be able to hear or locate him. Those machine guns on those trucks are probably just the tip of the iceberg. They're obviously very well armed." Hall crouched like an animal in the jungle. "We need to get closer."

Dan looked at the crosses again. There were ten of them, with seven people already hanging. Then, there was some motion and sound coming from the compound. He could see three people walking out of the facility. "That might be Walker," he said excitedly.

As they walked, one guard and then the other periodically shoved the center man, dressed in only a loincloth, arms tied together behind his back. Each time he was pushed, he stumbled and almost fell to the ground, catching himself instinctively before losing his balance. About halfway to the crosses, one hard push flattened him on the ground. With his hands restrained, he fell hard, twisting to the side but holding his head up. Dan jolted as if he felt the blow, "Dad!" he said, a bit louder than he intended. The guards picked Walker up and forced him back on his feet only to push him again.

"They're taking him toward the hill with the crosses." Walker did not struggle at first. He was doing all he could just to stay on his feet. But when he saw the other crosses, he tried to make a break for it, struggling to run away. The two guards caught him and turned him back toward "Calvary." Although his struggles became more violent as he approached the crosses, Walker was no match for the broad-shouldered guards. They muscled him down on a cross that had been lowered to a horizontal position and spent some time lashing his arms and ankles to the cross with ropes.

"They're putting Walker on a cross!"

At first, the cross was horizontal and pointed away from the compound. It gradually swiveled up as one guard turned a crank and the other pushed it up from the rear. When they finished their efforts, Walker hung on the cross, about fifteen feet in the air. Dan sat open mouthed as he watched his father, a man he had only recently been united with, hanging on a cross. Crucified.

Tears welled up in his eyes. "We've got to get him down!" Dan started to move toward the compound but Hall caught him by the arm.

"Stop!" Hall whispered as loud as he dared. "If you go in now, you'll be crucified on that cross right next to your father—and there's one more for me. Get back here!"

"We've got to get him down!" Dan insisted with clenched teeth. He wrenched himself from Hall's grip and ran across the cleared area between the bushes and the buildings, night vision instrument in hand.

"Dammit," Hall said to himself, watching his accomplice make the foolish move of a novice.

Dan knelt behind a Jeep in front of the compound and looked toward the crosses. The men who had raised Walker on the cross moved down the line, prodding each trainee with a wooden stick to make sure each was still alive. Each one groaned in pain when the stick was shoved into his gut while the guards laughed. In the quietness of the twilight, Dan could hear pleas for mercy.

But one man did not respond. Laughing harder, the guards prodded him again, but the man remained silent.

Dan couldn't hear the exact words, but the guards interacted as if they were arguing. One guard cranked the cross down as the other man helped lower the top when it got within his reach. They untied the man and carried him, one holding under the arms and the other holding the feet, the limp body hanging between them. They scrambled around to the far side of the buildings, nearly out of sight. Through the night-vision binoculars, Dan could see every gory detail, including the man's dead body dragging helplessly on the ground, bouncing over rocks and debris. They seemed to throw him into a hole, perhaps a mass grave for those who failed to meet God's favor and had succumbed to the torture of the cross.

As soon as the guards left, Hall ran up to Dan's position by the car. "Don't do that again, or you'll be up there with your father. Stick with me!" he whispered.

"That guy was dead. And they just threw him in the ground. I guess they're following history to the letter. Most people who were crucified in ancient times were given no 'proper' burial, they were just allowed to rot on the cross. Crow food."

Hall was silent.

"Walker will be dead soon if we can't get him down!" Dan's eyes looked desperate. "Let's move up to that window. It's protected by those bushes. Maybe we can look inside."

"Dan, no... just stay here!"

Dan ignored Hall's order. He crouched and scrambled across the empty dirt area between the vehicles and the bushes by the building. Hall followed, protesting. At the window, they kept their heads low, below the beam of light that poured into the darkness. Hall motioned with his hand for Dan to stay down and put his finger to his lips to emphasize being quiet. Then Hall fished into one of the cargo pockets of his camouflaged overalls, eventually pulling out a small mirror, only about one inch on a side.

Hall held the mirror up at an angle just above the windowsill, a move that allowed him to see into the room without showing his face. The room was full of trainees, sitting with their backs to the window in rows of seats like a classroom.

Hall put the small mirror back in his pocket and slowly raised his head to peer in. He motioned for Dan to do the same. In the front of the room was a large map of the United States and a list of important landmarks, including the Statue of Liberty, Golden Gate Bridge, the Arch of St. Louis, and the World Trade Center, which was crossed off. Another chart listed the most important U.S. Ports, ordered by total tonnage: Port of South Louisiana, Houston, New York, New Orleans, Corpus Cristi, etc. New Orleans was crossed off.

It didn't take Hall long to get his fill. He lowered his head back down, pulling Dan down with him.

"Those are the key U.S. targets for terrorist hits," Hall whispered. "I've been to the anti-terrorist office at Homeland Security, and this isn't it. These guys must have some links to terrorists activities, maybe Al Qaeda. We're going to need some help on this, Dan."

"But you said the FBI couldn't be trusted. Who will be willing to help us?"

"The local sheriff is an old school friend of mine. We worked together before I went to the Feds. I told him earlier that I might need help, but I had no idea. Let me see if I can call him."

Hall opened his cell phone but stopped suddenly.

"What's wrong?" asked Dan.

"Damn! I forgot! No service!"

Two guards walked in the space between the vehicles and the building and stopped suddenly.

"Hey, what's that sound?" Looking toward the dark area next to the window where Dan and Hall sat, the guards peered intently and squinted.

Hall held Dan's arm tightly, insisting that he remain still.

CHAPTER 74

"Here is your meal, ma'am and... sir." The waiter deposited hot plates on the table in front of Shannon and John. Shannon had suggested that they meet at Miguel's, a casual Mexican restaurant, and John happily consented. They seemed to be past their recent metaphorical sword fight. Each had made a point, and even though it had been difficult, each had had to admit the other's point as well.

Their relationship, which had begun to change in the quaint village coffee house, had progressed far beyond the happy-go-lucky laugh-fest they originally enjoyed. John knew that he had chemistry with Shannon at a more fundamental level, a level that seemed important to her. Nevertheless, he also knew that their disagreements on the religious matters could kill the idea of any long-term relationship. *We're making progress!* John thought. *I've been hinting about a dinner like this for weeks. Shannon is finally coming around!*

At the moment, the food took priority. Their meal was still hot but was cooling fast. So far, the conversation had dealt only with trivial matters. They were both cognizant of the tenuous footing of their relationship.

As they progressed into their meal, John was the first to deliver an olive branch. "Shannon, I know the last couple of weeks have been, well, differ—"

"No kidding," Shannon interrupted.

They both talked at the same time. "I wanted to talk—", they said simultaneously, then both giggled nervously.

"You go ahead," Shannon said.

"Ladies first," John said.

"All right. Ladies first."

John was worried about what Shannon would say. In a way, he regretted being so adamant that she go first. She took some time to formulate what she was going to say, her hand repeatedly folding her napkin.

"John," she reached for his hands and held them across the table. "I'm not sure how to say this."

She's probably having a hard time saying that she is deeply in love with me. "It's okay. I probably feel the same way. Don't worry."

Her expression became tortured—in sharp distinction from John's mental picture. *She isn't smiling!*

"John, I don't want to hurt your feelings..."

Oh, no! That isn't what she's supposed to say! "Stop, Shannon! Stop." *I don't want to have to hear this. It is too painful.* "Excuse me a minute." John got up from the table and found his way to the restroom.

He looked at himself in the mirror. *I'm an idiot! I should have known that it wouldn't work between Shannon and me... Evolution... She's right... But, I should still be able to be friends with her and maybe later... Dan... But Shannon probably needs someone who is more technical... I want a family.* John washed his face in cold water, dried off, and returned to the table.

"Sorry, Shannon. Look, I understand completely. Let's just be friends, okay?"

"That sounds good to me. Say, let's give Dan a call."

"Good idea."

Dan had convinced John and Shannon to stay out of the PIT infiltration effort, but it wasn't easy. Shannon pulled out her cell phone, scrolled to Dan's cell number, and initiated the call. She held it up to her ear and listened to the rings, then the announcement:

"Hi. This is Dan. I'm unable to take your call—"

"Straight to voice mail! It's been that way all afternoon!"

CHAPTER 75

A low rumble could be heard in the distance, approaching from somewhere along the entrance road. Headlights flickered over the top of the hill. The two guards turned from the sounds in the bushes and looked out to the road, then walked out past the parked vehicles. The approaching vehicles seemed to take forever to arrive, the sound and lights arriving far earlier than the vehicles themselves. Finally, two large SUVs arrived, rolling on large knobby tires and kicking up a cloud of dust. The trucks drove up to the facility, parking a bit to the left, the dust dissipating as a slight breeze blew to the right.

Hall reached for the night-vision binoculars. "Let me take a look." He focused on the vehicles. "The driver is getting out... He's opening the back door for someone... It's... it's the Bishop—Bishop Ward. There are some other people as well. They're heading into the first building."

Dan was having a hard time staying quiet.

Hall talked under his breath as he looked through the night-vision instrument. "Don't overreact. We don't want to get ourselves up on one of those crosses. Just wait until we can safely make our way over to that hill and have enough time to get Walker down and out of here. They're all going inside... even the guards."

Hall scanned the compound again. "Everyone seems to have been drawn into the compound to see the Bishop for some sort of meeting, maybe a church service or some sort of pep talk."

Dan held his breath to listen. "I can hear something, but I can't make out what's being done. They're responding to questions or maybe saying 'Amen' and 'Praise the Lord.'"

"Okay, Dan. This is our chance. Don't attract any attention. Keep an eye out for the guards and 'Ranch-hands.' Follow me and—*be silent*."

The two intruders left the protective bushes and crossed back over to the far side of the cleared area, then walked carefully around the compound. The camouflage hunting overalls faded into the darkness of the brush and trees.

About halfway to "Calvary," Dan didn't notice a small indentation in the ground; his foot gave way, and he went down. "Ouch!" He rolled on the ground, holding his ankle with his hands. "My weak ankles again!

I've twisted them a million times! Damn!"

"Shhhh! Dan, we have no cover here. Put your arm over my shoulder." The two men hobbled into the bushes. Hall set Dan down so his ankle could rest.

"We're only half-way to the crosses. The guards may come back out if we can't make progress soon."

Dan rotated and massaged his ankle. "It's feeling better. It isn't as bad as some twists I've had." He spent another minute or two resting, and then said, "I should be able to walk now."

"Good!"

They continued their journey toward the crosses, this time with Dan being extra careful and limping slightly as he tried to reduce the weight on his left ankle. They walked around the right side of the hill of crosses and then ascended from the rear.

Dan covered his nose with his arm. *This place stinks!* His nose reacted to the feces and urine that was an inevitable consequence of hanging people on crosses for any period of time. *If the cross doesn't kill you, the stench will! They never showed that in Sunday school!*

Dan stood behind Walker's cross so he would be at least partially hidden from any observer in the compound. "Dad... How are you doing?"

"Dan, is that you?" Walker said with difficulty.

"We're here to rescue you!"

"What? Don't worry about me! Get the hell out of here—*now*. I'm not worth getting yourself caught. These people are crazy. They're all brainwashed."

"Just relax. We'll have you down and out of here in no time. Agent Hall's with me. Are you okay?"

"It's hard, but not as bad as it could be. They didn't drive spikes through my hands and feet—thank God—they're just tied with rope. This little seat helps."

Dan looked at the "seat," called a *sedile*, a small protrusion from the upright of the cross that could be used to take some of the weight off of the arms and legs, a feature common in the torturing crosses of the medieval period, prolonging the punishment for hours and days.

Dan studied the mechanism to figure out how to lower the cross. The bottom of the cross was attached with a large bolt through a huge U-shaped bracket set in concrete. A diagonal support strut extended to the rear and a crank on that strut let an operator raise or lower the heavy cross. Because the crosses were constructed from huge timbers like telephone poles, it was more than any single person could lift, but he could see that the mechanical reduction gears should make it possible.

"Go ahead and crank him down," whispered Hall as he looked through his night-vision instrument at the compound. "I don't see anyone... Wait! A light just went on. Hurry, Dan. Take cover." They said no more and descended the back of the hill, directly away from the compound, back into the darkness of the bushes. They struggled to quiet their rapid breathing and to avoid crunching the leaves and bark on the ground.

A man with a flashlight approached the hill. His face was left in a shadow. The night-vision instrument was useless in this situation, overpowered by the glare of the flashlight. The man walked up the face of the hill and flashed the light onto each of the men on the crosses until he found Walker. The man held the flashlight steady on Walker's face. He spoke in a mocking tone of voice. "My dear friend George Stanfield, what sort of trouble have you gotten yourself into? My word, what on earth are you doing way up there on that cross?"

"Bishop Ward, I demand that you get me down from here. This is crazy," sputtered Walker.

"What's the matter? Lost your faith in God?"

"What is this place? What are you doing to these people?"

"Oh, my dear George. You just don't understand, do you? You were just the sort of person I needed; I had great hopes we could work together. Too bad you lost your head years ago. You couldn't learn those important lessons in life, could you? I told you, go along to get along. Don't buck the system; that's how you get ahead. But, that's not the way you look at it, is it? We've just barely cracked open the treasure chest here, and it looks unlimited."

"Great, you're playing army with disoriented youth. Perverted? Yes. But I can't see how that can be any gold mine."

The Bishop paced back and forth, playing with his long-sought prey, like a cat playing with a doomed mouse. Remarkably, he was willing to tell all now that Walker was doomed to die. "We're not just rescuing students here. We're training Christian Crusaders—patriots—willing to make the ultimate sacrifice to protect our way of life. And the Pentagon pays dearly for special-ops recruits that are willing to embed themselves and fight for what is right. The United States is a nation chosen and blessed by God. It has a holy duty to assume in the world.

"And it's a duty we must fulfill. It's hard work. Traditional military training can provide the understanding of weapons, tactics, and battlefield strategy. But, it doesn't motivate like our program. A soldier may know how to use an M-16, but he will he risk his own skin in pursuit of the enemy? The Islamic jihadists are willing to do whatever it takes. Without Christian training, our boys wimp out. Only one out of four will pull the trigger when the time comes. It's pathetic. You can't win this war with that. With our training here at the PITY Ranch, we get over ninety percent compliance. And, they're willing to sacrifice their lives. Our soldiers graduate as lethal killing machines—the kind the Pentagon wants and will pay dearly for. Our men become highly paid contractors, mercenary soldiers assigned to heart of the battle, crushing the enemy with the same terrorist tactics they've used on us."

"You can't be serious, Bishop. You're training suicidal mercenaries for the war with the Islamic culture? Don't you think this is going too far?"

"Not at all. This isn't really to win one little war against Islam. We're bringing peace to the world! Under our control, we'll make sure there's peace. Oh, by the way, this is not a war against 'terror.' That's stupid... just like saying a war against *bombs*. You fight ideas and cultures, not tactics. Our fight strikes against Islam. Oh, yes, we've been doing it for years, pitting one sect against another. Those car bombs you see on TV? Some of those are ours, of course. And the so-called terrorism in our county... the 9/11 attacks, anthrax, shoe-bomber, and exploding lotion... It's crazy if you think some small group of poor Muslims could pull those off. Fear gives us control. People are like little sinful children who need a strict father to teach them important lessons. The US must set a moral example in the world, and it's divinely ordained to do so."

Dan listened to the Bishop explaining his true agenda at this Ranch. Moral values? How moral is false-flag terrorism, mercenary armies, or even the worship of a cross—nothing more than a cruel torture device? Suicidal special ops-forces? The Pentagon was concerned that our troops would back down from missions that were certain suicide, and hard-core Christian culture was just what was needed to breed the new special-ops trooper. A trooper who would rather commit suicide than fail. A trooper who would think of the "passion of Christ" and feel good about sacrificing his own life. A trooper who would salute and perform his duty and not question authority—how can you question the authority of God?

Walker groaned with pain, coughed repeatedly, and then it seemed he was about to vomit. "I'm sure you overlook the absence of morality in the genocide of Native Americans, the age of slavery, the oppression of minorities, and rampant racism." Walker looked down from his perch. "What sort of moral example does the US make?"

"You just don't get it, do you, Stanfield. You're hopeless... hopeless!"

"Well, it looks like you've found a great niche to support the needs of our nation, Bishop. Very patriotic. Very noble. Great job. Now let me out of here. You don't need me for your twisted plan."

"Twisted? No, it's not twisted. It's straight and simple. We use Christian philosophy and the humility of the cross to inspire these youth to perform. Sure, the Pentagon would like mechanical robot warriors who operate without question. Our product is better. Compliant and willing youth are as obedient as their stupid robots. Plus, humans can infiltrate the enemy much better than any robot can.

"But it seems you'll never smarten-up, will you Stanfield? My poor, poor friend! You're so pathetic. You make me sick! Hah, hah, hah..." The Bishop was seething with a perverted satisfaction of finally capturing his archenemy. His laugh was worse than those of cartoon villains, he continued to laugh as he turned and descended Calvary at the PITY Ranch, drunk with satisfaction. "Oh, George, you'll understand after tonight... if you make it! Hah, hah!" The Bishop zigzagged back toward the facility, laughing and mumbling to himself, and then finally reentered the buildings.

"Dan, let's go." The intruders resumed their rescue attempt, climbed back up to the top of the hill and then waited just behind the crest for everyone to be drawn inside the compound.

Standing at the base of Walker's cross, Dan surveyed the situation again. The handle of the mechanism was in the rear, so it was only slightly soiled by the blood, feces, and urine that would run down the upright post. Dan flipped the ratchet switch to the position for lowering the cross and turned the crank. Each fractional turn of the crank made a loud click. Fast action was required. Anyone could notice the cross moving and the sound of the ratcheting crank. At first, the crank was easy to turn, but it required more strength as the cross came down, folding backwards toward a cradle in the rear.

Hall supported the top of the cross as soon as he could reach it, guiding it into the cradle. He slashed the ropes with his knife. Walker was in bad condition. The guards had jabbed him in the gut with the wooden stick, causing a large bruise. A crown of thorns made from a circle of rusty barbed wire was firmly seated on his head and dried blood from the punctures streaked down his nearly naked body.

Dan carefully removed the crown, trying to avoid reopening the puncture wounds.

Hall gave Walker a drink of water from a bottle he carried in his backpack and wiped some of the dirt and blood from Walker's face. Walker had only on a small loincloth at his waist, so Hall dug into his backpack and pulled out a lightweight jacket for Walker and helped him get it on.

Hall and Dan lifted Walker to stand between them, putting one arm over each shoulder. Walker could barely put one foot in front of the other. Dan's weak ankle wasn't helping either; he pointed out the hole where he twisted his ankle the first time.

They covered the distance from the crosses to their previous hiding place in only a few minutes. Remarkably, no one from the PITY Ranch noticed, still distracted by the Bishop and some sort of church-like service. The threesome took refuge in the bushes where they attended to Walker a bit more.

Dan massaged his ankle. "What about the others on the crosses? Shouldn't we get them down too?"

"They're happy to be there," Walker said. "They're brainwashed to believe that they must complete their 'cross training' so they can be better warriors for God. I don't think they'll willingly come down if you offered. This whole place must be shut down; it's a form of Christianity that no one ever anticipated, it and certainly doesn't represent the commandment to 'love thy neighbor,' or 'turn the other cheek!'"

Hall handed Dan squeeze-bags of antiseptic cream, like little packets of ketchup from a fast-food restaurant. "Dan, put this on those puncture wounds. Walker, I hope you've had your tetanus shots recently." Hall reached into his backpack again. "Here, eat this energy bar. We'll need your help on the way out to the car. It's at least a half-mile away. How are you feeling?"

"That small seat on the cross was a God-send. Without it, I would have probably given up long ago. In ancient times it was not uncommon for people to live for several days, as long as they had those seats. The fact that Jesus died in only a few hours, according to the popular story, was quite unusual. Indeed, that's a key reason rumors spread asserting that Jesus actually survived the crucifix—"

"Shhh! Keep it down." Hall whispered. "This is not the place for history lessons! Let's get going."

They lifted Walker back up on his feet and helped him place his arms over their shoulders. Retracing their original route, they walked away from the compound on the main road and turned up the arroyo path. They stopped at least a half-dozen times to rest, but the urgency of their retreat dominated their minds.

Hall pointed at the two rocks. "Here's the way to the fence. Let's rest just for a minute. Going through this brush is going to be the hardest." Everyone took a drink from a water bottle Hall passed around.

Hall opened his cell phone and redialed the number to his friend, Jack, a local sheriff. Dan looked over in earnest, hoping that the cell tower would be in range. Hall gave him the thumbs-up sign as soon as the phone rang. "Yes!" exclaimed Dan.

"Jack, Russ Hall calling." Hall looked around. "Not bad, until now. I'm going to need your help... We've gotten ourselves in pretty deep, but we're almost out. One man is with us who needs medical attention, and there are others who are near death inside the facility... We're off State Route 68, just after Cuyucos Creek... Yes... Yes, a fenced compound... That's right... Good. Bring all units available. They have a paramilitary group here with some heavy firepower... Thanks."

That sounded good, at least we would have some help, Dan thought.

Hall put his phone away. "Let's get going." They supported Walker again between their shoulders and turned to the side to get through the thick brush. They worked their way through the dense brush, back up the hill, and over the crest toward the fence. Although Walker's bare legs were being scratched by the brush, he didn't complain. Luckily, the jacket was keeping his chest and back from being further injured.

"Do you see where we squeezed through the fence?" asked Dan.

"Right behind that bush. We're almost there!"

The trip wire faded invisibly into the debris on the ground, a detail forgotten by the rescuers as they looked for the hole in the fence and supported the injured man. They walked directly through the tiny trip-wire, breaking it. Immediately, lights energized along the fence line; a siren and "whoop-whoop-whoop" alarm could be heard at the compound.

"Damn!" cursed Hall loudly. "I'm getting old... I can't believe I forgot that trip-wire! They'll be after us!"

CHAPTER 76

The threesome shuffled to the fence, now under bright halogen floodlights glaring from regularly spaced posts atop the fence. "Hold Walker while I open the fence." Hall released Walker to Dan's grip and pulled the fence fabric to reopen the hole. "I'll go through first. Then, we'll work Walker through," he said. The alarm continued to sound in the distance. Their adrenaline pumped. *At least the lights on the fence make it easier to see what we're doing,* Dan thought.

Dan repeatedly looked over his shoulder to see if anyone was coming. This part of the fence was not directly visible from the facility or the main road. He could see no one.

"They'll be checking the fence line soon. We must get through fast." Hall squeezed through the hole and pulled his backpack through. "Dan, lower him down and get his head through. I'll support him from this side."

They worked Walker through the hole in the fence. "I've got him; come on through!" Hall put Walker's arm over his shoulder, held him up, and walked down the small embankment below the fence line.

Dan squeezed into the hole in the fence. He crawled halfway through the hole and then lost his footing on the loose ground. When he got up, his back hit the upper part of the fence, snagging the roughly cut wires. He struggled to continue but was held firmly in the hole by the heavy-gauge wire. The alarm pealed in the distance, echoing through the valley behind them. Dan thought mindless paramilitary soldiers could be running up the trail behind them. He pushed again but could make no progress. "I'm stuck!" he yelled.

"I'll have to come back up." Hall lowered Walker to the ground, then walked back up the embankment. "I can see it... You're hooked in the middle of your back by the fence."

Dan tried to reach back but could not twist his arm to that position. "I can't reach it!" The alarm continued to sound.

"Wait, Dan. Stop pushing!" Dan stopped, and in a moment, Hall was able to pull the wire out of the camouflage fabric. Dan squeezed through the hole. They descended the embankment, put Walker between them, and hobbled down the sandy wash toward the car, wasting no time.

What seemed like a short trek on the way in now seemed like miles. *We might all be captured and crucified on mini-Calvary. We may not make it.*

"I've got to rest," Walker said, out of breath.

"We can stop at that rock up there." Hall led them to the rock. "Here, sit right here, Walker."

They gave Walker another drink of water. The alarm was not as loud here, but a minute seemed like an hour.

"We've got to get going," insisted Hall. "The car is not much farther." They hoisted Walker between their shoulders and rushed the final hundred yards or so to the car.

Hall opened the back door of the car. "Just crawl in and lie down on the back seat." They helped Walker get situated.

"I'm feeling sick," Walker said.

"Just lie down, Dad." Dan was still getting used to calling Walker "Dad," a habit he had given up twenty-five years ago. Doing so required an active thought each time.

Hall opened the trunk, dug around a bit, and then handed a blanket to Dan. "Here, cover him with this blanket. Climb in; let's go!"

The engine started easily, and the car moved slightly as Hall stepped on the gas. But then it came to a stop, engine roaring. "We're stuck in the sand!" Hall slapped the steering wheel in disgust.

"We'll need to let some air out of the tires. That way they won't dig-in so fast." Dan said. "It's a trick we use out in the desert."

"Good idea. You get that side; I'll get this side." They both let a few pounds of air out of the rear tires, letting the sides of the tires bulge out.

"Dig the sand out in front of the back tires and put these palm fronds down," yelled Dan. "I'll push from behind. Make sure you don't give it much gas—don't spin the tires."

They used their hands to dig the sand out in front of the rear tires, and then they placed palm-fronds on top of the sand. Dan put his back against the back of the car and held the bumper, pushing with all his might as Hall drove carefully out of the sand, climbing out on the palm fronds.

It worked. Hall drove all the way to the hard dirt of the tower service road before he trusted stopping. Dan ran along and jumped in as soon as the car was safely on the firm ground of the service road.

Hall drove carefully west, headlights off, toward their original entrance to this area. "Just over this hill, we'll be able to see the road into the Ranch. They'll probably be waiting for us."

CHAPTER 77

Hall pulled the car up a steep incline but stopped just short of the brow of the hill.

"Why are you stopping?" Dan asked.

"I'm going to take a quick look at what we'll be up against, and I don't want them to see the car. Wait here." He got out and quietly walked up the road toward the summit, hunching down, and staying in the darkness of the shadow of the bank on the right side of the road.

Dan waited in the car. Walker remained motionless across the back seat under the blanket.

After surveying the situation for a moment, Hall ran back to the car, got in, and closed the door softly. "I don't see anyone, but that doesn't mean they won't intercept us."

"How long before your friend arrives?"

"I'm not sure. He may be quite a while. We may as well try to drive out to the main road. If we can get that far, we'll be out of trouble—at least for a while.

"Okay, let's go!" Dan looked back at his father. "Dad, stay down and out of sight. They may not realize that you're missing."

Hall restarted the car and drove with lights off down the dirt tower service road, attempting to dodge ruts from memory and not having a great deal of luck. The high-voltage towers—monuments to high-tech industrialized society—soared overhead, a single red aircraft warning light blinking on the top of each one. The intruders rejoined the well-used part of the road with no problem. "Dan, keep an eye out the back window!"

They continued quietly along the service road under the high-voltage lines, up and down the hilly terrain to the meet the entry road. Turning south on that access road, they retraced their route back toward the paved road of Route 68.

"We'll be out soon!" Dan said. The entry road had fewer ruts, but it wound around great deal more to avoid excessive grades. The mile or so seemed to take forever. "The main highway should be right about here. I haven't seen anyone following us. We must have made better time than I thought."

"A gate!" Hall slammed on the brakes; the car skidded in the dirt and almost hit a heavy steel gate closed across the road. A heavy chain locked with a large chrome padlock joined the two sides of the gate.

As their dust settled, high-power halogen off-road lights from two Humvees energized, shining on their sedan. Bolts of guns could be heard. "Out of the car!" yelled a man. Dan could see the outline of Browning .50 caliber machine guns mounted on each vehicle—the same trucks they observed earlier at the compound. The safety mechanism could be heard as the soldiers took aim.

CHAPTER 78

The situation seemed hopeless. Hall yelled, "Don't shoot!" He spoke to Dan at a low volume keeping his head turned forward. "Dan, get out of the car. We were lost, okay?"

Hall and Dan opened their doors and put their hands up. Walker remained in the back seat under the blanket.

"What's the problem?" Hall said, innocently. "I think we must have taken a wrong turn or something. What is that alarm, anyway? Is there a fire or something?"

"What were you doing out here... and why are you driving with your lights off?" a gruff male voice said from behind the bright lights.

"Hey, we're just a couple of hunters trying to find our way back home. We heard the alarm in the distance, and we didn't want any bad guys to see us; we thought we'd be safer if they were off."

Dan cringed inside knowing the excuse was lame.

"We're sorry if we're on the wrong road. These dirt roads all look the same, you know."

The men in the trucks jumped out with M16 rifles, came over to Hall and Dan, pointing their rifles in their faces. "Down on the ground!" Before they could fully lie down, one man stomped on their backs and forced them to the ground as the other zip-tied their wrists together. The lead man walked down and gave Hall and Dan both a solid kick in the gut with his steel-toed boots. They writhed in pain.

Dan's cheek was firmly resting on the hard ground, rocks and gravel digging into his skin; he was still trying to restart his breathing. All he could see was about three feet of dirt road with black and tan service boots walking around.

A different voice was heard. "Hold it right there! Sheriff's Department. We've got you surrounded!" Dan could hear a voice from the bushes past the trucks, a voice that may be their savior. But the firepower of the paramilitary group far exceeded anything the typical rural Sheriff would have. Their only hope was that the paramilitary group really didn't want a run-in with law enforcement and perhaps still doubted that he and Hall were the people who set off the alarm.

"Back away from the men on the ground and leave the area. You don't want trouble from law enforcement. Leave now." The service boots stopped in unison and walked back to their trucks. The trucks backed away from the gate and spun their wheels as they accelerated toward the Ranch. Dan was surprised there wasn't any gunfire traded like he'd seen in movies, but he knew reality was far from those fictional scenarios.

Hall's friend, Jack Miller, walked out of the brush, cut their restraints, and helped them to their feet.

"Jack, I owe you, big-time," Hall said, shaking Jack's hand as he was helped up, brushing dirt from his clothes. "The 'PITY Ranch' is about two miles in and a half mile up near those towers you can see over there."

"You say, 'PITY Ranch?' Sure, we've known about that place for a while, but they don't seem to bother anybody," Jack said.

"It's a crazy paramilitary academy. They put trainees on Christian crosses so they can learn the 'humility of Christ.' We saw one die on the cross and they threw him into a pit or a mass grave. Dan's father, Walker, was kidnapped earlier today and hung on a one of those crosses. Walker's an eyewitness to their craziness. Dan, get Walker out of the car."

Dan went over to the car and opened the back door, ready to help Walker out. He looked in and saw nothing but an empty seat.

"He's gone. Walker's gone!"

CHAPTER 79

Dan spun around in dismay. "They took Walker back to the Ranch!" he yelled with anguish, pounding the side of the sedan with his fist. "No wonder they left without a fight. After finding Walker, they probably headed straight back to the Ranch to finish him off."

"Jack, where are your vehicles and the rest of your men?" asked Hall.

"We have two units out on the road."

"What? Two units? I said bring all you had! You can't fight these guys with only four officers!"

"Sorry, Russ, that's all we have right now. This is not New York City. Our department is small and underfunded, of course. Oh, sure, we know about communes and other wacko groups in the mountains that may not be following every law, but we don't have time to worry about those groups unless they pose a serious threat. We had no idea what to expect in terms of firepower. But it doesn't matter. Ever since the budget cuts, we've been operating on a shoestring.

"We were about to cut through those chains, but we heard the trucks coming, so we ducked into the brush. As soon as I saw the machine guns mounted on the trucks, I realized you weren't kidding when you called me. Even if we had more officers, it was too late to get any other help. We were hopelessly out-gunned and out-manned.

"Hell, we rarely ever use our guns around these parts. In fact, other than the practice range, I haven't even fired my pistol in the last five years—or more. We're definitely not ready for those military-grade machine guns and automatic rifles. Our only hope was to bluff and make our move when they were unprepared, so we spread into the trees and brush. After they captured you, they let their defenses down. By coming in from various directions, we made it appear that they were surrounded by a much larger force."

"Smart move, Jack," Hall said with a half smile. "But don't you think that next time you can move it just a little bit sooner. I could have done without that kick in the gut!" He held his belly and grinned.

"I beg to differ. You needed a good kick!" They chuckled with a moment of humor that seemed out of place to Dan.

"You guys are dreaming. They didn't leave because of your bluff," Dan said. "They obviously grabbed Walker, realized that they had what they wanted, and returned to the Ranch."

"Dan, we can't go after Walker until we have more reinforcements. They'll be ready for us. With that manpower and firepower, this could wind up escalating into a huge face-off. Remember Waco, Texas... David Koresh... that Seventh-Day Adventist sect, the Branch Davidians? That's what I'm talking about. ATF—Alcohol Tobacco and Firearms—blew that operation. The Davidians were breaking only superficial gun ownership regulations. Koresh purchased AR15 rifles—the civilian version of the M16—as an investment just before the ever-tightening gun control laws. He was a businessman with the intention to sell them after the price quadruped. The deaths of seventy-four men, women, and children in the inferno that resulted were totally avoidable. We may be up against the same thing here. Plus, with the reaction I've already had from the FBI, I know that nobody will take a risk. We need Walker to be able to generate a warrant. Without him, we have nothing.

"I just want you to be prepared, Dan. They'll use Walker as a hostage, a 'bargaining chip.' Without cooperation from other agencies, we may not even get that far."

"Jim, go ahead and cut that lock," instructed Jack. "Let's get out of here."

This is escalating out of control... I may never see my father again.

"Shhh! Quiet!" The officers grabbed their guns, spun around in different directions, reacting to the sounds coming from the bushes behind them.

They probably didn't actually leave, just set us up for capture when we didn't expect it. Dan ducked behind one of the vehicles. Everyone was quiet as they listened intently, guns drawn, ready for a final battle, taking cover behind the open doors of the sedan.

Crickets chirped all around them and then stopped suddenly, restarting after a moment.

"Ugghh, Dan! Help!"

Dan noticed that the grass was slightly separated going away from the car rear door. He followed the trail just beyond where the trucks were backed up into the bushes.

"Dan!" Walker whispered weakly.

"Dad!" Dan ran over to Walker, hugging him again. "You're safe!"

CHAPTER 80

"John, Shannon, come on in!" Dan pushed the door open and let his friends into Edgar's house, where they finally rendezvoused, on Friday, several days after the events at the Ranch.

"How is your Dad?" asked John, shaking Dan's hand.

"He's almost back to full strength. Look for yourself!"

John moved over to the fireplace where Walker was sitting in a reclining sofa-chair, soaking up the heat from the crackling fire.

Shannon gave Dan a big hug, making eye contact for an unusually long time. "Your story of adventure is unbelievable, Dan." She pulled him into the room by his hand.

It's really nice to see Shannon again, Dan thought, his heart beating and a shot of adrenaline adding to his excitement.

She moved over to Walker and crouched down next to his chair. "It's so good to see you alive and well, Walker! Dan told us the whole story on the phone. That place sounds horrible! I hope they won't be after you anymore. You've already suffered enough."

"I'm sure you saw the article in the paper," he said. "That suicide of the Bishop is bogus. The Pentagon probably had to take him out so he wouldn't blackmail them."

"I seriously doubt that's anything other than a cover-up," Dan said, mainly talking to his two friends. "The real story about the PITY Ranch probably will never reach the light of day.

"Is it considered homicide if people willingly submit to torture on a cross, and you simply provide the crosses for their 'enjoyment?' I'm sure some of those young students would change their mind once they got up on the cross. Is it murder if you don't take them down when they scream?

"One thing's for sure. They didn't want any of this activity to be scrutinized by the public. The media are heavily controlled by corporate and church dollars. They published a bogus story about a church bus crash on Route 68, claiming that the bodies of the youth were burned beyond recognition in the crash."

Walker talked with additional stops and pauses, a normal result of his injuries. "The government... is obviously behind this... from the highest levels, but... like everything else, it's swept... under the carpet. As long as it doesn't appear on TV..., the public will never know. Plus, they're busy with American Idol... and the latest sitcom reruns. This operation... was apparently funded by the burgeoning 'Faith Based Initiative' money, but... it was actually a Pentagon effort... an effort to train Christian terrorist soldiers. They want soldiers who could operate... like robots..., willing to go on suicidal missions, unflinching... even when their comrade perishes beside them..., following orders without question..., and willing to take... take life 'In God's Name' without batting an eye."

"This is probably an isolated case, though. Don't you think?" Shannon asked.

"The PITY Ranch... is just... just the tip of the iceberg. I'm sure... many other such training camps are in operation. You just don't hear about them on the news... or from NSA, FBI, or Pentagon officials, all for the sake of our precious 'national security.'"

"This whole thing is sick," Shannon said. "The evidence of planned torture at Abu Ghraib prison and at other detention camps around the world, like the US Naval Base in Guantánamo Bay, gave our culture a bad reputation about torture world-wide."

"Plus, the primary symbol of Christianity is the cross, a torture device," added Dan. "Renowned throughout history as cruel and unusual punishment, no modern civilized society would use it, or be caught worshipping it. Combine these factors and I can see why the Islamic culture is deathly afraid of unbridled Christian doctrine. The founding fathers of our country had it right to insist that church and state must be kept separate. The recent intrusion of the state into the church is the source of these sorts of distorted religious practices."

"You're making a sound point, but... I wouldn't make it... too loudly. Christian Evangelicals... they have a position of power and... they can be ruthless. Although the U.S. Constitution... stipulates that the U.S. is officially a secular state, the... the separation of church and state serve only to prevent... an official state religion. It doesn't prevent religiosity in government. The U.S. is clearly the most religious... of all the developed industrialized societies. Our experience with the PIT... it was just one example... one example of the sad truth... combining government institutions with religion is a very bad idea."

There was an uncomfortable pause as their minds processed the scope of the perversion.

"I hope we can get back to... to our earlier discussions. I've had some time to think... and maybe we can try again to put together... some sort of a model... a model that incorporates what we know from science and religion, but... without including the evil side of strict doctrine."

"Just relax, Walker," John said. "Sure, we can get back to those discussions, and it might be good to divert your attention from your injuries."

CHAPTER 81

It was a pleasant experience to get back to the comfortable seats around the fireplace of Edgar's mountain home. Of course, engaging in small talk over coffee now seemed impossible. Walker sat in a recliner at the end of the couch, where Dan sat the other day. Dan and Shannon sat side-by-side on the couch while John sat in a chair at the other end of the coffee table. Edgar made an appearance, but as before, mainly remained elsewhere.

This transition was really the best idea for Walker, who wanted to put the terrifying experience at the PITY Ranch behind him. "My dear friends, where were we?" he said, half smiling.

"I can get us back to where we were," John volunteered. "I must say that since that conversation, I've had a hard time thinking of anything else."

Dan recalled John's sudden departure, a departure prompted by his difficulty in accepting the stunning conclusions drawn by Walker, conclusions regarding Jesus and the "Christ cult" that arose in the first decades after Jesus taught in and around Jerusalem. Clearly, John had recovered and was ready for more. That was only a few days ago, but it seemed like an eternity to Dan.

John had his notepad, and he referred to it as he spoke. "Okay, I will agree that we found an amazing pattern match between the text in the J-Account and the facts of biology, including the description of DNA and how it all works. I'll have to say, Dan, you did a great job of pointing out the fact that Satan didn't enter the Bible text until much later. And my story of Lucifer—well, I admit that it's never found in the Bible. I did more looking, and I will submit to that conclusion, so you win on that one."

"The idea that it is a literal 'snake' makes even less sense," Shannon added.

"The match with DNA is truly astounding," John said. "Plus, the other matches explain verses I've never heard explained very well before."

"The multiple-point match makes it seems almost impossible that we've got this wrong," Shannon said.

Walker sat quietly, listening with curiosity.

"All the talk about our origins really got us nowhere," John said.

"I disagree, John," Shannon said. "I don't think people will be able to discount the theory that our planet may have been seeded by an ancient race."

"But that only pushes the question of origination further back, Shannon." John said. "And, as you so delightfully outlined, our current concept of evolution still needs refinement."

"Okay, John. Let's not get into it. Let's just leave it at that," Shannon said, sternly.

"Fair enough. I'd rather look in a different direction."

"Good... what's that?" Shannon asked.

"What I find more interesting is how our pattern match impacts the story of Jesus and how faithful people—Christians—can incorporate these startling facts into their religious beliefs. Walker, your research will obviously be quite challenging to Christians like me who are happy with the story as it is. Yet, I have to admit that our clear-cut pattern matching supports the concept that original sin isn't reality."

"And, it seems that your research on the life of Jesus and his teaching also supports the same conclusion," Dan said, talking toward Walker.

"It means..." John started, "that we must be willing to accept the possibility of a world without original sin. A world where people are naturally good, not evil."

"And a world where Christ's crucifixion must be considered an unimportant aspect of the teachings of Jesus," Shannon added.

"Don't blow this... out of proportion," Walker said. "It's really not as difficult as you're making it out to be... Being undecided and open to new ideas can be uncomfortable, but... it allows growth to higher levels of spiritual understanding. The first step in this is to... to acknowledge that everything... everything we assumed was true... might not be true at all."

"I do have a hard time with that. My faith has served me well."

"I understand, but... most of what you know is true from... from first-hand experience, will remain true."

"You're starting to lose me."

"Let me ask you a question. What is your first-hand experience... of being a Christian? In other words, from... from your experience, what does a Christian experience... that a non-Christian does not experience?"

John paused for a moment. "Sure, I can answer that. It comes down to how you center your life. Self-centered versus Christ-centered. You have to ask yourself: 'What will be the center of my life? Who am I going to live for?' The Christian centers his life on God.

"Once you have God at the center of your life, you think about the character of your life. You have to ask: 'What kind of person will I be?'

The teachings of Jesus are the guide to this. Your character is usually best exposed by the service you provide to others and how you interact with others.

"Finally, living in community and fellowship with other Christians demonstrates your connection to the family of God, to become part of the body of Christ. Don't worry about your job, school, or where you live. These are all secondary. Worry only about how God sees you.

"The Christian experience is directly related to that mind-set. As a Christian, you will pray and follow the opportunities that are part of God's will for your life. You will express humility in prayer with unquestioning belief that God will provide an answer." John paused for a moment. "Those are the main points, at least for me."

Walker shifted his position with a painful groan. "Uh, my first observation... is that none of those experiences depend upon... the concept of original sin... that you seem to find so challenging. Centering your life... on God does not. Maintaining a Christ-like character does not. Living in fellowship... with other Christians does not. Being successful in prayerful living does not. I'm wondering, what are you worried about?"

"Well, I guess you're right, original sin has little to do with these things, but it does bear upon *why* these things are possible—that is, why a person can be transformed by Christ from a sinful creature into a follower of Christ."

"Indeed. That's how it's taught." Frowning, Walker readjusted himself again, his bruised ribs making any position uncomfortable. Dan and Shannon tried to help Walker, but they could really do nothing to improve his situation. Finally, Walker started again. "John, let's back up a bit. I'd like to propose an alternative explanation... an explanation for many of the experiences... you have as a Christian. This was something I had... had to struggle with myself, starting years ago, when I also was faced with these questions. I can only make... some suggestions."

"I guess I'm open to improving my spiritual experience."

Walker turned his focus of attention from John. "Dan, have you run into... the theory of emergent properties?"

"Huh? ... Well, yes. But, that isn't really relevant, is it?" Dan looked puzzled.

"On the contrary, it is precisely where I want to go," Walker said.

"I'm sorry," Dan said. "It just seems so out of context. Fortunately, it's an area I've had some interest in, particularly with regard to *emergent intelligence*." Dan took on a professorial demeanor.

"The theory of emergent properties is encapsulated in the statement *the whole is greater than the sum of the parts*. That is, in a sufficiently complex system, the parts might each be relatively simple, but when viewed from the higher level, the system as a whole exhibits behavior or intelligence far beyond just each small part viewed alone."

"Dan, that's called *synergism,*" Shannon interjected.

"The artificial intelligence community is heavily involved in this exact area," Dan said. "They're trying to understand how the human brain works and how intelligent machines could be produced."

"I was wondering how you knew so much about this," John said.

"Let me fill this in some more. Conventional computers do poorly on tasks that we humans find second nature, like decoding a visual scene or understanding a conversation. Computer experts found that computer architectures are good for certain types of problems but almost worthless for others. At the same time the human brain can't do millions of arithmetic problems per second, but it can recognize faces easily, something computers can't seem to do well at all. The mind is good at just the opposite set of problems, the ones computers can't easily solve."

John said, "I'd say that's a good thing. Computers can't replace the lowly human yet, right?"

"True. But, it begs the question: Why are we so good at these hard problems? Computer architecture and neurology joined forces to consider that question, looking at the relative simplicity of the function of individual neurons compared with the complexity of silicon-based computers. Your brain doesn't require thousands of programmers to create a single program; you don't have to buy it, and there's no need for bug-fixes, upgrades, and unreadable documentation, or at least we hope not."

There was a chuckle from John and Shannon. Walker tried not to laugh. Whenever he started to, he grimaced in pain.

"Neurons can fire or not, and they may excite other neurons to fire—that's it, at least at the cellular level. Loops of neurons firing create attention and continuous thoughts. Neuron-A excites neuron-B, excites neuron-C, excites neuron-A. Saying something like 'pink elephant' means you can't forget that thought immediately. And trying harder doesn't help. The loop is established and will continue until some of the neurons in the loop stop firing."

"Before you continue," Walker said, "I want to make a comment about... about those mental loops. But don't let me go off... off on a tangent—a mental loop—and never return." Chuckles erupted lightly. "Mental loops, thoughts that... that won't stop, worries, and haunting memories, these can all be related... related to persistent loops of neurons firing. Most people can recall thoughts that... that just would not stop. These... these can be toxic.

"Stopping toxic and destructive mental loops is... is a very important skill. Meditation is extremely powerful in... stopping these loops... Eliminating destructive mental loops... this will allow the brain to... to think more clearly, more creatively, and... more simply, better. Meditative practices have been taught for... for thousands of years, mostly in the Far East, where... where Zen meditation, Yoga, and other techniques work to... defuse destructive loops. Prayer also has many of the same properties, both working to... to enhance alpha-wave activity of the brain when the eyes are closed and... and to allow those mental loops to... to relax and, when possible, stop. Advanced meditators report... a feeling that their brain has stopped thinking altogether, bringing it to a level of calmness and balance. Prayer groups also report similar results.

"I'm not saying that this is... is the sole property of prayer, but it's an important dimension. The act of praying, alone, and silently, is much... much like the ancient practice of meditation."

John said. "I pray about problems and situations even if prayers never seem to be directly answered. I've always had the hunch that the act of sitting quietly had a great deal to do with it. I've also heard of some Christian ministers teaching *meditative prayer*."

"I've been a meditator for... years. I certainly recommend that everyone should learn the practice," Walker said. "Meditation. It's a very natural state. Anyone can... can learn to achieve it. The results are amazing and heavily documented from... from a scientific standpoint. Meditators report higher test scores, better athletic performance, and even better relationships. Not something to... to shake a stick at.

"Okay, that's the end of... of my tangent. Let's get back off my mental loop...! Dan, what about 'emergent properties'...?"

"Hmmm. Okay... You're right, I got only to the point of setting the stage." Dan recomposed himself, holding his hands in the air to make his point. "Imagine a hundred billion neurons, all about the same, each able to stimulate ten thousand neurons nearby. Each neuron is simple, either firing or not. When it fires, it stimulates chemicals to traverse the synapse—the gap between one neuron and the next. The result is mental consciousness, our mind, our personality, who we are—much more than just a whole bunch of neurons."

"It's truly hard to imagine that my thoughts and consciousness arise from simple neurons that can fire or not fire," John said. "I can only take your word for that. It just isn't my experience of consciousness."

"Exactly my point." Dan slapped his hand gently on the table. "The emergent property of consciousness... they call it emergent because it isn't an obvious result. It never would be predicted by looking at the constituent parts. This is what I'm talking about."

"Yes, I think I understand the idea," John said.

"As another example, consider the humble ant. An individual ant is not too smart, that's for sure. Put one on the rim of a glass with a scent trail to follow and it'll walk the rim until it dies. But there are hundreds of millions of ants in a colony. These colonies have a remarkably high level of intelligence."

"Those ants drive me nuts!" Shannon said. "The little black ants around my house invade every spring. If there is food anywhere, they'll find it and create an ant freeway right to it. They're a real pain."

Dan used his hands to represent the colony. "As a whole, the colony clearly demonstrates a level of intelligence far beyond that of any single ant and far beyond what you would expect by randomly putting some insects together."

"Okay, I understand that example," John admitted. "Go on."

"Now, the human brain is a collection of simple neurons so highly connected that they result in an amazing thinking conscious mind. In the ant colony, individual ants are quite limited in intelligence, but when the colony is viewed as a whole, it's quite intelligent indeed. The same could be said for bees, termites, or any highly social animal. The whole is greater than the sum of the parts—synergism at its best."

"What about your body, how many cells are there?" Walker asked.

"About seventy trillion cells, seven hundred times more than the number of neurons in your brain," Dan answered. "Each cell is an intricate machine with every atom, every molecule placed exactly in the right place, as determined by the DNA code. The cell achieves a level of integration far beyond any computer or machine produced by human hands."

"Exactly what I hoped you would say. Those cells compose a... a unified colony, all working together for a common purpose, tightly coupled into tissues, organs, and structures. Does this colony of cells—the body—have emergent intelligence? Each cell has only... a very small intelligence of its own. Like a colony of ants or your brain, does it... exhibit intelligence beyond the sum of the parts? I claim that it does."

"That would certainly make sense." Shannon tapped her mouth with her finger.

Walker continued. "That 'body intelligence' is not centered in your brain. It's not in any particular organ. It's an emergent property resulting from combining those seventy-trillion cells in contact with each other in a cooperative whole."

"Walker, this is definitely a new idea. One that would be impossible to understand until recent times, when the fine granularity of our bodies was truly understood," Dan said. "And we would obviously need to understand the concept of emergent intelligence."

"I beg to differ. This is not a new concept at all. It's a concept that... that people have discussed for years... without truly understanding how it might come about. It's something that has been understood on... on an intuitive level for centuries. We all intuitively understand this intelligence. You see, the emergent intelligence of your body is simply your *soul*."

CHAPTER 82

"Oh my!" Dan leaned forward and readjusted his position so that he was angled toward Shannon and looking at Walker. He put his elbows on his knees and supported his chin with his hands, index fingers touching his lips. "The soul... understood by spiritualists for centuries, but never anchored in any scientific theory. Tossed around by ministers as either lost or saved." He leaned back, as if overcome with the weight of the idea.

The group felt the dwindling heat from the fire. John got up to add some logs since he was closest to it and since Walker was still recuperating.

"The soul. I've never heard anyone describe exactly how, on a scientific level, we could actually have such a thing," Dan said. "The soul... Yes. An emergent property of your body, a colony of trillions of cells, each contributing a tiny bit of intelligence... It matches the idea that the soul not located in any one organ or place in your body. There is a sense that, like a spirit or ghost, it exists somewhat apart from the physical structure of the body. That's exactly how emergent intelligence seems."

Walker said, "Think of the mind, our consciousness... compared with the structure of our brain. Our mind is not our brain. It's more than just a collection of neurons. Your consciousness seems to... to exist apart from it, in spite of the fact that... that we know our thoughts originate in our brain. Think of your soul compared with the structure of your body. Our soul is not our body. It's more than our body. Again, it seems to exist apart from it."

"True" Dan said, looking into space.

"John, what about you? How do you like this idea?" Walker asked.

"I don't see any big conflict. Although you're proposing a naturalistic rationale for the soul, that doesn't diminish the concept of the soul, at least not the way I think of it."

"It's a very cool idea," Shannon volunteered. "You can't explain the soul by looking at the components. It doesn't succumb to the reductionist view that physics and chemistry can explain everything."

"The existence of the soul was revealed to man by spiritual revelation, not through science. We can explain it only by looking at the higher level," John said. "No one would come up with the concept of the soul by looking at a pile of individual cells. But when you truly 'get' someone at their most fundamental level, isn't that the level of the soul?"

"Precisely. For example, knowing about the chemical building blocks of air doesn't explain how a hurricane works," said Dan. "A hurricane is like the emergent property of the complex system of the atmosphere. Picture the soul as a hurricane of communication among the cells in your body."

There was a nodding of heads and a bit of silent reflection.

"In that case, I'd like to... to move to the next level," Walker said.

"The next level?" they seemed to ask in unison. Dan felt some inner hesitation in his gut. In the short time they had been together, he had been through a lot with his long lost father, and if there was a next level, perhaps it was going too far.

"My friend Edgar revealed the possibility of this level in... in his description of our physical world, the understanding of the physicist. According to Edgar, the primitive particles—electrons, protons, neutrons—can be modeled as... as simple rotating donuts of stable charge."

"Right," Dan said. "They don't have absolute boundaries; they aren't restricted to exist in just one place at one time. They easily interact and blend with each other. An incredible amount of empty space exists between the apparent location of those particles, yet in that empty space, energy fields exist, electrical, magnetic and gravitational fields. And somehow, the particles themselves extend into that space. These are really still quite mysterious. No one has yet figured how to explain how those forces can permeate that 'empty' space."

"Add to this reality... a human being, a complex organism with... emergent intelligence on at least two levels—the mind and the soul. Because the human is made of those interacting donuts, the edges of... of the human being are not fixed. They bleed out into the sea of rotating donuts, interacting with that sea on levels we don't yet understand. We realize we are only a component of... of the larger natural world, a world where every part is reliant on every other part. To this image, add nearly seven billion individuals on earth. Is there an emergent intelligence of humanity? Is there a level of mind and soul above that of the individual?"

Dan mumbled a random word or two without making any sense. This level seemed to be exactly the level he frequently wondered about, a level that he understood without really knowing how it worked.

"You've probably guessed that I'm going to... to say that there is. This higher level of emergent intelligence is... is what some call the

'Body of Christ,' the 'Holy Ghost,' the 'Noosphere'—as Pierre Teilhard de Chardin wrote... in *The Phenomenon of Man*—or the... the Hindi *Brahman*, the *World Soul*. It's the seamless whole of... of the Ultimate Oneness underlying all apparent components. The separateness we see is... is only an illusion. We are all part of this larger whole..., like a wave is part of the larger ocean. This is the dimension where... prayer has effect; it's the 'Kingdom of God' Jesus spoke of, the field of possibility described by the famous classic book *The Magic of Believing*, by Claude Bristol.

Walker scanned blank faces and realized that his audience was likely missing some of his points.

"Dan, grab that red book... from the bookcase, right... there... I want to read the first paragraph." Dan got up and retrieved the book, locating it easily by following Walker's pointing finger. Walker opened the book and flipped the pages to find the passage he wanted to read.

"Listen to this:"

> *IS THERE a something, a force, a factor, a power, a science—call it what you will—which a few people understand and use to overcome their difficulties and achieve outstanding success? I firmly believe that there is, and it is my purpose in this, first complete exposition of the subject, to attempt to explain it so that you may use it if you desire.*

"If you haven't read this book," Walker waved the book in the air, "I sincerely suggest that you do. It explains this level of... of emergent consciousness so you can use it in your life. Many people who... who are highly successful credit the 'field' Bristol outlines in his book. I believe this is the same field that Christians call the Body of Christ... the Holy Spirit... the Kingdom of God.

"The concept of emergent intelligence is how I explain it to myself. You can use Christianity, Hinduism, Zen, Yoga, or many other belief systems. The fact is, we are all connected, not just humans, but all life. The belief that we are separate is... is only an illusion. The illusion feeds self-righteous individualism and related wars, conflict, and strife.

"Remember, your model of the world is completely your own.. You can change it at will, if you allow that as a possibility."

"Dad, these ideas are tantalizing, and I have some thoughts. First, the consciousness of the brain is highly evident, whereas the soul is less evident, and finally, this World Soul is even more subtle. I know the brain is designed for extensive communication among the neurons. They are tightly coupled, with each neuron touching to up to about ten-thousand other neurons. From it, we have a consciousness that is truly amazing.

"The body is more loosely coupled, with each cell touching only perhaps a couple dozen other cells. Although the consciousness of the soul is certainly more subtle, it is still clearly understood as a fact. Then, we may have billions of individuals in the world, but they are even more loosely coupled than that. As a result, the World Soul is very subtle indeed."

"No argument from me," Walker remarked.

"That does seem to be supported by scripture," John said. "Jesus said *where two or three are gathered together in my name, there am I in the midst of them.* This might be talking about the emergent property you've been explaining."

"Hmmm. Intriguing." Shannon tapped her mouth with the side of her pen. "It would be interesting if we could find a way to increase the power of the World Soul. The tightly coupled brain results in higher intelligence and thinking capability. Can we do the same for the World Soul?"

Because of his bruised side, Walker grimaced as he talked. "If the emergent property of the World Soul could be enhanced, we might find... some remarkable changes in the world—peace and prosperity, for instance—that might seem improbable. You sometimes get that feeling when people pull together after a disaster."

"I would like to see this emergent soul enhanced," Shannon reflected. "If it is possible, perhaps peace and prosperity could replace war, strife, and poverty. Is there any downside?"

There was brief quietness. Walker said, "It depends on your point of view, but yes, there is a... a drawback, a threat that you will lose your individualism. Just as you lose your individualism when you... you cooperate in any team sport, when you work in a large corporation or governmental institution, and when you enlist in... any branch of the military, you become part of the larger entity. This loss of individualism is not new. Some people enjoy the security and participation in the larger entity. If the World Soul was enhanced, reduced individualism would be a natural consequence. Personally, I don't buy into... into the idea of complete loss of your individualism, but some loss is a natural consequence.

"The other reason people fight this possibility is that the World Soul is inherently socialistic. You give for the benefit of the team, the company, the country. Your desire for selfish benefit must be relegated to a lower priority, or it will... ruin the cooperative nature of the body. Consider the cells in your body. They are not there for their own benefit; they exist for the benefit of the larger organism. Cells that selfishly reproduce for their own benefit are recognized as a terrible disease: cancer."

"Jesus taught a brand of socialism foreign to the capitalistic mind-set," John said, a bit unexpectedly. "Capitalism has worked well, but

I'm not sure it's what Jesus had in mind for us."

"Perhaps not," Dan said. "I can see that capitalism has been both useful and detrimental. Yet, it may not have a bearing on this question. I'm not sure if the economic system will prohibit the enhancement of the World Soul. I would think that getting the World Soul to emerge would require that we get as close as possible to our loved ones and form a tightly-knit community. Communicate more. Hug more.

"Love more," Walker said.

There was a knock on the door. Edgar emerged from the kitchen, and Dan rose from his seat.

Edgar looked through the peephole and then opened the door widely, "Yes! Hello, Russ! Glad to see you could make it for dinner."

Hall entered and warmly shook the hands with Dan and Edgar. He hurried over to the fireplace and kneeled before Walker. "How are you doing, my friend?"

"Quite well, given the circumstances. I can't thank you enough for your help. That's an experience with extremist Christianity I would rather forget. Unfortunately, I don't think I'll ever look at the Christian cross the same way. Crosses used to give me a good feeling. I can't stop thinking of the experience at the Ranch and the possibility of a government run amuck with designs of torture and control. I am certainly happy that the Bishop will no longer cause any problems."

"Although the media reported that he shot his brains out with a pistol, but I never saw any body. This corrupt administration probably provided the Bishop with a new identity and a pleasant retirement somewhere. How can you avoid corruption with political hacks and cronies all through the system?"

Hall stood up. "The heat was too much for me. I was planning to retire soon anyway, so I got out while I could. I'm moving to Montana where I can enjoy some serious fishing and hunting. I'm tired of the city scene."

Dan recalled Hall's professional capabilities during their rescue operation. *Hall won't enjoy complete retirement for long. Or, is Hall still working for the FBI or CIA in some covert capacity?* Dan tried to put it out of his mind. Hall had given him no reason to suspect anything.

"Are you sure you'll be able to adjust to that boring way of life, Russ?" he asked.

"I'm going to have to look for a ranch up in Montana, you know, a PITY Ranch. I want to become a recruit." Hall's mouth turned up slightly.

"Why wait, there's a cross in the back yard. Dan, John, go ahead and give our friend some humility, won't you?"

Hall's bluff called, they laughed in unison.

"You guys, this PITY experience was obviously traumatic," John said, "but it's nothing like what most Christians experience. That wasn't anything close to a normal church situation. Sure, I can see the danger of combining government and religion. It's just a very unusual thing, that's all." There was some silence. John seemed right, but they just didn't know if the practice was widespread or not. It seemed that mercenary training camps were becoming quite prevalent indeed, and the techniques they use come under almost no governmental scrutiny.

"My invitation to visit my church is still open. Shannon and Dan, I hope you'll consider checking it out."

Dan said, "John, I've been meaning to take you up on that for a while. With this evidence in Genesis, I'm going to have to start looking for a new church home, one that will embrace our interpretation and yet give me the opportunity to be part of a larger 'emergent intelligence.' I want to check that dimension out. But, all the hype over cross-worship, well, I've had enough of that."

"Me too," Shannon said. The animosity between John and Shannon had completely dissolved.

Walker's face darkened. "My friends, enhancing the... the world-soul can result in a wonderful, seemingly magical effect... of having intelligent beings interact... at a level far different from what you might observe. But there is a dark side, a side you must be careful to avoid. Charismatic leaders, they can use this effect to drive... destructive cults that encourage mass suicide or murder. Remember the 1978 *People's Temple* massacre in Jonestown, Guyana and the 1997 *Heaven's Gate* suicides? It seems that as some groups discover... the reality of the world-soul, they leverage it... to maintain their following. Mainstream religions do as well. Look at the growing... evangelical movement that's bent on erecting crosses... crosses on every hill, TV channel, and even in city hall."

"You know," Hall said, "I've frequently wondered how Bible-thumping Christians can allow the continued predominance of crosses in churches and on so many hill tops. The Second Commandment clearly disallows graven images of anything on earth or in the heavens. A cross is clearly a graven image of a worldly object, and so is a stone engraving of the Ten Commandments themselves—it's completely inconsistent."

"You're fooling yourself if you think that's the only inconsistency!" Shannon exclaimed.

"That exact issue caused a huge rift in... in the church in AD 726, known as the *iconoclastic controversy*," Walker said. "For a few centuries no symbols or icons were... were allowed in the church, including the cross. But it didn't last long. Those symbols were just too useful... especially during the Crusades. The Pope simply declared...

that these icons were not worshiped as graven images, and that was that. But regardless of their usefulness in the crusades to rally the troops, the cross is an obvious violation... of any literal reading of the Second Commandment."

There was a moment of silence when all present took stock in the personalities present and the pleasant evening.

"Dinner is served!" Edgar announced, standing over the table set for the meal.

Dan helped Walker up and over to one end of the rustic dining table. Edgar sat at the other, and Dan, Shannon, John, and Russ filled in the remaining seats.

"Dan, would you do the honor of opening the wine?"

"I'd be happy to help." Dan wasn't an experienced connoisseur of good wine, just a beginner. But he thought this bottle of Cabernet Sauvignon, from a world-renowned winery in the Napa Valley area of California, definitely looked expensive. Dan at least knew how to open the bottle without making a fuss. He poured a sample in Walker's glass for his approval.

Walker swirled it, sniffed the bouquet, and gave it a taste.

"Shall I pour?"

"Please do!"

Dan poured for his friends around the table, of course starting with Shannon, seated next to him.

Dan said, "I would like to propose a toast!" They held their glasses up. "To family, friends, and our journey to the field of emergent intelligence!" Dan took an extra long look at Shannon as he said the toast. Hall was obviously a bit out of step with the toast, but he accepted it nonetheless.

"Hear, hear!" John said, with the others.

They all clicked glasses and took a sip of wine, looking at the faces around the table, feeling that perhaps the emergent property of friends was also a part of the World Soul. They were friends—friends whose relationship had deepened during the last month, who had experienced more than anyone had imagined from a simple question, friends whose model of the world had been ripped to shreds and then reassembled with unexpected clarity. It was a friendship that could last forever.

"And don't forget," Walker said. "You're always right!"

"Absolutely!" They laughed.

THE END

SUGGESTED READING

Alighieri, Dante, *The Divine Comedy*, (1321, first printed in 1472), recent printing: NAL Trade (2003) ISBN: 0451208633. Dante (1265-1321) tells of the journey made by his sinful soul to eternal salvation, passing through the three realms: the inferno (hell), purgatorio (Mount Purgatory) and paradiso (paradise).

Asimov, Isaac, *Asimov's Guide to the Bible* Random House (1981) ISBN:0-517-34582-X. A historical and primarily secular treatment of the entire Bible, filled with maps and diagrams to explain the story of the Bible.

Asimov, Isaac, *In the Beginning...Science Faces God in the Book of Genesis*, Stonesong Press (1981) ISBN:0-517-543362. A great review of Genesis, with the presumption that the text was generated from earlier myths from the region.

Augustine of Hippo, *City of God*, Doubleday Publishing (1950, originally published AD 413) ISBN:0-385-02910-1. Augustine (AD 354-430) was a key contributor to Christian church doctrine; he coined the term "Original Sin" and authored the doctrine of original sin that would haunt theologians for centuries. See Book XIII: *Adam's Sin and Its Consequences*

Barber, Richard, *The Holy Grail*, Penguin Books (2004) ISBN:0-674-01390-5. Recounts the history of the Holy Grail, first introduced as a concept by a poet, Chretien, in unremarkable fictional poetry about the hero Perceval written in the AD 1100s.

Behe, Michael, *Darwin's Black Box: The Biochemical Challenge to Evolution,* Touchstone (1996) ISBN:0-684-83493-6. A case against Darwin's theory of evolutionary gradualism on the biochemical level.

Berkeley, George, *A Treatise Concerning the Principles of Human Knowledge*, (1710) Berkeley proposed that there is no physical reality, only our perceptions of it.

Berkhof, Louis, *Principles of Biblical Interpretation: Sacred Hermeneutics*, Baker Book House (1950) ISBN:0-8010-0549-3. Considers *Sacred Hermeneutics*, in that it assumes that supernatural influence exerted on the sacred writers by the Holy Spirit, by virtue of which their writings are given divine truthfulness, and constitute an infallible and sufficient rule of faith and practice.

Bouchard, Thomas J., Jr. " The genetics of personality." In Blum, K. & Noble, E. P. (Eds.) *Handbook of Psychiatric Genetics.* Boca Raton, Fl., CRC Press. Bouchard was principal investigator on the Minnesota Twin Registry.

Bristol, Claude M., *The Magic of Believing*, Pocket (1991) ISBN: 0671745212 [originally published in 1948]. This book postulates that there is a field that the human mind can tap into that we currently don't understand, but can work wonders if we just believe that we can indeed affect our world by thinking about it.

Cohen, Edmund D., *The Mind of the Bible-Believer*, Prometheus Books (1983) ISBN: 0-87975-495-8. From the introduction:

> *My contention is that the Bible is history's most successful psychological manipulation, achieving with uncanny facility what motivational researchers and psychological warfare experts of our own day have only dreamed of.*

Commission on Life Sciences, *DNA Technology in Forensic Science,* National Academy Press, (1992) ISBN:0-309-04587-8. Contains a great review of the issues surrounding DNA fingerprinting in forensic science, including the use of RFLP, PCR, and other technologies, the standards to be used for handling, testing and reporting.

Confucius, *The I Ching*, (400 BC) Modern version: General Publishing Company (1834, 1854, 1963) ISBN:486-21062-6 Translated from Chinese in 1854 and 1855 by James Legge.

Crichton, Michael, *Jurassic Park*, Knopf (1990) ISBN: 0394588169 Perhaps one of the first widely popular treatments of DNA concepts.

Darwin, Charles, *On the Origin of Species by Means of Natural Selection, or the Preservation of Favoured Races in the Struggle for Life*, (1859) First compelling evidence artfully presented with a full theory of evolution, based on the existing theory of the inheritance of acquired characteristics as published by Lamarck. This was one of the most important developments in the history of scientific thought.

Danzer, Gerald A., *Atlas of World History*, Borders Group, Inc. (2000) ISBN:0681465727. In the chapter entitled "The Rise of Agriculture and The Spread of Civilizations, 10,000 BCE to 500 CE" Danzer notes:

> *Note that the four primary civilizations in the middle latitudes of the Old World—in Asia and Africa—were set in riverine environments. The presence of a great river is often considered a major factor in the rise and development of these civilizations. The Tigris-Euphrates, the Nile, the Indus, and the Huang He are key geographic elements in understanding the rise and spread of these earliest civilizations.*

Denton, Michael, *Evolution: A Theory in Crisis* Adler and Adler Publishers (1985) ISBN:0-917561-05-8. Addresses the key weaknesses in the theory of Evolution in an easy-to-read volume.

Edwards, I.E.S., *The Pyramids of Egypt*, Penguin Books, (1947-1993) ISBN: 0140136347. One of England's leading Egyptologists provides the traditional interpretation of these ancient artifacts.

Forrester-Brown, James S., *Two Creation Stories in Genesis, The: A Study of their Symbolism*, Shambhala Publications, (1920, 1974) ISBN:0-87773-053-9

Fridell, Ron, *DNA Fingerprinting: The Ultimate Identity*, Grolier Publishing 2001 ISBN:0-531-11858-4. Easy-reading book hits the highlights of the history of DNA Fingerprinting as it relates to forensic science.

Friedman, Richard Elliott, *Who Wrote the Bible*, Harper Collins (1987) ISBN:0-06-0630350-3. Explores the authorship of the Old Testament, presents the

JEPD Theory and possible authors and dates.

Goldberg, David E. *Genetic Algorithms in Search, Optimization & Machine Learning*, Addison-Wesley Publishing Company, Inc. (1989) ISBN:0-201-15767-5. Provides a nice introduction to Genetic Algorithms and their application. The first few chapters are readable by anyone; only programmers will appreciate the remainder of the book.

Goldschmidt, Richard, *The Material Basis of Evolution*, Yale University Press (1940) Goldschmidt was an early contrarian to the neoDarwinians that predominated in the early 20th century. As professor of Zoology at the University of California, Goldschmidt used empirical evidence to support microevolution (evolution within a species) but to refute the claims of macroevolution (evolution between species). In this work, the term *hopeful monster* was first coined. He attempted to demonstrate that Darwin's theory was correct by considering animals that fossilized easily. He failed, and was a technical outcast for years. Today, his work still stands.

Gould, Stephen Jay, *The Structure of Evolutionary Theory*, Harvard University Press (2002) ISBN:0-674-00613-5. This massive book attempts to model evolutionary theory encompassing recent knowledge and debates. In its over 1,400 pages of fine print, Gould presents his life's final work, including the concept of punctuated equilibrium.

Hengel, Martin, *Crucifixion in the Ancient World and the Folly of the Message of the Cross*, Augsburg Fortress Publishers; 1st American edition (1977), ISBN: 080061268X. Crucifixion was anything but a bloodless punishment. From the whipping that normally took place beforehand to the way people were stapled onto the crosses, this was torture at its worst.

Hoffer, Eric, *The True Believer: Thoughts on the Nature of Mass Movements*, Harper Row (1951) ISBN:0-06-091612-5. This book is an amazing statement of truth about the nature of mass movements. Hoffer was originally speculating on the Nazi movement in Germany, but extended this to all movements, from religious to political.

Holldobler, Bert & Wilson, Edward O.; *Journey to the Ants*, Harvard University Press, (1994) ISBN: 0-674-48525-4. Describes the amazing intelligence of the lowly ant.

Hopfield, John J. *Neural Networks and Physical Systems with Emergent Collective Computational Abilities*, Proc. Natl. Acad. Sci. USA Vol. 79, pp 2554-2558, April, 1982. Biophysics. Also reprinted in the book *Feynman and Computation: Exploring the Limits of Computers*, Perseus Books, (1999) ISBN:0-7382-0057-3. The ground breaking work considering a large number of simple neurons to result in an emergent intelligence, the concept of "mind."

Hubbard, L. Ron, *Dianetics: The Modern Science of Mental Health*, Bridge Publications, Inc., (1992) ISBN:0-88404-632-x. Describes the concept behind the biofeedback methodology of Scientology. Describes that our mind is always right: "...the sentient portion of the mind, which computes the answers to problems and makes man *utterly incapable of error*." Hubbard goes on to say: "Man is good. Take away his basic aberrations and with them go the evil of which the scholastic and the moralist were so fond."

Human Genome Project, see www.genome.gov. This site provides the latest in genomic research, including the complete human genome and comparison with other life. Genetic textbooks online as well.

Josephus, *The Jewish Antiquities*, (about AD 90). Available as *Josephus Complete Works* by J. I. Packer, Merrill C. Tenney, Nelson Reference (1998) ISBN: 0785214275. Josephus was born in Jerusalem ca. AD 38 and became a historian writing principally about the Jewish people. He mentions Jesus Christ (i.e. the so-called Testimonium Flavinium) in two passages: Ant. 18.3.3 and 20.9.1.10

There does not appear to be anything in both of Josephus' accounts that would necessarily disagree with the Gospel writers. The problem seems to be whether Josephus actually penned the final form of the first passage (i.e. Ant. 18.3.3) as we have it today. The opinion of scholars, since the sixteenth century or so, has been divided. Some say that the saying as a whole is authentic. Others say that parts of the saying are from the hand of Josephus and that parts are Christian additions. And, thirdly, there are those who regard the whole statement as spurious—totally a Christian interpolation, as the flavor of the paragraph is in sharp distinction to the others.

> *Now there was about this time Jesus, a wise man, if it be lawful to call him a man; for he was a doer of wonderful works, a teacher of such men as receive the truth with pleasure. He drew over to him both many of the Jews and many of the Gentiles. He was Christ. And when Pilate, at the suggestion of the principal men amongst us, had condemned him to the cross, those that loved him at the first did not forsake him; for he appeared to them alive again the third day; as the divine prophets had foretold these and ten thousand other wonderful things concerning him. And the tribe of Christians, so named from him, are not extinct at this day.*
>
> — *The Jewish Antiquities, 18.3.3.*

Kant, Immanuel, *Critique of Pure Reason*, Prometheus Books (1990) ISBN: 0879755962 [Original published in 1781]. Widely considered the greatest single work in modern philosophy, Kant made a thorough and systematic analysis of the conditions for knowledge.

Korsmeyer, Jerry, *Evolution and Eden: Balancing Original Sin and Contemporary Science* Paulist Press (1998) ISBN:0-8091-3815-8. Korsmeyer examines how an evolutionary perspective impacts the traditional understanding of original sin. He reviews the history of the doctrine as well as the church's interaction with the theory of evolution. Using clues provided by evolution and process thought, the author suggests an interpretation of original sin that incorporates both modern Catholic scholarship and scientific evidence. Ultimately, he moves toward a theology of evolution.

Lamarck, Jean-Baptiste, *Philosophie Zoologique*, Flammarion (1997) ISBN: 2080707078, [Original publication 1809]. Lamarck (1774–1829) was a French botanist who proposed two ideas that had great impact in the theory of evolution. He did not believe in extinction, but that every member of a species would evolve into another species; he believed that change was brought about through use and disuse and inheritance of acquired characteristics.

Lawrence, Jerome, *Inherit the Wind*, (Play, 1960). A recounting of the famous

"Monkey Trial," a real-life case in 1925. Two great lawyers argue the case for and against a science teacher accused of the crime of teaching evolution.

Linnaeus, Carolus, *Systema Naturae*, (1735) Initially only eleven pages, Linnaeus proposed a new classification for the three kingdoms in nature: the animals, plants, and stones. The plant kingdom was particularly alarming, as plants were not considered living like the animals. His work was revised until it finally reached three thousand pages. Modern taxonomy information can be found on-line at the National Center for Biotechnology Information, Taxonomy Browser: www.ncbi.nlm.nih.gov

Lorenz, Edward, *The Essence Of Chaos*, University of Washington Press (1993) ISBN:0-295-97514-8. The original work on Chaos Theory by the scientist who coined the term. Fractals grew from this work as a means to predict the bounds of the outcome of a chaotic system.

Mack, Burton, *Who Wrote the New Testament: The Making of the Christian Myth,* Harper San Francisco (1995) ISBN:0-06-065518-6. This is truly an excellent book, broaching the taboo topic about the source of the *Christian Myth.*

Maharishi Mahesh Yogi, *Transcendental Meditation*, Allied Publishers (1963) Meditation is a technique utilized and improved for thousands of years in the East. Maharishi brought the practice to the West in a form suitable for use by cultures that may not subscribe to other aspects of religious practice.

Maynard Smith, John; Szathmary, Eors; *The Major Transitions in Evolution*, Oxford University Press (1976) ISBN: 019850294X. An important technical review of key problem areas in the present theory of evolution.

Milton, John, *Paradise Lost*, (1667) Epic poem drawing extensively on classical mythology, Homer, Vergil, Christian Scripture and theology, and British political events, to retell the Fall and explain abstract theological and psychological ideas.

Milton, Richard, *Forbidden Science: Exposing the secrets of suppressed research*, Fourth Estate Limited, 1995, ISBN:1-85702-302-1. In exposing taboo areas of scientific experimentation, Milton shows how findings that threaten scientific orthodoxy are systematically misrepresented, ridiculed, and starved of funding.

Muhammad, *Al-Qur'an* (Koran), Original from AD 640, English Translation: (1984) Princeton University Press ISBN:0-691-07329-5. This is the holy book of the Islamic faith as dictated to Muhammad by the angel Gabriel. Of interest is a section from *The Elevated Places*, verses 7.19-7.22, describing the Fall and casting the serpent as Satan:

And (We said): O Adam! Dwell you and your wife in the garden; so eat from where you desire, but do not go near this tree, for then you will be of the unjust. But the Satan made an evil suggestion to them that he might make manifest to them what had been hidden from them of their evil inclinations, and he said: Your Lord has not forbidden you this tree except that you may not both become two angels or that you may (not) become of the immortals. And he swore to them both: Most surely I am a sincere adviser to you. Then he caused them to fall by deceit; so when they tasted of the tree, their evil inclinations became manifest to them, and they both began to cover themselves with the leaves of the garden; and their Lord called out to them: Did I not forbid you both from that tree and say to you that the Satan is your open enemy?

Mundkur, Balaji, *The Cult of the Serpent: an interdisciplinary survey of its manifestations and origins* (1983) State University of New York Press. Technically sophisticated survey of the serpent in myths and cults throughout history.

Olson, Steve, *Mapping Human History: Genes, Race, and Our Common Origins*, Mariner Books (2002) ISBN:0-618-35210-4. Genetic research to trace the origins of modern humans and the migrations of our ancestors over the past 150,000 years.

Every single one of the 6 billion people on the planet today is descended from the small group of anatomically modern humans who once lived in eastern Africa... the old style humans eventually disappeared.

Peacocke Arthur, *Paths From Science Toward God: The End of all our Exploring*, One World Publications (2001) ISBN:1-85168-245-7. Renowned theologian and biochemist Arthur Peacocke "reunites the warring worlds of science and religion." Eloquently written, it nicely covers the history of science and proposes a method of dealing with theology that utilizes the trusted thinking patterns of science.

Penrose, Roger, *The Road to Reality: A complete guide to the laws of the Universe*, Alfred A. Knopf (2004) ISBN: 0-679-45443-8. Emeritus Rouse Ball Professor of Mathematics at Oxford University, Roger Penrose, known for "Penrose tiles," compiled this truly wonderful work. Most enjoyable by those with an understanding of advanced math topics such as calculus and complex numbers, it can be at least partially enjoyed by others motivated to understand these laws.

Plato, *The Works of Plato*, (Approx. 400 BC)

Polkinghorne, John *Science and Theology: An Introduction*, Fortress Press, (1998). Contains a carefully selected bibliography helpful to newcomers to the field.

Popper, Karl, *The Logic of Scientific Discovery*, Routledge; New Edition (2002) [originally published in 1934]. ISBN: 0415278449. In one majestic and systematic attack, psychologism, naturalism, inductionism, and logical positivism are swept away and replaced by a set of methodological rules called *Falsificationism*—the idea that science advances by unjustified, exaggerated guesses followed by unstinting criticism. Only hypotheses capable of clashing with observation reports are allowed to count as scientific.

President's Commission for the Study of Ethical Problems in Medicine and Biomedical and Behavioral Research, *Splicing Life: A Report on the Social and Ethical Issues of Genetic Engineering with Human Beings*, U.S. Government Printing Office (1982) LOC:83-600500. Governmental study in response to a request by the National Council of Churches, reviewing the ethical issues and made recommendations regarding the composition and focus of the Recombinant DNA Advisory Committee and the Genetic Engineering Commission.

Pritchard, James B., *Ancient Near Eastern Texts Relating to the Old Testament*, Princeton University Press (1969) ISBN:0691035032

Ryan, Thomas, *Prayer of Heart and Body: Meditation and Yoga As Christian Spiritual Practice*, Paulist Press (2001), ISBN: 080914056X. Describes how the Eastern practice of meditation can be effectively utilized by Christians.

Sagan, Carl, *Dragons of Eden, The: Speculations on the Evolution of Human Intelligence*, Random House (1977) ISBN:0-345-34629-7. Sagan reviews the structure of the brain and mind and relates it to other animals, and reflects on how such a brain may have resulted from evolutionary forces. Reflection on how well we adopt new ideas with suspicion and reluctance.

Salahuddin, Abubakr Ben Ishmael, *Saving the Savior: Did Christ Survive the Crucifixion?*, Jammu Press; First Paperback edition (June, 2001) ISBN: 0970828012. Presents the explosive theory that Jesus Christ survived the crucifixion, traveled across Asia, took up residence in Kashmir, India, married, had children, and lived to the ripe old age of 120 years.

Schroeder, Gerald *The Science of God: The Convergence of Scientific and Biblical Wisdom*, The Free Press (1997) ISBN:0-684-83736-6. Schroeder, a physicist from MIT compares popular scientific theories about the formation of the universe with the creation story in Genesis. He notes:

To account for life on Earth, scientific theories require that either life was planted on Earth from outer space or an exotic property of molecular self-organization rapidly joined the necessary chemicals into self-replicating molecules and then a yet-to-be-discovered series of catalysts developed these fecund molecules into life itself.

According to the fossil record, gradual evolution has been found to be false at every major morphological change. The fossil record regularly fails to give any hint at the basic anatomical levels that a change in morphology was in the offing. The record's leaps and bounds, Darwin claimed, were the result of its being incomplete.

One-celled organisms sprang to life as soon as water was present, 3.8 billion years ago. There is no clear-cut path from the primordial soup to life. 650 million years ago, simple globular forms formed, known as Ediacaran Fauna. 530 million years ago, the Cambrian Era was the start of all life extant today, simultaneously in the oceans. This explosion of life is one of the centuries greatest discoveries.

Smith, H. Shelton, *Changing Conceptions of Original Sin*, Charles Scribners Sons, (1955) ISBN:LOC-55-9682. This book provides a detailed review of the history of original sin, especially during the mid-1700s.

Smith, Joseph, *The Book of Mormon*, The Church of Jesus Christ of Latter Day Saints, ISBN:0-87747-643-8. Joseph Smith claims to have been visited by an angel named Moroni, who provided a set of gold plates with the book written on it, "giving an account of the former inhabitants of this continent, and the source whence they sprang." Of specific interest is 2 Nephi 2:17-19 on the Fall:

And I, Lehi, according to the things which I have read, must needs suppose that an angel of God, according to that which is written, had fallen from heaven; wherefore, he became a devil, having sought that which was evil before God. And because he had fallen from heaven, and had become miserable forever, he sought also the misery of all mankind. Wherefore, he said unto Eve, yea, even that old serpent, who is the devil, who is the father of all lies, wherefore he said: Partake of the forbidden fruit, and ye shall not die, but ye shall be as God, knowing good and evil. And after Adam and Eve had partaken of the forbidden fruit they were driven out of the garden of Eden, to till the earth.

Soros, George, *The Crisis of Global Capitalism: Open Society Endangered,* Public Affairs, (1998) ISBN:1-891620-27-4. Soros relies on several philosophical ideas to become one of the most successful investors. He defines *fallibility*, the claim that the human mind usually is in variance with the actual state of affairs; *bias*, the difference between the model of the mind and reality; and *reflexivity*, the idea that the defective human concept can also modify reality itself.

Sturtevant, Alfred Henry, *A History of Genetics,* Cold Spring Harbor Laboratory Press (1965, 2001) A classic work by a scientist who was present during the early days of genetics research, with the insights of a witness rather than a historian.

Tarnas, Richard, *Passion of the Western Mind, The: Understanding the Ideas That Have Shaped Our World View*, Ballantine Books (1991) ISBN:0-345-36809-6. A comprehensive history of ideas. Highly recommended.

Taylor, John, *Scripture-Doctrine of Original Sin Proposed to Free and Candid Examination* (1740). Touted as of the best books considering original sin. Suppressed by the church, it is very hard to come by, although the response by Jonathan Edwards—which supports conventional wisdom—is easy to find.

Teilhard de Chardin, Pierre, *The Phenomenon of Man*, William Collins Sons (1959) ISBN:LOC:59-5154 Translated from the French version originally published in 1955 after his death. Teilhard (1881-1955), a naturalist and geologist, was also an ordained member of the Society of Jesus. He lived in China for many years where he played a role in the discovery of Peking Man. This work considers the "Stuff of the Universe" and attempts to square evolution, atomic physics, and the facts of the geologic past with theology. This book focuses mainly on the concept that everything is intimately related and connected, and the "Noosphere" exists where we can access this "dimension." Finally, he introduces the Omega Point as a means to bring everything under one concept.

Tillich, Paul, *Dynamics of Faith*, Harper Row Publishers (1957) ISBN:0-06-130042-X. Describes the concept of faith, God, and the symbols of such a faith. Tillich uses a definition of faith that is based on "Ultimate Concern," and not the more simplistic concept of belief with uncertainty.

Towner, W. Sibley, *Genesis*, Westminster John Knox Press (2001) ISBN:0-664-25256-7. Provides a wealth of information regarding possible ancient myths that contributed to the stories found in Genesis, including the Enuma Elish creation myth, Enki and Ninhursaga Sumerian legend, Adapa Myth, and others.

Unknown, *Dead Sea Scrolls*, Recovered from caves near the Dead Sea. In 1947, young Bedouin shepherds entered a long-untouched cave and found jars filled with ancient scrolls. That initial discovery yielded seven scrolls and began a search that lasted nearly a decade and eventually produced thousands of scroll fragments from eleven caves.

Vorilhon, Claude (AKA "Rael"), *The True Face of God*, (1998) ISBN:2940252009. Describes an encounter with a flying saucer and aliens who described an alternative interpretation of biblical stories. A cult following of Raelians prepares for a landing of the aliens in Jerusalem and promotes the development of cloning technologies. With regard to the interpretation of the serpent and the temptation of Eve, the aliens say:

The "serpent" was this small group of creators who had wished to tell the truth to Adam and Eve and as a result they were condemned by the government of their own planet to live in exile on Earth, while all the other scientists had to put a stop to their experiments and leave the Earth.

Watson, James D., *DNA: The Secret of Life*, Knopf (2003) ISBN: 0375415467. Overview of DNA from one of the key discoverers.

Wecht, Cyril, et al, *Mortal Evidence: The Forensics behind Nine Shocking Cases* Prometheus Books (2003) ISBN:1-59102-134-0. Overview of the O.J. Simpson trial and its attention to the issue of DNA evidence.

Wendt, Herbert, *In Search of Adam*, Houghton Mifflin (1956) ISBN: LOC:56-7241. Background and narrative history the key players as they strive to understand our biological roots, including Gregor Mendel.

White, Andrew Dickson, *History of the Warfare of Science with Theology in Christendom*, (1898). An amazingly thorough work reviewing theological criticism and scientific theories as of 1898.

White, Ellen G., *The Story of Patriarchs and Prophets* (1890). Organized what eventually became known as the Seventh-Day Adventist Church, Ellen G. White (1827-1915) was regarded by supporters as a modern-day prophet. From Chapter 3, "The Temptation and Fall," she writes:

In order to accomplish his work unperceived, Satan chose to employ as his medium the serpent—a disguise well adapted for his purpose of deception. The serpent was then one of the wisest and most beautiful creatures on the earth. It had wings, and while flying through the air presented an appearance of dazzling brightness, having the color and brilliancy of burnished gold. Resting in the rich-laden branches of the forbidden tree and regaling itself with the delicious fruit, it was an object to arrest the attention and delight the eye of the beholder. Thus in the garden of peace lurked the destroyer, watching for his prey.

Williams, Patricia, *Doing without Adam and Eve: Sociobiology and Original Sin*, Augsburg Fortress (2001) ISBN:0-8006-3285-0. Williams suggests that the entire story of Adam and Eve should be ignored and forgotten, and replaced with the scientific view of evolution.

Woodward et al.,. "DNA sequences from Cretaceous period bone fragments." 1994 Science 266: 1229-1232. Scott R. Woodward, a geneticist from the Brigham Young University, claimed that he was able to extract and amplify DNA from two eighty million-year old bone fragments of a large skeleton found in the roof of a coal mine. Later, others refuted his claims, asserting that his experiments were contaminated with human DNA.

Wooldridge, Dean E., *Mechanical Man: The Physical Basis of Intelligent Life*, McGraw-Hill Book Company, (1968) LOC:68-11240. Contains nice summary of organic vs. inorganic and molecular structure of proteins and DNA.

Yan, Johnson F., *DNA and the I CHING: The Tao of Life*, North Atlantic Books (1991) ISBN:1-55643-097-3. Yan considers the correlation between the sixty-four codes available to the three-position codons in DNA and the sixty-four elements of the I Ching. He attempts to pair the I Ching patterns with DNA codons by considering the frequency of each codon and the spacing of prime numbers.